MEET ME
IN THE
GREEN GLEN

Meet Me in the Green Glen

ROBERT
PENN WARREN

RANDOM HOUSE NEW YORK

TO ARNOLD
AND BESS STEIN

Love, meet me in the green glen,
  Beside the tall elm-tree,
Where the sweetbrier smells so sweet agen;
  There come with me.
    Meet me in the green glen.

                              —John Clare

My love is of a birth as rare
As 'tis for object strange and high:
It was begotten by Despair
Upon Impossibility.

                         —Andrew Marvell

BOOK
🌲🌲🌲🌲 I 🌲🌲🌲🌲

CHAPTER ONE

✝✝✝✝✝✝✝✝✝✝✝✝Far off, up yonder, the mist and drizzle of rain made the road and the woods, and the sky too, what you could see of it above the heave of the bluff, all one splotchy, sliding-down grayness, as though everything, the sky and the world, was being washed away with old dishwater. Out of that distance, she saw him come.

She did not know how long she had been at the front room window. She stood there, with one hand holding back the tatter of lace curtain, and stared across the yard and over the fallen-down picket fence and down the road where it ran alongside the creek. The creek was now a tumble of red-clay-colored water with white slashes and swirls of foam.

She had begun by staring just at the creek; for there were some days when her staring seemed to start near and then wander off, away from her, just as there were days when, even though she knew it was hers, it seemed to start far off and be coming toward her, secretly, creeping closer and closer. At those times the staring was like a hidden animal creeping up that never took its eyes off her. Yet all the time, whether the staring started near or far, she knew it was her own, even when she felt that the staring was at her.

Today she had begun by watching the flood. The water would crouch and heave at a big boulder fallen off the bluff-side, and the red-and-white foam would fly. It reminded her of the blood-streaked foam every heave would fling out of the nostrils of a wind-broke horse. It reminded her of the time Sunder, out of his crazy devilment, had tried to race a storm home, and had come beating up the road, and the mare, that he was too heavy for anyway, had come down on her knees there at the gate, red streaks in the snorted-out foam. Sunder had disentangled himself from the stirrups, gone into the house, come out with a 30.30, pumping a cartridge into the chamber, set the muzzle just at the left ear—that side being toward the house—and pulled the trigger.

Now, standing at the window, staring out at the creek, she thought she heard Sunder's voice call. It came, she thought, from back in the dark hollowness of the house, that sound that was not words, the only sound he had been able, for years, to make.

But this calling now, she realized, was only in her head.

It was funny, even if so many of the things she heard every day were just in her head, she always thought at first, before things got sorted out, that they were outside her head. She stood now, and clutched the lace curtain, which, in spite of the heavy dampness of the air, was dusty and prickly-dry with age, and wondered if there were people who always knew, right off, what was inside and what was outside their head.

Now she was staring at the spot by the gate where the mare, all those years ago, had come down on her knees, and again she thought she heard the voice of Sunder. But this time she knew, right off, that it was in her head. It was exciting to know right off that the voice was inside and not outside her head. Suddenly she found spit coming into her mouth, and had to swallow, and her breath came quick with the dizzy happiness she sometimes got when she found herself staring as far off as she could.

Suddenly she knew what she was staring at.

Out of the distance where bluff, woods, and sky dissolved into the drizzle that made the far-off near and the near far-off, floating out of distance toward her through the gray air, not seeming to touch the ground, he was coming.

She did not know how long she had been seeing him, but she did know that she had been seeing him for a time—how long you couldn't tell, a second or a thousand years, for time got funny when the staring came on you.

Then she heard the words inside her head: *I see a man and he is coming down the road.*

Long ago a great stream had cut through the heaved-up limestone to make this valley. The valley had been made, and now the great stream was shrunk to a creek that rose in the hills to the southwest, then swung northerly. The creek was nothing to what the great stream had been, but in flood, even now, it would come roaring down the boulder-strewn bed. On the left bank of the stream, to the west, reared the bluffs, sometimes showing the gray of limestone, streaked black with lichen, and sometimes covered with woods; opposite the house there were woods from the creekbank willows to the skyline, where now the grayness of sky tangled in the bare, black boughs of oaks. On the right bank, around the house, the land spread out level, then sloped up in the distance. Fields had once been on the slope, but now were gone to weeds and brush, with faraway woods scarcely visible in the slow-coiling mist and deliquescent torpor of the land.

A road lay between the creek and the old fields. A man was coming along the road, moving southward against the direction of the creek's flow.

The man was trying not to think of anything. Even with the rain on the back of his neck, he kept his head down. His eyes were fixed on the pointed tips of his patent-leather shoes as they were set, one after the other, neatly in the mud. He could not take his eyes off those pointed tips that were taking him down this road that would keep on going nowhere, forever. The feeling had come over him, though he did not have the words for the feeling, that this was what his whole life, all twenty-four years of it, had been.

He had never seen a place like this; and in this place everything that had ever happened seemed as though it had not happened. Even things like girls or whiskey or driving a car very fast or getting into fights, or standing in front of a mirror naked to the waist and combing your black hair till it gleamed smooth as silk—none of those things was like going down this road in the rain. And not one of them, now, seemed ever to have happened at all. Only one thing was real: you bowed your head down to watch your patent-leather shoes, one after the other, squish the mud while the rain ran down the back of your neck.

So now he kept his eyes on the tips of the patent-leather shoes as they lifted and moved forward to be set in the red mud, then lifted again. In that rhythm, he did not feel afraid, angry, or sad anymore. He felt instead a peculiar freedom, strength.

He thought: *Eccomi, Angelo Passetto. Me, and I walk on this road.*

Then, for no reason he could think of, he saw in his head the picture of his father sitting in the smoky kitchen, in the falling-down house, in Savoca, in Sicily, on a mountainside high above the sea, the big body hunching forward and the face stiff and gray when the pain hit him, but the jaws clenching together, and the breath coming hard and slow.

His father had died eleven years back. For a long time now he hadn't even thought of him. But Angelo Passetto was not dead, was in a place they called Tennessee, and was moving down this road in the rain.

There was a sharp stir in the creekside brush, and then, all in the same instant, out of the brush the creature's great leap unspooled in a flashing trajectory above the road. He saw it all at once. There on his right was the clump of brush on the bank above the roaring water. There, on the left, was the wet, dark hulk of a house set between two big cedars. And there, in the air, over the road, seeming, for all its flash of speed, to float timelessly and without substance as without effort, was the creature. For that instant, as Angelo Passetto froze in his tracks, it was unidentifiable.

Then he thought: *Sandy Claws!*

And he half expected to see a whole string of such creatures floating in the air and behind them the sleigh with the fat little red-nosed, red-dressed son-of-a-bitch grinning out. Just like Christmas time in Cleveland on Euclid Avenue, with the windows of the big stores shining in the dusk, and music blatting out till you couldn't hear yourself think, and people shoving, and the snow falling.

But now there was no music blatting. No people. No snow falling. Here, under the lowering sky, there was just that creature suspended in the air at the end of the leap, with forelegs delicately probing down to touch earth where the ruin of the flattened fence lay. And then, just before those delicate forehooves touched earth, there was, suddenly, that *zing* and stab across the air.

He saw the shaft of the arrow set deep in the side of the creature, just back of the left shoulder, angling downward, still quivering.

The buck was in the air again, but with the big rack jerked to one side, and the forelegs making an awkward pawing motion as if they were trying to climb up a wooden ladder into the air, and the slick hooves couldn't get a purchase on the wood, and kept slipping off. All at once, that ladder you could not see, broke. The buck came crashing down.

Then Angelo Passetto turned to another sound. There to his right and high over the creek, at the near end of a ruinous footbridge of wire cable and boards, a man stood against the grayness of bluff and sky, a bow in the left hand, held high. Angelo Passetto knew that the sound he had just heard, a guttural, rasping cry, was the cry of triumph uttered by that man.

Now the man was plunging recklessly down the board steps to the road level, then across the road, toward the buck that lay just beyond the rotting ruin of the fallen fence, still kicking. But even in his passage, that burly, booted figure turned, for a split second, and exultantly flung out the words: "The bastard—did you see me snag that great big white-bellied bastard!"

Angelo Passetto stood there, holding in his hand a parcel wrapped in disintegrating newspaper, feeling the rain soak through his coat to chill his shoulders. The man had flung his bow aside, had seized the hind legs of the buck, had started to drag it out into the road. For a moment the body slid. Then the big rack caught in the ruin of the flattened-down old paling fence. The man grunted and pulled. When he released the

hind legs to get a better grip, one of the legs jerked spas-
modically. The man pulled again, grunting. The snagged
antlers held. The buck's neck bulged out under the strain. The
man swung his face toward Angelo Passetto.

"Hey," he cried, "grab a-holt and help drag!"

Angelo Passetto never knew what he might have done. For
the moment, he stood there without will, sunk in the gray
blankness of the land. From the man's hairy, grizzled face, the
red-rimmed eyes glared commandingly at him. In a moment
that angry force might enter into him, and his body would
move as that force dictated, but it would be only his body, not
Angelo Passetto, moving.

He managed to draw his gaze away from the man's gripping
glare. He looked up the road. Fifty yards on, the road swung
right, following a bend of the creek, away from the fields, again
in woods on both sides. It was getting dark already there
in the woods. Beyond that point the bluff began to sink toward
a notch, with hills rising beyond. Above the limestone-colored
cloud that lay in the notch, the sky was lightening toward a
slatey-blue. The underside of the raveling tufts of gray cloud
in the high sky bloomed faintly pink, catching from below a
light from the sun that would be setting, beyond the cloud-
blocked notch. The top of the low cloud-mass in the notch was
thinly outlined in a tracing of orange foil. He thought of being
beyond the notch, in a country where you would be seeing the
sun go down clear and calm.

For a moment Angelo Passetto had forgotten the man.

"Durn it," the man ordered, "lay holt and drag!"

But suddenly, from off to the left, the other voice called. "You
won't drag a thing, Cy Grinder."

Angelo turned. A woman was in shadow on the porch of the
dark hulk between the big cedars. The face, very white,
seemed to be floating there, bodiless.

The man kept his grip on the buck's hind legs. "It's my deer," he said.

"Not and you shot it on my land," the woman said.

"I shot it in the big road," the man said. Ignoring the woman, he crouched lower and gave a great heave. But the rack held.

"Cy Grinder," the woman said, "I told you to stop dragging."

The man looked up from his crouch, still gripping the buck's legs. "Who are you, Cassie Killigrew, to be tellen folks to stop? Even if old Sunderland Spottwood did marry you?"

But she was not there. The white face that had seemed to float bodiless in the shadow of the porch had been there, and now, on the instant, it was gone.

Cy Grinder, lost and spent after his outburst, stared at the place where the face had been in the darkness of the porch. Then, jerking his eyes away, he looked down at his hands, now loose on the hind legs of the buck. With an un-definable cry of anger, he seized the legs anew, and heaved.

The rack jerked free. The buck slid out into the road. He dragged it across the road, to a hackberry tree. The weight left a smoothly graded shallow trough in the mud, sym-metrically scored down the center by the prongs of the antlers. He dropped the legs, gave a great puffing exhalation, drew from a pocket of his mackinaw a length of small rope, and flung an end over a bough of the hackberry. Then he crouched again to lash together the legs of the buck.

He was crouching there when, again, the voice came.

"Listen!" Again, suddenly, the voice called. "You say you shot that deer on the road?"

The man looked up at the place across the road where again the white face floated in shadow.

"Yeah," he said.

Then the voice said: "You—you standing there!"

Angelo Passetto realized that the face was now toward him, and that the words were coming toward him.

"You were standing there the whole time," the voice said, "weren't you?"

Angelo Passetto looked at the woman. He looked up the road, where it disappeared into the woods again.

He looked back at the woman. "Who? Me?" he said, and dropped his gaze.

Over to the right he heard, at his words, the rasping exhalation, the same cry of triumph, but in a lower key, that Cy Grinder had uttered when the arrow smacked home.

But the woman was saying: "Look here, look at me!"

Angelo Passetto raised his eyes. He had not known that at that distance eyes could stare right into yours. The eyes were dark in the white face, but even at that distance, beyond the fallen fence, in the shadow, they burned at you.

"I was looking out the window," the woman said. "I saw you coming up the road. You stood there and looked when the arrow hit. Why don't you tell the truth?"

Angelo Passetto looked down at the pointed toes of the patent-leather shoes, set in the red mud. He saw, with sadness, how small his feet looked with the pointed black patent-leather shoes set in the red mud. He knew he was not a small man, he was a big enough man, but he felt small, all of a sudden. He felt how big the world was. Red mud was messed over the patent leather. He loved patent leather because it was black and shiny, and now the red mud was smeared over it.

"Are you going to tell the truth?" the voice demanded.

He lifted his head again, but did not look at her. He looked up the road where it disappeared into the darkening woods. His feet, moving in the mud, would take him there. That was the way it was. He thought how, if a man's life stretched out like that ahead of him, there was nothing to do but go on.

That thought hung in his mind, with a slow, dawning, glowing surprise. He had never before had a thought like that—about the way life was.

Yes, he had, he remembered. Once, in a bar, with a jukebox going, a girl who was with him had said that life was just a bowl of cherries, and had giggled, then leaned at him for him to light her cigarette, and had suddenly opened her eyes, wide and fake-scared, to look up at him: and those words had kept going over and over in his mind, that life is just a bowl of cherries. Every now and then, for three days, the words had come into his head. It got so he would say them out loud to hear how they sounded. When he said them he felt free, like a bird. Then, on the night of the third day, he had got at the girl.

There had been nothing wrong with the girl. She had been OK. But, when everything was over, he had been sad. He had wanted to cry, like long ago when he was little and had wanted to run to his *mamma*, there in the stone-floored kitchen, in Savoca, far off in Sicily, and it was night, and everything had gone wrong that day. This feeling, a feeling he had forgotten for years, had come on him because that girl had put the words in his head that life was just a bowl of cherries, and then, suddenly, after he had had all there was to get out of her, he had known that life was not like that.

But now, standing in this road in the rain, he was suddenly thinking what life was: it was the road with the dark woods and the slate-blue patch of sky lightening over the notch between the hills where the gray mist slid down, and your feet would move forever. Now, thinking what life was, he felt a burst of cold joy.

"Are you going to tell the truth?" the woman's voice demanded.

He swung toward the shadows, where the dark eyes were burning at him. The burst of cold joy was in him, a bleak strength.

"That—that—" he began, but could not think of the word for what that thing was. "That Sandy Claws," he said then, "he not in road when that thing come. That thing they shoot."

For a second there was silence, silence except for the steady roar of the creek which, in its steadiness, was like silence. Then there was the man's voice: "You son-of-a-bitch!"

And the man had taken two plunging strides across the road, and Angelo Passetto had switched his parcel from the right to the left hand, and dropped his right hand toward his pocket. Then he remembered. There was nothing there.

In that same instant, to his left side there was a crashing boom, and he saw the mud blast up at the very feet of the man. The man, eyes popping, was staring across the road. His red-weathered face was streaked white.

Angelo Passetto turned. The woman stood near the edge of the porch now, with the shotgun still half raised. The blue smoke frayed out from the muzzle, motionless in the heavy air.

"You tried to kill me!" the man cried. "Cassie Killigrew, you tried to kill me fer a durn deer!"

"I didn't try to kill you," she said. "I didn't try to do a thing but what I did do."

With that she began to laugh, a clear, girlish laugh which, swelling from the shadows into the dripping air, made Angelo Passetto think of children playing far away. And with that thought the image came of children playing on a summer night, far away under a streetlight, long ago in Cleveland, singing, *"Giro, giro, tondo,"* holding hands and dancing in a ring. Angelo Passetto felt like crying.

"You're crazy," the man, standing there in the mud, still streak-faced and unsteady, was saying to the woman.

"If I was you," she said, mastering her laughter, "and I figured Cassie Killigrew Spottwood was crazy, and she had a shotgun in her hand and one barrel still loaded, I'd just drag that deer back where it belongs and put my string in my pocket and pick up my little old bow and arrow and get on back fast as I could where I came from—back to Gladys

Peegrum, that tow-headed, buttermilk-smelling yap-gal you wound up getting yourself married to."

Cy Grinder's mouth worked as though he were about to say something. But nothing came out.

"That's what I'd do," the woman said, seeming, all at once, to be drained and blank.

That was what the man did. In silence, except for the squish of boot in mud, he dragged the buck back across the road, stuffed the rope into a pocket, picked up the bow. In silence, the broad back, covered in the worn red mackinaw cloth, moved off. The water in the road slowly flowed into the tracks the man's boots left in the red mud.

Angelo Passetto watched the water flow into and fill the tracks. He did not know what this fact meant—the water flowing into the fresh tracks—but he felt somehow that it confirmed the new bleak strength in his own being. Soon he would go up that road, and the water would flow into the tracks made by the pointed toes of the patent-leather shoes, and he would not look back to see the water fill their emptiness.

The man was high on the suspension bridge now. He was looking back, standing there against the darkening sky. His rasping voice came out of the grayness, above the steady sound of the water. "Yeah, Cassie Killigrew," the voice yelled "if I knowed Mrs. High Muck-a-Muck Sunderland Spottwood was so pore-hungry she'd kill a man fer a deer, I'd sent you a bait of sowbelly!"

High on the bridge, over the sound of the water, he screamed with laughter. The laughter was muffled in the wet air. The man disappeared over the bridge, into the mist of the bluffside.

The woman had come off the porch and was standing by the buck, looking down at it. Then she looked up at Angelo

Passetto, a critical, assessing look—at his face, at the pad-shouldered, tight-waisted, big-plaid sports jacket, at the narrow black trousers, at the patent-leather shoes, at the soaked and disintegrating newspaper parcel in the left hand.

"If I don't tend to it right away," she said, "it'll ruin. Can you help me?" She hesitated, again looking at him. Then added: "I can give you a quarter. No—a half-dollar."

He said nothing. But he stepped delicately forward, over the fallen fence, moved to lay his parcel in the protection of one of the paint-peeled, square boxed columns of the porch, and turned to her, waiting.

"I'll get some rope," she said, and moved away, a thin figure swathed in a too-big, old-fashioned, dark brown, button sweater, a man's sweater, that hung down over her hips. She had a lot of dark hair piled up loose on her head, and the drizzle was falling on it.

He watched her cross the yard to an old barn, more ruinous than the house. She came back with a length of rope. "This old plow-line," she said, "maybe it'll hold." She held it out to him.

He took the rope, and waited for her to speak.

"What you waiting for?" she demanded. "Drag him under that big cedar, please. Throw the rope up. Then hoist him." She paused, then added, as though in apology: "It's the dragging and hoisting I can't do."

He obeyed. The buck hung head down, the narrow heels ceremonially bound together, the rack clearing the ground by a full foot, the gold-speckled eyes bulging and fixed. Unsagging, back of the left shoulder, the arrow protruded upward. At the base of the shaft, a little blood oozed. Angelo Passetto waited.

"It's a big one," the woman said, studying the creature hanging there. "A hundred and seventy-five pounds, maybe. Eight points."

"What?" Angelo Passetto asked.

(15)

"On the antlers," she said. "He's eight years old."

She stared at the buck. She reached out and touched a finger to the left side at the soft juncture of the haunch where the nut-brown shaded to the cream of the belly; then ran the finger, meditatively, down the side. The finger touched the blood of the wound.

"Eight years," she said, "and him running round over the whole country, and then Cy Grinder shoots him with a little old piddling bow and arrow."

She withdrew her finger, looked at the blood on it, then wiped the blood on the lower edge of the old brown sweater.

"Lady," Angelo Passetto said, "and now what happen? *Cosa fare?*"

She seemed to discover him.

"You know how hunters say it?" she demanded.

He shook his head.

"It's not like a lady is supposed to talk," she said, "but if you do a thing it don't matter much, I guess, how you say it. They say, bleed, nut, and gut." Her gaze swept the buck, from the sack of testicles, hanging forward now, down the cream-colored muscle-bulge of the belly, to the black muzzle. A little blood now drooled from the muzzle.

"I'll get a knife," she said, and was again gone.

She brought the knife, and handed it to him. He moved to the porch and, under her gaze, laid down the knife, took off the plaid sports coat, folded it, with a certain lingering loving motion, and laid it at the driest point within reach on the porch floor. He stood there, rolling up his sleeves. The flesh of his forearms was swelling and slick, brown against the whiteness of his shirt.

He picked up the knife, tested the edge on the hair of his left forearm, approached the buck with his delicate tread, as though the ground were uncertain or he wanted to spare his shoes, and stood by the buck; with a sudden ease he had seized the rack, had lifted it to make the throat bulge taut, had inserted the knife and slitted across, had stepped back from the gush of blood.

He stood leaning toward the buck, in the pose of a dancer, still holding the rack up to keep the neck taut and the slit open to facilitate the gushing of blood. The blood kept on coming. It sluiced the old cedar droppings to make little dams and dikes, which the steaming red flow then would break through.

"If you know how to do things so well," the woman said, "how come you asked me what to do?"

"Before I never do it to a—" He stopped. "To a Sandy Claws," he finished.

"Where did you learn what to do?" she asked.

"My *zio*—" he said. Then: "He had a what-you-call—a farm. I learn in my uncle farm."

He did not say how, when his father died, they sent him to America, to his uncle in Ohio, and he had worked on that *maledetto* farm, and he had hated the uncle and the farm and himself and the whole world. Till the day he knocked the uncle down and ran away to Cleveland and found the bright exciting things like whiskey and girls and cars and his own face in the mirror while the comb moved through the black silkiness of his hair, over and over again.

"What's that way of talking you've got?" she asked.

"Me *Siciliano*—Sicily," he said.

She was studying him. He stood under her gaze, under the darkness of the big cedar, his arms hanging loose at his sides, the knife hanging loose in the right hand, a pool of blood soaking into the earth at his feet.

"Is that why you are so brown-complected?" she asked.

"*Siciliano*," he said, not even sullen, simply waiting.

The gush had stopped. Only a few drops fell now. They fell off the now-drenched muzzle, one by one, into the pool.

"Where are you going?" she asked.

He looked up the road, not saying anything.

"The road, it doesn't go anywhere," she said. "It just peters out. Time ago, there used to be some nice houses up there. But the land, it washed away, everything petered out." She paused, seeming to forget him.

"My family's house was up there," she began again. "It was a real nice house. A nice big farm. When I was a girl."

She stopped, and he looked at her and wondered what she had been like as a girl, and wondered how long back that had been. He tried to think of her as a girl, but could not. She was what she was. Her face was white and withdrawn now, the eyes veiled.

Then, with a shocking directness, she lifted her eyes to him.

"There's not any house up that road, anymore," she said. "Except for Cy Grinder." After another pause: "He was the man killed that deer. Do you reckon he's holding up supper till you get there and he can ask you to come in and pull up a chair?"

She laughed, again with that sudden burst of swirling girlish gaiety, the dark eyes flashing.

She stopped laughing, and her face was, again, white and still.

"You can stay here," she said out of that white face, distantly as if nothing in the world mattered. "There's plenty of rooms to sleep in. You can have your keep. I'll pay you what I can. I need somebody to help. One time there was lots of hands on the place, but they're gone now. The last one left last spring. Just an old colored man that happened to stay on. In that old shack up the hill. Then he up and left."

He looked off again, up the road.

"You can always leave when you want to," she said, listlessly. "You can always say your kind goodbye and set your foot in the big road."

He looked back at her. Her hands were behind her, and she was leaning back against the corner of the porch, as though spent. From the slumped shoulders the old brown sweater sagged loosely about her thinness. Her face was whiter than ever, and the eyes in it were veiled with indifference. The drizzle fell on her bare head. A few strands of the dark hair had slipped down from the loose pile on her head and were plastered across the left cheek. She did not seem to know or care.

"OK," he said. "I stay."

He would stay. They would never think of finding him here.

CHAPTER TWO

☘☘☘☘☘☘☘☘☘☘☘☘**M**urray Guilfort nursed his shining new white Buick Roadmaster convertible up the rutted and rocky road, beside the creek, under the brilliant blue of the autumn sky. Even if he allowed himself a new white convertible, and kept the top down as much as possible, and laid his hat aside to get what tan he could, he always wore a dark gray suit well buttoned up, a dark tie, and black shoes. Except, of course, in hot weather. But now, though the weather was bright, there was a chill that streaked the heat of the sun. Whenever the car passed into shadow, or drew near the creek, or found a downdraft of air from the bluff, there was that cold finger brushing you, as when you swim in a warm pond and hit a current from a secret spring. So Murray had not been long in the valley before buttoning up his dark gray herringbone tweed topcoat. He set the gray felt hat carefully on his head, under the blue sky.

Murray Guilfort allowed himself the shining white convertible. But looking into the triple mirror in the shop of the best tailor in Nashville, or even in Chicago, and seeing the incipient bulge of his belly, the paleness of the face that always seemed to underlie what the sun or sunlamp had done, and the round, balding skull with the silky hair brought somewhat forward, he had long since decided that he could not allow himself any other than the dark gray suit.

Not that his decision was ever in words. It was in a flow and flicker of feeling: in a small sadness like water rising in a dark cellar; in an undefined, unaimed anger that might, to his great surprise, edge his voice as he spoke to a fitter; in a hopefulness that made him steal a glance at the profile caught in one of the side mirrors and think that his nose was good and strong; in a stoicism that made him suck in his belly; and, during one period, in a sweet pity that came as, looking down at the gray, or bald, head of an old fitter crouched to measure the length of trousers, he wondered when that fellow had last had a piece of tail.

Murray could remember, though he tried valiantly not to remember, the event that had laid the groundwork for that sweet pity that later would come on him as he looked down at such a crouching old figure, with its arthritic motion.

He had been at the meeting of the Bar Association, up in Chicago, where he had gone alone, his wife being unwell. One evening he had a few drinks, late, with Alfred Milbank, a very successful patent lawyer from Washington, D.C., a horsy, red-faced, burly man, handsome and with prematurely white hair, who liked to be mistaken in public places for Stettinius, then Secretary of State; and Milbank, after some moments of silence, setting his empty glass down on the table with a sharp click, as though definitely settling a weighty matter, had said: "This city of Chicago has a population of three million, and one half of that count is cunt, and I am going to get some."

With that Milbank had drawn a little black morocco leather book from an inside pocket and begun riffling the pages. He had laid the book flat, marking the page with a large, well-manicured forefinger. "Say, Guilfort," he had said, grinning out of the raw, fevered face, "you look like you need a piece."

And before Murray could pull himself together, Milbank went on: "Yes, Guilfort, you are getting into middle age. You owe it to yourself. Your wife—no disrespect to a fine lady—is getting into middle age. You owe it to her. Yes, Guilfort, if you'll hone yourself on Matilda or Alicia"—and he tapped the page with that manicured forefinger—"you will go back to Tennessee all edged up to give the little lady a real whack. She'll appreciate it. She'll start reducing. She'll fix her hair different. She'll begin listening when you have something to say, she'll—"

Suddenly, with a sad guiltiness that became a flash of resentment, Murray had thought that Bessie was a lot overweight—hell, fat—that the bed sagged on her side, that when she held up the bridge cards to study them her fingers looked puffy, that she had acquired a habit of sucking her gums.

And Milbank's voice had been saying: "—and as for Alicia, she is a cross between a she-catamount and a summer cloud. Your soul will expand when she breathes upon it. She has, my dear Guilfort, that rare art of making a man feel loved for himself alone. *Qua* man. No—*qua* that unique individual *esse* said to be precious in God's sight. *Qua*—in your case—Murray Guilfort."

And at that moment Murray, looking into the bottom of an Old Fashioned glass, where the orange rind lay scarcely awash, had been wondering if he—he, Murray Guilfort—had ever, ever, been loved for himself alone.

And Milbank had been saying: "With Alicia, the performance is, as I said, art, not nature. For, my dear fellow, it takes art to complete nature, and what passionate sincerity can make a wife do for a man a time or two in his whole married life, art can enable a pro to do every God-damned time she un-limbers your jock."

He laughed a sudden, raw, neighing laugh, and rolled his eyes.

"Yes, Guilfort," he went on, "art is all, and a good lie is worth a million facts in any court. Or in any bed. Illusion, Guilfort, is the only truth. And as for me, I solemnly affirm that, within the hour, I shall lay out one hundred dollars for a big juicy chunk of illusion. With"—and he laughed again in a coughing heartiness that sent a blast of whiskey-heavy, hot breath across to brush Murray's damp brow—"hair on it!"

At that blast, Murray had lifted his gaze to confront the red, strong-jowled face leering at him from under the glossy, bar-bered mass of white locks. He had felt a cold, sick chill up his spine. He had felt, painfully, the surprising erection trapped in his tight shorts. He had been afraid that something might hap-pen, as though he were a kid, then and there. He had hoped that that man would not see his fingers trembling on the Old Fashioned glass.

"How about it, chum?" the voice had said, and the heavy lips of the red face had drawn back to expose, in a leer of con-temptuous challenge, the strong, yellowing canines that stood too far out from the gums.

But in that instant, Murray had not seen the aging, saturnine face of Alfred Milbank that was thrust at him, but the face of Sunderland Spottwood, young, ruddy, leering at him in the same contemptuous challenge. It had seemed to Murray that he was trapped in something that had been long ago and would never end. He would, forever, have to live with such a face be-fore his eyes—the face of Milbank or the face of Spottwood, did it matter which?—to live under that amiable contempt, to live in his envy of that face, to live, in fact, by the image of the life of that face which was the face of another man.

"Well, he's dead," the man said, offhand and curt, as though dropping a soiled object.

The man turned away, leaving the space of air where he had stood.

Later that day, after making some discreet inquiries and cutting the afternoon session to hunt up files of the Washington papers in the Public Library, he learned that Alfred Milbank had had a heart attack in a hotel in Scranton, that an unidentified woman in a leopard coat, and a pulled-down blue felt hat, had given the alarm to a bellhop and dashed out into the night, that the stricken man had died three hours later at the Moses Taylor Hospital in that city. The woman, in her haste, had left a pair of stockings and a brassiere in the hotel room.

That evening Murray got a plane back to Tennessee.

At home he came down with a severe gastric disturbance, which the attending physician diagnosed, somewhat dubiously, as pancreatitis. Some five weeks later, however, the patient was well enough to make a trip to Chicago.

Murray had, however, long since lost track of Sophie. Upon learning from Mrs. Billings, Milbank's Chicago "connection," that Sophie was no longer available, he had had the wild impulse to track her down, to get a divorce, to marry her. But common sense had prevailed, and in recent years a certain Mildred, who had come to him well recommended by Mrs. Billings, had proved a very satisfactory surrogate. All he had to do was to send Mrs. Billings a wire (never sent from Parkerton and signed only Charlie), with date of arrival. Mildred had fallen easily into his ritual—the dimly lit sitting room of a suite, the bottle of Piper-Heidsieck, the muted conversation, then the silence as she sat on the couch by his side with her head on his shoulder.

At the end of the ritual Murray always closed his eyes and waited for the image of Sophie to pop into his head. Then he would be ready.

But on this, his last, trip to Chicago—the last he was ever to make there—Mrs. Billings told him that Mildred was unavailable, that, to be exact, she had got married. To a very sweet man, Mrs. Billings added, a retired dentist. Mrs. Billings was saying something else, about a sweet and competent girl named, it seemed, Charlotte. But Murray, in a faint, dreamlike motion, was replacing the phone on its cradle—the phone was blue, the suite was done in blue. Mildred always liked blue.

It was only 2:00 in the afternoon. There was the whole afternoon to live through. The afternoon was supposed to be a period of anticipation. He stood in the blue suite and wondered why he had racked up the phone. What was wrong with Charlotte?

But at the thought of Charlotte, a nameless fear gripped him, and the strange discomfort which the doctor had said was a symptom of pancreatitis again began. He thought, then, that he might call up one of the lawyers he knew in Chicago —one who had been very nice to him and wasn't too "toney." But that thought made the pain worse.

So he went for a walk along the Lake. It was spring—an early spring—and people, some of them young couples holding hands, were walking in the park by the Lake. He averted his face from them and walked on, north. He walked for hours. It was long after dark when he got back to the Loop, where he found a French restaurant and ordered an expensive meal and a bottle of Bordeaux, even more expensive. He ate little, but he drank the bottle. Then he had coffee, and three enormously expensive brandies, thinking grimly, as he sipped the brandy, that a man had to have something, anyway.

Back in the sitting room of the suite, he heard, with some surprise, his own voice saying, into the blue phone, that they should send up the bottle of Piper-Heidsieck. When the wine came he tipped the waiter exorbitantly. Then, in solitude, he sat on the couch and, sip by sip, drank the wine. That took him two hours. The last sip gone, he leaned back and closed his eyes. It was after midnight when he rose, moved somnambulistically across the room, entered the bathroom, and masturbated.

He stood before the mirror and stared at the new-ravaged face. He had not done that, he told himself, in twenty-five years. He said it out loud, in a husky awe-struck voice: "Twenty-five years." As he said the words he felt that a great black wind was sweeping over the city, through the thick walls of steel and stone, into this very place of glittering privacy.

Then, as he stared in the mirror, he had the idea. He would get on the Supreme Court of Tennessee. If he were on the highest bench of his state, even if it was only Tennessee, then nobody—like that lawyer from Washington, that high-toned son-of-a-bitch—would look at him with that queer fish-eye chill, and then turn away.

Moving along beside the creek in Spottwood Valley, under the brilliant blue of autumn, with the top of the shining white Roadmaster convertible down, Murray was thinking that he might, really, get on the bench. He was prosecutor now—and didn't that prove he had popular appeal? And they owed him something. He had put his shoulder to the wheel. He had put his hand in his pocket. He was favorably known in the state, even over in East Tennessee, after that Franklin Lumber case. And an appointment from the Parkerton-Fiddlersburg section was long overdue.

His eyes were fixed up this road that he knew so well—and had known all his life—but his vision was inward, fixed, as it were, on a single point of acute light in the darkness of his being. It was the point of light in a camera obscura, and he was inside the dark box.

That point of light was, somehow, the idea of himself as a

judge. Sometimes he did have the actual image of himself sitting on a high place, surrounded by clouds that softly glowed in a sourceless, transfiguring light. But more often the thing he had in his head was, simply, the point of brilliant light. He had the feeling that, when he was judge, he would be able to stare unblinking into the very heart of that point of light.

More and more, it seemed that, when, in his inwardness, he stared at that light, his vision dimmed for the world of things around him. He was, in fact, alone. He had no close friends. Bessie was dead, four years now, and at night he came home to eat alone in a shadowy house, served by a manservant named Leonidas whose foot made no sound and whose black hand was anonymous on the edge of the plate offered him. He did not sleep much, and often at night would get up and wander the house, half expecting to see, suddenly on some wall of darkness, that pinpoint of brilliant, apocalyptic light. For on those occasions, it seemed that he was not wandering the darkness of the house but the darkness of his own head.

As the world of the present grew less real, his whole being became more sharply focused on some redeeming future. He could not bear to think of the past—or could bear to think of it only because, with his gaze fixed on the point of light in darkness, he could repudiate the past. Someday—soon, soon—he would be free of all the past, transformed and redeemed, his true self at last unhusked, to exist forever in an ecstasy of triumph.

No—of vengeance.

Vengeance on what? For what? He did not know. He did not, in fact, even know that it was vengeance. He knew only, and denied the knowledge, that sometimes, rapt in the dream of the future and his mystic transformation, his muscles would go tense and strong, his breath would come fast, and there was a deep image and enactment of striking and striking and striking again, in darkness.

. . .

Up the road, on his left, across from the old suspension bridge, he saw the house. He thought of Sunderland—young Sunder—booted, spurred, young, whooping as he rose in the stirrups, galloping down that road, and the fields were green, and fat cattle stood on that green, and the sunshine that was over all was the sunshine of nearly forty years ago. In that vision the house glimmered white between the dark cedars.

But the house did not glimmer white now. Looking at the paintless weatherboards, the broken glass of an upper window, the sagging ridgepole of the ell, he told himself that the house had never been anything very great anyway—just a big log house to begin with, in the time of the first Spottwood; then, later, weatherboarding had been nailed on, then the ell built, then, in the day of Sunderland's grandpa, the two-story porch hung on. But the pillars were just square boxes set around props of hewn cedar. You could see that clearly enough now, with the boxing rotted away.

And he thought of the house he now lived in—the old Darlington place which had become his when he married Bessie Darlington. Yes, that was a house for you, brick, with the high white portico, with Corinthian columns—he loved to hold the word in his mind, *Corinthian*—and everything spic and span, for he had been able to foot the bill to put it back in shape.

Hell, he'd bought it twice over, the money he had poured into it. And that expenditure seemed, far back in the shadowy logic of his being, part of the necessary price you paid to be a judge on the Supreme Court of Tennessee. Perhaps marrying Bessie Darlington had been part of the price, too, but that thought was something that hung always to one side, just out of range of vision. He had never turned his head enough to see it directly.

With a sad contempt for the boy who had once thought the Spottwood house grand, he closed his mind like a valve on all recollection, and said to himself that the government ought to take over this whole poverty valley, where the soil had leached away and the fences were down. They ought to turn the whole thing into a timber and game preserve.

But if they did, where then, he thought, would Sunderland Spottwood go?

Then he asked himself, with sudden anger, if it mattered where that hulk of old flesh lay? And he asked himself, even more savagely, why he was coming all this distance, losing the better part of a day, when work was piled up at the office, especially since he was now prosecutor in addition to his private commitments, to stand and look down at that hulk which could give no sign of the imprisoned, dwindling life except the throaty, rasping exhalation that made the listener himself feel strangled.

And his mind, do what he would, turned again to the past, to the image of what Sunderland had once been, a powerful, big-footed, big-handed, ruddy, disheveled young man, with a mass of curly yellow locks and slightly protruding insolent blue eyes. In his first year at the university in Nashville Sunder had worn to class—when he went to class—an old hunting coat, stained with the blood of many seasons. He had carried a frog-sticker with a five-inch blade, and sometimes during a lecture would flick the steel out and do an extremely scrupulous job on his nails. He did not shave regularly. He paid little attention to the sprinkling of co-eds, but every Saturday night went down to one of the whorehouses back of the Capitol. He had pledged a good fraternity, as the name Spottwood, the rumor of Spottwood money, and his own arrogant masculinity would guarantee, but before initiation he got roaring drunk at the house, fought a senior, and got his pin jerked.

"Screw you!" he told them, one and all, "you bunch of mule-buggers!"

By April he was a legend.

By May he was expelled. He had ridden his motorcycle across the campus, buck naked at 4:30 of a fine spring afternoon, the soft-aired hour when old ladies tooled their electric broughams slowly along to admire the magnolia blooms that adorned the academic scene. That evening, when Murray came to sympathize with him about his expulsion, he found him seated on a bed, between two suitcases into which he was flinging whatever came to hand. A half-empty clear glass bottle of white mule—this being back in Prohibition—was on the floor at his feet, surrounded by books, face down, ripped apart. When Murray said he was sorry about things, the big blue eyes, now red-rimmed with drink, popped bigger in their arrogant unforgiveness and fixed deep in the very soul of Murray Guilfort.

"Screw them all!" Sunderland yelled in manic glee. "And screw this whole mule-buggering university!"

So he had gone back to Spottwood Valley, and here he was now, in that house which Murray was approaching, as so many times, summer and winter, over the last years, he had approached it. He would draw up to the place where the gate had once been, get out, and with a slight constriction of breath, move toward the rotting steps.

But now, all at once, he noticed that the steps had been repaired. The boards were not new, but looked sound, and the work was neat. Then he saw a hammer, saw, and metal square against the wall of the porch—old but with some of the rust off from recent use. The brown blade of the saw was, he observed, smeared with grease, to loosen the rust.

He picked up the saw, and smelled it. Yes, it was bacon grease. He and Sunder, boys together, had once built a skiff for fishing. The saw they had used to build the skiff—it, too, had been brown with rust, and they had put bacon grease on it to keep it from binding. He laid this saw down and went to the door.

Why was he here, he asked himself. Why the hell was he
here?

The door opened. In the shadow of the hall, the whiteness
of the face floated before him. For an instant, before the
words would come, he stared at that whiteness. Staring at it
now, he saw the face of the girl—whiteness swimming at him
in the shadow of the hall—who had opened the door when he
came to this house almost twenty years ago, to the funeral
of Josephine Killigrew Spottwood, who had been the first wife
of Sunderland Spottwood. Out of the shadows, shyness, and
distance, the face had floated at Murray Guilfort, who, in that
instant, twenty years ago, had, inarticulately but with an angry
wrenching of the heart, recognized his destiny. The girl, with
one white hand clutching the time-darkened oak of the door,
had said: "I'm Cassie Killigrew. I was nursing my aunt. It's
my aunt Josie who is dead."

Now, so many years later, standing at the door that would
open upon the same dark hall, he saw the vision of a white hand
clutching the door. The varnish on the door had long since
swollen in tiny yellow pustules that, broken, had left white
streaks, now dry and scrofulous, and the hand was more bony
now. But staring at the face, Murray knew that, on that day
long ago, he had already known all that would be brought
forth by time. Why did a man have to know ahead of time?
Why wasn't the last knowing, when things finally came true,
enough for a man to have to endure?

Like that time when Sunder, only a boy then, had come
pounding up the lane on that great gray beast of a stallion
named Stonewall, and had swung off the saddle, himself wall-
eyed and heaving like the big gray, and said he double-dog
dared Murray to get on? Why had he—Murray Guilfort—had
to know, even as he set foot to stirrup, all that would happen:

the image of himself in the moment when Stonewall would rear, and plunge forward, and the world would go reeling into blackness? Why did you have to know?

Why couldn't you be like Sunder, who had known nothing, who cared nothing, whose own image of Sunderland Spottwood was that of an angry, laughing self clamped astride a great beast that reared triumphantly against a world of nothingness, and who had plunged ahead into the darkness of time, his eyes bulging bright and lips damp with the spittle from a last yell of manic glee?

Then, as Murray stood at the door of the house, that flash was gone. It was as though he now remembered nothing, had asked himself nothing.

The door opened, and there, in the shadow, was the woman.

"How are you, Cassie?" he was saying.

"I'm all right, thank you," she said, and held out her hand.

"How's Sunder?"

She shrugged, ever so slightly. "How can he be?" she asked, and fixed on his face a look that, from its still distance, was asking how could anything be but what it was, how could Murray Guilfort be, how could the world be?

"Yes," he murmured, "yes," and followed her down the hall.

She pushed open a door, and entered the front room, which he knew would be unchanged. There would be the holes in the red carpet, strands of fabric showing gray, the boards staring up from beneath; the big sepia engraving above the fireplace, the "Horse Fair" by Rosa Bonheur, splotched with damp, now scarcely identifiable as a picture at all; the long, ponderous rosewood piano by Chickering, toward one corner, the gap-toothed blackness where ivories were missing and the remaining ivories yellow as old cheese; the tattered and yellowing lace curtains that hung inside the dusk-streaked red velvet drapes; the marble-topped table with the big black leather

Bible, in which the names of all the Spottwoods were written, in ink long since gone brown, the black leather binding gone brown too; and, by the black cave of the fireplace, propped on an easel once gilt, the oil portrait of the first Sunderland Spottwood, burly, black-coated, red-faced, with a clipped gray Vandyke stuck on the massive chin, like some whimsical afterthought of the artist, as irrelevant as the end of a lady's feather boa hanging over the edge of a limestone cliff—old Sunderland, who had grabbed the land, built the house, beat the niggers, and gone to Congress, and whose flat, painted arrogance of eye refused, in this dimness, to acknowledge what, over the years, had happened in his house.

Murray saw it all, just what he had known he would see, and thought how nothing changed, not anymore. Then, with a flicker of terror, he knew that everything, even as he looked, was changing. The shreds of the carpet raveled under his eyes, writhed like worms in anguish, burning in their lightless combustion. The leather of the Bible disintegrated and fell, like pollen, on the white marble of the tabletop. The paint scaled off the eyes of old Sunderland Spottwood, the arrogance fell away from those painted eyes in miniscule pale flakes that lay on the dark brick of the hearth, like dandruff. Everything was nothing.

Then Murray got hold of himself, and turned toward the woman.

"I see you're getting some repair work done," he said, heartily. "The steps."

She nodded.

"Must be hard to find anybody qualified out here," he said. "But I want you to know my offer of last spring, it holds good. To get a real carpenter from town, and a couple of helpers, and get some basic repairs done here. It's a shame to let property go to pieces. Property has rights of its own that a man has to respect. If you'll just let me, Cassie, I'll—"

She was looking at him. "What difference," she said, "would it ever make to him—to Sunder?"

"But property," he began, "it's sound property and—"

She wasn't even listening to him. He knew she wasn't. That was the way she was. She would be standing before you, even looking you in the eye, and you knew, suddenly, that she wasn't there. But he asked anyway, in a sharp voice that might stir her: "But who did the work? This work?"

She wasn't even looking at him now, but at some spot beyond him.

"Who," he repeated, even more sharply, "could you get out here to do the work?"

She let her gaze come back to him. "Angelo," she said.

"Who's he?"

"I don't know," she said.

"What do you mean you don't know?" He heard the thin, sharp tone that he always tried to keep out of his voice when he was examining a witness in court. He tried again: "You mean he wasn't from around here?"

"He came down the road, in the rain," she said. "His name, it's Angelo."

"But Angelo—that's a first name. What's his real name, his surname?"

"I don't know," she said.

She seemed to be falling away from him again. So he said, very gently: "These days, Cassie—how are you feeling these days?"

"I'm feeling fine," she said. "Except for a headache. Now and then."

"I'm sorry about the headache," he murmured. He waited a moment. "Now this Angelo," he asked, "where does he live?"

She studied him. "You thought you were being clever,"

she said. "You thought you were being smart and tactful. Like a lawyer. Changing the subject and asking how I've been feeling. Then coming back to Angelo. But I've told you all I know. He came down the road, in the rain, wearing city clothes, all wet, with a paper package in his hand. Newspaper, soaked and giving way. It looked like he just came, all of a sudden, out of the rain and mist. Then he helped me dress the deer."

"What deer, Cassie?"

"The one Cy Grinder shot."

"Cy Grinder—oh, yes, that fellow."

"Yes, Cy Grinder, and he shot the deer on my land. With a little old fool bow and arrow, and I made him give it back to me. Angelo was there, and he said it was on my land, too, and Cy Grinder got mad, and I shot off the shotgun." She paused, then added: "I didn't shoot so as to hit him. But he brought the deer back."

"Shooting at people," Murray said tartly, "it's against the law."

But he saw that she wasn't listening. He leaned at her, and almost in a whisper, said: "Angelo—where does Angelo live, Cassie?"

"That's what you asked me," she said. "I don't mind telling, he lives here."

"Here?"

"Yes," she said. "He dressed the deer. He couldn't remember what to call it—in English, I mean—but he could dress it fine. As soon as he knew it was done like a hog or a beef. And he's killed my two hogs, too. Just last week when we got that meat-frost, and put it in the smokehouse. He lived on his uncle's farm, that's how he learned how, and—"

"Where was his uncle's farm, Cassie?"

"I don't know," she said. "And he fixed the porch. He cut the winter wood, too, and—"

"Could I see him—talk to him?"

(37)

"He's gone to Parkerton," she said. "He fixed the car, so it'll run. He had some business in Parkerton, and he'll get supplies, too."

"Could I see the room he's in?" he asked.

Without a sound she led him into the hall, down to the cross hall that came out of the ell, up the cross hall and into a room. It was bare except for an old walnut tester bed, a mahogany dresser with a marble top and carved scrolls of leaves and fruit around the time-splotched mirror, and by the bed a split-bottom chair, on which stood an old electric table lamp, with no shade. One windowpane was out, repaired with a piece of cardboard, water-stained. The door to the closet was off. A strip of burlap had been tacked over the opening, to hang for a curtain. The burlap looked new.

Murray stepped to the closet and lifted back the burlap. A coat was there, on a hanger. He brought it forth, and examined it, a coat of bold plaid, black and gray, with heavily padded shoulders. "It's good material," he said, fingering the fabric. "It cost money." Then added: "Tailor-made."

"I wouldn't know," she said.

He looked inside the inner pocket, then at the spot under the collar where a label might be. "No label," he said. Then added: "Secondhand, no doubt."

He carried it back to the closet, inspected the pair of black serge trousers, and adjusted the coat over them on the hanger. He picked up one of the patent-leather shoes that sat neatly side by side on the floor and examined it. It was wadded with old newspaper to hold its shape, and had been wiped with something that looked like vaseline. "He hasn't got a big foot," he said. "Is he a little man?"

"No," she said, "he's right good-size. Bigger than most."

"What's he wearing now?"

"He looked so sad," she said, "trying to do things in his good clothes. So I found some old things of Sunder's, and cut 'em

down to fit. He's not as big as Sunder, even if he is good-size."
She paused. "Not that they fit so good," she added, "even after I
cut 'em down. But they'll do for work."

"Do you feed him, or does he cook for himself?"

"I feed him," she said. "Why wouldn't I feed him, when he
comes in from work? But I don't eat with him. I never sit down
and eat with him. I eat in there with Sunder, I mean after I've
got him fed. If that's what you want to know."

"Listen, Cassie," Murray said, hoping to make his voice just
right, "don't be annoyed I'm asking questions. You know how
concerned I am about you and Sunder. That's all I'm concerned
about, and—"

"Look at me!" she commanded, with sudden intensity.
"Would he be concerned with me? If that's what you are concerned about. He's young. Look at me, I'm old!"

He couldn't help but obey, despite some distress, repugnance, and fear, that forbade. The brown sweater, with faded
streaks, hung shapeless about her, the white face looked dead
again, and distant.

"I was young," she was saying, in a voice listless and thin,
not directed at him. "But it was only a little while. Then, of a
sudden, I was old. There wasn't anything in between. What
most folks have in between, what might have been in between
for me—it was like somebody just blew it away. Puff! Like
blowing off dandelion fuzz."

"Hush, hush," Murray commanded, in a harsh, urgent whisper. "Hush—you aren't old!"

She began to laugh. Then she was scrutinizing him.

"What makes you look so funny in the face?" she asked, and
laughed again.

She came close and peered into his face. "Why, Murray,"
she said with a quick girlish giggle, "why you—you're old too!"
She kept looking at him. "Didn't you know you are?" she demanded.

"Sure," he said, with forced heartiness. "A man doesn't get any younger."

Foolishly, he discovered that he still held the patent-leather shoe in his hand. He was grateful to discover it in his hand. Now he would have to lean over and set it, carefully, beside the other, on the floor, behind the burlap curtain.

She led him back to the parlor. He stood there, reached into his inner pocket, took out his wallet, and began to count out the bills. He held the money out to her. "It's a hundred dollars," he said. She took it, saying, "Thank you."

He laid a receipt on the marble top of the table, and a fountain pen. She went to the table and signed it. He picked it up, put the receipt in his pocket, picked up the pen.

"I wish you'd keep a checking account," he said, fretfully.

"It would just be trouble," she said. "Trouble for nothing."

"I expect you'll have more income soon," he said, not knowing on what impulse he said it. "I'm making a new investment for you."

"We've got all we need," she said. "Just to hold out."

At this, some dark anger stirred in him. He felt defensive, caught out, vengeful. "You could at least allow yourself a little comfort," he said, his voice shaking despite his effort at control. "At least a few little luxuries. At least, a—"

She was looking at him. "You have to lead your own kind of life," she said.

And Murray thought: *What kind of life must I lead?*

Yes, what kind of a life, indeed, coming out here, year after year, bringing money that he had to pretend was from an investment, putting those receipts in a file in his office to get yellower year by year, telling the lie, even beginning to believe the lie, feeling himself caught in the lie. But what kind of lie? He did not know.

His mind closed against thought. He braced himself, squared his shoulders, drew in the slackness of belly, said: "I reckon we can see Sunder now."

She nodded, pulled aside the weighty, dusty-red remnants of old velvet curtains to expose a door, between the fireplace and the inner wall, opened it, and with the money in her hand, led the way.

As a boy, whenever he was with Sunder, he would pull back his shoulders and suck his belly in. Now following the woman into the room where Sunder was, he did that.

The room had been the dining room of the house, a big room with wainscoting, and a floral paper, and with a crystal chandelier, once for gas but now showing empty electric sockets, in the middle of the ceiling. The wainscoting had lost its varnish, the floral paper had long ago faded like a garden stricken by the final frost, the plaster of the ceiling had fallen, here and there, to expose the laths, and what plaster remained was cracked and crazed, waiting to fall. The big fireplace, back-to-back with the one in the parlor, had been covered over with tin. A pot-bellied iron stove was connected by rusty black pipe to a flue, crudely knocked out and mended with fire clay, above the old mantel shelf. On the mantel a damaged Dresden bowl held a handful of spills, of twisted newspaper. Against the outside wall a big dining table was pushed to give floor space, and on it was piled the detritus of years, old papers, a rolled piece of carpet, a saddle from which the long-dry leather was peeling off the frame, several large crocks and a crock jug, a dozen empty medicine bottles, a length of pipe. There, too, was a stack of bed sheets, clean and folded, but not ironed.

Near a door, over to the left, was a narrow iron cot, neatly made up, the pillow plump and white in the general gloom. In the middle of the room stood the old brass bed. By the bed was a slop-jar, with a white enamel cover. An enamel bedpan was visible just under the foot of the bed. On the bed, under a quilt, was the immobile thing.

The slow wheezing sound drew across the silence.

Murray stood and tried not to hear that sound while he waited for the woman to do what she always did. She went to remove a brick over at the right side of the fireplace. From the hole beyond it, she drew out an old black leather purse, and put the bills into it.

"You really ought to have a bank account," Murray said.

"Out here?" she demanded. "Who's to cash checks for me?"

"Where you spend the money—that store at the Corners."

"I get stuff at Parkerton now," she said.

"They'd cash a check."

"I don't go," she said.

"But you just said you—"

"I didn't say I went," she said.

"Well—"

"I make a list. I give him the cash money," she said. "It's him goes. Every two weeks. Since he fixed the old car up. He can fix anything. It's him who—"

"Him," he echoed, with distaste. Then seeing the old black purse, he added, fretfully, "At least you might get a purse that'll hold together. That's got a hole already—"

"I don't go anywhere with it," she rebutted, and crammed it back in the hole, and replaced the brick.

She turned to face him, nodding across the room toward the bed.

"There he is," she said.

Murray looked across at the figure on the bed. He was not yet ready.

"All these years," she said.

"You have been a devoted wife," he said, mechanically. He

was leaning over the inner depth of himself, straining to see, to
hear, something in that darkness, waiting for something to
happen there.

Sometimes it did not happen. Sometimes nothing happened
at all. On the visits when nothing had happened, he would get
into his car, and drive down the road, and the land would
seem empty, and he would feel empty, emptiness moving
through emptiness. On the visits when it did happen, there
would be, after it was over, a misery in him as he moved across
the land, but it would not be the misery of emptiness. Instead
it would be a gnawing, like remorse. Then he would think,
quite irrationally, of the receipt in his pocket. For that would
mean, at least, something.

Even if he didn't know exactly what.

Now he stood and stared across the room, at the thing under
the quilt, and thought that today it might happen. He took a
step toward the bed, experimentally, then another step, avoid-
ing a rocker that stood in the center of the room. A gray tiger
cat was asleep in the rocker. He took refuge, for one instant, in
the sight of the cat: yes, yes, that was what life was, a cat
asleep in a rocker, and outside was the blue beauty of the autumn sky, and your heart steady and slow in your bosom.

But abruptly he shoved the rocker aside, and passed on. The
chair was rocking slowly behind him, the cat's gaze indifferently
on him, as he approached the bed.

He looked down at the shapelessness, then at the face. The
face, upward, was still somewhat fleshy, but not ruddy now,
paleness streaked with red. The flesh looked soft, so soft that
it fell away from the nose and chin, lying in folds and drooping
furrows down the throat and jowls and cheeks, leaving the
chin and nose as unnaturally sharp protuberances out of the
sleekness of flesh. The sharpness of nose and chin gave the impression that a thin, frail man was sunken and trapped in the
slow-sagging flesh.

(43)

"He's not as big as he used to be," Murray said.

"He keeps right on losing weight," she said. "It's a God's blessing, I reckon. For me, I mean."

He looked at her.

"Used to be I could hardly move him any," she said. "To take care of him. I had to strain and struggle. Now I can manage."

Murray was looking into the man's eyes.

The eyes, a clear boyish blue, stared up at him. He could see nothing in them. Something might be there, if only he could read it.

Then the shadow came over the eyes.

The left side of the face began to twitch, the shadow in the eyes darkened, like storm over water. Then the heavy, pale lips parted and the sound came. It was a grinding, rasping exhalation. It came three times. It was merciless and unappeasable.

It stopped. Then Murray knew that today it was going to happen. He felt, deep in himself, that stir, then that burst of cold, justifying joy. He had felt the moment that justified all.

It was Sunderland Spottwood who lay there.

CHAPTER THREE

✝✝✝✝✝✝✝✝✝✝✝✝**E**very morning she heard it. She would lie on her cot, over near the hall door, on her back, the quilts tight to her chin and clutched there, eyes fixed on the ruinous plaster of the ceiling, and listen. First, there would be the creaking of the door down the cross hall. Then the silence, and in the silence she would wonder how far he had come down the hall. Then she would hear the creaking of the loose boards where the cross hall joined the main hall. Then, again, in the silence, she would wonder how far he had gone down the main hall. Then there would be the sound of the door out to the back porch.

He would be going out to the privy.

After a time, there would again be the sound of the back door, followed soon by the first clank of the iron lid of the cookstove in the old kitchen. He would be making the fire.

But, one morning, it was different. She heard the creak of

the door of his room, and then, in the silence, while his feet were, she knew, coming down the cross hall, she set her own feet suddenly to the floor, and moving so quickly she fluttered the old gray flannel nightgown, reached the door of the hall and laid her cheek against it. In her mind, she saw him moving down the hall toward the back door.

She opened the door, ever so little, and peeked out. She actually saw him, just as she had seen him in her mind: an erect figure wearing a woolly red bathrobe corded very tight at the waist to make the shoulders look bigger, with the black hair smooth on the skull, just the back of the head visible, moving out a door at the end of a dim hall, into the grayness of a winter dawn.

The red robe had belonged to Sunder once, and she had cut it down. She had, she saw, made it too short. The length of bare shank between the hem of the garment and the old brogans in which the feet were set looked frail and boyish against the gray light beyond.

Then the figure was gone. She shut her door carefully, and stood there with her cheek pressed against the wood. She was standing there when she heard Sunder. He needed attention.

At the first moment of waking, Angelo always expected to see what, for the past three years, he had seen every morning; but seeing the room in which he now lay, feeling himself sunk in the featherbed, covered by the weight of quilts, he could not, in that moment, believe it. He would try, then, to sink himself deeper in the feather ticking, under the quilts, into the unreality, to hide himself more perfectly in this unreality, thinking: *They no find Angelo here.*

For how could they, who belonged to the real world, ever enter the privacy of a dream? For this was a dream: Angelo

(46)

Passetto had walked up the road, in the mist and gray rain, and suddenly he was here where nothing resembled the real world he had known. Here were the hollow shadows of the house, with the scurry of rats in the rooms overhead. Here the always shut door to the room where he had never been and from which he could hear, sometimes, that sound. Here that woman with the shape you could tell nothing about because of that old brown sweater that fell over everything, and with all that hair piled up, dark hair that, in a crazy way, you wished were gray, and with that white face that turned those black eyes on you like you had done something and they saw right into you.

Nothing seemed real here. At night, when she had cooked food and set it before him, and then stood over there beyond the direct rays of the bare bulb hanging from the ceiling and looked across at him as he moved the fork to his mouth, he was always surprised to find the food had substance and flavor. He had expected his jaws to close on the resistlessness of shadow.

He fled every morning from the house. In a fury of activity he could restore something that he felt draining away from him when he was in the house. Once, in the early weeks, he had, literally, fled: across the rising fields back of the house, where briars and scraggly vine now encroached on pasture, across the higher fields where long sunken furrows, years ago gone back to turf, tripped you like the scraggly vine, up the hill where the gray rock stuck from the ground and the cedars began.

That had been the day of the hog-killing. By the time of his flight the blood had long since soaked into the ground. The entrails had been drawn, purged, put into a big pan to be cleaned for sausage casing. Under the great black iron pot, big as a cookstove, the fire crackled, and from the water the steam rose up pale in the chill, bright sunlight. The carcass of the hog, the harslet out, the skin scraped, pink and fresh as a baby, hung head down from the slaughter beam.

All morning Angelo had been working, the woman, wordlessly, working beside him. He had been moving in a trance, his hands performing the motions learned long ago on his uncle's farm. It was as though the memory of the past and the motions that were the present now merged into the same unreality.

Then, all of a sudden, the woman straightened up from the big pan of entrails, fixed her gaze upon him in a moment of recognition that became, in a flash, non-recognition, and moved toward the house. He straightened up too, saw the bulk of the house floating dark and motionless in the chill brightness of air, saw the figure moving away from him, saw the darker spot where the earth had soaked the blood, saw the scraped baby-pink of the carcass.

He turned and fled.

At the top of the hill, deep in the cedars, winded and with blood pounding in his head, he lay on the ground, on the mat of dead cedar needles, with his eyes closed, and thought that he could not stand it. He did not know what it was, but he knew that he could not stand it. He would get up and go away. Now. Anywhere.

But where could Angelo Passetto go? For this was the place he must stay. They would not find him here, hidden in the cedars.

Under the cedar droppings there was stone, the great darkly-humped limestone that was the hill, and he became aware that the hardness of stone came up through the mat of needles and numbed his flesh. With that awareness, he stretched out his arms and pressed his body hard against the earth. The hardness of the secret stone seemed to reach the very bone of his body. He thought of nothing being left of his own body but bone, bone against stone. He lay there for a long time. His breastbone now ached from what pressed up against him out of the earth. There was nothing to do but get up, and go down the hill.

As he entered the backyard, coming from behind the old barn, which he had hoped would screen his approach, he saw the face in the kitchen window, shadowy white behind the glimmer of glass.

The flight up the hill to the shadow of the cedars had been his only literal, declared flight from the house, and the memory shook him. It shook him because he did not know what it was in the house that he fled from. Then, later, it shook him because he became aware that he had fled from something just discovered in himself that he did not know the name of. Something had stirred in the depth of black water, for an instant glimmering white like the belly of a fish, as it turns. Something had breathed in the dark.

That was the only literal flight. But every morning was, in its own way, a flight into occupation. He sought the task to perform, and ferociously performed it. He cut enough wood for two winters, and stacked it neatly on the back porch, racked square at the ends. If one stove-length stuck out or if its shape broke the rhythm of the stack, he would undo the work of an hour to get it right. From old boards found in the barn he rebuilt the rotting square pillars of the front porch. He mended the fence of the barn lot. He rebuilt and rehung the barn door. He replaced the broken windowpane in his own room. He had begun mending the harness found hanging in the barn, using an old awl. He rebuilt the fallen picket fence, measuring, sawing, nailing, caught in a passion for accuracy. He had to cling to a task, to live by the law of an occupation, the exact measurement, the nail driven straight. If the nail bent there was no telling what might happen.

The woman had begun by paying him a dollar a day. When on the seventh evening he had finished eating, she laid the money on the red-checked oilcloth table cover, beside the vinegar cruet, the big glass salt shaker, and the cracked blue china sugar bowl—seven dollar bills, each laid carefully down as though to allow slow wit to count during the process. With total indifference, even with an air of incomprehension, he looked down at the money. Then he slowly raised his gaze to her face, as though trying to infer some relation between what was on the table and that face that hung there under the blaze of the electric bulb, whiteness backed by shadow.

After a second, she spoke. "Take it," she said.

On his first trip into town, he bought a sack of nails. He had used up all the nails he could salvage around the place. On his next trip, two weeks later, he came back with a bucket of white paint. The paint went on the rebuilt box pillars of the front porch, absurd and glaring in the general dun of weather and time. The next time Wednesday came around—he had arrived on Wednesday—she laid a five-dollar bill and five ones on the table after he had finished eating.

She had long since ceased to suggest occupations to him. He went his way and did the things he did, and said nothing. Once, while painting a porch pillar, he had looked up and seen the face at the window.

The tasks became harder to find, or to improvise. When it rained, and the gray underbelly of sky seemed to be snagged on the black trees that crowned the blufftop, and the creek roared and slashed, he would retire to the barn, and try to sort out the contents of the old plunder room—bolts, nuts, old plow points, a mowing blade, an ax head, steel traps, a grandfather's clock with no hands and the side knocked in, a beaver muff, a little round tin box with the names Agnes, Mabel and Becky stamped on it. His breath came white in the chill dimness of the plunder room.

By the end of November, when it rained, he would go to his room, lie on the bed with a quilt over him, his brogans still on, and stare at the ceiling, smoking a cigarette, trying to think of nothing. He was very successful at that. He had had three years of practice. During those three years if certain thoughts or images came into his head, he would start sweating and shaking. Therefore, it was wise to cultivate that blankness of being.

But even with three years of practice it is not possible to caulk every crack, nail up every rat-hole, seal every window casing and perfectly defend the dark inner nothingness. So one afternoon in early December, Angelo Passetto hurled the quilt off him and stood in the middle of the floor. He saw that the windowpane no longer ran with rain, that the gray sky was breaking up into blue. At the door, he stopped, hand on the knob. If he went out into the world he knew that the fear would jump on him, like a cat jumping on your shoulder from behind, in the dark.

But it was not dark. Sunshine was pouring over all the land outside.

But that made everything worse. They could see you in the light.

But he could not stay in the room.

Beyond the barn and the old field, he crossed the ridge and moved south, following what seemed to be an old cattle track, screened from below by a tangle of leafless sassafras, elder, and sumac, the sumac with the wind-battered rusty heads still hanging. In the woods, the track swung right. It began going downhill. He moved into the dripping gloom. High above, in the patches between the black boughs, hung the blue sky. The wet leaves were soft under his feet. Here the path, whatever path there was, was indicated only by the absence of larger growth.

All at once, he saw the structure. It was of gray stone, some thirty feet long, almost roofless, but with the ridgepole and many rafters yet in place. As he drew near, he saw, at one end, the opening where a door had once been, and near the door a low arch in the wall from which issued a clear stream. The stream moved over stone and gravel, wandering slow in a dense dark growth of some low-lying water plant.

He came to the wall and knelt to inspect what grew there. He plucked a stalk of cress and put it in his mouth, but even as he bit into the succulence and recognized it, he heard the noise. It was a soft clinking, from inside the structure. He made a dash for the cedars, and crouched there, waiting.

She came out of the open door-space in the stone wall, a slender figure, a bucket in each hand. Then his mind said what his eyes had known with blazing immediacy, before they knew anything else, what his body, too, had already known— *ragazza: girl.*

She was very slender, young but well put together. *OK*, he thought, *OK—bella.* Her face, with the black hair pulled back and tied with a red ribbon or strip of cloth, looked OK, as far as you could see at that distance. Maybe *Italiana*, from the shape of the face, from the color. Maybe *Italiana, Siciliana.*

And at that thought, the fear was suddenly on him.

Siciliana: and he crouched against the cedar. He felt his member shriveling at his crotch.

But then he thought there could be no *Italiana*, no *Siciliana*, in this place into which he had wandered in the rain and mist. There would be no *ragazza*, standing in the door of a ruined structure, in a clearing among cedars, with a bucket hanging heavy in each hand, here in Tennessee, in this spot *dimenticato da Dio.*

This spot was forgotten by God.

Then he thought: *nera, negra.* Then: *nigger.* Yes.

The girl was moving away up a path—clearly a real path over there, different from the old trace he had been following. She was going across the little open space into the woods beyond. Now and then water sloshed from a bucket. The buckets were heavy, and at each step that weight threw a hip into added prominence, first one, then the other, in a rhythm of swell and recession that affirmed flesh, the deep inner texture and flow of flesh, under the dark cloth. He watched that motion as it withdrew from him across the air.

The narrow shoulders were bowed with the weight of the burden that pulled the arms down. He felt the very weight that pulled the arms down taut from the shoulders, pressing flesh against flesh, tightening the darkness of armpits where the dark hair would damply crinkle.

He thought how it had been three years.

He thought: *tre anni.*

He thought he was going to cry.

She had disappeared into the woods.

Crouching, he ran around the back of the structure, and still crouching, crossed the open space beyond, and entered the path. It was darker here, almost nothing but cedars. The well-worn earth was damp and soundless. He was moving forward in long strides, holding himself back from running, waiting to catch a glimpse of that motion under the dimness of trees, that flux and flow that would be the girl. In one sense, that was now all she had been, she was not real to him, only an abstraction of motion, a fleeting, flowing sign in the shadow of trees. It was as though his mind, his very being, refused to entertain more than that innocent abstraction.

Then he saw her. Up the path, moving with her burden, she flamed into reality.

He blocked himself from racing after her. Then he was

afraid she might turn and see him. He slipped off the path and moved along the screen of cedars, faster but with no noise, gaining on her, spying on her every motion with an anguishing avidity. But he kept telling himself that he had to be careful, that if anything happened there was no way to know what would then happen to him.

Enough had already happened to Angelo Passetto. God would not let anything else happen. He found himself saying his own name. It was as though he crooned to himself, in a voice not his own, assuring himself that everything was going to be OK, OK, for Angelo Passetto.

Once the girl stopped and set the buckets on the path. But she did not release the handles. She was leaning over, still holding the handles, too tired, it seemed, to let them go. Crouching in the cedars, only twenty feet away now, he saw how the black hair was crisply drawn together and tied with the red ribbon at the nape of the neck. He saw how the bunched bouquet of hair lay on the forward-hanging nape of the neck. He saw how humble and defenseless the neck was.

He thought how a girl like that would do anything for you. Because she loved you. She would crouch on the ground—oh, so sudden and awkward—and clasp your knees and press her forehead against your knees as you stood taller than God in the shadow of the trees. You would look down and see that little bunched red ribbon that tied the hair lying on the narrow nape of the neck.

Her hands still gripping the bucket handles, her arms drawn taut by the yet unbudged weight of the buckets on the path, the girl lifted her head, her face upward as though yearning at the sky, and thrust cleanly downward with her thighs and legs. The buckets, swinging a little, rose from earth. The rhythm of her motion resumed. Then he realized that she had stepped out of shadow into an openness just this side of the road.

Beyond, then, he saw the house, if it was enough of a thing to call a house: a structure of boards and battens, unpainted, with a tar-paper roof now glittering black in the wet light of late afternoon, and a rubble chimney piled against the near gable. But it had a porch; and remnants of vine, yet clinging to old sections of chicken wire hung from the eaves, showed how, in summer, the porch had been sunk in green shadow; and on the floor, at each side of the board steps, stood a big flowerpot, stalks of dead geranium yet protruding. The earth between the girl and the porch was bare and clean, as though swept, and a dampness gleamed on it. A white hen moved across that space, from left to right, and a faint reflection of the whiteness moved with it, swimming faithfully across the damp gleam of the ground.

The girl moved forward again. She crossed the space, mounted the porch, entered the house. The board door closed behind her.

Smoke curled from the chimney. There was life in the house.

So it began.

In the afternoons he would leave whatever work he was doing and slip off up the path, not going there directly but going into the barn, then out a small side door away from the house.

He would reach the old dairy house—for after careful inspection he was now sure that was what it had been—and crouch in the cedar gloom, waiting. Even in the rain he would crouch there, not caring. He would crouch there and warn himself that if something happened there was no way to know what would then happen to Angelo Passetto.

She would come, get the water, and go back up the path; and he would follow, silent among the cedars. He would keep his gaze on that flicker of motion beyond the screening growth, thinking: *tre anni.*

But the day after, well before she emerged from the woods, he was sitting on the log, singing. As usual, he had spied her as she left the house and had raced back here to be ready. Now as she came out of the woods, he sang directly at her, this time a gay song, lifting his right hand toward her and waving it in the air. She moved on down the path, paying no attention.

When she was opposite him, he stopped singing. "'Allo," he called, "you no hear me?"

She paused and faced him. "Do you think I'm deaf?" she demanded tartly.

"Sì," he said, "yes," and began to laugh.

She averted her face. He stopped laughing, and sang again as she moved on into the dairy house. When she came out, burdened, he asked her if the water was good. She said it was good, and with a flirt of her head, moved on.

The next day was like the first. He was not there when she came out of the woods, but when she came out of the dairy house, there he was, not singing now, just sitting in the chill sunshine, idle and easy, as though it were summer. He said, "'Allo," and asked if the water was good.

She deliberately set both buckets down, and put her hands on her hips and looked him over. "You're sure one thirsty-thinken kind of a man," she said, with tremulous, head-flirting boldness, "always asking if the water's good."

"Sì," he said, laughing. "Sì—thirsty. You let me drink? Out your bucket?"

"No," she said, and picked up the buckets, and went on.

As she reached the edge of the woods, he called: "You leetle-a girl—two bucket too heavy."

She had looked up, fleetingly, and gone.

The next day was his day to go to Parkerton—he went every other Tuesday—and with the image of the dairy house and the cedar path in his mind, he almost forgot that he had to go. Then, remembering it, he thought, with terror, of what might have happened if he had forgotten. Then he thought, collecting himself, that he had remembered in time; and besides, it was all right to make her wait one more day. He began to smile, thinking of tomorrow.

He began to feel *fortunato*.

Lucky.

The next day she did let him carry the buckets. As they drew near the clearing where the shack was, she abruptly stopped. Not thinking, watching the narrow heels move before him on the path, he almost bumped into her. He stood there, the water still sloshing in the buckets.

"Give me the buckets," she said, almost whispering. "Don't come any closer."

He did not surrender the buckets. He looked her full in the face, into the gray eyes that showed pale against the tint of her skin. "I don' know you name," he said slowly. "What you call?"

"Charlene," she said.

"Char-leen-a," he repeated, studying her as though the name made her different. Then, very soberly, he said: "Me— I have name Angelo. That mean angel, like fly in Heaven, but" —and he paused again—"Angelo, he not so bad man. You got *papa*—me tell 'im Angelo not so bad."

"Give me the buckets," she said sharply.

He looked at her slowly, thinking: *She no want me go in. She no told.*

With that thought, his heart leaped.

Then the word came in his head: *Poveretta.* Thinking that he knew her better than she knew herself, he felt strong, he would save her from all evil. His heart melted in tenderness: *Poor leetle-a girl.*

So he set the buckets down, smiling, and stepped back. She

immediately seized the handles, lifted her head to the sky to get a better balance, thrusting down with her thighs and legs to make the buckets rise. He saw that motion, and in it knew the fluid but hard reality of muscles sliding within soft flesh, of thrust and strain and torsion, in darkness. She was real. He suddenly realized with a painful stopping of his breath, that she was real. Not a dream.

"Your *papa*—Angelo tell 'im," he said again, firmly, when his breath came back, still seeing in imagination her face lifted toward the sky in the moment of effort, the lips slightly parted, damp.

"No," she said.

Then a part of him was thinking: *Bene*. Thinking how he had guessed right, she wouldn't let him talk to her father, thinking that Angelo Passetto was *fortunato—fortunatissimo*—for if she had said yes, what was there for Angelo Passetto to say to her father?

He was lucky, she would keep him for her secret, for the song coming from far in the woods.

So feeling very strong now, knowing he was lucky, he looked her in the face, pleading with his large brown eyes: "Listen—I talk to *papa*."

She turned away, sloshing the heavy buckets with the abruptness of her motion.

Over her shoulder in a blaze of anger, she said to him: "I ain't got no father!"

She moved away as fast as she could with her burden, sloshing the water. Across the space, toward the shack, he watched her motion flowing from him, like music into distance.

But there was no sadness in him now.

He was thinking that Angelo Passetto was lucky.

·   ·   ·

For two days he did not show himself. Then he appeared, and carried the buckets. Under the shadow of the cedars his eyes were fixed on the flicker of her heels, the flow of her haunches. As before, but farther from the clearing, she suddenly stopped. As before, she commanded him to give her the buckets.

"No," he said, smiling, "no. You too leetle. I take to house."

"The house," she suddenly blazed at him, and her pale eyes glittered in the shadow, "you don't want to go to the house. You say it, but you know I don't let you go to the house. So you grin and lie and say you want to go. Oh, I know!"

But how did she know, he wondered, how? He was overcome by weakness, by a sense of paralyzing guilt. He had never had that feeling before, not in all his life. Except that day when Guido Altocchi had jumped up and pointed at him, crying out: "*Traditore!*"

She was staring at him, seeing deep into him, knowing him for what he was. Then, in cold, controlled intensity, she said: "Put down the buckets."

Very slowly, he lowered them to the path. The buckets, one on each side, touched earth well clear of his feet. Carefully he released the handles. They fell. She was not far from him. One step—one leap—and he could do it. Have hands on her. Before she could make a sound.

Then the fear had him. He felt it running cold down his spine, like cold sweat.

She was saying: "—and I don't ever want to see you grinning and smiling again, and I don't ever want to hear you singing off in the woods. Go away!"

It was not the fear he felt now, but the sadness. He thought: *tre anni*. He looked at the paleness of the angry eyes, and wondered what they would be like if that angry glitter were gone, if they swam with tenderness.

(61)

She was, at that moment, staring back at him.

"What are you?" she asked.

"Why?" he asked, feeling, at her question, the sadness and lostness clot in him and intensify and darken.

"You talk funny," she said, twisting her mouth in malice and satire, "that's why!"

He looked numbly at her.

"What are you?" she demanded, triumphantly.

"*Siciliano,*" he said, trying to think what the word really meant, a word he had said all his life and now realized, among the darkening boughs of the cedars, that he had no meaning for. To give it meaning, not for her, for himself, he added: "From *Sicilia*—Sicily."

"Well," she said, and gave a thin, twisted laugh, quickly bitten off, like a thread, "go back there. Wherever that is."

"Long time I don' see *Sicilia,*" he said, finding that thought strange and sad.

"Well, go anywhere!" she burst out. "Just get away from here. Quit grinning with those white teeth you're so fool proud of. Quit singing off in the woods. For listen"—she hesitated, took a step toward him, lifting her face, thrusting it up at him, saying with a sharp expulsion of breath—"I hate you!"

At those words, it was as though a force that had been held down in darkness in him, leaped up into full light.

"Is true?" he demanded, shaking with desire, his muscles tightening, his breath sharp. "Is true you hate Angelo?"

And he took a step toward her.

She did not retreat. She was looking him straight in the eye, mimicking him, saying, "Yeah, is true I hate Angelo." And then when he moved, ever so little, she burst out: "You touch me, and I call the Sheriff—if you don't go away, and for good, I swear to God I will!"

She stood an instant, not retreating, so close he could have touched her, and then, with body still erect, she bent her knees

(62)

—there before him, under his face, between his very hands, as though she knew that all strength and danger had withered in him—and with her face still lifted to gaze at him with that pale-eyed anger, let her hands grope for the bucket handles.

She rose with the weight of the buckets pulling her arms taut, withdrew her gaze from his face, like picking up a coat from the dirty ground, turned with a calm contempt, and moved away.

Standing on the path, he stared into the emptiness of space that spun away from his eyes toward the clearing, toward the shack. It was the space which the motion of her withdrawal had occupied and then left vacant. Now staring into it, he had, like the realization of a doom, the recollection. It was a recollection which, all day, his mind had been refusing. It was a recollection of what he had learned that morning, but what he seemed to have known for a long time.

For how long? It could not be that he had known it forever. That was not possible. But standing here with the event in his head, his feeling had the weight of foreverness. With his eyes fixed on the vacancy left by the girl's passage, it seemed that the withdrawal of her body from sight had, as though it were a weight tied to a cord laid over a pulley, drawn up out of the darkness of willed forgetfulness the vision now in his head. He had the feeling of the inevitability of what had happened— the replacement of her presence by the recollection—as though all were as simple as that simple physical law: the greater weight draws up the lesser.

Yes, in the feeling of inevitability he knew that one thing drew on another. He was breathing painfully, as though a pressure were on his chest, feeling how things were tied together, how one thing drew on another, how his spying on the girl in the woods had, in the dark tissue of law that was the world, brought on the spying on him in the house. For he had, that very morning, discovered the secret eyes upon him.

Suddenly he felt spied upon now. He felt eyes peering from the dimness of cedars. In a flash of panic, he thought: *They know—they know Angelo here!*

Then he told himself that they could not have found him, not here. He told himself that they would never find him here. But he looked carefully around as he moved back into the woods. Dark was near. Darkness reached out at him from the cedar boughs.

He remembered how, that morning, her eyes had been watching him.

The eyes of the woman.

That very morning he had become aware of it, or acknowledged it to himself, for the first time. Just after dawn, going down the hall, toward the back door, he had reached into a pocket of the red robe for a cigarette, and had paused, just before laying hand to the knob of the door, to light it. In that instant he had heard the noise. Bending to light the cigarette, careful not to turn fully, he had seen the crack in the door, and had caught, he was sure, the glimmer of the face, the dark gleam of eyes.

There she was.

He laid hand to the door and stepped out, closing the door behind him; and instantly was crouching to peer back through the old keyhole, which had no key in it, there being only the slide-bolt inside. He saw the gray flicker of her movement in the hall, then down the cross hall. He rose, dropped the cigarette, and crept along the wall of the house, out the ell. There was the window of his room. He could identify it by the new putty, where he had put in the pane.

Very slowly, he lifted his head to get his eyes above the level of the window ledge, then moved carefully to the right to get one eye at the glass. From this angle, however, he could see nothing. His breath was white in the cold air, and he was shivering inside the old red robe. He was afraid to move his head farther. But he was sure she was in there.

He tried to imagine what she would be doing. He tried to make his mind blank for a picture to come there to tell him. But the only image that came into his mind was of the whiteness of the face that, now and then over the weeks, he had caught behind the glimmering of the glass of a window peering out at him.

So he jerked back from the window as though the face had, actually, appeared on the other side of the pane.

He crouched under the level of the window sill, afraid to try to spy again. He knew she was in the room. And in that certainty he felt trapped, violated. She was in the room, and he had to crouch out here, his breath white, his bones shivering.

He crept to one side, rose, and went on to the privy. With his hand on the spongy old wood of the door, and with the first intimation of the odor of that place, he felt a stir of nausea.

CHAPTER FOUR

✝✝✝✝✝✝✝✝✝✝✝✝ **T**hat night, the night after the morning when he had found himself spied on, the night after the girl had thrust her face at him and told him she hated him, he had the dream. He had had it many times before during the three years. Even in broad daylight, with his eyes open. The difference between daylight and night was that at night you had to endure the sudden waking in the dark and the sweating, and if you had the dream in daylight, with your eyes open, it simply faded out on the air, and though the sweat started it did not come as strong.

But now, for weeks, he had not had the dream. He had, instead, been dreaming about the girl, about her moving down the cedar path and suddenly stopping and turning to him with a smile coming on her face, like a light in the gloom.

That had never happened except in a dream, but when he

was waking up after the dream, coming suddenly awake in the dark, he would be feeling such happiness that it was like the dream coming true. If he was very careful, if he moved his hand very slowly to the pack of cigarettes on the chair by the bed, if he lighted the match as quietly as possible and focused his eyes so intently on the flame that he saw nothing illuminated by it, if then he lay absolutely still, on his back, and took slow deep drags and let the smoke simply drift upward out of his lungs, out of his mouth, into the darkness—if he did all these things and did not think of anything, then he might make the happiness last a little longer.

The happiness would be all through his body. It ran through his body like his blood. It was going everywhere in the dark inside him, lighting up the inner darkness with a glowing, and he knew that if you should prick his skin anywhere, a little drop of happiness would ooze out and glow in the dark.

But the girl had thrust her twisted face at him, suddenly not beautiful—no, more beautiful but in a different way—and said she hated him, and that night he did not dream of her. Instead he dreamed the old dream. He woke in the dark with the old guilt and terror, sweating.

There, again, was the courtroom, and there, again, was that lawyer pointing at Guido Altocchi and saying—saying to him, to Angelo Passetto—"Is this the man who held the revolver?" And again he heard, far off, his own voice saying, "Sì—yes." And the figure of Guido rose suddenly from the hands that tried to pull him down, Guido's face above all the other faces turning at him—at Angelo Passetto—and Guido's eyes flamed across the distance at him, while his lips cried out the word: "Traditore!"

Immediately, in the dream as it had been in actuality, Guido Altocchi would twist back his own neck, so that the muscles bulged, and he would draw his own forefinger slowly across the bulging throat.

Now, under the dust-smelling quilts, Angelo knew where he was, and knew it was only a dream, and knew that Guido Altocchi was dead—dead a long time now.

But now, here it all was, happening again. Angelo lay in the predawn dark, and thought what a fool he had been to think that it had ever stopped happening. It was happening now, in the dark, just beyond the corner of his eye. He fumbled for the cigarettes on the chair by the bed, then was afraid to strike a match. If he struck a match, he might suddenly see it all, by the flame of the match: and the face of Guido Altocchi.

But finally he lighted the cigarette. He smoked another, then another, and another, waiting for light to grow at the window. Then he remembered what had happened yesterday morning, how he had been spied upon. Then he remembered what had happened in the afternoon, how the girl had thrust her face at him and said she hated him. He felt the two things tied together. He thought of the morning that now was coming on.

He thought of all the mornings to come.

Then it was light, and he got up, shivering in his nakedness before he fumbled into the red robe, set his feet into the brogans, which had once belonged to another man, and went out into the cross hall. He moved at his usual pace, down the hall, across the boards that creaked, down the main hall. Suddenly, he again remembered how the girl had thrust her face at him and said she hated him. The remembrance filled him with a numb portentousness. His movements felt slow and wooden, but inevitable.

Before the back door, he stopped and lit a cigarette, standing at an angle that would let him see, out of the tail of his eye, the door to that room. Yes, it was opening, ever so little. So he went on out, casually.

Once out, he flung the cigarette away and, across the dawn-glittering hoarfrost, raced back to the window of his room, kicked off his brogans, vaulted over the sill of the window he had carefully left open, and leaped into the closet behind the burlap curtain. The curtain was still quivering when he heard the creak of the door.

Through a tiny opening in the weave of the burlap he saw her.

Barefoot, the gray flannel draped loose about her, the dark hair loose and tangling heavily down her back, her face whiter than ever in the dawn light, she moved toward the bed. Coldly, contemptuously he thought what a fool she was, she ought to know the man—*the man*—might forget something and come back.

He thought: *the man.* For he did not, in that moment think of himself, Angelo Passetto, as the man who had risen to go, presumably, to the privy, the man who had stopped in the cold hall to light a cigarette and catch, from the tail of his eye, the opening of the door to that secret room, the man who had vaulted into this room and now stood behind the burlap curtain. No—Angelo Passetto was not in this body that had done those things, and would do what it had to do. Perhaps nothing was in that body, nothing but the need to do what was, inevitably, to be done.

There was the woman, who did not know that *the man* might come back and stand, in secret, behind the burlap curtain.

The bed was set out from the wall opposite the window and the closet, diagonally across from the closet, to the left of the door from the hall, and now he saw *quella cretina* move toward it. He saw her lean over the bed. He saw her reach a hand down, gently, to touch the pillow where his head had lain. At that, at the gentleness of that motion, rage seized him. He could not bear the sight.

(69)

Full of his coldness, contempt, distance, and distaste, he thought: *cretina*.

Suddenly, all in a loose, disorganized motion, as though she had been felled by a blow from behind, the woman dropped across the bed, face downward into the pillow.

She lay there for a moment, then whatever force held her in that position, gave way. He saw the knees sag into the empty space below them, the released weight of the haunches dragging the upper torso across the bed, the face down, both arms stretched out on the bed straight above her head, being dragged too, all as though some contemptuous power had her by the heels.

Then the body reached a point of rest, like a bank of loose earth sliding down to strike the final grade. The left leg was crumpled sharply under the body's weight; the right leg, toward him, was thrust sidewise, with the knee bent; the face was down, buried suffocatingly in the feather ticking exposed at the edge of the bed; the right arm hung nerveless by her side, but the left arm was still outstretched on the bed above her head.

Cretina, he breathed.

Then the hand at the end of the outstretched left arm on the bed, moved feebly. Through the burlap he saw it. He saw the fingers strain and reach, fumbling the air in a weak anguish of effort. He saw them touch the pillow, where his head had lain, and close on the cloth. He could see the tightening of the knuckles, the skin go suddenly slick and bright. He saw the hand, in a slow weakness, begin to drag the pillow, as though it were a great weight. Then the pillow had reached a point where the woman's face could press against it.

He felt suffocated. His heart fluttered in weakness, then, all at once, was bursting with a strength of rage, and was free. All at once, in a dimension beyond will, or even awareness, it happened.

He stepped out, beyond the burlap curtain.

He had not even bothered to lift a hand to push it aside. He would not have been able, in fact, to do so, for, in that instant, even as he thrust through it, his arms were down, and back, to shake off the red robe. As he stepped clear of the burlap, the robe fell to the floor behind him. She had lifted her head. The eyes were wide. She did not utter a sound.

Nor did she utter a sound when he stood above her. She had, as a matter of fact, closed her eyes, and let her head again fall against the edge of the bed. It was as though she had seen nothing, or as though she had managed to deny all she had seen, had withdrawn totally into that downward slack weight of her own body, which, in that moment when he stood towering above her and stared down, was sliding a little lower, twisting to one side within the gray flannel.

Nor did she utter a sound when he leaned and seized the left arm, which was still stretched above her head on the bed, the hand still clutching the pillow. Nor when he dragged her, quite literally, from the bedside, dropped her on the bare boards of the floor, and jerked up the gray flannel, ripping it. Nor when he dropped himself upon her, letting his dead weight drop brutally as though he, too, had been felled. Nor in that instant when he, angrily, drily, joylessly, almost without sensation in that unremitting thrust except for the slight tearing of his own tissues, penetrated her.

He gripped her shoulders with his hands, threw his weight at her, and ground that passivity and blankness of her flesh upon the unswept boards, until the spasm. The spasm seemed impersonal in its automatism, not involving him, as though it were not even happening to him. Only when he again stood above the flung-down body, exposed there unmoving in its abandoned awkwardness, did he have some actual awareness of her.

For in that moment, even though the eyes were still closed,

she became real to him. The body which beneath the old brown sweater he had never sensed, and which in the blank act on the unswept boards he had not seen, was, he suddenly saw, beautiful. He looked down at the glimmering whiteness of the body and knew that it, in spite of—no, because of—the crumpledness and distortion, had a grace that glowed through everything. In the recognition, he felt a dusty pain in his chest. He felt cheated and deprived.

He seized his clothes—not the old clothes she had cut down for him, but the city clothes in the closet—and stepped naked from the room, hoping that those eyes would not open until he was out the door.

Hoping, in a numb rage of frustration, that they would never open.

It was, in the end, the bright cold moving in from the open window, creeping along the still air to occupy the room and envelop her nakedness, that made her open her eyes. She rose from the floor.

The old gray flannel of the nightgown fell about her body. Automatically, she made little patting, prinking motions to adjust it, as though she were a young girl putting on a new dress. Then her eyes fixed on the big new rip upward from the hem, and suddenly, she was shivering.

She went to close the window. For a moment she stared through the glass at the world beyond. She saw the things that were in the world—the old busted black iron kettle flung down by the roots of a hackberry tree, the old chicken house with the roof now glittering with frost, the two rusting plow points hung on a wire to pull shut the gate of the chicken yard, the grindstone under the hackberry, one leg about rotted off, about to give down and pitch the whole contraption.

If she could name those things—the kettle, the chicken

house, the plow points, the grindstone—the world would be as it had always been.

Then she knew she was hearing, far off, the sound Sunder made. It was outside, not inside her head. So she went to attend to him.

Afterwards, she went into the kitchen. The fire was burning. She stared at that remarkable fact. He had made the fire. He had stopped to make the fire. She began to get breakfast. She set the usual place on the table, set out butter and jam, made coffee, made corn pones, cut off slices from the smoked hog-shoulder hung in the corner and put them in the iron skillet. When the meat was done, she poured off some of the fat from the skillet and cracked three eggs into it. At the end she settled the coffee with eggshell. She did everything as she had grown accustomed to doing—today with special care, even. She served the plate, poured the coffee. But she knew, in a flash of vision that made her stand stock-still in the middle of the kitchen and stare at the steaming plate on the table until it seemed to be infinitely withdrawing into distance, that nothing she had prepared would be eaten or drunk.

She knew this, for she knew, all at once, what her life was. It was a going away. Life was the way things went away from you, and left you standing.

She went out to the barn. The car was gone.

Long ago—how many years?—Cy Grinder had gone away from her. That fact had had, so long ago, at the time of its occurrence, all the unbelievableness of the sudden wound from the knife that slips or of the first cool feel of scalding water spilled on you, which, in the instant before pain begins, you look down at and see, but in the seeing refuse to recognize as happening to you. But now, as she knew in a flash, the un-believable had become the thing most believable, and she knew that if reality is the inevitable, even if it is unbelievable, then you must believe in it.

She had come back to the kitchen, and now, at this moment when she knew what at last, at this long last, had to be be-lieved, she felt the walls, on all sides, wherever she turned her eyes, withdrawing from her, she felt distance bleeding out of her and fleeing infinitely away. Wherever she looked, her eyes bled distance—no, it was bleeding out of her at every pore.

The knowing filled the hollowness of her head like a swirl-ing vapor, and all at once she realized that, in the middle of the vapor, there was a light, and realized that if it were not for that coiling, dizzy vapor, the light would be intolerably bright. Then, as she suddenly knew that the light was the very center of herself, and of the whole world that fled away from that glowing center, she felt something like rapture begin. She was in awe of what was happening inside her head.

She knew at last what was real—totally real, as though, after all the years, the news had just reached her that Cy Grinder had gone away, had gone out West, never a word, never a letter. She knew at last that this was true, and at last she knew that she could bear it.

She could, at last, even bear the fact that once there had been a slim, strong young man, just twenty-one years old, with an arrogant carriage of the shoulders, when he thought to jerk them up, and a mouth that, though already set in a bitter sullenness, would smile when he looked down at her. When he did smile, she knew that the bitter sullenness that made him clamp his jaw and thrust out the lower lip and draw down the corners of his mouth, was the face he turned to the world, and this fact made all the more preciously her own that smile that privately he bent on her. When he took her face between his hands and looked so searchingly into it, as though seeking there the thing he had never found anywhere else in the world, that smile was innocent of all the things the world had done to Cy Grinder.

And not a thing had been his fault.

It was not his fault that Old Budge Grinder lay drunk in the shack up the hill while the soil washed away down the creek, nor that young Budge, Cy's big brother, on one of the rare occasions when he could summon up his energies for sustained effort, had been detected, in the middle of the night, at the wrong corncrib getting a load of raw material for his manufacturing operations at the still up the cove, nor that his older sister Mabel had walked barefoot down the creek road to the highway and hooked a ride in an automobile, and had, according to common report, paid in kind for transportation to Nashville, where she was to learn to wear shoes and where, not while wearing shoes, had earned her small fame. And it was not his fault that he was cursed with the need to bend over the book in the slab-side, one-room schoolhouse, and try to wrench from those pages the mysterious secret that might free him from Spottwood Valley and, in fact, free him from the curse of being himself. It was not his fault that, in school, the pale, quiet girl stared at him out of those dark eyes, and he dreamed about her at night. She was the only girl in school who was nice to him.

She continued to be nice to him a few years later when he had found a job in Mr. Rawbock's sawmill and was making ten dollars a week and was saving five of the ten and taking a correspondence course in engineering from the Worldwide Correspondence School, and sat up at night, by a kerosene lamp, sweating to make sense out of the pages that he had so little preparation to understand. He would literally sweat, even on a winter night.

In this struggle his whole body took part, for that body was, he deeply felt, his real self, the only thing he was sure of and could depend on, and be proud of; if the sweating strength of that body could only come to grips with the nameless adversary of the world, all would be well. So his muscles went tense and his breath came hard as he wrestled with his angel, and the dollar alarm clock, that would wake him at 4:30 the next morning, sat on the table and stared grimly at him and ticked away the night with a sound like the stroke of hammer on anvil. It was as though his very being were on the anvil for the stroke, and would be struck and then renewed to await the next stroke. And sometimes, as his fantasy came clearer, it seemed to be his genitals laid on the cold block of steel, waiting.

Sometimes on a Sunday afternoon, in good weather, he would meet Cassie Killigrew, in a corner of the lane bordering her father's farm, and hand in hand would walk with her along the creek. Now and then he managed to borrow a car from one of the workers at Mr. Rawbock's mill, and took her to Parkerton or Fiddlersburg, to a movie and an ice cream soda. It was always the kind of old car a hillbilly mill hand in Spottwood Valley would have, but Cassie always seemed proud and happy to sit by him as the car banged, coughed, and chugged over the ruts. The expeditions were infrequent, for they were possible only when she could work out the deception of staying with a girl friend, Gladys Peegrum, who was socially frowned on by Mrs. Killigrew but was Cassie's only confidante and confederate. Poor Gladys, who was a fat, slow girl whom nobody wanted to take out at night and handle, and whose only excitement was her vicarious participation in what she was sure Cy Grinder did to Cassie Killigrew when he got that manageable slenderness, so different from her puffy bulk, out in the dark.

The hands of Cy Grinder did know every inch of the body of Cassie Killigrew, and sometimes, in a sunset dell by the creek or in the back seat of a mill hand's car in the dark, she would cling to him, weeping and breathless, trying to tell him that she loved him; but Cy, despite the obvious lack of resistance, had done none of the things that Gladys Peegrum attributed to him. In an obscure way he felt that that was something he could not have until he got the certificate with the gold seal to say that he was an engineer; until he was, in fact, translated out of himself, no longer the son of Old Budge, but an untarnished Adam walking the new earth with the breath of the Worldwide Correspondence School blown into him.

He felt, even, that despite the straining and distress he endured in the sunset dell or in the midnight back seat of a mill hand's car, he would, if it came to the point with Cassie Killigrew, be incompetent. Not that he had ever been less than competent with the kind of girl who would h'ist her skirts and prop it up for the likes of the son of Old Budge. But with Cassie Killigrew it was different. Or might, disastrously, be. Until he got that certificate that would give him a new self.

The technical virginity of no girl was ever safer than was that of Cassie with Cy. But this was not the view held by Mrs. Killigrew once she learned, finally, that Cassie's presumptive evenings at the Peegrum house—a place disgraceful enough— was only a way of kicking up dust in her eyes to conceal something far worse. As was inevitable, the mill hand's car with bad brakes and dim lights and with Cy's right arm around the girl to fold the hand back over her breast, had a smash on the highway, and Cassie got two ribs and a collarbone broken and was hauled, by the State Highway Patrol, back to Parkerton, to the hospital.

When Mrs. Killigrew, Sunday black hung on her attenuated person, her very bones clattering in the general vibration of rage, eyes glowing with the elated justification of a deep-held faith that no good would ever spring from the loins of her husband, Gustavus Adolphus Killigrew, entered the ward where Cassie lay, she spied Cy Grinder leaning against the wall near the head of the bed, stunned and still, and for all his breadth of shoulder, looking frail and sick. To the credit of Mrs. Killigrew's warmth of heart it may be said that she had already been informed that her daughter was in no mortal danger; and so without any compunctious visitings, she could, seeing Cy Grinder now so defenseless there, turn to deal with the clear and present danger that her daughter, also the granddaughter of Abbott Gillswaith, Gillswaith being the glory of her family name, might fall into the hands of the son of Old Budge Grinder.

In that moment, she did not even see her daughter, much less speak to her. Instead, she was immediately informing Cy Grinder that little more than what had happened could have been expected of the son of Old Budge, that he had probably been drinking rotgut, that even sober his least touch would be a contamination, that his brother was a felon and his sister a woman of ill-fame, that since he and all his tribe were pore white trash, he might more properly have devoted his time to debauching that fat, slug-white slob Gladys Peegrum, if he hadn't done that already to make her help him get at Cassie Killigrew, and that if Cassie Killigrew had stooped so low as to let him touch her, it was only the natural result of the fact that she herself had had the misfortune to permit Gustavus Adolphus Killigrew to sire that creature that now in shame, and she hoped remorse, lay upon that bed.

All of this was uttered in loud, clear tones, in a single sentence and in the presence of one nurse, one intern, three extremely interested patients in neighboring beds, and a Negro orderly who, it was obvious, was merely making work for himself in the vicinity so that he might miss nothing.

Meanwhile, Cy Grinder, not now leaning against the wall, stood erect, his arms hanging at his sides and his big hands

twitching and working, his face even more strained and his
eyes sick, and felt a coldness like death filling his very bowels,
and knew that he had lived among shadows and delusions
and that the words that fell from that bony apocalyptic face
were the blaze of truth.

Nothing he had done, or could ever do, would change the
truth. When Mrs. Killigrew at last paused for breath, he moved
forward, brushing her aside, not in rudeness or violence, but
simply because he moved in the unwitting trance of a man
stunned by truth, and made his way to the door, and out into
the dawn.

That was the last time Cassie Killigrew, or Spottwood Valley,
was to see him for eight years. There was no word of goodbye, and no scrap of a letter to come, just the remembered
glimpse of the frozen face that passed her, then the stiff
shoulders retreating across the ward from her bed, the back of
the well-shaped head retreating across what, at the moment,
seemed infinite distance. If he had turned even once and
looked at her, she would have risen from the bed, taped and
plastered as she was and wearing that hideous white sack the
hospital had put her in, and run after him and would never,
never have left him. But he did not turn his head.

And as she saw the door close after him, she thought: *He
loves something else better than me.*

So night after night, living over the past that had somehow
culminated in that stiff-shouldered withdrawal across the distance of the ward, she felt a sudden revulsion from all the
clutching and pressing and probing she had so faithfully endured, and an even greater revulsion from the recollection of
her own hot breath and wet lips and shudders and tears. She
would lie in the dark and feel cut off from that person she had
been. It was as though that other person—that then-Cassie—

had been abandoned forever on the turf of a sunset glade by the creek, or left huddled, in the dark, in shame, on the back seat of a hillbilly mill hand's old car. She could shut her eyes and, quite literally, see that abandoned body of the then-Cassie, flung down like a doll. And in such a vision she would feel, mixed with her revulsion, a sad, distant pity for all the passion and yearning that had come to naught.

As for Cy Grinder, he had headed West that very day, as soon as he could find the mill hand whose car he had wrecked and give him two hundred of the five hundred and seventy-seven dollars and forty-three cents he had saved in the past two years. But he did not set out before taking the books and papers and study guides issued him by the World-wide Correspondence School and carefully disposing of them down a privy hole. In the blaze of truth that had come to him about himself, and about the world, he felt that he would never again need such props and toys.

He walked out of Spottwood Valley. He would ferociously act out his destiny, which, as he now saw, was to need nothing. And when, in the end, after all the repudiations and angry risks of his eight years in oil fields, mines, wheat fields, lumber camps, and Tarawa and Iwo Jima, he came back to Spottwood Valley, that act was merely to prove that Spottwood Valley was now nothing to him.

He could move through it, now, spit on its earth, and not see it. And one morning, not long after the return to the Valley, living in the shack where Old Budge had lived, humped for his morning defecation on the very hole down which he had once thrust the books sent him by the Worldwide Correspond-ence School, he got, like a lightning flash, with a burst of laugh-ter that he had trouble to control, the idea that would crown the destiny he had been struggling to fulfill: he would marry Gladys Peegrum.

.   .   .

When Cy Grinder came back to the Valley his presence made no significant change in the life of Cassie. His presence merely marked a stage in a long and secret process, like water finding its way in the dark of earth, the process by which the unbelievableness of his old withdrawal would someday, after all the subterranean darkness, become the believableness of life. Even the marriage to Gladys Peegrum did not stir her. It seemed merely the predictable course of the world.

Her old role and that of Gladys Peegrum were now reversed: she now the imaginer, Gladys the imagined. But Cassie could, without bitterness, even appreciate the irony, just as without pain she could view the drama of darkness enacted in her imagination. That drama, played again and again in her head, was without pain, for she could intuit the combination of repugnance, gleeful wrath, and bitter satisfaction in the ful-fillment of an ordained role, with which Cy Grinder would wreak himself upon the puffy, clabber-smelling unmanageable-ness of Gladys Peegrum; and in her intuited understanding of the vengeful alienation of Cy Grinder from himself implicit in the act performed upon Gladys Peegrum, she found con-firmation of her own rejection of that other Cassie who had been her then-self, and who had once quivered under his touch.

What a little fool that then-self of Cassie had been! Not to have known all the time what, night after night in that cabin above the creek, was now being sweatily demonstrated—that Cy Grinder was perfectly designed for the likes of Gladys Peegrum. All fell into place in the great charade of the world.

By the time of Cy's return, Cassie had been married eight years.

In the year after Cy Grinder's flight West, Cassie lived under her mother's eye, and tongue, with the sense of having no role in the world, no identity. The discovery of Cy Grinder had been her only way of discovering those things, and now that he was gone, her own reality had been withdrawn. And sometimes her fingers, touching a simple object, might go as numb as her heart. Then she was sent to take care of her aunt, her father's sister, who was married to Sunderland Spottwood, and who had developed consumption.

The fact of this connection of a Killigrew to the name of Spottwood was the only thing Mrs. Killigrew found bearable about her husband, the feckless and failing Gustavus Adolphus; and to cement this connection, she proposed sending Cassie to the Spottwood house. Over the ineffectual resistance of her husband she rammed the policy through.

"What reason," she demanded of Gustavus Adolphus, "can you possibly have to deny your own blood sister the decent care and comfort that your daughter could bring—in place of those incompetent Negroes?" Gustavus Adolphus did not deem it decent, or politic, to name the reason. He knew that the very reason he did not want his daughter in the Spottwood house was the reason, unacknowledged even to herself, that his wife did want her there: as one bond with the Spottwood house rusted and flaked away, another would be forged.

Mrs. Killigrew succeeded more promptly than she had ever anticipated. Within three months after the consumption-wracked remnants of Josephine Killigrew Spottwood had been laid in the burying ground of the Spottwood family, now hard with January frost, Cassie inherited the place in bed the deceased had once enjoyed beside the bulk of Sunder. Mrs. Killigrew never allowed herself to define the expectation on which she had built her hopes, and which common gossip has long since accepted as an accomplished, if as yet unsanctified, fact. Sunderland Spottwood was not, as everybody knew, a man to let decorum, decency, or legality stand between him and a whim.

The reputation borne by Sunderland was for directness, callousness, idiotic courage, and amiable bestiality; and by and large, the reputation was justified by the record. The narrow world of Spottwood Valley had demanded little else of him. But, as no carrier of common gossip would have guessed, Sunderland was, in special circumstances, capable of some subtlety in pursuing his ends.

For the first two weeks after she had come to nurse her aunt, the pale, timid girl moved noiseless as one more shadow among the shadows of the house, standing back against the wall for Sunderland Spottwood to pass or sitting at supper with downcast eyes. He treated her with a kindly, absent-minded respect; it was as though he were living only in the numbness of heartbreak. He would come out of his distance only to ask: "How is she?" Or: "Is she suffering more?"

That was the first two weeks; but in the next phase, he treated her to pathetic attempts at entertainment and gaiety, as though he knew that a young girl could not be expected to live on a diet of grief. He would tell some anecdote or some innocent joke, all the more touching for the fact that, falling back into the grim reality of his thought, he might forget the point, then have to rouse himself and, with a gallant smile, try to repair the defect. He had now begun to call her "little Cassie," or "my dear little Cassie," and to study her out of his great blue eyes that always seemed moist with tears.

One evening in the fifth week, in early December, when Dr. Tucker had said there was not much longer to wait, Sunder asked her if she would sit with him in his "office." Then before she could answer, he burst out, "I know you don't want to—not with an old man like me—but I just can't stand to be by myself!"

In the course of the evening, there by the dying fire, after one of his gallant sallies at anecdote had broken down, he began to weep. Most appallingly he swayed in his chair. Out of dark eyes gone suddenly wide, she stared at him. Suddenly he slipped off the chair to his knees. He seemed about to pray. But he did not pray. Like a giant crab, or a wounded bear, he floundered the few feet to her chair. For an instant, as he raised the grief-torn face up toward her, she again thought that he was about to pray. Then all at once, he had thrust his face into her lap.

The tears, she knew, were soaking into her clothing. She could feel the big chest heave with the almost soundless sobs. The big shoulders shook. She did not know the name of what she herself felt, but it was tearing at her heart, the tragedy and power of life. Without intention, even without knowledge of the fact, she laid a hand on the thick tangle of yellow curls. On the instant, as though she had closed an electric circuit, she felt his arms clasp around back of her knees and under her thighs, and he uttered a deep groan of unfathomable grief.

Of a sudden, he blundered up, saying, "Don't—don't touch me!" in a hoarse, strangled voice which, years later, his rasping wordless exhalation was to remind her of.

She sank back in her chair, and watched him stumble from the room. Then she shut her eyes, her senses reeled, and it was as though out of that dark of her shut eyes, she might at that very moment, feel on her face the breath of Cy Grinder.

When Sunderland Spottwood came to her bed in the middle of the night there was little resistance. It was like a dream—a dream she had had long before.

The marriage took place in late April, 1938, in the living room of the Killigrew farmhouse, with no one outside the family present except the Methodist minister and Murray Guilfort, who served as best man; and who kept stealing glimpses at the downcast face of the bride to try to read her history since the day of the funeral when the door had opened to him and the whiteness of her face had seemed to float toward him on the tide of shadow, and his heart had been stabbed with a pitying and clairvoyant, but unspecifiable, sense of her destiny, and his own. Looking at her as the Methodist minister droned on, he felt that she herself already had some sense of her destiny.

But he was wrong. She was moving through this day with no sense of any future. She moved in the hypnosis cast on her by the collusion between the tear-swimming gaze of Sunder's eyes in firelight and the ghostly breath of Cy Grinder which had seemed to fan her cheek when, left alone in the "office" that night, she had closed her eyes and let her head fall back against the chair, as once it had fallen back against the seat of a mill hand's beat-up old car.

If, when the marriage took place, Cassie had no sense of the future, by June she began to know its shape all too well. Out on the porch, in the summer evening, Sunder, with the glass of bourbon and water in his clutch, would sit staring out under the trees where the fireflies pricked the hot darkness. If he said anything at all, it was to tell her to fetch him a pitcher of fresh water. That was all he would utter until the time when he heaved his bulk from the chair and said: "Come on."

But some nights he would not even say that much; he would heave up from the chair and fumble his way alone into the dark house. On these nights she might sit for hours afterwards, alone in the dark, watching the fireflies. Far off, down the summer-shrunk creek where the water was now scarcely audible in the dark, the bullfrogs would grumble and grind their gums.

On December 7, 1941, at 2:00 p.m., Cassie and her husband were eating their Sunday dinner. The day was unseasonably warm, and only a smoldering heap of ash lay in the dining room fireplace. Sunder's jaws moved with massive deliberation on the beef and potatoes in his mouth. His lips glistened with gravy. His blue eyes, slightly bloodshot, bulged arrogantly in their sockets, seeing nothing, rapt in the process of ingestion. He had had three drinks before dinner, this being Sunday. The radio was turned on, with ear-splitting volume, to a hillbilly band from Nashville. The radio suddenly stopped.

Then the voice spoke: "The Japanese have attacked Pearl Harbor, Hawaii, by air, President Roosevelt has just announced. The attack was . . ."

Sunder's bulging eyes fixed on the radio, over there by the fireplace. The jaws stopped their massive grinding, the eyes glittered. All at once, the jaws moved again, once; and the gullet jerked with an effort of swallowing the half-prepared mass, and the man rose from the table, knocking his chair back. "Kill the bastards!" he yelled. "Kill the little yellow bastards!"

His eyes flashed. While the voice from the radio continued he paced about the room. All at once he dropped into a crouch, his eyes blazing blue and about to burst from his head, and drawing his lips back over the big teeth, he swung an imaginary machine gun slowly from side to side and back again, all the while uttering from between tight jaws: *tat-tat-tat-tat-tat*.

Then suddenly, directly across the table, at her: *tat-tat-tat*.

He stopped, and glared across the table.

"I ain't forty," he proclaimed in a loud, public voice, "and strong as a bull!"

She was looking at him, her face impassive.

"God damn it," he said, "you know I'm strong as a bull. God damn it, say it!"

"Yes," she said.

"You won't say it," he said, glowering. "Just trying to cut me down, not saying it. You know I'm strong as a bull, but you won't say it. Cut a man down—yeah, that's what you want to do. Say it, God damn it," he commanded, "say it. Every damned word of it."

(86)

"You're strong as a bull," she said, flatly.

"You're damned right I am," he said, "and you sure ought to know!"

With that he began laughing. He laughed and slapped his thigh.

He stopped laughing and took a few paces about before he again wheeled at her.

"I'm strong as a bull," he said, "and I'm gonna kill me a passel of those little slit-eyed yellow bastards, I'm gonna shoot off their yellow asses—*tat-tat-tat*. I'm sick of this stinking farm, and sick of this stinking house, and sick of—"

He swung his bulging, blue-flame gaze around the room, with a force that seemed to scythe out beyond the walls, over all the land; then swung it back to her. He seemed about to say something, staring at her, but did not.

Instead, he went to the sideboard, and poured himself half a tumbler of straight bourbon. He turned on his heel and, carrying the glass, stalked out of the room.

Later, as she washed the dishes, the cook being off for the day, she heard him tramping about upstairs. Now and then, muted by walls and distance, she heard the sound: *tat-tat-tat*. Then laughter.

The next day he drove all the way to Nashville, straight to the big gray stone building where the gay and violent posters were stuck to the billboards outside, and forced his way, out of turn, to a desk. "I want to join the Marine Corps," he said. "I want to be an officer." The man gave him a form to fill out and motioned him to a table where there were inkwells and pens. Sunder sat there, clutching a new Post Office penstaff that somebody else had been chewing the end of, and began to sweat.

It felt like being in school again. It felt like they were getting ready to do something to him. The rage was mounting in him. He snapped the pen between his powerful fingers, then stared at the ruin. "Strong as a bull," he said, out loud; gave a couple of hacks of laughter, picked up the functional half of the broken pen, dipped it, and began to write.

At the medical examination they told him something was wrong with his blood pressure. They advised him to see his personal physician. "Screw you," he said to the appalled examiner. "And screw your whole damned mule-buggering Marine Corps."

He stayed in Nashville a week. He tried the Navy, the Army, and even the Seabees. He had high blood pressure, they told him. He should, they told him, see his personal physician. They were all mule-buggers, he told them, and went on to Memphis. In Memphis, all the mule-buggering bastards told him the same thing.

Back in Spottwood Valley, in his black mood, he sat by the fire or paced the house, flinging his bloodshot glance from side to side. Or he would, suddenly, burst out of doors, saddle his horse, and be off, God knew where, gone all day and maybe half the night. It was one afternoon during this period that, racing a storm home, he had ridden his mare past endurance and she had fallen at the front gate, knees in the red-clay mud and blood snorting out of her nostrils, and he had stomped into the house to get the 30.30.

Sunderland Spottwood never said a word to his wife about what had happened in Nashville and Memphis. He said nothing to her about anything. And all the time he never laid a finger on her. Lying awake in the dark beside that bulk, she would hear the faint rasp of breath, and would know that he was not asleep.

(88)

. . .

One afternoon in April, she was sitting by the window of their bedroom upstairs, mending. Out of the tail of her eye, she saw a figure—a woman—moving across the yard toward the back porch. Since the woman was going to the back, she assumed, without thinking, that it was the cook coming back. Then she realized that it was too early to start supper. She got up and started downstairs. She was halfway down when she heard the knock at the back door.

At the door she found not the cook, but that Benton woman, Arlita.

"Come in," Cassie said, feeling, even as she looked into the woman's face, that the moment was portentous, feeling a light-headedness, a bright giddiness that was almost like joy.

She had never before seen the Benton woman's face. She had merely seen the figure, the shape of a young woman, moving down the road, on foot or in an old Ford, going to and from the tenant house where she lived with her husband—the husband who, only three months back, had run off and joined the Army, right at the beginning of spring, when hands were hard to come by anyway. Now looking at the face, she realized that she had never really seen any Negro's face before. This face was yellow-brown, but the color seemed, in a peculiar way, clear and transparent, as though the air were yellow-brown and what brownness the face seemed to have was the brownness of the air it was seen through. Not that she was, exactly, seeing a white face beyond stained air; she was simply seeing *face-ness*, the fact of a face, some reality she had never guessed. She had the crazy impulse to reach out a finger and touch that face to see if it was real.

Instead, she said: "What do you want?"

The young woman looked at her, as though she, too, were musing on the strangeness of something. Then, driving herself from her musing, standing in the quietness of the empty house while bright leaves were shifting in the sun outside, she answered: "Doan you know nuthen?"

"Don't you know you ought to say *mam* to me?" Cassie said, hearing, with surprise, these words come, for they had not been in her head, where, in fact, there was only that bright giddiness, like the movement of air turning the bright new leaves in the sun outside.

"Yes 'um," the Benton woman was saying, softly. "Yes 'um, I knows that, Miz Spottwood." Then, in her steady watchfulness, added: "I 'pologize." Then, when Cassie found nothing to reply, the woman again said: "Doan you know nuthen?"

"Know what?"

"My husband done left," the woman said. "Gone to de wa'hr."

"Yes," Cassie replied, tartly, "ran off and left right when plowing was to start, and hands hard to come by." But these words, too, she realized, were a surprise to her; they hadn't been in her head, just suddenly there in the air asking to be said.

"Doan you know nuthen?" the woman demanded more softly, leaning at her, peering into her face. "Doan you know what been going on here, all up and down this here valley, all these years?"

Then, even before the woman could speak again, Cassie knew everything, and the bright leaves were fluttering in her head, in sunshine. It was funny how knowing something, having something rear up out of the dark of nothing, even if the something was awful, was this giddiness of joy. It was like yourself coming true.

So that night, after supper, while Sunder was still at the table, drinking coffee, she said: "Listen, Sunder."

"What?" he demanded.

"I know," she said, and saying it, was surprised that she wasn't afraid to tell him. She felt bright and free.

"Know what?"

"That Benton woman was here this afternoon."

"Well," he said, studying her, "what made you ever think that the thing you're sitting on was the only cunt in Cardwell County?"

He gave a burst of his rasping, croupy laughter, then took a draught of coffee.

"You don't understand, Sunder," she explained patiently. "It's not that I care what you do. I don't care even if you beat me, or something." She felt the brightness and freedom coming back.

"What the hell you mention it for?" he demanded.

"Just this," she said. "You can't drive that Benton woman off the place. Like you drove her husband off. And her pregnant with your baby. You've got to do something for her. Now if you—"

He was laughing. When he had controlled the laughter, and with the back of a hand wiped the tears of mirth from his eyes, he said: "So you think I'm rich! So that's the reason you and that bloat-bellied mule you got for a ma wanted me to marry you? Oh, yeah, you didn't think I knew. Well, the joke's on you. I'm pore and getting porer every day, and don't give a damn. But—" and he heaved up from the chair and again roared with laughter, "never let it be said that Sunderland Spottwood does not know how to behave like a gentleman. When he wants to. I'll make amends, like a gentleman. In fact, I am a gentleman."

He squared his shoulders, assumed an air of comic dignity, then proceeded: "I'll pay off the black bitch, and furthermore, since you love her so much, I'll make you and Arlita neighbors for life. I'll give, transfer, and name in fee simple to that black bitch, that shack and the best piece of land I've got, that forty acres up there. Yeah, you two can be neighbors," he said, "and talk it over behind my back."

He began laughing.

She watched the laughter, and when the first strength had gone out of it, said: "Sunder."

He looked at her.

"Sunder," she said, "it has just come to me. You aren't a bad man. It's just something happened to you that you can't help. It's just that you're crazy, Sunder."

He was still looking at her, but in a new way, a slow, dawning way, a way that was, all at once, glitter-eyed, and for an instant reminded her of the way he had looked at her, that night by the fire, in the office, when he jerked his head off her lap and rose up and stood above her.

"Listen," he said now, staring down at her with that damp brilliance of blue, "it's you that's crazy. You—you're bottled-up crazy."

Then he was looking down at her, again in a slow, dawning way. He said: "You know—you know why I ever laid into you?"

She said nothing.

"You know why I ever wanted to lay into you, Cassie Killigrew?"

She said nothing.

"Well, it's no wonder you don't know, for I didn't know either. Not till just this minute. But it was because I could see you were bottled-up crazy, and I thought it might be fun to make you blow the cork."

He laughed again. Then stopped.

"You know why I'm laughing?" he demanded.

Then, when she said nothing: "I'm laughing at myself. At old Sunder, the Human Pile-Driver. Yeah, he thought he was a real man. Well, girlie, he wasn't man enough to bust that cork."

Quietly, almost tenderly, even wistfully, he looked down at her.

She felt a shy stir of feeling, as on that first night in his office, as though all afterwards had been a dream, her bad dream.

But then, again, he was laughing.

He was saying: "Boy, if you ever do blow that cork!"

Her mother died in the early fall, after a brief illness. At the funeral, she could not shed a tear. She felt that something would burst if she did not cry, but she could not. Not even when they put the dirt in. She thought how people could cry, how tears ran down their cheeks in that bliss of being themselves and having had something to lose.

After she got home from the funeral, she felt something coming on. At first she thought it was going to be tears, and felt excited. But she began to laugh. She was laughing because she hadn't been able to cry at the funeral of her own mother. Once she got started laughing, it looked, people said, like she couldn't ever stop.

Shortly after Christmas—the Christmas of 1942—they carried her to the mental sanatorium of Dr. Spurlin, near Fiddlersburg, for treatment.

In the spring of 1946 Sunder had his stroke. Cy Grinder, back from the war, passing down the road with a load of corn, saw the body on the front steps, managed to drag it into the house, and telephoned Dr. Tucker, who, after he had done what he could, notified Murray Guilfort. There was nothing

anybody could do for the hulk that had been Sunderland Spottwood—except, of course, to see that food and drink were
placed in that mouth while the eyes, now clear and blue as a
baby's, stared upward at you, and to remove excrement, and
to wash the flesh as often as decency required.

But there was no money left to hire this done. So Murray
Guilfort called on the director of the sanatorium. Mrs. Spottwood, the director admitted, was much better. She might,
he admitted, even improve further, with simple, routine
responsibilities.

So she came home.

And now, more than twelve years later—years which, in one
sense, had not been time at all, had merely existed and then
were gone—she stood in the kitchen, on a bright winter
morning, with food laid on the table and coffee steam rising in
the air, and had the vision of her life.

She was the fixed point from which there was forever the
going-away. She stood there and experienced the pure joy that
comes only with the full, free recognition of destiny, which is
the recognition of the self. Standing there in the sunlit kitchen,
she felt calm and immortal. All was fulfilled. And Angelo
Passetto would not come back.

But he did.

BOOK
II

CHAPTER FIVE

✝✝✝✝✝✝✝✝✝✝✝✝ It was dark now. The big electric bulb that hung from the middle of the ceiling—there had to be a big bulb, the kitchen the size it was—blazed. You could see the freckles of flyspeck on the glass of the bulb, and the streaks where the grease-laden air had made deposits to settle and run down. Sometimes in the kitchen at night, she might suddenly stop whatever she was doing and stare at the blazing bulb. Sometimes it came closer and closer, so close she could see the flyspecks big and clear, but no matter how close it got, it never got to her and only kept coming. But sometimes it seemed to be going away from her, spinning away forever but never getting out of sight, never even getting smaller.

Tonight, she was staring at it, standing motionless with an empty saucepan—the one she meant to boil the potatoes in—hanging from her hand as though the wrist were too weak to support even that small burden. This was one of the times when the blazing bulb seemed to be going away from her, and though the going-away was awful, something else was growing in her head too, the notion that if you got to know that the way things happen to you, no matter how awful, couldn't happen any differently and that the way they happened was, really, just part of the way you were you, then you could keep forever this new feeling of strange joy.

She stood there, the saucepan dangling, bathed in that bleak whiteness of light that kept pouring from the bulb, even though the bulb was spinning away forever, and knew what joy meant. It meant that things would never again tease her and scare her by coming closer and closer and yet not coming. From now on everything, like that bulb there, like the walls of the kitchen, like the trees outside in the dark, and the hills, would keep on spinning away.

The going-awayness would never change—now, at last, she knew that, and suddenly, she felt the joy so strong she was dizzy and her eyes blurred.

But, of a sudden, she heard the noise. The door, the door to the back porch, was swinging slowly inward, open. There he was.

In her sight, he seemed to sway and swim there, as though the darkness from which he had come were a medium like water sustaining him. It was as though the pressure of all that darkness flooding down from the hills and woods had just pushed the door open, and in one second more, would come pouring in, filling up the room, washing him at her. She was sure that she saw the darkness swirling about his knees, ready to lift him off his feet, and flood in, bearing him to her, with his eyes fixed on her.

But that was not what happened. While he stood there, and the eyes kept looking at her out of his face, his hand went behind him and, though his body never moved, shoved the door shut. It made a little slam. The latch had caught. The dark would not come in.

But something else happened. She looked, one split second, at the electric bulb, and it was not going away now, it was coming back and she could see the flyspecks on it clear as could be.

She had been wrong. The going-awayness was over. The coming-closerness had begun again.

Then she was looking back at him, and his face was coming closer.

The eyes in his face were looking at her, and the mouth said: "'Allo."

She felt her own mouth trying to move, but it wouldn't. His face was coming at her. She could see how the bristles that hadn't been shaved off today stuck out stiff and black around the pinkness of his mouth. His legs were moving, but it seemed that he was coming faster than the legs, faster than the walls were coming, or the stove, or the electric bulb, or anything. He was right at her when she closed her eyes.

She stood there in the darkness her eyelids made. Then she knew that the sound of him—no, it was the feel of him—had gone on by. She opened her eyes.

He was past her, over by the old zinc sink, by the window, running a glass of water, like he was nothing in the world but a man who had come in late and was thirsty.

Everything now had stopped coming at her, and had gone back where it belonged. Everything was like a dog you had told to go lie down.

He was looking at her face so hard it was as though the flesh would begin to hurt if he didn't stop.

"Did you go to Parkerton?" she said, and heard her voice way off asking that fool question.

"Yeah," he said, "Parkerton."

His gaze shifted from her face. She followed his eyes as they turned to look at the table she had set. There it was, as always, the red-check oilcloth on the table, the knife and fork and spoon, the coffee cup, the same pink-and-white plate, the last of the set of what they called Haviland china left from the old days, from her Aunt Josephine's time, from the set that had come as a wedding present and her aunt had been so proud of. It was the plate she had got in the habit of setting out for him to eat on.

He was staring at the plate, then strangely at her. "I go wash me," he said finally, and went out the door that led into the hall.

As she stood by the stove she did not feel anything. If she did not feel anything, then nothing would have happened, ever. And if nothing had ever happened, then she would not have to feel anything.

He was a long time coming back. She was glad of that, for now everything was ready, the mashed potatoes, the two porkchops, canned peas. In his chair, he looked down at the food on the plate, making not the slightest preparatory move to touch it, then up at her as she stood above him to pour the coffee. He looked down at the coffee, while the vapor rose thinly into the blank whiteness of the light of the bulb that hung almost directly above him. She had gone back to stand near the range, watching him.

All at once, having touched nothing, he shoved back the chair, with a scraping noise on the boards, and rose. Ignoring her, he went to the old electric icebox in the corner beyond the sink, got a tray of ice, put three cubes into the glass, poured it two-thirds full of water, and carried it back to the table. He set it carefully beside his plate, sat down, and, never having looked at her, having, in fact, mysteriously denied her presence, her very existence, by every motion made, drew a bottle of whiskey from his right hip pocket. He poured the glass nearly full.

Then he looked at her. He thrust the glass toward her, staring at her with bloodshot eyes.

She shook her head.

"You no wan', eh!" he said, and gave a sharp, bitten-off laugh. He took a long drink, then began to eat, not with appetite but in a slow fastidiousness, looking critically at each mouthful after he had lifted the fork, then chewing the food with a mincing motion of the jaws, the lids of his eyes lowered to shroud them from her sight. Each time, after he had swallowed, he took a delicate sip from the glass. The coffee went unnoticed.

He was more than half through the food on the plate, when he lifted his head. She stood frozen in the sudden unveiling of his gaze.

"You stand there, why you stand there?" he demanded.

She tried to think why she was there. Every night after she had dished up the food, she had stood here by the range to watch him eat it. She had seen the light on his wet slicked-down hair like black enamel. But that was not an answer, she knew it wasn't, and she felt as she used to feel in school when she was a little girl in that schoolhouse up the road that wasn't there anymore, and the teacher asked her the question and the answer wouldn't come out of her mouth.

He was staring at her. "You no eat?" he said.

She shook her head.

"Why you no eat?" he said.

"I can't," she said.

"Why you can't?"

It was like school, and the answer wouldn't come. Always after he had finished eating and had left the kitchen and she was alone, she would warm up something to take to Sunder.

After she had fed him, she would sit there by his bed and eat something.

But was that the answer?

"Why you no sit?" he was saying, with the bloodshot eyes on her.

She didn't answer.

"That chair, see?" he said, pointing to one by the wall beyond the sink. "You bring here now, eh?"

She brought the chair and placed it opposite him.

"*Bene,* sit."

She sat down, under the white glare of light.

He began to eat again, not noticing her. He finished, gazed directly across at her. Under that light her face was chalky white, but, as he stared at her, the flush began, first just a touch on each side, under the high cheekbones, the spot hectic and sudden like fever. As the cheek mantled, as she seemed about to lower her head, her eyes, from the dusky shadow of the sockets, suddenly met his with a look both bright and distant, like pleading.

Her eyes were there only an instant. Then her head dropped to press the chin on the breastbone. It was enough, however, to make the anger flash up in him.

"Why you no talk?"

He leaned at her.

"Talk," he commanded.

She did not stir, and suddenly, his right hand leaped across the table and seized the wrist of the arm that lay opposite, humble, weak, and indifferent. His grip closed tight, lifting the arm from the table, holding it a foot or so above the surface, in the empty air.

"Talk! You talk!"

But nothing happened, and he flung the wrist from him, in despair and outrage.

He rose from the table, seized the bottle, and stood there.

"Who you?" he cried out. "*Porca Madonna!* Who you are?"

By the time she had raised her head to look at him, to try to find something to say to that question that was filling her head, he was gone. Rather, his back was going through the door into the hall. Then the door closed.

He stood in the dark of the hall, breathing hard. If she had just said something. Then you would have known she was real.

Slowly, not bothering to turn on the light, he groped his way down the hall, turned the corner into the ell, and found his door. In the dark, he lay down on the bed, all his clothes on, even the shoes. He took a drink from the bottle, set it on the floor by the bed, lit a cigarette, and lay on his back, staring up into the dark.

When he took a drag of the cigarette, he held it between thumb and forefinger, cupped so that the brightness of the tip was concealed from his eyes, except for the faint bleeding away of pink glow upward into the darkness above the edge of his palm and little finger. When he took a drag, he kept his eyes on the upper darkness, aware of the glow but not looking at it.

After a while he took another drink and lit another cigarette and kept on staring at the darkness where the ceiling was.

It was raining again.

When he first jerked awake, he did not know where he was. But his thumb and forefinger hurt, and he knew. He had gone to sleep, and the cigarette had burned down to the fingers. The butt was there on the blanket, smoldering. He crushed it out, and spat on the spot on the blanket, and rubbed in the wetness. Then he put his hurt fingers to his mouth, and with the other hand fumbled on the floor for the bottle.

He found it. When he shook it in the dark there was a slosh, but not a big one. He drank what there was.

He lay there and thought: *Santa Madonna, sono tornato. Back.*

He was lying there in the dark, the empty bottle loosely between his fingers, on his chest, as though forgotten. He was remembering all that had happened—or rather, he was seeing things happen in the dark above his wide-open eyes—when he heard the sound.

It was the sound that came from that room down the hall. It was like the sound he remembered from his uncle's farm in Ohio, when you butchered a sheep. You hoisted the sheep up by the hind legs and slit the throat and suddenly the last bleat with the blood in it was like the sound from that room. But when the sound came from the sheep, it did not keep on, the way the sound from that room did sometimes. With the sheep dead the sound stopped.

The sound was loud now in the dark, louder than he had ever heard it come to this room. He made a move to rise, but the sound stopped, so he dropped back down. Then he decided he'd get up anyway, to go outside to relieve himself, rain or not. He tiptoed down the hall, to the back porch, to stand on the edge under the eaves.

He had got back to the door of his room, when he realized that just a minute back, when he came out, the door had been open. That was why the sound had come so loud. Now he stood there in the dark and tried to remember whether he had shut the door upon entering the room after supper. Every other night, always when he went in, he had shut it. He stood there thinking about the door.

Why was he worried about having left the door open?

There was nothing here, nothing but the woman and the noise in that room, and the rain falling outside, and upstairs the weight of darkness. He stood there, his hand on the door-jamb and looked upward toward the darkness of the ceiling, thinking of the rooms up there that he had never seen, of those spaces filled with darkness.

He could have gone up, any day or night, and nobody would have ever known or cared. There were the wide stairs in the front hall. He had wandered into the hall, just as he had wandered idly into the room where the piano was. But he had never even thought of going up those stairs. He hadn't had the curiosity even to open the two other doors in the ell, on this floor, assuming that nothing, not here or upstairs, would be different from the room he was in.

But that was yesterday. And this was tonight, and what had happened had happened, and he was back here in this house, and he was standing in this dark hall, and the need was grow-ing in him to know what was in this house, to touch every door, to go into every room, to stand in every room and breathe the dark there, to know—. To know what?

He groped into his room, found the old syrup bottle he had stuck a candle in to go out back at night by, lit it, lit a cigarette, which he let hang from the left corner of his mouth, came back into the hall, and shut the door carefully behind him, as was his custom, and tried the door opposite his own.

He had been right in his assumption. It was like his own room, only more ruinous. The other door in the hall was to a bathroom, a big zinc tub set in a varnished wooden boxing, a marble surface on top about the tub. There was a zinc basin, set in a marble slab, with heavy brass fixtures, like those of the tub. There was the toilet in the corner near the window, with a pipe going up to the old-fashioned flush box, up near the ceiling.

Christ-a Jesus, he thought, *and ever' morning, Angelo—he go out to stink-house.*

But when he tried a faucet in the basin, no water came. He

leaned and held the candle over the bowl of the toilet. It was dry and dusty.

He came back into the hall and went toward the corner where the ell joined the main hall. He paused for a moment at the door of the room where the sound would come from, standing very still while the candle flame grew steady on the wick and the shadows froze to the walls as flat as black paper pasted on.

Then he turned right and moved the three paces that led to the door cutting off the front hall. He was still wearing his own clothes, the town clothes, and he set the toes of the patent-leather shoes down without sound. He looked down at the shoes and saw that they had no sheen in the candle light. There were getting dry and cracked. Despair flooded his bosom.

But he laid hand to the hall door, entered, and ascended the stairs. The carpeting on the stairs was frayed through to the wood. Halfway up the stairs, he looked back. His own shadow, cast by the candle held breast-high before him, made the darkness darker behind him. There his shadow filled the air, enormous, hovering over him. When he had turned again up the stairs, he felt the weight on his shoulders.

He wandered the rooms. Out of the darkness, the furniture swayed slowly at him, swaying into the light of the candle like clumps of waterweed in the backwash of a sluggish current. In one room, a mattress, still on the bed, had been cut open by rats or squirrels, and the gray, clotted viscera spilled out over the floor. Standing there, he was aware, through the thin soles of the patent-leather shoes, of the gritty feel of dry rodent droppings under his feet. A moldy odor, streakily mixed of dust and damp, filled his nostrils. Here the sound of the rain was louder.

The last room he entered was toward the front, over the parlor, he calculated. It was much larger than the others, with a fireplace and, as he noticed, a marble mantle, this on the inner wall to the left, and a big tester bed jutting out toward him from the wall he faced. He moved toward the bed, and stood beside it.

He looked up at the canopy. Some of the fabric had given way, slowly giving down of its own weight, hanging in motionless, raveling strips. He held the candle closer to a strip, studying it. It had once been rose-color, as even in candlelight, he could tell from a few streaks not yet faded to a pinky-gray. He lifted his hand to touch the fabric, but in the air the hanging cobwebs which he had not seen caught his hand in their dry, sticky tangle, with a contact more loathsome for its feebleness. He withdrew his hand, not having touched the hanging strip, and wiped it against his trouser leg.

He looked down. There were two thick mattresses of gray-striped ticking. He saw the bolster of ticking, and the two pillows, in their places. He had never seen a bed like this. He wondered what it would be like to sleep in such a bed.

He thought how people had really lain in that bed, on that mattress, sleeping while the rain came down outside as it was doing this very minute, or had waked to turn and clasp each other in the dark.

That thought filled his head. It was the kind of thought he had never had before. It was, literally, filling his head with a pressure that hurt.

Here me, he thought, and put out his hand to touch the mattress.

All at once he jerked his hand back, and still looking at the bed, the very spot on the mattress where his hand had been in contact, withdrew a couple of slow backward steps.

He moved from the bed, and moving, caught the glint of the candle flame in a mirror, the tall mirror of the armoire across the room—the candle flame and then, in the same instant, the shadowy image of a man with the flame glimmering pale on his face. His blood froze, for in that instant he did not realize that there was a mirror, that the shocked, forward-thrust, wide-eyed face, glimmering so pale in light, with the cigarette hanging from the corner of the mouth, was his own.

Then he knew, and knowing, moved toward it, the knowledge itself not merely knowledge, but, after the chill of the shock, a bemused wondering. A pace from the mirror he stopped, and stared into it, studying the image.

Me, he thought, in a wondering that grew more powerful and benumbing with the confrontation, detail by detail, of the knowledge that this image was, really, himself.

The light on the face in the mirror flickered. The candle in the mirror was, he suddenly saw, guttering. He was staring at the face in the mirror when the flame flared up and then, all at once, had died. In the mirror there was only the tiny illumination of the cigarette that hung from the left corner of the mouth. It showed faintly the little area of the cheek and the left corner of the lips, where it was burning down to the very flesh. That was all you could see in the mirror.

With his tongue tip he pushed the butt free to fall, then delicately set the toe of a patent-leather shoe on the glowing spot.

He stood before the mirror, which he could not see now, and breathed, slowly and harshly, the dark air.

Whatever broke it, what was broken was the dream, with a sense, on waking, that something had been literally broken, like a plate dropped, or like a windowpane shattered because an old rotten window-cord snapped when you touched the sash, and the sash fell. In that instant of waking, even before any consciousness of what the dream had been, she was flooded by that sense of brokenness, of irremediableness.

Then, in that awareness she knew what the dream had been. It had been a dream of Cy Grinder, not the thickening man in the torn red mackinaw standing on top of the bridge over the roaring creek, waving a bow against a darkening sky and calling to her some insult she could not make out, but of Cy Grinder young, towering above her as she lay at his feet, smiling down at her with the smile that had always made her want to cry with joy, now towering above her while his nakedness, which she had never seen and had dreamed only now, glimmered white against the darkness of the world.

He had been about to reach out to her, to say her name, but then the dream broke, and there was the wild sadness, followed by the flash of rage that she had had to have the dream at all. For she hadn't dreamed of Cy Grinder all these years. Oh, why did everything have to begin again!

Then, in that moment of waking in the dark, she thought, with a grim satisfaction, that the noise that woke her had been Sunder. But she could hear his breathing, and though it was ragged, it was not the kind of ragged it was after he had made his noise. So she lay listening.

Then she heard the noise again, knowing suddenly that it was the same kind of noise that had waked her. Somebody had bumped something, somebody upstairs, toward the front of the house. Even before that thought was framed, however, the cold prickles ran down from the back of her neck down the spine.

For she knew who it was. Her mind saw what it was: *him*.

Him, for he didn't have a name, at least not in her mind. Even if he had told her his name, as she knew he had, she never called him by it. He was no name, he was the shape with no name: *him*.

She lay under the weight of the blankets, staring up where the ceiling was, listening for something to move far off up there in the dark hollowness of the house.

There it was. Closer.

.   .   .

After he had fumbled his way down the dark stairs, he stopped in the hall outside the door to that room, and listened.

There was no sound. He shrugged his shoulders. What was behind the door? Just that woman. And whatever—whoever— made that noise like a sheep being slaughtered.

All at once in the darkness of his head, as in the darkness of a closed room, he saw the woman, this very instant, standing behind the door, just the other side, listening. He knew she was there.

He moved down the hall to his own door, and then, with his hand yet on the knob, was, on the instant, totally convinced that when he had entered the room tonight after supper, he had closed the door.

Somebody had opened the door while he slept. He could see it as though it were happening this very instant.

The face, faintly white in the dark hall, had leaned close to the panel of his shut door, listening for his breath. The white hand had been laid to the knob, it had begun to turn the knob without any sound.

He shivered.

For he was seeing, suddenly, the place laid for him tonight on the table, the pink-and-white plate, the knife and fork and spoon, the cup, all there on the red-check oilcloth that was beginning to show gray where it was cracked, the table and everything there under the blankness of light. All had been ready.

So she had known he would come back.

And as the knowledge of her knowledge filled his head, he felt totally without defense. He felt tied up by ropes. He felt he was being put in a dark room and a key was turning.

When, at first light, his throat dry and head throbbing, he woke up, that same thought was already in his head, as though it had been waiting for him to wake up. She must have known everything. If not, why, when she knew that the car was gone, hadn't she telephoned the police? There was a telephone. How could she know he wasn't running away with her car?

Suppose she had called the police.

He lay there sweating, thinking how near he had actually come to running away. He had got a hundred miles, up into Kentucky, running blind. Running blind, not from anything, not to anything, just blind, to be away. He had got up there in Kentucky before he remembered what day it was. It was the day to go to Parkerton.

So he had turned around and gone to Parkerton.

Suppose he had forgot Parkerton, and everything, running blind. He started sweating again.

"Well, Puss-Face," the man had said, cocking back in the swivel chair and removing the cigar from his mouth, "so you made it?"

"Yes, sir," he had said.

"Well, five minutes more and I'd a-been long gone, Puss-Face. You expect me to wait round all night for you, Puss-Face?"

"No, sir," he had said, and later, down in the street, he had felt faint. He had leaned for a full minute against a building. He hadn't eaten all day, but he knew that was not the reason. It was the idea of coming here, and finding the door locked.

But on the way back from Parkerton to the valley, he had to keep fighting the impulse to turn off the road, to run blind, anywhere, let anything happen, no matter what. Then he kept thinking a drink would help. He hadn't had a drink in three years. He had got so he never missed it. But now the need was growing in him. The spit grew at the base of his tongue. There was a package store on the highway.

Back in the car he unscrewed the tin cap of the bottle and was about to put it to his mouth, when he decided he'd better get off the highway before he had the drink. So he waited until he had reached the Corners, and had turned off the highway up the valley. Then he took two deep drags, with no chaser, burning, raw.

He drove on up the valley, the feeble lights of the car muffled in the ground mist. It was going to rain, and he kept thinking how it had been raining the first time he came up this road, walking beside the roar of the creek. The creek was roaring now, and he was coming back.

He drove slower and slower, so slow the old car began to jerk and heave in high gear. He was approaching the spot where that damn Sandy Claws, *quello dannato*, had come flying in the air, and the arrow had whanged.

There was the house looming ahead, on the left. Slowly, the tires slipping and sliding in the muddy ruts, the car moved on. He felt like a man who lets the reins go slack, lets the horse follow its head, in the dark.

The car had gone on past the house. It went up the valley. Until he saw the light of the shack he refused the knowledge of where he was. Now he pulled on past the shack, found a place to turn, turned, and came back past it, his lights off. Then he stopped. He fixed his eyes on the shack yonder. Between him and the light there, he saw the faint glint of reflection on the slick, wet ground of the yard. He felt for the bottle on the seat, found it, and with his eyes still on the spot of light, drank.

He sat there a long time. Now and then he took a drink. He thought of himself, alone in this car, watching the light over there, through the rain, in the place where the girl was.

He finally tore himself away. He drove slowly back to the place where he now knew he would go. He didn't even bother to put the car in the barn, just got out of it and walked away from it toward the back of the house, where light shone from the kitchen window. He stepped under the protection of the deeper dark of a cedar, and stared at the woman in that other world beyond the glass of the window, standing by the range, with a saucepan hanging off her limp hand. Suddenly he knew he was trying to know what was going on in her head.

Christ-a Jesus, he thought, peering in at her from the darkness of the cedar, *Christ-a Jesus.*

If that morning, she had only said something. If she had moved. If she had fought him. If she had scratched him. If she had cried out. If—if anything—

Then, standing there under the cedar, peering in at the woman by the range, who was wrapped in that old baggy brown sweater, he saw the image of the body glimmering on the floor, motionless, as it had been that morning, when, after it was over, he had risen and was looking down at her, where she had been dropped to lie in limp and awkward beauty. Her eyes had been closed. She had never even opened her eyes.

It was like she was not real.

No—and at the instant of that realization his breath froze in his throat—it was like you, you yourself, were not real.

Then, through the window, he saw the table, under the electric bulb, the plate laid on it. He stood there and waited, but he knew that he would, in the end, go in. And she—she had known it all the time.

He lay there in bed while the dawn light hardened into day, and again, in his head, saw everything that had happened. It was all happening again—right up to this very minute, this very second. And he thought: *If I stay in this bed right now, nothing never happen no more.*

He lay on his back and pulled the sheet up to his upper lip, just under his nose, drew it tight, and closed his eyes. This way, nothing could happen.

But, in the end, he got up.

He put on the old cut-down red bathrobe and went out into the hall, stopped before opening the back door, lit a cigarette, and knew that that door behind him had come open, and the eye at the crack was watching him. He went on out, to the privy.

On his way back to the house, he stopped, lit another cigarette, and stood there. The morning was clear and bright. The puddles from the rain of the night before, standing among the brown, sparse stems of grass, now glittered with skim ice. He stood there in the brightness of the world, with the smoke oozing slow from his nostrils, to pale to nothing in the sunlight. He stared at the window of his room. This side of the house was in shade, and the window was, in the gray paintlessness of the wall, a rectangle of darkly glimmering opacity.

He had to stand out here in the cold, not even dressed, waiting—waiting for what?—because that *cretina*, she might be in there, in his room. With anger there grew, too, a bitter stubbornness. He would go to the kitchen, he'd make the fire, he'd sit there and wait, he'd eat something, anything, to hell with coffee even, and wait till she came. He'd outwait her. That would show her.

He would not even go to look in the window to see if she was there.

But he did.

And there she was as before, crouching on the floor, wearing that faded flannel nightgown, mended now, he could see that much, her head leaning against the side of the bed, the eyes closed.

Idiota, he thought. He'd show her. He'd go to the kitchen and wait.

That was what he would have done. If she had not risen on her knees and, with eyes still closed, groped for the pillow where his head had lain.

(1 1 4)

The hands found the pillow, and drew it toward her. Then, still on her knees, the eyes closed, she buried her face in it, in the very spot where his head had lain.

With his vision of this act, another kind of anger rose in him, more murderous but mixed with desolation, powerlessness, and yearning.

Then he was racing toward the back door, then down the hall. He did not hear what noise his feet made on the boards.

All happened as it had happened before.

With one difference:

Afterwards, the clothes he seized were not his own, the town clothes, but what she had cut down for him to wear here.

He went to the kitchen, dressed, made the fire, and went out and busied himself splitting stove lengths until he calculated that breakfast would be ready and his place laid.

If, earlier, work had been a flight, a refuge, now it became a fury. That was all the days were—a blind occupation. He had long since replaced the broken pane of the window in his room. Now he set about doing windows wherever needed, and many were needed. He prowled the attic on rainy days to spot leaks, and on his next trip to Parkerton bought five bales of shingles and patched the roof. He bought paint and began painting the outside of the house—the part, at least, under the protection of the high porch. When he got beyond that, he found too much clapboarding in need of replacement, and all the wood too soggy with damp to take paint. He would have to wait for warm weather to dry things out. But nevertheless he gave a second coat to the wall under the protection of the porch, put a few boards in the porch floor, and laid on blue deck paint. Then he began, bit by bit, to replace the worst pieces of clapboarding.

But he interrupted that to work on the bathroom. One morning, high on the ladder, ready to set a length of clapboard, he remembered the bathroom he had found the night he came back and wandered in the dark house. Immediately, on impulse, he came down the ladder, got the car, and drove to the Corners, where the store was, and bought a flashlight. He came back, found a board-covered opening in the rough stone foundation, and crawled under.

It took all day to trace the pipes that led to that bathroom. For one thing he began by wasting time on those that led upstairs; for another, there was painfully little space for crawling. In some places the heavy timbers came down so low he had to inch along, belly down, thrusting himself forward with elbows and toes, driving his head forward through the veils of ancient cobweb that hung down into the jerky beam of the flashlight.

Now and then, he would roll over and stretch out to relieve the cramp of his muscles. Once, lying on his back with the light out, breathing the dry, cool dustiness of that secret earth, not drowsing, wide awake in that darkness, he felt a lassitude creep over him, rising from the earth beneath him, like water rising, and then, as the deliberate flood seemed to close over him in the dark, he knew that it was peace, a nothingness that was, strangely, a kind of sweetness. It would be sweet to lie here forever.

Flickeringly, he remembered what life had been long ago, the burning of whiskey in the throat, the smell of a girl, the roar of the exhaust as a car plunged at night into the tunnel of its own flung beams, the excitement of a fight, the sight of his own face in the mirror as the comb moved glossily through the blackness of his hair, the sway of colored lights in a dance hall while the music kept on and on. Like those flickering lights in the dance hall—that was what his whole life, what everything, had been.

Was that what it had been? A bright whirling and swaying, a hunting for something, a running after something, a going and coming and not knowing why? And now was everything this easy, after all? To lie in the dark, and not want anything?

He must have dozed off. For suddenly, he jerked into wakefulness, in the dark, not knowing where he was, then knowing, and knowing that the flashlight was gone, and knowing that the mass and weight of the house was over him, was coming slowly down on him.

He was groping wildly for the flashlight. He found it, and the beam struck forth to show, in their actuality and not in his nightmare vision, the timbers, the earth itself which, because the flashlight lay so close to the surface, was marked by unpredictable pools of shadow reaching from him, and the gray draperies of cobweb receding, timber after timber, into darkness.

He knew it had all been crazy, that panic.

I fix pipe, he said to himself. *Me, I fix.*

If he just kept his mind on that, everything would be all right.

He found where the line from the kitchen had been disconnected and capped. Then he found the old leak. You could spot it by the delicate concentric circles where, long back, water had dripped on the undisturbed earth.

The work on the line meant two trips to Parkerton, to get pipe and rent tools to cut and thread it, and then carry the tools back. The work meant cutting off the water for the house. He had traced the supply line, a gravity feed from a big spring with a stone storage basin, up in the woods on the rise beyond the house. There was a valve there, beat up and corroded, but still workable. When he told the woman to stock up on water, he was going to cut it off to do some work, he made no further explanation.

He never explained more than he had to. If he did not explain, he protected something. He protected the fact that he was himself.

The first morning after he had fixed the line, he woke up with the immediate thought that now he could go to the bathroom, he would not have to go down the hall, would not have to stand to light a cigarette at the porch door, would not have to know that that other door was opening a crack, would not have to suffer the eye at the crack spying on him. Then, back from the bathroom, standing in the hall, he wondered if, when he opened the door, she would be there.

His hand on the doorknob, he thought back on his confusion of feeling the first time he had not found her in his room when he opened the door. He hadn't known what he felt. He had dressed and gone to the kitchen, and there she was, silent, the eyes on him, the place laid for him. For five days it had been like that, and he had adapted himself to it, had found some relief, a sense of hope that life would offer something new, unexpected, and even joyful, though what he could not know.

Then one morning, the fifth morning, she had been there again, and he knew it had been her period. So everything was as it had been, and he did not know what he felt about that, either.

Now, with his hand on the knob, he remembered the first morning when she had not come, and opened the door.

But there she was. On the bed, on her back, the sheet to her chin, her eyes closed, lying like dead, waiting for the violation, waiting to be used, dropped, flung aside, all in silence except for the labor of breath, her own breath tight and hissing with the effort of control.

The bed—for long back now, that had begun. One morning he had opened the door, had seen the form crouching beside the bed, and had felt the burst of anger, had heard his own voice saying: "You crazy?—you do all time on floor? Get on bed—if you wan' Angelo do you big—"

He used the dirty word, saw her eyes snap open, staring up at him, dark eyes sudden in the white face, and, in that instant wide, wild, and glittering as though surprised at seeing him and his obvious intention.

"Bed," he said, "you get on bed."

With a cranky, tentative motion, like an old woman, her face now averted from him, she obeyed.

But otherwise, the ritual remained unchanged.

The ritual of work remained unchanged, too. After breakfast, with the last gulp of coffee still hot in his throat, he would shove the chair back and go out the back door, not even pausing to light his cigarette until he was free. If it was raining, he stood on the back porch, sucking on the cigarette, waiting for a break that would let him go to his task. If the break did not come, he would put on the old black slicker he had found in a closet and tear out for the barn to skulk there in that shadowy dampness, pretending to sort the debris that, over the years, had accumulated there.

Pretending, for he had already done all that was really needed. Not that the pretense was designed to deceive the woman in the house. No, he was not concerned to deceive her, but he had to deceive his own hands, make them think that the movements they made had a purpose. For if he deceived the hands into making those movements, then they, by those movements, could deceive him and he would not be left, oc-cupationless, to sit in the chill shadows of the barn, with a cigarette in his mouth, with the cigarette butts accumulating on the packed earth about his feet, staring out the half-open door, up the slope where the woods were, at the gray, sopping sky. If he did not play that trick on the hands, then they would not play that trick on him, and if they did not, he would have to sit and think how things had once been and how they could never again be anything but what they now were.

Sometimes at noon, whether it was raining or not, whether he was in the barn or doing some job outside, he did not go to the house to eat. Not that he would have had to see her, for from the first, even if she had been visible outdoors, hanging wash, she would always be put out of sight by noon. In the kitchen would be the cold food laid out, a pot of coffee keeping hot on the back of the range, the kitchen empty and silent. Even so, he might keep at his job, or if it was raining and he was in the barn, he might keep watching his hands make those careful motions which pretended to be a job.

But the time always came when he would have to go to the house. He would avoid the kitchen, now that he did not have to get water for washing, and enter by the door to the back hall, and go to the bathroom which he had brought back to service. He would strip to the waist and wash himself, then lay out his razor, hoping that some water was still warm in the coil built into the kitchen range. When the shaving was over, he would comb his hair and then lean forward to inspect his face in the mirror—oval, olive-swarthy, dark-eyed, even-featured except for a fullness of the lips. Looking at it, he would think: *Puss-Face.*

That was what that man always called him. Someday he would kill that man.

After shaving he would take a drink from the bottle he now kept in his room, just one good one, put on a town shirt, and go to the kitchen. His place would be laid, one place on the red-check oilcloth. The woman would be over there by the range, waiting.

But one night he took three pulls of the bottle before going to the kitchen, and when he entered and saw her staring at him, he went straight toward her, seized her and pressed his mouth hard and probingly against hers.

Releasing her, he stared into her face.

"*Santa Madonna*," he cried out, "why you no talk?"

Nothing changed.

"*Santa Madonna*," he cried, and heard his own voice thinning as into a wail in distance, "who you, please? Who you are?"

Just then the sound came. If he had not left the door open to the hall, they could not have heard it.

"Who that is?" he demanded, seizing her by the shoulders and shaking her. "You think Angelo stay here and no know!"

Then he shoved her from him. "I go see," he said, and strode toward the hall door. At the door he paused, and looked back. "I go see," he affirmed.

If she had said for him to stay, or even to go, he would have gone. But she said nothing. So in his rage and humiliation, he closed the door and went to sit down at the table.

After supper, he always went immediately to his room. There he lay down, and by the bare bulb of an old table lamp he had found in the barn and now kept on a chair by the bed, read one of his magazines. He had found them, stacks of them, in the armoire in the room upstairs with the tester bed—*True Detective, Argosy, Black Mask, True Confessions, Gangland, Ellery Queen*, dozens of titles, hundreds of copies, some dating back thirty-five years, none more recent than 1945, the pages gone yellow, the paper ready to flake under a touch, the colors of cover illustrations fading out, the dresses of girls and the shapes of cars in the pictures all looking funny now. He had brought the magazines down to his room, load after load, to stack along the wall, to the right of his bed. Now dozens of them were on the left side, where, at random, they had been flung. For when he had finished one, had really finished it, reading it steadily, even the advertisements, he flung it over to the left side.

It was not that he would have been able to identify a single story read a week, or perhaps even a night, earlier. He sensed this fact, but sensed, too, that the very blur of similarity, was something he craved. The excitement evoked in the blur of violence and lust was allayed only to be re-evoked by a new story which, in turn, would be nothing more than the old cycle repeated, the tale always empty of meaning but charged always with the heavy atmosphere of gunsmoke and sweetly sweating flesh.

For it was all a dream, like the dream his own past now seemed to be, and the two dreams could merge into one dream, not to be differentiated, and in that dream he was strong, he was real, men fell beneath the impact of his fist or the bullet he fired, and white arms stretched toward him, and red lips gone slack and distorted with yearning piteously called out his name—Angelo, Angelo.

Sometimes he would lie on the bed and think how there had once been somebody named Angelo. People had called that name. But now only in a dream.

At a certain point, it might be in the middle of a story or while his eyes were fixed on an advertisement, he would let the magazine fall to his chest, and would fumble to locate the little radio he had got secondhand in Parkerton. Lying there, propped on a pillow, with the cigarette hanging from his lips, he would hunt for a station, and when he found the music he wanted, with the radio turned down till the music was little more than a whisper in a dream, a murmur coming from beyond the further edge of silence, he would lie back and watch the smoke unspooling upward in the naked light. He would be thinking what it would be like to be in a world where that music was.

He would lie there with closed eyes, while the music murmured from beyond the further edge of silence, and try to remember something—anything—that had once happened to him. Shapes, gestures, sounds would come into the darkened theater of his head, but colors, they never came. He knew that there had been colors, but the colors had been bleached away, and behind the shut eyes he watched the gray flickering of a world that had once been real.

Or as he watched the flickering, he would try to remember what feelings he had had in that world when it was real. But it seemed that all feeling, like the colors, had been drained away from these stances and movements of memory. Then, one night, listening to the rustle of music from the radio, he became aware that he did not even know what feelings he had now.

He was suddenly aware of this, but was not aware that he had been trying, in fact, not to have any. Day by day, he watched his hands in the fury of occupation, and tried not to have any feeling. He ate food and tried not to taste it. He looked at the woman standing by the range. He rose in the morning and evacuated, he came back to the room to find her there, he did what he would do, and everything was like everything else.

Was this the way things always were in the end? If all you had out of living was the memories you couldn't remember the feelings of, did that mean that your living itself, even now while you lived it, was like that too, and everything you did, even in the instant of doing, was nothing more than the blank motions the shadow of your body made in those memories which now, without meaning, were all you had out of the living and working you had done before?

He thought how his mother's hands had always been moving, all the years, and how he had watched them move. He thought of his father's hands. He had watched their hands moving, and their eyes as they looked down at their hands, and he had sworn that he would never be like that. And he had not been, not for a while, but now he himself was like that.

He remembered how, in the last years, his father had sat in a chair in the kitchen, far off in Savoca, in Sicily, a dying hulk, and the hands had not been moving then, lying swollen on the knees. But a foot, always the right foot, had always been twitching, just a little, inside the torn felt slipper, with the big toe sticking through, twitching with a rhythmic regularity. The old man sat with eyes fixed on the floor, and everything, everything in the world, was just that twitch that you waited for, and then it came, always in that feeble and merciless regularity that made you want to get up and yell and run out into the street, into the fields, up the mountains, anywhere.

Now night after night, remembering his father and the motion of the foot, he would rise from the bed, and go from the room. He would go upstairs and wander about, and in the end, shut off the flashlight and stand breathing the dark air that was harsh with dustiness and cold. It was always the big front room with the tester bed where he cut off the light. In the dark he would move toward a window and look off in what he knew was the direction of the ruined dairy house.

The first night when he wandered upstairs, he came back to his room, to find the radio still emitting its whispery music. He seized it, lifted his arm high as though to hurl it from him. But he lowered it, turned it off, and in the silence stared down at it, there in his hands.

On subsequent nights, if he had forgotten to turn it off, he merely picked it up, turned the switch, and then undressed as quickly as possible, and lay down to sleep.

At least, in this world of changelessness, where nothing had ever happened and nothing would ever happen, he could, if he waited long enough, sleep. For he knew that the dream that used to wake him in the sweat of fear and guilt did not come now. The dream might be there, waiting in the dark to be dreamed. But now, night by night, he closed his eyes and knew that, at least not yet, he would not have to dream it.

He knew that he was living another dream, and the living of that dream was the price he paid not to dream the other.

Back in the fall, sorting out the plunder in the barn, he had found a 12-gauge shotgun. It was old and rusty, but he dismantled it, soaked it in kerosene, worked it over with steel wool, and oiled it. Now in the protracted spell of hard clear weather that came in January, he would slip away in the afternoon and go hunting for rabbits. He felt some uneasiness in breaking from the rigid ritual of his occupations, but now, in this new brightness of sky, he could not stand the proximity of the house. When he came into the kitchen at dusk and flung down a couple of rabbits, gutted and peeled, he was doing something that seemed to expiate whatever had, in the afternoon, needed expiation.

The first day he wandered over the ridge east of the house, and into the woods and old fields beyond, but each day as he made the loop homeward, he moved closer and closer to the other woods to the south and west, toward the road. On the fifth day, it was still daylight when he crouched behind deadfall at the edge of the open ground where the dairy house was.

There was no movement in that space. A squirrel chittered somewhere, far off. After a time, a single crow, very high above the spot where he crouched, labored, in a stubborn, methodical motion, across the visible sky. At that height, the sun glittered on the blackness of those moving wings. Then the crow was gone, and lowering his gaze, he realized the thickening shadow of the woods around him.

He rose and took the track toward the house.

When he came around the corner of the barn, he saw the big white Buick convertible. He had seen that car three times before. It had come every month. Peering out from the protection of the barn, he waited until the man in the gray suit and gray overcoat came out and got into the Buick.

Suddenly, with the powerful glide of its take-off, the car disappeared beyond the house, so suddenly he was not sure it had been there at all. Staring at the place where it had been and was not now, he thought that if he had not gone away, or if going away, he had not gone into those other woods, then the car would not have been there.

But he knew that thinking that was crazy.

The car came every month.

CHAPTER SIX

✟✟✟✟✟✟✟✟✟✟✟ **T**hat night, before going to
the kitchen, Angelo took two drags from the bottle. The car
had come, that was what made him do it. It came from that
world where the music was that tonight he would hear
whispering from the radio, and where the colored lights swept
the dimness of a dance hall while you smelled the girl's hair,
and where he would never come again.

But why did it come here, that *macchina maledetta*, to
make him stand in the middle of this room and shiver and not
know why?

It was then that he took the second drag from the bottle,
before he went to the kitchen, where the woman, while he ate,
stared at him more mercilessly than ever and with a brightness
in the eyes that, even in this distance, he knew had never
been there before.

He did not finish the food on his plate but went to his room,
lay on the bed, turned on the radio, picked up a magazine

from the nearest stack to the right of the bed, and began to read. He read doggedly, his lips moving without sound, making the shapes of the words that now, tonight, even as he shaped them, carried no images, and had no meaning; and he felt, somewhere deep in himself, more clearly than ever before, both the burden and the hope of the ritual: if he read all those words on that rotting paper stacked along the wall to the right of the bed, then maybe something would be over, and something would again be real.

Suddenly he could read no more. He snapped off the radio. But he could not bear the silence. He rose and went upstairs and wandered those rooms until he came to the big room where he had known he would come. He stood in the middle of the floor, flashlight off, and breathed the dark air, his eyes closed, steadfastly refusing to go to the window where he knew he would, in the end, go.

When he went to the window, he pressed his face against the pane as hard as he could without breaking the glass, and peered out into that forbidden direction. To the flesh of his brow, the glass was cold as ice. It was like the ice that cut him off from the world outside, and cut him off from all the time that had been and might ever be. Then, as he peered out, he saw that his own breath, condensing on that icy glass, had fogged all vision. He could no longer see whatever lay beyond.

He went downstairs, and got into bed, shivering at the contact of the sheets. He left the lamp blazing on the chair by the side of the bed, and again turned on the radio. Even if the sheets had lost their initial chill, he still shivered.

Then he heard the knock on the door.

"Come in," he said. There was nothing else he could say.

At the further perimeter of the light cast by the lamp on the chair between him and the door, there she stood. He saw that she was wearing some sort of dingy-dark woolly robe which he had never seen before. He could see, below the robe, the grayish hem of her flannel nightgown, and then, the white of her feet and ankles. He looked at her face, hung white against the darkness of the hall.

Now she come my room, he thought. *Now, at night.* He was cold with rage.

But it was not as he had imagined. She stood there motionless in her distance, with the lips going strangely full and soft in what looked like a smile, and the eyes again had a misty brightness that earlier tonight, in the kitchen, he had noticed and that had disturbed him, and disturbed him now.

"What you want?" he demanded.

"May I come in?" she asked, framed there against the darkness of the hall, waiting humbly for his answer.

"This house," he said slowly, "she yours."

For a moment she regarded him with the undiminishing brightness, then said: "I wish you wouldn't say that."

He wished she would not look at him in this new way. For things were changing, something was changing now this minute, just when he thought they would never change again, just when he had found a way to live in that changelessness.

So now he felt the need to make her angry, make her look different from the strange new way she was—make her do something. All right—make her throw him out. He had the sudden image of himself walking down the road in the dark night, wearing his town clothes again, as he had come, feeling the now-frozen mud sharp against the thin soles of his patent-leather shoes as he set them down in the dark. He felt a kind of angry glory in that image, a sense of being himself again, free again. Maybe for the first time, ever.

So, before that feeling faded, he said: "What the hell you want me say?"

"I'd like to talk to you," she said.

Something was going to change.

"May I sit down?" she asked.

"This house," he repeated, and fixed his eyes on the ceiling, detaching himself, "she yours."

The light on the ceiling suddenly shifted, a shadow swung across, then retreated, sank, and settled. He did not look but he knew what had happened. She had put the lamp on the floor between the chair and the stacks of his magazines, and had sat down, on the chair, by the bed. He waited for her to say something, keeping his gaze upward, hearing the slight rustle of her breath.

If she was waiting for him to look at her, she could wait forever, he decided.

She did not wait that long. She said: "Mr. Guilfort—Murray Guilfort—he came here this afternoon."

He knew something was going to change.

After a moment he heard her voice.

"Tell me your name," the voice said.

When, that afternoon, Murray Guilfort had first mounted the porch steps he carefully scrutinized the glistening blue deck paint on the floor, then examined the putty job on the panes in the front windows of the parlor. Everything was even more workmanlike than he had remembered. Preoccupied, refusing for the moment to inspect the nature of his feelings, he let the big brass knocker bang twice, then stood listening to the hollow echo from beyond the door. He thought of the dark hall beyond the door, with the sound waves swelling in the dusty air. He wondered if sound waves actually moved things. Would they agitate the motes of dust that hung in the shadowy air beyond the door?

Nobody came. So he entered.

"Cassie!" he called, then entered the parlor to his right, beyond the foot of the stairs. He stood for a moment surveying it, the portrait on the easel, the rosewood piano, all the dim decrepitude that had once been pride.

The door to the room that, long back, had been the dining room but was now the room where Cassie and Sunder lived, opened, and there she was, as always, with only the difference that the sleeves of the old brown sweater were pulled up near the elbows and her hands were wet, and in the right hand was a safety razor, with a fleck of soap on it. She was looking at the razor.

She lifted her head.

"I just cut him," she said.

"You were shaving him," Murray said, aware, even as the words were uttered, of the idiocy of the remark. But he was just realizing that, after all the years of his coming here and looking down at what was Sunderland Spottwood on that bed, he had never seen the face with more than a day's growth of stubble. But he had never thought, not even once, how that face had been shaved, day after day, over the years.

"You want to wait here," she was saying, "or come in while I finish?"

"I'll come in," he said, with the sudden need to see her performing that task.

She was again by the bed, about to lay a wadded towel to the blood that was spreading thin and bright down on the neck from a good gash across the jawbone.

The towel in place, she looked up at Murray, and said: "I never cut him bad but once. Long back, near the start, when I was using the big old straight razor you had to strop, the one he always used before, his beard being so tough, he said. He must have jerked, and I nearly took a big slice off. On the jawbone like now. But the slice, it was sort of hung on by a hinge of skin, and I put it back down and taped it. It grew back."

She lifted the towel. The blood had not yet stopped, so she put it back, and again looked up.

"It left a good-size scar," she said. Then added, with an air of courtesy, "You can see it, if you want. On the other side."

He could think of no way to refuse, so crossed around the foot of the bed and looked. There it was, the thin white line, circular like the better part of the circumference of a twenty-five-cent piece, defined merely by its slickness against the whiteness of the face. Murray looked at the tallowy whiteness of skin, and thought how, in the old days, that face had always been flushed as with a fever, and full-fleshed. Now the white skin, in folds and pouches, hung off the bone, and out of that minutely downward dragging of flesh what had once been the strong full thrust of the nose, now pinched thin and waxy, pointed upward, in pitiful assertion.

Murray became aware that the fingers on his own right hand were lifted to prod the flesh of his own face. *Fifty-four*, he was thinking, *I'm fifty-four.*

Then with a desperate joy: *But he's older than I am—he's two years older!*

The woman's voice cut into that thought.

"I reckon the blood's stopped now," she said. She looked at the stained towel in her hand, then hung it on the back of a chair, and added: "I've got to bring my chair around to the other side."

"I'll do it," Murray said, and came to pick up the chair, on which was a tin basin of water with a film of soapy iridescence on the surface, and a big, old-fashioned shaving mug with the scrolled initials S.S., in marred gold, and a shaving brush stuck in it. Carefully, he set the chair near the bed on the other side, and looked down. On the right cheek of the face on the pillow, the stubble stood out, yellow as wheat, no gray showing.

The woman brushed lather over the cheek, jaw, and chin,

and then, delicately, in small patches, began to work on the stubble. "It's awful tough for this razor," she said, not looking up, "but I'm afraid of the other kind, he jerks so sometimes. His head does, I mean."

But Murray was not hearing her. He was watching the delicate motions of her fingers. As a slow pain grew in his chest, he thought how, day after day, year after year, she would lean in her devoted occupation, how that man there on the bed could, even now, exact such devotion. At the thought, with a sudden grinding access of pain, he knew why the devotion could be exacted—no, why it was so freely given.

And he had the vision of Sunder, not that bundle of bones wrapped in slack skin there on the bed, but the man as he had been when Cassie first came to this house—Sunder riding up at dusk, swinging from the saddle, the big body tingling from autumn chill and the plunging gallop of the beast, the face fevered and the eyes focused to a blaze of blue that, in the vision, seemed to light the way into the dark house. He saw Sunder surprising the girl in the hall, himself surprised by the sudden impulse, seizing her, stifling her cries, dragging her into a cold bedroom to do what would, in its ruthlessness, paradoxically earn this abiding devotion now past all excitements and satisfactions of the flesh.

The thought that the very bed thus disordered in the cold room of the vision had been freshly made up for guests who would come to arrange the funeral of the woman who, at that very moment, in another room of the house, would be spitting away her last life—this thought somehow confirmed, for Murray Guilfort, the devotion he now saw manifested before him. The flushed face, the blazing glance, the ruthless self-fulness had been, it burst on him now, its own confirmation, the fulfillment of life beyond all the deceptions and niggling of the world, and in that thought, the pain in his chest became almost unendurable.

Then he thought that maybe it hadn't happened like that at all, that maybe it all happened another way, that he didn't really know how it had happened. But somehow, with that thought, there was a numbed sense of loss that seemed worse than the pain it had succeeded.

It was the sudden cessation of the scraping sound of the razor that drew him out of himself. The woman was cleaning the razor.

"I'm done," she said, "except for washing his face." And she took the basin and mug and went out, leaving the door open back into the pantry and kitchen.

As soon as she went out, Murray approached a step closer to the brass bed and leaned to look down into the eyes.

Long back, whenever Sunderland Spottwood got angry or excited, the big blue eyes would blaze like a Bunsen burner when you brought the flame to its sharpest focus. Like the flame of a Bunsen burner—that was the idea that, once, back in college when they had shared a table in the chemistry lab, had come into the mind of Murray Guilfort.

But now he looked down into those eyes, and saw that they were the sad, sick blue of skimmed milk, and for an instant, he felt a surge of dizzying elation, a sharp catch of the breath, as if justice had, at last, been achieved. He straightened his shoulders, feeling strong.

Then he realized that the eyes were looking at him. They were alive. They knew him. They knew all he had been, and now was.

God damn him, he thought, in a flash of rage, *why can't he die!*

If Sunder Spottwood were dead, then there would be nobody who could remember the Murray Guilfort who had once been the boy who had been afraid to mount the gray stallion, who had been afraid to dive off the high bluff to the deep pool of the creek, who, no matter what, under the amiable leer of

Sunder Spottwood, he forced himself to do, had remained afraid
—of what? But if Sunder Spottwood was dead, there would
be nobody to remember that earlier self whom Murray Guilfort
now sought to forget, expunge, bury, or absorb into the man
who was now called Murray Guilfort, and to whom people
bowed respectfully on the street.

No—there would be one person left to remember.

And he named the name to himself: *Murray Guilfort.*

So he stood there with a sickness in his stomach and looked
down at the knowledge in those eyes that, in their paleness,
were mercilessly fixed on him.

When Cassie came back, he turned to her. "Does he know
things?" he demanded.

"Sometimes," she said, standing there with the basin of hot
water, from which vapor rose athwart her face. "Sometimes it
looks like it."

She set the basin on the chair, picked up the washcloth,
and began to rinse off the face.

"I pray that he does," Murray said. "That he does know
things." And as he stared with a painful avidity at the occupation of the woman's hands, he heard, as from a distance, his
own voice continuing: "For then he can know all you have
done for him all these years. Can know how devoted you are,
know how you give your life to him, know how—"

She was looking strangely at him, and water from the
washcloth forgotten in her hand slowly dripped to the floor,
the drops making a darker spot on the old, colorless carpet.

But his voice kept on. He wished it would stop, but it was
keeping on: "—know how you are capable of such devotion,
how you can remember so deeply all the happiness you all
gave each other—I hope he knows, for even now, even the
way he is, that must be a last happiness for him—for then
you know that what you are doing isn't wasted, it has meaning
—yes, we must find meaning in life—for if we don't—"

A great stone was growing in his chest, pressing on his breath. The stone was getting bigger. It stopped his breath.

The woman was again leaning over the face, carefully washing it, her own face hidden. She was like this when his words gave out.

He was panting softly, trying to think what he had meant to say, waiting for things to settle inside him, for things outside to come back into focus.

Out of her averted face she was saying, very slowly and distantly: "I try to do what I can."

She began to dry the face.

He pulled himself together, and squared his shoulders. With his air of business, he drew out his wallet, then said: "Here is the usual amount, Cassie." He laid the crisp new bills on the big table, on a small bare space among the accumulation of junk. Then he produced his pen and a sheet of paper. She came, and put out her hand for the pen. "Better read it first," he commanded. "It's more—more businesslike," he said.

She obeyed him, signed the receipt, went to put the money in the hole behind the loose brick of the chimney.

"I want to say something," he then said, clearing his throat, preparing for utterance.

She didn't seem to hear, stooping before the stove over there that now substituted for the fireplace, putting in a stick of wood.

"I have something important to say," he repeated.

"Yes," she said, and came to stand before him.

"It's about—" he began, then stopped, and looked significantly toward the bed. "We'd better go in the other room," he said.

She led the way, then paused while, with an air of courtliness, he opened the door to let her pass into the parlor. They stood facing each other across the marble top of the table. He let the fingers of his right hand touch the marble, and cleared his throat. This was a way he had in court. He liked to begin things in a low key. If you began low, it gave you somewhere to go. It suggested confidence.

He cleared his throat again, and then waited to let her wandering gaze fix on his face. It was difficult sometimes to keep her on a point.

They stood there in the dimness of the parlor, and from their faces the breath, in the chill air, rose white.

"Tell me your name," her voice was again saying.

So he told her. "Angelo Passetto," he said very slowly, not looking at her, keeping his eyes upward.

"Angelo Passetto," she said, slowly to herself, syllable by syllable, as though trying out the words.

Hearing her voice repeating, in that slow, inward way, the syllables of his name, he rolled over and pushed himself up on his right elbow, the cover sliding off his naked shoulder. "You—" he burst out, "this long time and no know my name—and no ask!"

As she looked at him, the new softness and fullness of the mouth was making the smile; but now, suddenly, the look of the eyes was brighter, and mistier, too. Very slowly, she was shaking her head, looking at him from what seemed to be a great distance.

This, too, fed the rage, and he pushed himself up further, his voice sharper: "And you—you do all what you do—long time with me, and—nothing! What my name? Who me?—You no care."

His rage went weak, or rather seemed irrelevant under that steady distant look.

"No," she said, "it wasn't like that. I knew your name, but—"
She stopped.

He had dropped back down now, on his back, and drawn up the covers, smoothing them carefully under his chin.

"But now," she said, "I want to hear you say it. Exactly how it sounds. Exactly how it ought to be."

"What you want for now?" he demanded, turning at her.

"It's different now," she said calmly, patiently, looking straight at him with that bright, naked, new way that made him angry and, somehow, afraid.

"What you mean?" he cried out. *"Porca Madonna,* what you mean?"

"Back then," she said, "I didn't know."

"What not know?"

"He came this afternoon," she said, now calm and factual. "He said how you had been in jail. At Fiddlersburg. In the penitentiary. He said how—"

"Oh, he say how! He say how!" the man on the bed cut in, the bitterness bursting up out of his lips.

"Hush," she admonished.

"A man like 'im," the man on the bed said, with no passion or bitterness now, quite coldly, putting the words out into the air, "with suit-clothes like 'im, face like 'im—I know 'im, I know 'em all like 'im, and—"

"Hush," she said.

"He say me go," he said.

"All right," she said, "but—"

"All right," he said, and pushed himself up, "and you go out this room, and I put my clothes, I go!"

"Hush," she said, almost whispering. "Hush and lie down."

It was not what she said, it was the whispering, the fact that he scarcely heard the words at all, the fact that he had to strive to hear them, like the whispering from the radio at night —that was what made him lie back down. Very slowly, he let himself down again and drew up the covers and stared at the ceiling.

He lay there for a moment forgetting everything, for he was remembering the flight of the crow he had seen that afternoon —now seeing it again, high over the woods that had grown shadowy, the crow coming into vision southward, to move slowly across the cold, empty height of sky, with the last light of the sun glinting far up there on the blackness of the deliberate, laboring wings that were moving beyond vision, steadily, over the woods, northward.

Now, for the moment, that cold height of sky and the distant glint of the wings filled Angelo Passetto's head.

Then the crow was gone. His head felt enormous, clear, and empty, like the sky.

She had been saying something, he did not know what. Now the words began to come to him: "—and I told him no, it wasn't your fault, and now they'd let you out of jail, it wasn't fair to start worrying you all over again. I said I wasn't going to tell you, even. When you came in to eat supper I didn't mean to tell you. But I went to bed, and I got to thinking. I thought how you were locked up all that time, you just a boy, and it wasn't your fault!"

Her voice was, all at once, a wail of pain, and without thinking, without remembering his resolve, or rather, his bitter need to look at the ceiling and not at her, he had turned his head. She was leaning at the bed, and everything was worse— the smile, the softness, the sadness that was not sadness, the glitter in the eyes, brighter than ever, but mistier.

Then she was saying: "Oh, Angelo—just a boy, and they did it to you!"

He turned his face away, and lay rigid, his eyes shut. For one instant he again saw the crow in the high, empty sky, with the light cold on the moving wings. Then it was gone.

He kept his eyes shut.

"But I won't let them," she was saying. "Not ever again."

He felt a hand on his forehead.

The voice was saying: "—not your fault—nothing was your fault—not anything, ever—"

In that instant, even as he felt the cool softness of the hand on his forehead, even as the voice was saying that nothing, nothing, had ever been his fault, he saw the face of Guido Altocchi, contorted in rage, glaring at him, Guido struggling to break from the hands that held him, struggling to get at him, at Angelo Passetto, and everybody in the courtroom looking while Guido got one arm loose and pointed at him, crying out in outrage and accusation: "*Traditore!*"

He had seen that scene a thousand times, in the middle of the night, the finger pointing. Then the next second, that finger would draw like a knife across the throat of Guido Altocchi, which Guido thrust forward to the promise of the blade, while Guido's mouth twisted to make a parody of the sound of gargling anguish.

So here, lying on this bed with the cool hand on his forehead, the old dream had, in that instant, come back, and the old sweat was starting.

But the hand was moving on his forehead, gently, gently, and the voice was saying: "—not your fault—not your fault—oh, no—it wasn't—"

And Guido Altocchi—he had to hear the voice. For Angelo was crying out to him: *Senti, Guido—listen—non è colpa mia —she say not my fault—she say me innocente—innocente—*

The sun had been already low toward the ridge across the creek when Murray came out to the car. For a moment before he touched the starter, he looked up at the western horizon, beyond the roar of the creek. The leafless timber along the crest of the ridge showed in black detail against the cold flush of the sky. Staring at the sky he was thinking, or rather was trying not to think, that nothing had turned out as he had expected.

With that he touched the starter and, at the instant response, slammed the accelerator down.

The cracking of skim ice and the slewing of the car in the half-frozen mud jerked him out of himself. What a fool she was! Who else but a fool would keep a convict in the house, a man convicted of armed robbery and accessory to murder?

What if he was out on parole? He was a convict—and Italian, a dago, to boot.

Then he thought how he, he himself, had been a fool. All he had needed to say was that the man was a convict. But he had let her make him blabber out the whole business. How this Passetto was only twenty at the time, how he claimed he was just going along to New Orleans for a job maybe, didn't know Guido had done time for armed robbery or that the car was stolen, was surprised when they pulled into the filling station. How, after the police softened him up a little, he had decided to cooperate and told where the weapon was thrown out, into the creek ten miles down the highway, and clinched the case.

"But he was innocent," she had said, the fool.

And he had said: "He may have been guilty as hell, and probably is, but he clinched the case—"

"But there was nothing against him. Except being there."

"For God's sake, Cassie, just being there is a lot, that's the way criminals—"

"But he didn't do anything—and they locked him up—"

"All right, all right, take it another way and it's not very nice. He squealed."

"Squealed?"

"Betrayed his friends. Got them executed. Is that pretty?"

"But he told the truth—"

"Oh, for God's sake, Cassie!"

Yes, going over it in his mind, he knew that he had been a fool. Then losing his temper to compound the foolishness. But how could a man keep his temper when she always slid off at a tangent? Of course, that Passetto had done a lot of work around the place—he knew where his bread was buttered.

And when he'd told her it was because that dago knew where his bread was buttered, she'd just looked at him and said: "You don't know what it's like to be alone. Like this. In a place like this. And nobody to do anything."

That would make anybody lose his temper, especially since he'd tried to make her bring Sunder into town, there were decent cheap apartments there now, and she could get some help. Sure, he'd lost his temper then. And gone crazy like a millionaire too, he now said to himself, telling her how if she wouldn't come to town, he'd send a crew out here to put the place in shape, how he'd find a good practical nurse to send out there.

Hell, he'd talked like a multimillionaire, with every penny to come out of his own pocket, since Sunder Spottwood didn't have a dime and hadn't had a dime for a long time, and every penny for everything to come out of his own, out of Murray Guilfort's pocket, and nothing to show but a stack of receipts Cassie Spottwood had signed. He had been a fool, and not just beginning now!

But a lucky fool this time. For she had turned down that millionaire offer he had babbled out. She would stay in that falling-down house, just as it was, with Sunder—and that criminal.

She would stay, she had said, and all at once, she had stepped toward him, thrusting her face at him, looking him in the eye with that sudden way she had, demanding: "Look at me—look at me, Murray Guilfort—what would that man do to me? I'm an old woman."

And he had looked at her, seen what she was, that old brown sweater bagging off her and the dark eyes staring out of that face that was white as chalk and you wondered how it could be that white, you tried not to wonder if the skin kept on being that white after it went under whatever it was she was wearing under that God-damned sweater, you tried not to wonder if it was that white in the dark, shining in the dark at night.

And he had burst out: "Old! You're not old!"

Then looking at the whiteness of the face, he had thought, as though the thought had always been waiting in shadow and now slipped calmly out into the open place of his mind, how Bessie was dead, how Bessie, after all the years of painful skinniness had gone fat, how Bessie, with the diamond rings cutting into the swollen flesh of her fingers, was not anywhere anymore, how she had gone away forever with her fatness and swollen fingers. How if you shook that God-damned bag of a sweater off this woman who stood before him, she would be slender, slender but not skinny, Cassie Spottwood had always been slender—

And now, in the dusk, he had pulled the car off to one side of the road. It stood on the side away from the creek, in the gap that had once been the entrance to a drive. The drive had led to the old Guilfort place.

For years now, there had been no house there. It never had been much of a house, in fact. Murray did not like to remember, ever, what it had been like—not a shack, no, a good, decent house, but not the kind of house he wanted to remember. Nor did he ever want to remember what had gone on in that house. Not because anything terrible had ever happened. Not because there had been unkindness. Merely because there had been, for him, only nothingness, a movement of shadows.

If only something had been terrible.

He could still lie awake at night and wish that something terrible had been there. But it was nothing, nothing at all, that had happened there.

Now at the very spot where he, in those years long ago, a boy, had passed a thousand times, he was sitting in the expensive automobile which was the mark of his success, and while the muted roar of the creek filled his ears, he stared down the road where dusk now gathered.

She had said: "Oh, I know you're important. I know you're rich, and got elected prosecutor or whatever they call it, and I know you can make people do what you want."

Hearing her say that, he had felt, for a moment, free and strong.

But only for a moment, for she had said, "Yes, Murray, you can. But, Murray, if they make him go away, or do anything to him, I'll know it was you."

So, suddenly, he had stared at her, and had felt trapped and found out, for that very thought was in his mind, all he had to do was pass on the word to the parole officer.

But that had not been all, for, not stopping, she had gone on: "And if they do that—listen, Murray, I mean it—I'll never see you again."

Hearing that, even before the meaning of the words took shape in his mind, he had felt stripped and naked. For here she was talking to him that way as though she had the right to, as though she were his sweetheart and could threaten and boss him and he was powerless.

But who the hell did she think she was? Did she think she was young and beautiful? What was she but a middle-aged woman in that God-damned brown bag of a sweater standing in that moldy and ice-cold wreck of a parlor! He had looked at her there beyond the marble top of the table, and in his rage had thought: *Christ, for her to put on airs when I've had the women I've had.* Thinking of Chicago, of what had happened in Chicago, saying this to himself as he had the vision of himself in the expensive suite in the hotel, with the gleam of that spurious elegance, the bubbles of champagne rising in the light, the perfume of a woman's hair in his nostrils, not seeing Mildred, seeing, rather, a thousand different Mildreds, each one beautiful, leaning against him, embracing him, lifting the parted lips, seeing a succession of images in glittering sequence, like mirror after mirror visible through arabesques of smoke.

In the instant of power he had stood there, and cold and contemptuous, had stared across at the aging female who was Cassie Spottwood.

But she had stared back at him, and now, by the roadside, in the dusk, seeing in his mind the eyes that had fixed mercilessly on him, he took the hat off his head, let it drop, and leaned until his bare forehead pressed against the upper rim of the steering wheel. His hands were tight on the wheel, as though to control the car at a desperate speed. But the car was motionless, and closing his eyes, he felt the reality of the hard cold arc of plastic against his forehead, and inside the shell of bone that was his head he was reliving an event he had once lived, seeing himself in the doubleness of the living and the reliving.

It had been the fall after Sunder's marriage to the girl, and he—Murray—was out here for a weekend of bird-shooting, even if Bessie disapproved of Sunder even more than she disapproved of bird-shooting, and there had been a quarrel, and she had stayed home. After the day in the field, and dinner, Sunder, Cassie, and he were sitting by the fire, in the lassitude of food, warmth, and whiskey, when Sunder poured himself near a half-tumbler, and not bothering with ice or water, downed it in three gasping gulps, and without warning, rose, leaned to seize the girl's arm, and almost jerking her from the chair, said, "Come on."

Then he dropped the arm, nodded a leering goodnight to Murray, and in casual confidence that the girl would follow, moved, with scarcely a sway in his stride, out the parlor door into the hall. The girl, with a single quick, sidewise glance at Murray, a glance he tortured himself to interpret, followed out the door.

Murray continued to sit there before the fire, his half-empty glass going tepid in his grasp, and heard, despite the carpeting, the weight of the man on the stairs, then, after a moment, the sharp, authoritative sound of a door being closed.

That was the door that, later, when he was on his way up to bed, with a head now humming with whiskey like wind on a million telephone wires, he would stand outside of, in the dark hall.

So, with his forehead against the steering wheel, he saw himself standing outside that door, in the dark hall. Then, as distinctly as a voice, the thought was in him: *There are beggars and buyers and stealers and pickers of remnants, and you are among them.*

Then: *There are seizers and takers, and you are not among them.*

The voice seemed to come from a great height, down to him, and hearing it, he thought how only the takers are real. His body, leaning forward in the dark, felt as though it were nothing more than smoke. He wondered what, if it were Bessie alive and he dead, she would remember of him. He thought of Mildred, who had married the retired dentist, and wondered if she ever remembered Murray Guilfort.

Then he wondered if Cassie—if long ago things had been different and she had married him and not Sunder, and if he now, and not Sunder, lay motionless on a bed—he wondered if

Cassie, day after day, year after year, would bend above him, with that devoted and studious care, to shave his face.

With his eyes closed and his forehead still against the wheel, pressed hard there to give him one point of painful contact with the reality of the world, he shifted his right hand to finger the stubble of his cheek. He thought of fingers moving over his face as he lay triumphantly motionless in the joy of having had joy.

"Hey, mister," a voice said, breaking in on his inner darkness, and the voice, he knew, was real.

He jerked his head up from the wheel. The dusk had now thickened into first dark, but he could make out the dim figure of the man there by the car, a shotgun under an arm and a dog, even more dim in the deeper darkness, at his knees.

"You all right, mister?" the man was asking.

He managed to say yes, he was all right.

"Just wanted to know if'n you was all right," the man said, and Murray started to say something, to try to explain how he was just a bit tired, nothing was wrong, but the man was already moving away, facing into the darkness he had come out of.

Then, just before touching the starter, Murray thought, yes, everything would be all right when he got on the Supreme Court.

A man had to have something, he thought.

Angelo Passetto had been asleep. How long he did not know, but even before he opened his eyes, he was aware of the coolness of the hand on his forehead. For an instant his muscles tightened and he was about to jerk free of the touch, but in that awareness there was the fleeting recollection of a night when, as a little boy after he had been sick for a long time, he had waked up in the dark and the fever was gone and he felt weak and sweet and floating, and a hand, his mother's, had been on his forehead.

Then the recollection was gone. He opened his eyes.

But he did not turn his head, even when the voice said: "You went to sleep. You slept a long time."

"Yes," he said, not looking, trying to think what he felt now, lying there.

"Do you know why I came down here tonight?" the voice asked.

"No," he said, to the air above him.

"I hadn't meant to come," the voice said. "I hadn't meant to tell you, not anything Murray said. But I lay in the bed and I couldn't go to sleep. It was something I had never thought before."

The voice paused.

Then: "Do you know what I was thinking?"

"No," he said.

"I was thinking," the voice said, "of how they locked you up and you lay there in jail at night. It started with me thinking just that. But then—do you know what I thought then?"

"No," he said.

"It was all of a sudden," the voice said, "and I thought how all my own life, it was like that, like being locked up, and lying in the dark, how it had been—"

The voice stopped.

Then it said: "Do you know what happened?"

"No," he said.

"Angelo," the voice said, "it was all of a sudden then that I knew—I really knew—how you felt. It wasn't till I knew how I had been always locked up that I knew how you had felt— and I jumped out of bed, and I grabbed that old robe and I ran down the hall just barefoot, and then—"

He thought, suddenly, of how she had stood in the doorway and he had seen the feet bare. The white feet had run in the dark down the hall, toward him, on the cold boards.

"—but then I was afraid to knock, I felt weak and funny, everything was swimming in the dark, but I had to knock. I knew I had to tell you how it was, that I really knew how it was for you to be locked up and lying in the dark."

He was trying not to hear. He lay rigid and his breath came hard and slow. He was trying not to let happen what was happening to him.

But the voice cried out, "Angelo—do you wake up now in the dark and not know where you are and think you are still there, and locked up? Angelo, do you?"

He was trying hard, and his breath came hard and slow. But, all at once, as though something inside had cracked like a piece of dry, dusty wood under a great slow pressure, his own voice said: "Yes."

And her voice was saying, "I don't want you to wake up that way—not ever again, not ever."

He was holding on. Something had cracked, but he held on.

He held on until, after a long silence, the voice, very low, almost whispering, said: "There's something else I don't want, Angelo. Do you know what that is?"

"No," he said.

"I don't want you ever to wake up right here, in this house, and feel you are locked up."

That was what the voice was saying.

"I want you to feel free, Angelo," it was saying. "I don't want you to feel caught and locked up. Not ever again. I want you to feel free. To go out the door if you want."

It was then that whatever he had felt crack in him before, broke completely. It just gave way, inside him. He rolled over, and pushed himself up, and looking at her, seeing her sitting there in the chair, her hands folded on her lap, with the light striking harshly up from the floor, from the lamp he could not see down there, throwing her shadow beyond and above on the ceiling, so that her face was white against that blackness of her own shadow—it was then that, uttering a sound like a groan, he reached out toward her.

After an instant, looking at him from her bright, misty distance, she gave him her hand.

He seized it in both his own, letting his body fall forward on the bed with his face pressed into the palm of the hand.

CHAPTER SEVEN

✟✟✟✟✟✟✟✟✟✟✟ **T**he spot shouldn't have been there. It was in the wrong place on the ceiling. That was the first thing she thought when she woke up. That spot should be farther away, above the stove.

But, all at once, she realized that it was on a different ceiling.

Then she thought: *It is a different me, too.*

Very carefully, she brought her hands out from under the covers, one hand on each side, to touch her cheeks, light as a feather. Under the touch the flesh tingled. When the touch was lifted, the tingle stayed on.

She thought of the air touching her face all over, molding it, giving it a shape, making it alive. She thought how she had never thought that before. How you were a shape where the air was not, but the air touched you all around and its touching made the tingling that was your shape and made you know that you were alive and were you.

She shut her eyes and thought that thought. All she wanted to do now was to lie with her eyes shut and watch that one thought glowing in the dark inside her head, with the dark all around it spreading out forever in all directions in her head. But then it seemed that the thought was not in her head, that she herself was the thought and was lying somewhere in a darkness that spread out all around her forever, and she was glowing in the middle of that darkness, for she herself was the thought.

She opened her eyes.

Now, with her eyes open, the world seemed to be glowing too.

Beyond the window, she could see the high branches of the oak tree with frost over their blackness, and they were shining with light. The top part of the roof of the chicken house— which was all she could see of it without turning, and she was not yet ready to turn—was shining too. The wall opposite the foot of the bed, where the light struck, was shining. Out of the tail of her eye, to the right, she could see the chair by the bed, and it was shining. The old gray robe, flung over the back of the chair, and the old flannel nightgown, they were shining, too.

Everything simply was, and was shining.

She turned her head.

At first she was surprised. It might have been somebody else, lying there sound asleep, everything was so different. It was the hair, she decided. She had always seen it combed down smooth and glossy-black, tight to the shape of the skull, and now it was mussed up in all directions. Then she decided that that was not *the* difference. It was only *a* difference.

(152)

He was lying on his side, facing her, the knees drawn up a little, the shoulders a little hunched. Very carefully, she turned her body toward him, not near, but so she could look more directly into his face. The flesh seemed smoother and softer on the bone, even if the face wasn't yet shaved and had black bristles. With the eyes closed and not dark and watchful and hard-bright like a bird's, the face was defenseless. The lips were lax, and from a regular, infinitesimal motion, sensed rather than seen, she knew that the breath was going in and out, slowly, between them.

It was the face of Angelo Passetto, but it was not his face. As she stared at the mouth and saw that tiny motion of the lips moving with the breath of sleep, she knew that it was the face of Angelo Passetto when he was a little boy, a little boy asleep, and somebody else had been watching him.

At that instant he woke up, and saw the glimmering softness of the gaze upon him.

They lay there facing each other across the distance, looking at each other.

Then, very quietly, she said: "I feel I just got born."

He said nothing.

She slipped her right arm out from under the cover and pointed toward the window. The arm was bare. "Look," she commanded. "Look, everything is shining. It's like the whole world just got born."

He rolled his head and lifted it a little to peer out at the frosty brightness. Then she was aware that he was looking at her bare arm lifted to point, and she lowered the arm and drew it under the cover.

He had turned his head and was again looking across at her. "You," she said, "you are just born, too?"

The discomfort, not fear, not pain, not yet more than a discomfort without name or focus, began to grow in him. He shut his eyes not to see her, but immediately opened them.

When he opened them, he saw that the arm was reaching toward him, the forefinger extended. It touched him on the lips, and very lightly traced the shape of his mouth. Then it withdrew and the arm went back under the cover.

"You look different," she said. "Maybe it's because I never saw you before."

She paused, then said: "Maybe I never saw anything in the world before."

He knew that the discomfort was increasing.

"You," she demanded, even more quietly, speaking out of that distance across the glimmering whiteness of sheet between them, like a field of snow where nobody had walked yet, "are you just born, too?"

He said nothing. He wished that she would stop looking at him.

"Tell me," she said, her voice only a whisper now.

"Tell what?" he demanded, savagely.

"Are you just born, too?"

"OK, OK," he finally said, low and harsh, hearing the sounds which were the word after a long minute during which she had kept looking at him as though time didn't matter and she could wait forever, for she knew that he would say it in the end. With her eyes on him and that shining soft look in them, it seemed to him that the tight feeling in his chest might be better if he said it and got it over with.

It was in the silence after he had said it, as they lay there still looking at each other across the distance of white sheet, that the sound came.

Her face was, all at once, as it had been in the past, not the way it had been just now.

She pulled away, and with the top blanket drawn about her shoulders to cover herself from him, set her feet to the floor, and sitting on the edge of the bed, reached out toward the chair. She got the gray flannel nightgown she had been wearing last night, and still keeping the blanket up, managed to get it on. Then, without even a glance toward him, she put on the old robe.

The sound came again, and she went out the door, on bare feet, the way she had come last night. For a split second, she had stepped out of sight in the hall. Then she was again there, framed in the doorway, as the night before.

"I want you to come," she said.

"Me?"

"Please," she said.

In the second before he replied, she added: "Please, I'll wait."

She again stepped out of his range of vision. But he knew she was there, waiting. He thought: *What she hide for?*

Then, in a flash, he knew why she had slipped beyond eye-range of the door. So she wouldn't see him get up naked to dress. He remembered how she had sat on the edge of the bed, hiding herself from him with the blanket.

Cretina, he thought, but, to his surprise, the word, the thought, did not have that hard contempt it used to have when he thought it. He now felt his face softening, against his will, into a smile.

He stopped the smile.

He slipped on the old red bathrobe she had cut down for him, and went out the door. There she was, waiting. She turned down the hall, and he followed.

Just as she reached out to lay hand on the knob of the door of that room, he said, "Listen here. Other night I wan' come in here, you no let me. What you let me for now?"

For a moment she looked up into his face. Then, very slowly, still looking up at him, but standing well away from him, she said: "So you'll know."

"Know what?" he demanded.

From her distance she studied him in a slow, curious way. Then she said: "Me."

Abruptly, she turned away and entered the room, with an air of certainty that he would follow, leaving the door wide open behind her. He stood there, filled with a sudden resentment, feeling that she knew what he would do even before he knew it, and even if he thought he was going to do something different. But he crossed the threshold and was in the room.

She was standing in the middle of the floor, staring toward the brass bed. He came to stand near her, but not too near.

She nodded toward the bed, saying, "That's my husband. His name is Sunderland Spottwood."

Angelo looked across at the man on the bed, then at the woman. He looked at the very white face out of which the black eyes regarded him. He looked at the bare feet sticking out beneath the old gray bathrobe, white against the time-stained carpet. He looked at the woman's face. In the silence of the room, he heard the small, ragged, raw sound that was the breathing of that man.

He moved toward the bed, stood at the foot, and looked down.

"What happen?" he finally asked, not taking his gaze from what was on the bed.

"He had a stroke."

"What that?" he demanded, not shifting his gaze.

"In your head," the voice was saying, "something breaks, then you fall down. You can't ever move again."

He was staring at the two hands out on the blanket, each connected to a length of arm, nothing but bone with dry skin on it that disappeared into a baggy faded blue sleeve that was crooked thinly where the elbow was. Each hand, bony but enormous on the coarse dirty-brown of the old army blanket, lay palm down, the fingers spread and slightly bent.

Each hand looked like a spider, an enormous, bleached-out, sick-white spider suddenly exposed to light. He thought of the time he had disturbed a heap of damp old rubbish and rags in the cellar of his uncle's house. There had been the white spider, the legs long and weak-looking, more horrible for that impression of weakness, and very white.

The hands were nothing but bone now, bone covered with that waxy, sick-white skin, but they were very big. He looked at the length of bone under the blanket, then at the width where the shoulders were. And on the thin neck, the head, which was nothing but skull with the skin sagging off the face and the nose pointing up at the ceiling, was very big. It was still big, looking even bigger on that neck that had gone so thin.

"Big man," Angelo Passetto said. "Big man one time, huh?"

"Yes," the voice said.

"'Im," he said, "you love 'im one time?"

She met his eyes, then turned to study the man on the bed.

"Love him?" she said, finally, still looking across at the bed. Then, after a moment of waiting: "No, I hated him."

He looked down at the man on the bed, the long bones under the weight of blankets. He went around to the far side of the bed and leaned a little so that he could look down into the face. He saw the sagging skin, all white, sprigged with the coarse yellow stubble. He looked down into the empty blue of the eyes.

But the eyes, he suddenly knew, they were looking up at him, they were alive, they were sucking him in. It was like losing your balance, falling into a deep hole.

He jerked back, then looked across at her.

"Me—" he demanded, "you hate me?"

He heard the urgency in his own voice, for the crazy thought, which he knew was crazy, was somewhere in his head that the man with all that yellow hair, who had once been so tall and big, a lot bigger than he was, than Angelo Passetto, was lying there now like dead, but worse than dead because you had to stay alive just to keep on suffering the being dead—that the man was there because that woman had hated him.

But the woman, standing there, wrapped in the shapeless dingy garment, with bare feet against the dark dinginess of the carpet, was just looking at him from her distance, across the body on the bed; and staring back at her, he heard his own voice again demanding: "You hate me?"

Waiting for some word or sign, dizzy at the edge of a depth he could not fathom, the depth now being her gaze on him, he felt the sweat gathering cold under his armpits. Daylight was pouring into the room now, defining the objects of the ruinous and dusty disorder, but as he waited, those objects, the room itself, seemed to fall away into distance, to leave him alone to confront that gaze he could not tell the meaning of.

"No," she said at last, "I don't hate you." Then, after a moment: "I love you—Angelo Passetto."

She said the name very carefully and slowly, as though trying to say it right, the way it ought to be said.

Day after day, the world glittered in the iron-hard and ice-bright winter of January. As he moved about his work with a tingle of blood, in the brightness of air that seemed to glow in the lungs as you breathed it, all the objects of the world seemed to stand clear and separate. At noon he would go to the empty kitchen, put a couple of lengths of wood onto the half-banked coals in the range, heat up the coffee, and then, in the silence in which the clock ticked, he would stand by the range and eat the food left for him. Out the window he could see the glitter of the world.

By February he had already repaired the roof of the
chicken house, and now was clearing out and fixing the nest
boxes and resetting the roost poles. Mending the chicken-
yard fence would have to wait, for you couldn't set a post-hole
digger into this iron ground. Anyway, there was no need for
the yard now. What there was need for was an incubator, so
he mended the wreck of one found in the barn, and on his next
trip to Parkerton got the eggs, four dozen, Plymouth Rock,
guaranteed. It was the kind his uncle had kept, good layers,
and meat on the bone.

He had told Cassie nothing about what he was doing, and
when he came into the kitchen that night, and laid out the
stuff he had brought from town, she cried out, "Four dozen
eggs—we'll never eat that many!"

"Wait," he commanded, and with flashlight in hand, went
out.

Through the window she saw the spot of light moving toward
the barn, then after a little, jiggling along, it was coming back.

The door pushed open, and there he was, carrying the thing.

"This thing, where I put?" he demanded.

"What is it?"

"To hatch eggs," he said. "I fix."

"Oh, Angelo," she said, "that old incubator in the barn!
You're so smart. Now, let me see—" and she flustered about,
trying to pick a spot.

"Here," Angelo said, not waiting for her, and carried the thing
across the kitchen and made space for it against the wall toward the pantry.

"Not wall outside," he said, "and no near stove. So here."

Then he got the eggs in place, got a can of kerosene he had
left on the back porch, filled the tank of the incubator, waited
for the kerosene to work down the line, and lighted the heater.

"OK," he said, "I wash me."

He went out the door to the hall. He was humming as he went. After he had left, she strained to hear him, but he had closed the door.

When, ten minutes later, still wearing his town clothes, his hair damply slicked down and glistening, he came back, she smiled at him out of the vapor that rose from a pot just lifted from the range.

"Stew," she said, bringing the pot toward the table.

"OK," he said, "OK by me."

He set the unopened bottle of whiskey on the table, picked up his glass and went to the electric icebox. When he got back, she had already served his plate and was ladling stew into her own.

He picked up her glass.

"You take whiskey?" he said. "I fix."

"No, thanks," she said, smiling.

He sat down, fixed his drink, stirred it with the handle of his fork, and sampled it fastidiously.

"My biscuits!" she exclaimed, leaning over the pan before offering them to him, inspecting the dozen biscuits, plump to bursting, evenly golden-brown on top and shading to pale gold at the sides, flawless in shape. "Oh, look," she wailed. "Looks like they keep getting worse on me, not better."

"OK by me," he said, and reached for a clutch of three.

When the meal was over, she stood by the range, coffeepot in hand, and asked if he wanted more.

"You bring," he commanded, and when she had refilled the cups, he added: "Now you sit, you."

He took a long drag on his coffee, got up, and came around to stand behind her chair. "You sit and no move," he said sternly.

He drew out the few pins that untidily held the mass of

black hair piled on top of her head. It fell about her shoulders. Running his fingers delicately through it, he spread it, very evenly, over the shoulders.

"What are you doing?" she asked.

"You no move," he said, and drew a comb from his pocket and began, with finicking, even strokes, to comb the hair. That done, he drew a brush out—the brush from his room— and began to work.

She stirred. "What are you going to do?" she asked, a faint trace of alarm in her voice.

"No move," he said, more sternly than before.

When he had finished the brushing, he said: "Turn chair leetle-a bit."

She obeyed, and he came around to stand in front of her, some five feet back, studying her.

"Sweater," he said, "you now take off."

Not rising from the chair, she worked it off.

"Face, now up," he said.

Under the harsh light from the bulb directly above, her face was chalky white. The face wore an expression of puzzlement, even supplication. Ignoring her, as though she were an object and nothing more, he went again behind the chair, and began to gather the hair together, encircling the mass tightly with his left hand, just above the height of her shoulder, while with the right hand he fumbled in a pocket.

"Now shut eyes," he said. "Shut!"

He arranged the hair forward over her left shoulder, came around in the front, still keeping his grip on the mass of hair, and with his free hand got the red ribbon in place, and worked at the bow. His fingers were deft. His forehead, where the glossy olive-colored skin was ordinarily so smooth and un-marked, was drawn into a sharp vertical V of concentration between the eyes. Now and then, for an instant, he would interrupt the manipulation, to look down at her lifted face.

From the slight contact with the head or shoulder, he knew that the body there under that shapeless dress, was stiff as a board. Her breath came in small, sharp inhalations.

When he had finished the hair, he said: "No move." He drew the lipstick from a pocket, and putting his left hand firmly behind her head to brace it, touched the stick to her mouth. She stirred, the mouth moved, she began, "But—"

His hand instantly tightened on the back of her head, just at the base of the skull, and with a sudden, whispering ferocity, he said, "No move! No open eyes!"

She was again frozen, the eyelids tight shut. He pushed her head backward a little more, so that the light fell more bleakly over the face, and began to outline the mouth. He pressed the lipstick down hard, pressing the lips back against the teeth, pulling the mouth sidewise with the slow movement of the lipstick. At each point, after the pressure had passed, the flesh of the lips lifted, seeming swollen now, the color thick and dark on it.

He stepped back to examine his work, came forward and again put his left hand firmly behind her head, and pressed the stick against the mouth. He had thickened the lower lip a little more.

"Eyes," he said, "you no open!"

He went to the wall and took down the mirror. He came and held it before the immobile, chalky face. The eyes were closed and the depth of the sockets was such that, even with the face slightly lifted, there was shadow under the eye-arch.

With a kind of cold avidity, he was studying the face.

"Now," he said, suddenly. "Eyes—you open!"

For a moment, her eyes, coming open into that harsh light, blinked. Then they fixed on the mirror. Over the top of the mirror, Angelo Passetto, with that cold avidity, looked down into her face.

It was as though he spied on her through a window from

the dark outside, because, for all his whetted intensity of attention, she was not aware of him. Her own gaze never wavered from the mirror. As she stared at what was in the mirror, he stared down at the real face—the black-red lips that were full, almost lax-looking, almost sullen, the red ribbon binding the black hair at the left shoulder, the black hair over the white face, the hair seeming heavy and loosely held, ready to slip unbound and fall about that whiteness of face from which the black eyes stared out.

Then he could see the eyes brighten under the electric light as moisture gathered in them. The black-red lips trembled for an instant before the words would come out.

Then she lifted her eyes, discovering him, and said, "But I never felt pretty—not before—and a girl ought to feel pretty —and it's awful to be old and of a sudden feel pretty. And I'm old—I'll be forty-three—forty-three, in two weeks, Angelo —oh, Angelo!"

She was weeping now. The tears came welling out of the eyes that were unwaveringly fixed on him. They flowed glistening down her lifted face. Her hands lay helpless in her lap, and she did nothing at all about the tears.

Then the words came: "Angelo—you made me pretty—and oh, I can't stand it!"

He looked down at her, at the mouth, at the glistening flow of tears unimpeded and shamefully unashamed, at the naked depth of the eyes, and for an instant he was swung dizzily upward in the unanticipated burst of his own feelings. For a split second, he saw the image of one of those little white plastic balls, like a ping-pong ball, that dance on a jet of water against the black background of a shooting gallery. In that split second, he not only saw the white ball dancing there, but was himself the little ball dancing on a jet of his own feelings, white against the blackness, weightless and vulnerable, waiting for the crack of a marksman's rifle.

He did not know what made him a little white ball, suspended and swirling in that vulnerability.

How high he seemed to hang above the white, tear-glistening face!

Suddenly he thrust the mirror at her, saying, "Take!" and dashed out into the hall.

When he came back, he had the radio. He set it on the table, among the dirty dishes, connected it, and fooled with it a moment; then the music came. He seized the mirror from her, shoved a place clear for it on the table, and then stood over her.

"Now up!" he said.

The face, eyes fixed upward on him, rose toward him. The face came swimming up at him, and the body, helpless and irrelevant, was being drawn up after it. Then she was standing before him. He slipped his right arm around her body, his hand low at the waist, the fingers spread, and with his left hand he seized her right.

"Now," he said, "dance," and took the first step.

"But I—" she began.

"Dance, you!" he said, in his ferocious whisper.

He led her into it, holding himself back from her body, but feeling its stiffness, trying to control its movement with the tips of the spread fingers of his right hand set low at the small of her back, just where the swell began. "Easy—easy—you take easy," he was whispering. "Come with Angelo—e-e-easy!"

Her face was looking up at him.

"I was just a girl," she was saying, "just a girl when I danced the last time—it was so long back, and I never danced good—oh, I can't!"

He stopped abruptly, pushed her down into the chair, and kneeling before her, began to unlace one of the brogans. He flung it over to bang against the woodbox. "*Santa Madonna,*" he said, "these things and nobody dance!"

He flung the second brogan after the first and drew off the black cotton stockings and let them lie tangled on the floor where they fell. The feet, drawn back toward the chair and held close together in a position of modesty and weakness, were white in the shadow. He leaned and seized a foot in each hand, slipping the hand under it so that the sole was to palm, and pressing the feet close together, lifted them to meet his bowed face, and kissed them.

Looking up at her, he said: "Leetle feet—you got so leetle feet!"

All at once she was weeping again, in the same overflowing inner abandonment, as though there was nothing to be done, not anything in the world, about a trouble so deep and inexhaustible.

Letting the tears flow as they would, not looking down at the man crouching there, but at some indefinable distant spot across the kitchen, or across the world, she was saying, "But nobody ever did this—not ever—"

"But Angelo—yes!" he exclaimed, and was suddenly standing before her, drawing her up to him. "Yes! And me Angelo."

When he had put his arm around her again, the first thing he was aware of was that now, without those brogans, she seemed smaller. He had to bend his head to look down into her face, and even the face looked different. In that moment of looking down at her, he felt a thrill of strength, and new possession.

She was moving more easily now. The stiffness was thawing a little. Under the cloth, he could feel the freer flow and play of the delicate musculature where the fingers of his right hand were spread down at the point where the waist broke. He was holding himself a little back from her, as before, and as they danced, he stole a look down, now and then, to catch a glimpse of the bare feet moving white on the time-darkened boards.

Then he would steal a glance at her face. It wore the expression, intent and yet remote, of a person trying painfully to remember something. Watching that intentness, he felt, again, the thrill of strength and possession. She was trying so hard, *la piccola.*

"E-e-easy," he whispered, "take easy."

She shut her eyes. She was trying so hard, *la piccola.*

He was going faster now, but she was there, she was with him. He was aware, all at once, of the flow and spin of the kitchen around him. The range, the table, the sink, the old clock on the wall, the window glass glittering like ice over the depth of darkness beyond, but reflecting the light of the room, reflecting her, reflecting him with his arm around her—everything flowed around him, went away, came back, and again flowed away to the sound of music.

The window flowed back again, then again, and faster, and he saw how far her head was below him, the top of her head no higher than his chin, and that was what did it.

He pressed her close to him.

He spun her around, then again and again, and each revolution was bringing them nearer to the door to the hall. As they danced close to the door, he slowed enough to reach out his left hand to jerk the door open. But he caught the beat, swung back into the kitchen, then suddenly, laughing out loud, he swung her into the dark doorway, and they were gone.

The emptiness of the kitchen, drenched in the raw light of the hanging bulb, was reflected in the icy blackness of the window above the sink. Nothing moved in that reflected world. The raw light of the kitchen entered the darkness of the hall, but the shadow defined by the clean knife-edge of the doorjamb struck down positively across that light.

On the table, between the face-up mirror reflecting the coldly blazing bulb hung high above it, and the bottle of whiskey, among the cups and platters and plates where the gravy of the stew stiffened into grayness, the radio stood.

Over by the woodbox, on the boards of the floor, were the brogans. One lay on its side, the sole exposed toward the room. A small hole was worn through the middle of the sole. The leather heel was worn down much more on one side than on the other, and there the metal nailheads made little spots of brightness in the light.

The waltz had long since been finished. Now, in the instant when a voice had just stopped but the announced music had not yet begun, there was the sound of slip and settling in the firebox of the range. The cold had crept into the kitchen. The cold stood there like a presence in the emptiness.

The radio began again. A drum was beating, and now a horn cut anguishingly across that rhythm.

On the night of Saturday, February 15, he parked the car in front of the house, just outside the gate he had repaired and rehung. He took the bundles from the seat beside him, and with the aid of the flashlight picked his way around the wing of the house, to the left, and entered the door that gave on to the little side porch there. With great stealth he tiptoed down the hall to his room, laid the packages on the bed, and as silently retraced his steps down the hall, and out. Then he drove the car around to the barn, deliberately making a great racket. He went to the house.

He set down his grocery sack. She was there, but even as he kissed her in greeting, his glance was on the clock on the wall. Yes, it was early enough. She hadn't really begun. So he told her he was going to cook supper tonight, that she cooked all right, but she could just watch and maybe she would learn something. He made her sit at the table, and he set about making the sauce. Once the preliminary frying was over, he allowed himself a drink of whiskey.

He sat at the table with her, taking finicking little sips to make the drink last, and now and then stole a glance at the clock. They found nothing to say. An indefinite weight hung in the air. But that pleased him. That was what he wanted now. He would steal secret glances at her, and think, *la piccola,* she didn't know, she didn't guess, she'd be wondering. He hugged his secret in sly glee. Now and then, he went to stir the sauce.

When the clock said twenty-to-seven, he went to the range, stirred the sauce, inspected it, and turned toward her.

"Why tonight you no fix-a hair?" he demanded.

"You came so early," she said.

"Go fix now," he said.

As she rose, he said: "Go my room. You find-a something. You put on. You come twenty-five minute. No soon, no late."

His voice was very stern.

When, exactly at the time specified, she came back, he was at the range. He heard her enter, but deliberately kept on stirring the sauce, not turning his head. Then, still not turning, he lifted the lid of the pot and peered in. He kept occupied until he heard her voice.

"Angelo," the voice said, at last, sounding weak and far away.

OK, he thought, feeling good, but not turning, not saying anything. Let her stand there just a little longer, *la piccola,* with that funny face, like she didn't know what had happened.

Then he turned.

The dress was red, and shiny like silk. The belt was black

patent leather. The stockings were black and shiny. The slippers were black patent leather and pointed, and the heels were very high. *OK, OK,* he thought, thinking that she was tall and slim with the shoes on, but you take them off she would be little, like a surprise you could hold in your hands.

"Happy birth-a-day," he said.

He served the spaghetti and meat sauce. In the middle of the table were the flowers, stuck in a tall glass, red and yellow plastic roses he had bought at the dime store, bold and glittering under the naked light. He poured the red wine into the two wine glasses. He had bought the glasses at the dime store, too.

He made her drink the wine.

After the spaghetti they drank the rest of the wine, and he made her drink her share. Then, when they began to dance the wine made her relax more. She was easier to handle, even in the new kind of dance that came on the radio. She laughed, she was so pleased. She laughed like a girl.

During the day when he was away from the house, he might stop what he was doing and think of her.

But it got so that he left earlier in the morning. When she got up to answer the noise from the room down the hall, he would pretend to be still asleep, keeping his eyes closed so as not to see her there in that old dingy robe, for if he saw her like that, in the morning light, he might not remember her the way he wanted to during the day. Something might happen, the bottom might drop out of everything, he would feel himself shriveling away to nothing.

He kept his eyes shut, and as soon as she got out the door, he would dress and hurry to the kitchen. The dishes from last night, with the remnants of food in the stiffening grease, would always be on the table, and the used pots on the shelf by the sink, for he never let her take time to wash things up at night, that would ruin something. So, in the morning light, he would keep his eyes from those things, quickly make up the fire and get the coffee on, go out for stove wood, come back, grab some cold food and the scalding coffee, always too weak, for he would be in a hurry, and get it down, and go.

He did not scrutinize the impulse, he merely acted upon it.

Then, after a time, it got so he was even afraid, when he was away from the house, to think of the nights there. All day long he would be waiting for the night, but if he thought about it, something he did not want to think about might come in too. Something might happen, he did not know what. Like what might happen if he opened his eyes in the morning when that rasping bleat came from down the hall, or what he felt in the morning, in the kitchen, when he saw the old grease from the night before gone gray on a plate. He knew that he had to keep the night separate from the day, like a dream, and in the day not even think of the night.

He had his own interests in the day now, and he could live in them. He began to create a Time of which the days would be a part, a Time in which things could exist and change, a Time that would stretch backward and forward and that you could think about. There were things you could do that would help make a picture of yourself in Time, and therefore make you real. Like fixing the old John Deere Model A tractor he had found in the barn, half overwhelmed by junk, shrouded in cobwebs, the green paint long since scaling with rust. Now he had cleared things away from it, and was scraping it clean, with an old wood chisel, steel wool, and kerosene. He had already taken the head off and drawn the pistons and cleaned them with penetrating oil, and all that it needed now to be good as new was to finish the paint job, do the rewiring, and get a generator. He figured he might find a generator second-

hand at the junkyard in Parkerton. He knew all about the old
John Deere. That was what his uncle had had long back, in
Ohio.

He liked the picture of himself sitting on the tractor and it
shining with new paint. He could feel the sense of power as
the plowshares sliced solidly through the earth and left it
folded behind him, open and shining in the sun with the polish
left by the sharp steel. He decided that he would put that
field back of the house into corn. You could see the old furrows
where corn had once grown. It would be feed for the chickens.
In his mind, he saw the runs he would build, full of chickens.
He would sell the eggs in Parkerton, and fryers and broilers.
He saw the cow yard clean again, with Jerseys standing there,
their jaws moving slow in the evening light, waiting to be
milked. With the tractor he could cut and bale the hay.

Now and then, in the evening as they sat at the table, he
had the impulse to tell *la piccola* about the tractor, about
sitting on the tractor, about plowing the field, about the chickens, about the picture in his mind of the Jerseys standing in the
evening light. The impulse would come over him so suddenly,
and so powerfully, that with only the greatest effort could he
master it. But he had to master it. For the tractor was real,
the field to be plowed was real, the cows would be real, and
deeply, darkly—in something like despair—he knew that you
could never carry what was real, and belonged to the day,
over the secret line into the world that was a dream and belonged to the night.

So he kept for the day what belonged to the day. He had
found the rule of the game.

At dusk, after the work of the day, he would come to the
house. He would stand on the porch for an instant before he
opened the door, and in that instant the Time that belonged to

the day and that gave him a sense of reaching out backward and forward from the day—that Time would simply fall away. It fell like something off your back that should have made a great racket falling, but did not make any sound at all, as though you had already entered the world of dream where things fell with no sound.

It fell, and you stood there in a sudden emptiness of no-Time, in the dusk, and you opened the door to what you would see there in the middle of the kitchen floor, under the cold blaze of timeless light from the bulb hanging from the ceiling, fixed and frozen like something in a lighted store window at night, but actually there in the kitchen that was like a box of light suspended and floating in the timeless dark of night that stretched away in all directions over the land.

Her hair would be bound by the red ribbon. She would be wearing the red dress that was shiny like silk. Her face would be wearing the smile that was not quite a smile but was like the expression on a young girl's face, a little girl's face, that would suddenly be a smile if you said something nice to her, *la piccola.*

So he would try to think of something nice to say. But sometimes he couldn't. It seemed to get harder to do, sometimes. His head would be blank.

But he would try to say something.

If he was coming back from town, he would have something to give her, not much, but something he had bought for her. He bought her the glass beads. He bought her the ring with the red stone in it. These things did not cost much, but she gave that smile when he held them out to her, and later on, when it got so he could not always think of something to say it was better to have something to hold out, not being able to think of a thing to say.

Also, those things like the beads and the ring with the red stone looked good on her, and that made him forget that things

were a little different sometimes from what they had been only
a month or so back. The red paint he bought to put on her
fingernails had been very good for that. He had been walking
down the street in Parkerton, and in the window of the Rexall
store had seen the advertisement of a woman with long black
hair down over bare shoulders, holding up one of her hands
with the fingernails all red, and that picture had made him
stand there staring, and suddenly he was getting a hard on, so
he had gone in and bought that stuff.

He had made her put it on her toenails too. When, at night,
she pulled off the shiny black stockings—or maybe he would
pull them off—he would be waiting for the flash of the red.
That was something to look forward to.

Another day, coming down the street, he had seen, in the
window of Grant's store, which was a lot better than the dime
store, a wax dummy, naked except for the black lace panties
and the black lace brassiere. So he went in. As soon as he got
home that night, he had made her put those things on, even
if she was already dressed in the red dress. He had waited in
the kitchen while she went back to his room to do it, so it
would be more of a surprise when he saw it on her later. That
night when he was eating, and then when he danced with her,
as he sometimes did, though less and less as time went on, he
was thinking of the panties and the brassiere black against the
white skin in the dark under the red dress. He thought of the
black lace slipping back and forth over her skin as she moved
in the dancing.

He kept her dancing a long time that night, for he wanted
to keep thinking and wondering what it would be like when
she slipped off the red dress.

More and more he found reasons to go to Parkerton, or
would seize on reasons to go sooner than really necessary. One
day, right in the middle of rehanging the door from the kitchen
into the back hall, he remembered that he would have to have

wire for the tractor, and so headed to town right away, leaving his tools on the kitchen floor, and all the way to town he was explaining to himself how he really ought to get that rewiring done now, a man ought to do things when he felt like it, when he was hot, he got more done that way. That was the day when, coming down the street in Parkerton, he saw the advertisement in the drugstore window for the red paint for fingernails. He did not admit to himself that, after he had got the coil, he had been walking up and down the street looking for something, he didn't know what. As soon as he had the red stuff for the fingernails, he went directly to his car and started to drive back to the Valley. What he had come for and not known he was coming for, was done now.

Sometimes he did not even go to Parkerton, he would go down to the general store at the Corners. The first time that happened was only a few days after the birthday party. He was moving in the dusk toward the house, where he could see the light from the kitchen window. Then through the window he caught the flash of red, the red of the dress, and came closer to the window. He stood concealed in the shadow of the cedar tree, and peered into that box of light.

She was standing by the table where they ate, leaning over to put the plates and cutlery on. She was there alone under the light, and he suddenly knew, with a cold, disorienting shock, that, even if he had spied on her before, he had never, never once, thought of how she really was when alone. He had never wondered what she was when alone, and now she was there, under the light, alone and the way she could never, never be if she were not alone. This thought struck him, suddenly, with terror. With terror, for there was no other word for what he felt as he saw her lean over the table and saw something in her posture, some hint of age or creakiness or strain, that he had never seen before. Or if he had seen it, he had not known what it was, for she had not been wearing the red dress and whatever it was would not have mattered if she was not wearing the red dress.

He turned and, almost running, went to the car, backed out of the barn, and headed for the Corners. He was lucky. He found the beads there, and they were only fifty-nine cents. When he got back to the house, he slipped to his room, washed and put on his town clothes, and then went in and gave her the present.

To give her a present: out of some darkness in himself into which he never looked, the need would begin to rise, shapeless like a vapor at first, seeming nothing more than part of the darkness from which it was emerging. It might take a couple of days for him to really know, days of that growing unease. Then he would know what he had to do.

But he didn't know what would happen if he didn't do it. He merely knew that something might happen.

La piccola, she was the *leetle-a one.* Sometimes, looking at her with the hair on her left shoulder tied by the red ribbon, he would remember the woman he had first seen, that day when he had come up the road in the rain. While the last blood dripped from the slit throat of the buck, the woman— the woman with the old brown man's sweater hanging loose on her and with the drizzle wetting that loose pile of black hair on her head—had looked across at him. The look had come to him across the patch of earth where the blood of the buck was washing the pine needles into little dams and dikes. She had said: "Where are you going?"

He hadn't been going anywhere. He had been coming from somewhere. There hadn't been any place to go, and he had stayed right here, and that woman who had looked at him out of her distance and indifference and age, for she had been old then, was now standing before him, but was somebody else.

(175)

There had been the old woman with the rat's nest of hair matted down by the rain, and now there was this girl with the red ribbon, waiting to smile.

For she was a girl. She was more like a girl than any girl could be, more shy, more blushing, more fearful, and more anxious to please him, more grateful and shaking when you really made her feel good and she let go—more than any girl of sixteen or seventeen he had ever taught things to. It was because she was both a girl and not a girl. She had been that old woman, in the brown sweater, all frozen up in her ignorance and hopelessness, and that fact had kept the girl inside her more innocent and tender and yearning than any girl who had never been hidden that way inside an old woman could ever be. Now she would suddenly press her head against him and hold onto his coat, and would say, "And I saw you coming down the road in the rain and oh, Angelo, I didn't know who you were. I didn't know what it was to be alive. And there you were coming down the road."

She would clutch his coat like a child trying to keep somebody from going away.

She was ignorant as a child. Like that morning after the first night she had spent in his room, when sitting up, she kept the blanket around her shoulders while she struggled to get on that old gray nightgown.

What a *cretina* he had thought her at that time—all that fuss not to have him see her naked after he had been slipping it to her for three months and her shutting her eyes and pretending it wasn't happening. But now he had begun to realize that what had been happening in the time before didn't have any meaning now. It was like it had never happened. Rather, it was like it had happened to somebody else she had never even heard about.

That was it. For *la piccola* had only then, that very morning, come to exist. She had said: "I feel I just got born," and she was just born and didn't know anything.

In the end it was her ignorance that possessed him. It was the emptiness that he had to fill up. That was the putty, the clay, he had to handle and mold. It was also the air he breathed, it was the bread he ate.

Filling it up, molding it, breathing it, eating it—that was his way of being alive. He lived by her ignorance. When he taught her something, he felt the thrill of his own knowledge, his own power, and she tried so hard to do what he wanted, and with breath coming sharp and shallow, she would whisper, "Like this?—you mean like this?"

As the presents he brought her were a kind of magic to keep something from going away that had happened, or to keep something from happening that had not happened, so was the teaching. In the middle of the night he would wake up, and try to remember something some prostitute or some woman had showed him, or something somebody had told him about, or something he remembered from the dirty snapshots he had bought from that man in the bar in Akron when he was not much more than a boy and then his uncle had found them and beat the *merda* out of him, and then later he had caught the uncle with them in the cellar, and the uncle had beat him again. Or he would try to think up something new, something he had never heard about.

For there always had to be something new. Whatever was new became, always, suddenly old, and even if it had been new last week, this week it was not new, for now she would know it, and would not whisper, with her breath coming that way: "Like this?—you mean like this?—Oh, Angelo!"

Meanwhile he lived by the filling up of that ignorance, by

the planned surprise, the calculated torsion and tension, the withholding and retardation, the pleading, the contrived frenzy, the collapse, all the while finding in himself, as a result of his calculated manipulation of her passion, a colder and more powerful passion beyond appetite.

But now and then the thought would come chillingly into his head, what would he do when there wasn't any ignorance left for him to fill up? As soon as that thought came, however, he had to push it away. It was like the thought of lying frozen forever, like that man in that room yonder. He could not bear to think of that man.

Then one night, as he was coming down the dark hall from his room, where he had just gone to wash and change his clothes, he heard the noise. He stood there staring at the pencil of light that showed under the blackness where the door was. Without thought, as though he were a toy on wheels being pulled by a string, he moved toward the door and entered.

He closed the door behind him, blinking in the light. Then he approached the old brass bed. An old floor lamp with a tasseled silk shade, split here and there, cast a light over what was on the bed. He stood at the foot, but not too close. There was nothing to be afraid of, he knew that, but he did not want to get too close. He stared at the man, and was aware that his own breath was difficult.

All at once it came to him that the man there with all that yellow hair, the man who had once been so big, was the one who was supposed to have taught that woman something. And hadn't. Hadn't even known anything to teach her. That man there was like all those big yellow-headed men—they always looked at him, Angelo Passetto, like he was dirt, like he was nothing, *niente*, was *merda*. And all the time all they were was big and yellow-headed and had money, but they didn't know anything, and that man there, he had never made that

(178)

woman cry out his name, but Angelo Passetto had, he could make her do anything for him and call out his name, he could make her crawl on her belly, if he wanted to.

Suddenly, he wasn't afraid of the man on the bed. He looked down at him from a dizzy height, and felt nothing but contempt. He wasn't afraid that he—Angelo Passetto, who was, all at once, as tall as the house, as tall as a tree, and as strong as God—would ever lie on a bed and not be able to move.

He moved down the hall, and opened the door of the kitchen.

"Hey," he said, urgently, "you come here. That stuff on stove, you push back—you come here."

"What—" she began.

But she did not continue the sentence. Instead, she was coming toward him across the kitchen, her eyes fixed on his face, and he knew that she knew.

She stopped a couple of feet from him, still looking up into his face. Framed in the doorway against the darkness of the hall, his left hand still on the knob, he moved his right hand slowly out, and the thumb and forefinger touched the bulge of the shiny red cloth over the left breast, and then, slowly and with remarkable precision, closed firmly over the unseen nipple.

Increasing that pressure, he stared into her face.

After a moment, he said, his voice a slow whisper, "Now you tell me, you tell me what in a minute I do you."

She was looking up into his face. She did not say anything but the tip of her tongue had come out to move over the dark, wounded-looking color of her lips.

"Tell me," he said, his voice even lower, the pressure of thumb and forefinger increasing ever so little.

Looking up into his face, her eyes bright out of the darkness of the sockets, her voice dry and thin, she said it.

"You'll fuck me," she said.

And he slowly moved backward into the shadow of the hall, drawing her after him by that precise and delicately placed grip of thumb and forefinger.

Spring was coming on. The willows down by the creek had long since put out their furry buds. One day he cut a half-armful of the straight shoots, then found, in the barn, a brass vase as big as an umbrella stand, and put them in it, and set the thing on the side table in the kitchen, next to the incubator. He had never done a thing like that in his life. He was half ashamed of having done it and more ashamed at the kind of pleasure she showed.

What was she acting that way for?

Along the creek the maples were budding, too, and far off at the margin of the woods, their buds made a red haze against the blackness. Day after day, when the great flocks of grackles swung blackly across the damp blue of the sky, you could hear the ceaseless whish of wings coming down from a great height. You could see the stippling, fleeting shadow sweep the new grass. One morning, early, when he went out for the firewood, a flight of duck was going over. The creek was in flood, and at night, he listened to that rushing roar off in the dark, muted by distance.

It was up in March now. Dawn light was coming earlier; and earlier every morning he would get out of the house. The air was bright and soft, but still streaked with cool. He would draw the air deep into his lungs, throw his head back and look up at the sky. Then he would plunge into some task that would give him the sense of time reaching back into the past and into the future, too.

But each morning he had to choose among the possibilities.

The tractor was not fixed yet. It had proven tougher than he had foreseen, and he had stopped work on that to put the old garden patch into shape for early peas and radishes and greens. Then, except for the rainy days when he would be in the barn with the tractor, he took to working on the chicken yard, for now you could get a post-hole digger into the ground.

He was dimly aware of some need to grasp first one project, then another, as some new image of the future. The activity of the day itself—even though it became more and more obsessive—was not enough. To get through the day, he had to pack it with moments that seemed to be stolen from the future, that seemed to promise a world that would have a future.

But always, at last, dusk came, and he would stand on the porch for a moment before opening the kitchen door to enter. In that moment at the door, he was like a man taking a last breath before diving down into a great depth. He was about to dive into a depth where, if he forgot and made a gasp for breath as he would in the world up above where Time was, he would die.

He was about to dive into that depth where there wasn't any Time, and he would at last lie on a bed, staring at the ceiling washed by a raw light cast from below, from the unshaded lamp set on a chair by the bed, and now and then put a cigarette to his lips to draw the smoke into his lungs and then expel it deliberately from his nostrils in two curling, grayly exfoliating, vanishing stalks. Now and then he would put a bottle to his lips to let the brown-gold liquid seep burningly down his throat, while beside him, under the sheet, tne woman lay, her eyes, too, fixed on the ceiling. Now and then he would set the cigarette to her lips for her to draw the smoke in. Now and then he would set the bottle to her lips to let the brown-gold liquid seep down her throat.

And all the while the radio on the chair beside the bed

would emit the whispery music, and in the darkness under the sheet his hand would be on the softness of the woman's belly, and he would try to think of nothing whatsoever.

But that secret world of no-Time, which had seemed to be safely boxed inside the walls of the house, and which he entered only at night when he set hand to the knob of the kitchen door—that world had begun to bleed out into the outside world. It spread slowly outward from the kitchen door, as though the fluid seeped under the door all night. It spread out like a stain, on the grass. When, in the morning, he opened the door to go out, it followed him like thin smoke. It spread around him. You could see through it so easily you did not at first realize it was there. But things seen through it looked different. They would curl and waver, like paper being burned by a flame invisible because of the brightness of the sunshine.

He would stand there in the morning light and not be sure what he had intended to do. He would look at something he had done—at the new roof on the chicken house, at the new posts for the unfinished cow yard—and it would seem incredible to him that he had done that, had had the image in his head of a thing to be done, and had lifted his hands to do those things. He would stand there in the sunlight, and a great lethargy would flow over him.

He would look at the objects of the world around him and, for a moment, he would not be able to understand their relations. A tree, a post, the broken old grindstone, a puff of white cloud on the blue sky—any one thing seemed to be all alone, to hang in an infinite vacuum of namelessness, and he would have to struggle to know what it was. Out of range of vision, off in the cedars, he might hear a jay call. There would be the clear, brassy brightness of sound, and he would marvel at it.

For an instant he could not remember ever having heard that sound before.

He might stretch out his hands, and stare at them.

Then he might cross the yard with a sudden air of purpose, pulling himself together, feeling strong and on the verge of making an important decision. But, as likely as not, he would start some task, pick up a tool only to drop it and then stare stupidly at it. Or he might simply sit on a pile of old lumber, and stare up the slope at the line of leafing woods.

The eggs in the incubator hatched. One night, coming into the kitchen after having been to his room to wash up and change, he found *la piccola*, in the red dress, sitting on the floor, knees bent, and legs to one side, light glinting on the black patent-leather slippers that she had kicked off, and yellow chicks, some still damp and tottery, some brisk and chirpy, around her knees or on her lap. She held one in her hands, and was touching her cheek against that softness.

Still holding the chick, she looked up at him, her glance glittering with excitement, and cried out: "Look, Angelo—look how sweet they are!"

He was studying the look on her face.

"Come here," she was saying, "lean down here."

He leaned down, and before he knew it, she had put the chick against his face.

That touch on his cheek converted some inner tightness into sudden anger. He jerked back, crying out, "That fool thing —you think I want on my face!"

He stood there panting, not knowing what had happened to him. When he had breath, he said: "We no keep them things here. I fix room across hall."

He went and sat at the table, and waited sullenly until she had served the food.

. . .

The next day he went, on sudden impulse, to Parkerton. He needed some things, he told himself, if he was going to get back to work. He felt he had to get back to work. In town, he bought five pounds of staples, a roll of barbed wire, a second-hand generator that he was lucky enough to find in the junk-yard, and last, a bottle of perfume. Passing the Rexall store, he saw the advertisement for a sale of genuine French perfume, it said. After he had bought it, he felt better.

When he came out of the Rexall store, he saw the first flake of snow. Here it was well up in March and a snowflake. He stood on the pavement and realized that he had come all the way into town and not noticed how it was getting cold, how the sky was gray and low. He looked down the street, and there, against the darker color of the land and woods, where the town broke, he could see the veil of thickening white. By the time he got out of town, snow was falling steadily in big flakes that stuck to the windshield faster than the old wiper could get them off. It was a slow trip back, and by the time he pulled into the barn, snow lay even and thick on the ground. In a feeling of strangeness, as though he had never been here before, he made his way toward the house through the falling flakes, guided by the light of the kitchen window. An excite-ment was growing in him. Everything was strange and fresh. Everything was going to begin again, like new.

When he got inside, he did not at first give her the present. At supper he had it in his pocket. He was going to give it to her after supper. If he gave it to her before, it might be, he felt, somehow wasted. During the meal he got more and more restless. He could think of nothing to say. He kept watching the big flakes of snow coming suddenly white, with no noise, against the black window glass. Now and then his hand touched the little package in his pocket. It had cost some money. It had cost $2.49. Thinking of that, he felt excited.

He did not give the little package to her until they were in the bedroom. She seemed glad to have it, and she smiled sweet like she used to, and she was *la piccola.* He told her to put some in her hair, and to put a drop or two on her breasts. He got quickly into bed.

He didn't feel restless and unsettled anymore. He watched her as she undressed, and then as she turned toward the bed and approached, naked, shivering a little, her arms hanging straight down by her sides, the palms of the hands turned a little forward, the light white on her body, the red ribbon still binding her hair at her left shoulder.

He had not yet smelled the perfume. When she had opened it and, according to his instructions, touched it to herself, he had stood back from her. He had not wanted to smell it yet. Now, when she let her head fall on his arm and he looked down into her face and untied the red ribbon to let the hair slip loose, he caught the full scent.

At first he did not know what was the matter.

Then he knew. He had smelled it before. He had smelled it on a girl back in Cleveland a long time ago. She was the girl who had said that life was just a bowl of cherries, and he had been crazy about her. She had acted crazy about him, and she had the smallest waist he had ever put his hands around and she had put that same perfume on her breasts. She had left him for a guy with a yellow Lincoln Continental convertible that was only three years old.

That was what was the matter, and it was plenty.

Nothing worked.

It was after 2:00 when he got up and put his clothes on. Enough light was coming in the window for him to see, for there was a moon. The snow had stopped.

She was asleep. But he hadn't been asleep. He had been lying there for hours, his eyes shut, trying to think of nothing and go to sleep.

He made his way down the back hall. When he got out into the open, he looked up. The moon was big and bright, and the air brilliantly cold. Shadows lay across the whiteness of the snow like spilled ink. He looked toward the barn and saw that the tracks he had made in the snow coming toward the house that evening were filled up now. He stood there and looked at where they had been and now were not, and it was as though nothing had ever happened, nothing in the world.

Finally, he moved toward the barn, went beyond it. He bore to the right and angled up the slope of the field, feeling the ridges of old furrows underfoot, but not looking down, keeping his eyes on the distant shadow of woods.

At the edge of the woods, he turned and stood staring up at the blank and glittering face of the sky. The world seemed to fall away from him. He stood face to face with the sky, and could stand there, looking up, and never have to move or remember.

But he did look away. He looked back down the slope where the whiteness of snow was washed by the whiteness of moonlight; and out of that whiteness, his tracks, dark against it, emerging from the invisibility of distance, marched up the slope at him. They came, sharper and darker, to the very spot where he stood, walking mercilessly at him, and all at once, as though his shoes had come alive with a life of their own, or the earth were alive under the shoes and seized the shoes and moved them forward, he was moving into the shadow of the trees. So he moved forward into that crazed geometry of white moonlight and black boughs and black shadows on the whiteness of snow which was the woods.

He came, in the end, to the open place. It was brimming with moonlight, the snow white on the ground, the stones of the structure white in the light, and the winding stream glossy black except where fringed with skim ice. Beyond the open whiteness, the boles of deciduous trees and the bulk of cedars stood black.

He entered the openness.

He went into the doorway of the dairy house. Through the ruined roof moonlight fell to lie in jagged white patches on the stone floor. In the stone trough, the water slid blackly with no sound. For a full minute he stood in silence; then, as silently, came out again into the open. Scarcely masked by the snow, the path to the shack led into the cedars and disappeared in their shadows. He moved forward, staring intently at the ground he was about to tread.

Then he found one.

It was a little off the path, where under the snow, the frozen mud was a jumble. What he found was a single foot track, small, perfectly formed, in what had been the spongy turf beside the stream. Water had seeped into the track, and now the water was frozen, and the shape was there, clear and perfect in the moonlight.

He crouched beside it, and stared at it. The track was pressed sharply into the turf, no doubt by the weight of full buckets, for the track pointed away, toward the path into the cedars. He brushed the little snow off the ice that covered the print of the track. A single stalk of cress, encroaching from the stream to the soggy ground, had been caught by the passing foot, and pressed down. The tip of the stalk of cress, clearly visible in the moonlight, was frozen into the skim ice that, now that he had brushed away the snow, so brightly defined the shape of the foot that had trodden there.

With one finger, he touched the free curve of the stalk that arched from ice back to its root. Carefully, he pinched off the stalk at the root and began to lift it. The foot track of bright ice came with it, keeping its shape. He held it high, letting the moonlight shine on it, then through it. He lowered the ice into the flattened palm of his left hand, and slipped his right hand below the left as though to help support a burden. He lowered his head to let his lips touch the ice, as lightly as possible.

Then, all at once, with a fierce exhalation, he thrust his now parted lips against the icy shape. It shattered soundlessly beneath that kiss. He shut his eyes and held his face pressed against the fragile coldness. He held it there until the ice had completely melted and his face was wet.

The next morning, at first light, well before she woke, he was out of the bedroom. He had had less than two hours of sleep, but felt calm and detached. The earth was white, and the air was cold and bright. You felt that if you weren't careful the very air would crackle and craze beautifully, like ice. You felt calm and old, as though everything had happened to you, and it was all beautiful and nothing would ever happen again, if you were very careful, and lucky.

As he moved cautiously through the brightness of air, toward the barn, he was thinking that now he would finish fixing the tractor. His mind focused sharply on that. Nothing else mattered. If the tractor was fixed, everything would be all right. He did not think what would be all right. He moved through the icy brightness of air.

When he entered the barn, he saw, there beyond the car, the tractor, with the tools laid out neatly on a board where he had left them—he was always careful about tools, he couldn't stand people messy about tools—and the parts neatly on the tin tray made by the inverted top of a big lard can. His heart melted, suddenly, in gratitude.

By noon, he felt sure that he could finish the job that day. He felt no hunger. Out the door of the barn he saw that the snow had all melted, all except for the patches of deep shade. Now the air was sweet and silky.

At 3:00 he began the test. He went around to the right side of the engine, and as he braced himself and laid hand to the flywheel that stuck out there, he found himself shaking with excitement. "Christ-a Jesus," he said out loud, and spun it. Nothing happened, and he remembered how he used to fight the damned thing, and curse it, back yonder in Ohio.

It took ten minutes before the engine gave the first cough, and the first blue-black, acrid smoke burst from the exhaust. Five minutes later he dared to cautiously turn the valve that shifted the feed from gasoline to kerosene. He nursed the engine for a couple of minutes, then mounted, and very carefully backed it out into the drive at the end of the barn toward the road. He made it move back and forth on the snow-soggy drive, testing the controls.

When he stopped, he found that he was shaking even worse than before he began. He stood there and stared at the tractor shining in sunshine with its bright, new green paint, bright as new leaves would be, and heard the steady beat of the engine, and was shaking in the silky air, with the patches of snow yet visible in the shade of cedars, but the sky blue and soft above him, and wondered why he was shaking. He wondered if anybody else—his father, his uncle, people he had never known—had stood this way, shaking for nothing while the sky was blue and the air like silk. His throat was parched.

Leaving the tractor running, he went to the house for a drink of water.

She was there in the kitchen when he entered.

For a split second he did not recognize her. For weeks now what he had seen upon entering the kitchen, always at dusk, had been the red, silky-shining dress, the black patent-leather belt, the slippers, the red ribbon binding the black hair at the left shoulder, and now what he saw, standing there in that peculiar desertedness of an afternoon kitchen in spring, was a woman in an old brown, too big, man's sweater, brogans on feet, and black hair piled untidily on the head like an enormous rat's nest, staring at him from a bright and pitying distance, with a pity that, in that moment, seemed unforgivable.

With her gaze upon him across the kitchen, where the afternoon sun slanted in to show the graining of the worn boards of the floor, and where the sound of the ticking of the old clock on the wall dripped time away, he knew that that look was the same that had been upon him the night when she sat by the bed and said, "I want you to feel free, Angelo," and something had cracked inside him and bled into sweetness.

But nothing cracked now. In fact, he felt nothing, nothing at all, as he stood there and stared at her, and saw her, exactly what she was, every detail.

And seeing, he realized that everything else—the red dress, the black patent-leather slippers, the black lace of the panties and brassiere on her white skin, the bottle of whiskey held to her lips, the wrenchings and contrived tensions, the forbidden words she had humbly learned to utter, the calculated frenzy —all had been a lie.

It had all been a lie, a lie he had told to himself.

But, suddenly, as he looked across and saw exactly what she was, and saw that look from her bright and misty distance for exactly what truth that look was, he knew that the dry and grinding pain that had come with his recognition of the lie, was gone.

He looked across at her and thought, marveling, how he had never really seen her before. Then he thought how he had never seen—not really seen—anybody before. He had never seen the truth before, about anything. That thought filled him with awe, and with a sweetness.

He moved across the kitchen toward her.

"Cassie," he said, and the word felt strange on his lips.

Then she said: "That's my real name. You never called me by my name before."

He wanted to say something to her, but he had no words for it. So he put his arms around her, and sank his face into her hair.

Everything might have been all right, if it had not been for that perfume.

There it was again.

He jerked his head back, his arms fell away from the embrace. Suddenly, he was at the door. He flung from the house. The engine of the tractor, there on the drive, was still running. He plunged on past, not even looking at it, reached the barn, and was gone.

After he was gone, the sound of the engine kept raveling upward, into the emptiness of the soft blue sky.

It was just after dark when Angelo stood under the denser darkness of the cedar in the yard and peered through the window into the lighted box that was the kitchen. Under the blazing bulb that hung from the ceiling the table was set. For a moment that was all he could see: the light falling on familiar objects rigid in the mute emptiness.

Then she moved into his range of vision. She was wearing the old brown sweater. Her hair was pinned up in the old loose tumble on her head. All was as though nothing had ever happened. So he went in.

If she had been wearing the red dress. If her hair had been tied in the red ribbon. If she had been wearing the patent-leather slippers. If things had been that way, he did not know what he could have done.

But now he could go in. Nothing had ever happened. He made his mind think of nothing, and went in.

They sat at the table and, without speaking, ate the food. He tried to think of nothing, but something kept happening in his head, and it was everything. When, after leaving the house that afternoon, it had happened, it was like a dream, but at the same time, it was the only thing real.

It was real that very instant, he knew. It was still happening. It was happening right there in his head.

She is standing in the path with an empty bucket hanging down on each side. He stands before her, and says: "Why you hate me?"

"You're white," she says, "ain't that enough?"

He pushes the sleeve up on his left forearm, reaches to seize her right wrist, making her drop the bucket, pushes her sleeve up, and holds the two forearms side by side. "Look," he says. "You more white."

She jerks her arm back, and says: "Mine—I wish it was black."

"OK, OK," he says, "but why you hate me? I no hate you because you *nera*. One time me—Angelo—had a—"

She slaps him ringingly on the cheek.

He stares into her face. He begins to smile. "I no care," he says. "You do again, you see I no care."

The hand swings toward his face again, but stops in the air. He is smiling. He feels the smile on his face, and is happy. The hand is there in the air, waiting, and he reaches out and seizes the wrist.

She tries to jerk free.

But he holds tight, looking at the hand, then into her face, saying: "This leetle hand give me slap?"

She is staring wildly at him.

When he draws the hand to him and kisses it, she bursts

into tears. He releases the hand, and she stands there weeping.

"I don' like you cry," he says. "I like you put head here—" His right hand reaches across to touch his left shoulder. "Please, on shoulder," he says, "and Angelo sing."

Now, sitting at the table, with his jaws working on the food, he dreamed the dream over again, seeing nothing there on the table before him now, for the dream was the only real thing. In the afternoon they had gone into the dairy house, he and the girl, and had stayed there a long time, and when they came out, it was getting toward dark. So sitting there at the table he dreamed it again.

She is standing by the little stream that flows out of the dairy house. She says: "That song—the one you used to sing, way off in the woods—"

Interrupting her, standing there in the first dusk, he lifts his head to sing:

'Nta 'stu curtigghiu c'è un peri di rosa.
Nun la tuccassi nuddu, che è la mia.

He stops. He looks at her in question.

"Yes, that one," she says. "What does it mean?"

He thinks a minute. Then he says: "A man make song. He say is a *curtigghiu*—is a *cortile*—like a yard. Is a *rosa*, but nobody touch, she *la mia*."

"*La mia*," she repeats.

"*Sì*," he says, "mine! She my *rosa*."

And she says: "Sing the rest."

"It sad," he says.

(193)

"But it sounded sweet," she says, "coming off in the woods. Sing it."

So he sings, and he comes to the end:

Dunn avi li peri, la testa ci posa.
Jeu eu lu giuru, pi'la parti mia.

"And that—" she asks, "what does that mean?"

"It mean sad," he says.

"But tell me, tell me," she says.

"The man, he say, in the place for the *peri*, for the feet—the *rosa*, she put the *testa*. She put head down. Down there in the place for feet. She dead! That what the man say, *lu giuru*, he swear. He say, I know it myself, *parti mia*, she dead."

He looks at her face. Her eyes are swimming with brightness.

"But your face," he says, "she not rose, she up here high, not on ground."

He reaches out and touches her cheek.

"I don't care, I don't care!" she cries out. "I don't care how sad it is—it's beautiful!"

He shut his eyes, sitting there at the table, and in his mind he saw the girl's face as she said the words.

Then he felt a touch on his hand, and opened his eyes, and looked down to the hand laid on his, there among the dirty dishes. He lifted his head and looked across the table at the woman.

"Angelo," she said, "please don't worry."

He continued to look at her.

"Angelo," she said, the hand pressing his, "everything will be all right."

The hand held his harder.

(194)

"Don't you know that?" she demanded, smiling.

"OK, OK," he said.

It would be OK if he could just learn not to think of what had ever happened, and not to think of what would happen.

That way it could be OK.

CHAPTER EIGHT

ჄჄჄჄჄჄჄჄჄჄჄ Տhe had not even taken her
clothes off, all night, waiting. He had left early yesterday morning, Saturday. She had not even seen him after he got up, just
heard him in the kitchen while she was in Sunder's room, then
the ax splitting wood, outdoors. A little later, she heard the car
start.

In the kitchen she found that he had not even grabbed
something to eat. The coffeepot was boiling on the stove. She
went to his room. His town coat was gone, and his tie, but his
town pants and the patent-leather shoes were still there. He
had gone off, of a sudden.

There was a whole day of wondering. When she wasn't going
to look up the road, she filled up the time of wondering by
doing things for Sunder. Twice during the day she washed
him. She had shaved him in the morning, but she did it
again at night. If she was with him, she could do things that

made part of her feel the way she had felt before she ever saw Angelo Passetto coming down the road in the rain.

At night, she sat in the cold parlor, in the dark, holding aside the prickly dry lace curtain that raveled apart under her fingers, and stared up the road. She kept thinking about the first time when he came down the road in the rain, setting his feet down in the mud, finicky as a cat, holding a newspaper package in his hand. That was afternoon, but now it was night, and he never came.

She decided that if she stopped watching, he would come. She went and lay down on the bed in his room. She pressed her face into the pillow where his head had been, and smelled the smell of Angelo Passetto. She wondered how long it would take for that smell, that was all there would ever be of Angelo Passetto if he never came back, to go away.

That thought was so awful, she could not stay on the bed. She went back to the parlor and put her face against the windowpane and looked out into the darkness. She was looking up the road like that when she realized that, long back, daylight had come, and in that light the road was emptier than it had ever been.

Then she heard Sunder.

In a way she was glad of that.

It was Sunday.

It was early afternoon, and she was again lying on the bed with her eyes tight shut and her face in the pillow that had the smell of Angelo Passetto, when she heard the car. But she was sure the noise was in her head and not in the world outside, so she carefully did not go look. She did not even open her eyes. Not even when she heard a step in the hall, and the door creaked. She could not bear to open her eyes and find the truth. She knew it was only in her head.

But it was not.

Suddenly she knew it was not, for with no warning, something fell heavy across the bed. It jounced her eyes open, and she saw him.

He lay there on the bed, and his eyes were closed. He was lying almost on his back as he had fallen. She thought he was dead.

She stared at his face. It was as though there were two faces. There was one face that was watery-white like skimmed milk, but over that face there was the other face that was the pale brown he usually was, but that face was so thin and transparent that you could see the water-white, blue-pale face showing through it, and she knew he was dead. She had shoved herself up on the bed, on her right arm, and held her hand over her mouth to stop the scream, while she looked down into his face.

His right eye was bruised blue, and swollen. There was a cut on his head at the edge of the hair on the left side of the forehead, and dried blood. The right side of his mouth was swollen and black, with fresh blood there, and a slow bubble of blood and spit that expanded and broke with his breath. It was the bubble that made her know he was not dead.

She scrambled off the bed and got a wet towel from the bathroom and shoved the lamp off the chair by the bed, and sat there and wiped his face with cold water. When nothing happened, she ran to the kitchen and got a bottle of vinegar. She dabbed the towel, and leaning over him, wiped his face and held the towel to his nose. After a little, his eyes came open.

The eyes were looking up into her face, but the eyes did not seem to know who she was.

"Angelo!" she cried out, feeling that her heart would break for joy that his eyes had come open, and for sorrow that the eyes did not know who she was.

She saw his lips were twisting to say something even through their thickness, so she said, "Be quiet, be quiet, you're all right, everything will be all right—everything!"

After she had managed to get him undressed and into bed, and had him lying as comfortably as possible, on his left side, with the hot-water bottle against the place above the kidneys where he hurt worst, and had got some coffee down him, he said that just after dark he had been forced off the road and held up. The bruised lips twisted slowly and a little more blood, diluted with spit, ran down from the right corner of the mouth, but the words came out clearer now, saying how they had beat him and knocked him down and kicked him when they found he didn't have much money. It was the kick in the kidneys that made his back hurt so.

She made him stop talking, heated milk and made him drink some, and got an old army blanket and hung it over the window to darken the room, and sat by the bed holding his hand. After a while he went to sleep. She was dizzy with happiness as she sat there, holding the hand and listening to his breath. She was happy because he had come back and now she would never let anything happen to him again.

The breathing was so soft she had to strain to hear it at all, but that straining was part of the happiness. She thought that this was what she had been waiting for all her life, just to sit here and listen to his breath. She felt ashamed that he had had to be hurt to make her know how much happiness there was in loving him, but then the shame got to be part of the happiness, and she thought how, if she loved him this much, maybe she could make up to him for having to get hurt. She sat there with her heart inside her bleeding happiness like a great big plum oozing gold juice in the hot darkness after the sun goes down.

She shut her eyes so that nothing would ever change.

In the middle of the afternoon, sitting there with her eyes closed, she heard the noise from Sunder's room.

When she got there and looked down at him on the bed, she felt, to her surprise, a sweet pity for him. She felt it because she suddenly knew that he, too, was part of all that had happened to her and that if what had happened had not happened, then she would never have known what the happiness was that now filled her.

Looking down at him, she remembered that she had not fed him since morning, so she went to the kitchen and stirred up some fire to warm the pot of soup. She stood by the range, waiting for the soup to warm, thinking, too, that she might get Angelo to take some. But she wouldn't wake him up for it, she would feed Sunder and then see if he was awake. She filled the bowl for Sunder and turned from the range.

There was the woman, standing in the open doorway to the porch, looking right at her.

No: what Cassie saw was only a dark shape against the bright spring light of outdoors. It was a shape that her mind was not giving a name to.

Her mind would not say, *It is the woman,* but she knew that her breath had stopped and her skin was prickly cold all over, and sweat popped out on her temples. It was as if she knew something was going to happen, but her mind was not going to say it. No, it was like something that had already happened, and her mind was trying not to remember it.

The woman was looking at her. She saw the woman's eyes shining white in the head that was part of the dark shape against the brightness, and she knew that the woman had been watching her. She stood there holding the bowl of soup.

She said: "You been watching me."

"Yes," the woman said.

"How long you been watching me?"

"Since you stirred up that fahr."

"Whyn't you knock?" Cassie demanded, in outrage, surprised at her own fury and strength. "You've got no right not to knock! You've got no right to be watching me."

The woman came inside the door, closer, moving silently in the old tennis shoes, each shoe split above the little toe where the bunion must be. The woman stood and looked at her with shining eyes. Not against the light now, the face was not dark, it was yellow, and now it was not the whites of the eyes that were shining, it was the other part, which was yellow. The eyes were yellow and were fixed on her.

"What you watching me for?" Cassie demanded, standing there with the bowl of soup in her hand and the spoon now rattling in the bowl.

"Jes watchen," the woman said, very slowly. "Jes watchen to see what kinda woman caint keep holt on no man."

Cassie retreated, sidling off to the left, turned, and clutching the bowl of soup in both hands, made for the pantry door, which was open, saying, "It's getting cold—the soup's getting cold," not saying it to the woman, not even to herself, just saying it to fill up the time and space until she got into the pantry away from those eyes. Her feet, moving as fast as they could without making her spill the soup, got her across the pantry. Then she was in the shadowy safety of Sunder's room.

Beyond the bed, she turned, but there was the woman on the other side, not near it, merely standing there in those old bunion-split tennis shoes.

"Get out!" Cassie commanded.

"I'se here," the woman said softly.

"Get out of here!" Cassie again commanded, her voice now thin and cracked.

"Feed 'im," the woman said. Then: "If'n you kin hold that spoon."

Cassie looked at the spoon, which jiggled in the bowl.

"Feed 'im—Cassie," the woman said, more softly now. "He's all yore'n now—Cassie."

The spoon suddenly stopped jiggling in the bowl. Cassie felt still, very still all over, and cold. She looked across the distance at the woman.

"Yeah," the woman said, "you hear'd right."

She came around the foot of the bed, and stood before Cassie. "Yeah," she said, "it was *Cassie* you hear'd me say."

Cassie felt her mouth start to move, then stop.

"Listen," the woman said. "I come here, sixteen-seventeen—years ago, and I slip and doan say *mam* to you, and you ketch me up, and me, I 'pologize. Well, Cassie, I ain't 'pologized since. Not even to God."

The woman began to laugh. Cassie watched her laughing.

Suddenly the woman stopped laughing, and said: "You know why I'm a-laughen?" And when Cassie did not answer, she said: "I'm laughen 'cause I wonder if that time back yonder when I fust came here—I wonder if you thought when I was layen up in baid with him"—and she jerked her head toward Sunder—"I used to say mister."

There was a split-bottom chair there, and Cassie sat down on it. She set the bowl on the edge of the big old table, the spoon was rattling so.

The voice took on a mincing, falsetto girlish tone: "Oh mister, please, oh mister, please go easy on this pore leetle nigger gal—oh mister, you break my pore leetle back—oh, please!"

"Hush!" Cassie cried out. And pressed her hands to her ears.

But the voice had stopped, the woman had moved soundlessly to the bed. She stood there looking down at Sunder. "Him," she said, studying him, "he won't break no more backs."

She swung her gaze from the man, and moved toward Cassie, a couple of yards from the chair. "You think I come here 'bout him?" she demanded, jerking her head toward the bed.

"Naw," she said, answering herself, "you can have him now. You kin keep holt on this 'un, now he caint play with hisself even." She was looking down at Cassie with the unswerving yellow stare. "But that other one," she said. "It's him I come about—that other feller you got now and caint keep."

Cassie's hands were again pressed to her ears.

"Mought as well git them hands off," the woman said, very loud, "I'll yell so you caint he'p hear."

Cassie took the hands down.

"OK," the woman said, "you knows that I mean. That Eye-tal-yun you got—yeah, that what he call hisself. Eye-tal-yun—which is what would'n no nigger be."

She laughed quick and dry, like ripped paper.

She began again, "You know whar yore Eye-tal-yun was last night?"

Cassie opened her lips.

But the woman said: "I doan mean no lie he tole you—whatever lie 'twas, and now you set thar yore mouf dry-gapen at me lak a fish out-a water, fer you know it's a lie." She slid closer. "But the truth," she said, "that's what I'm tellen you."

"They robbed him—" Cassie burst out, rising in the chair, her face coming alive, her eyes bright. "They robbed him, they beat him, they—"

"Set down," the woman said. "Set down and I'll tell. He seen my Charlene pass down the road, yestiddy mornen, she walken down to the Corners to git the bus in. To visit her gal-cousin. And that Eye-tal-yun, he grab the car and chase her and tole her he was goen to Parkerton and she got in and it was half a day till they git thar, and in town he got in a fight and got beat up. And Charlene caint drive no car, and he kept fainten, but he got nigh my house. Charlene, her cryen and goen on so, she made me drag him in. He looked lak daid and—"

The words stopped. The woman stood there panting. Then said: "And I wish he was. Wish he was born daid."

Cassie, sitting very still in the chair, was looking down at the dingy, dark gray skirt she wore, watching her fingers smooth the cloth toward the knees. All at once, she looked up at the woman, with a bright, girlish expression. "I don't believe a word of it," she said.

"I doan keer what you believes," the woman said, the yellow eyes coming sharply to focus on Cassie's bright, polite, little-girl smile. "All I keer is, you keep that Eye-tal-yun off my Charlene."

"Why don't you keep your Charlene off the road?" Cassie asked, happy for an instant, hearing her voice so bright and sure.

"Listen," the woman said, "I caint do nuthen with Charlene." Her voice was suddenly flat, and her face bony, grayish, and spent. "That gal, she done gone crazy. This mornen, I beg her. She won't listen. I locks her up, she beat the door with her haid till it bleed. I say I whup her she see him agin, and she walk to the kitchen stove and git ready to lay her finger on the stove lid to show me she doan mind me hurten her, and I know she gonna do it, and I snatch her off."

Cassie, not smiling now, was leaning forward in the chair with her clenched hands pressed hard against her body just under the bosom, for the pain had suddenly come on when, in her head, she saw the girl walk right up to the stove ready to put her finger on the stove lid, she loved him so.

"Listen," the woman said, her voice again savage and strong. "I doan keer what that Eye-tal-yun do to you. I doan keer, Cassie Spottwood, if'n he rake you back-ards and far-ards lak a bed-harrow busten dry clods. But listen—you keep him off Charlene." She turned away, with a motion of weary in-difference, saying as though over a shoulder, "Done said my say. He come round agin, I fill him full of buckshot."

Cassie kept her hands pressed against that spot where the

pain was, and rocked back and forth, ever so slightly, in the chair.

The woman, on the noiseless shoes, was beyond the old brass bed, one hand on the far bedpost, at the foot. She was again staring down at the man.

Cassie heard the voice flat and far off, say: "Him."

She stopped the rocking motion and straightened up.

"Him," the woman repeated. She had moved up the bed on the far side, and stood staring down at the upturned face. "He was shore-God much-man," she said.

Her right hand reached out and hung in the air above the face.

"Don't!" Cassie cried out. "Don't you dare touch him!"

She leaped to her feet.

But the forefinger of the yellow hand had touched the forehead.

"Look," the woman said, fixing her gaze now on Cassie. "I done tetched and nuthen happened."

"Get out!" Cassie cried.

The woman was looking across at Cassie, the yellow face smiling from its distance with something almost like pity.

"I'll git," the woman said, softly, "in God's own time."

The tennis shoes made no sound as she went slowly through the open door to the pantry, and beyond.

There had been no sound of the going, as there had been no sound of the coming. The woman had just suddenly been there, out of the air, and now she had not gone, she was simply not there, and the air had closed over the space where she had been.

Nothing had happened. At least, nothing new, no coming or going, for whatever had happened had happened a long time back, and that woman had come in this house a long time back, and all this was only a remembering. A remembering had stepped out of her head—out of Cassie Spottwood's head, like suddenly coming out of the air—that was all.

Cassie sat in the split-bottom chair and smelled the spring air that came in through the open kitchen door and on through the pantry into the room. She heard the drowsy, late-afternoon quarreling of a robin somewhere among new leaves. Nothing had happened.

Nothing except the pain inside her bosom, where her hands, made into hard fists, were pressed.

Then she saw the bowl of soup at the edge of the table. She had been about to feed Sunder and she had set the bowl down and it had got cold, and now she would heat the soup. She would feed him. Everything was as simple as that. That was what you did, and it was as though nothing had happened.

Except the pain.

But the pain was very strange. It lived all by itself. It stayed in its own dark hole and had no relation to the world outside.

After she had finished feeding Sunder, she stood by the bed, the empty bowl in her hand. She looked at the empty bowl and remembered she had meant to make Angelo some. So she went to the kitchen and filled another bowl.

As she approached the door to his room, the pain was, all of a sudden, worse. The pain had swollen up, and was pressing up against her lungs so she couldn't breathe. She put a hand on the knob of the door, bracing herself to stand, and at the same time trying to make the hand turn the knob, for she knew that if she didn't go in now, she would never go in.

He was still asleep. So she sat in the chair, holding the bowl in her hands. He opened his eyes, and in that instant the pain leaped up in her and clawed at her insides, trying to get out,

like a cat in a sack. It was clawing upward, it was going to
jump out of her mouth, and jump on his face with all its claws
and tear it, and tear it, the poor hurt face that was so beautiful
—oh, Angelo!

Then she heard her voice asking if he wanted some soup,
and he said yes, and so it was all right.

He smiled out of his poor hurt mouth when he got through,
she was sure it was a smile, and when he went to sleep again,
she held his hand, and watched the light get dimmer in the
room. Nothing had ever happened.

This was all, and this, she knew, was happiness.

It was well after dark when she went to shut up for the night.
When she went to lock the back door, she remembered how
she had seen, in that doorway, the dark shape against the light,
and so the pain came back. She locked the door, and for a
moment leaned against it, as though the weight of her body
would help to keep something out.

After a little, she felt better, but when she went into Sunder's
room, everything started up again. She looked down at him
lying there, and the pain began to swell and claw. But she
kept standing there, hanging on to the bedpost at the head of
the bed. She stayed there and forced herself to keep looking
down at him and see the yellow finger reaching out to touch
his forehead.

She was discovering something. If she could stand being in
here, in this room where Sunder was, the thing inside her
would get tired of clawing, and when it stopped, she could go
back to the other room.

She had discovered something, for when, in the dark, she
felt her way back to the other room and lay down fully
clothed, careful not to waken the sleeper, the clawing did not
start up again. The thing that was inside her stayed curled up,

furry and soft and tired, and went to sleep. So she went to sleep, too.

Before dawn, however, it woke her. She wondered how long it had been awake inside her and trying to wake her up.

She left the room, softly, and wandered about the house, the hall, the parlor, even the room where they had kept the chicks till they got big enough for the chicken yard. She even went out to the backyard. She saw the lighter-looking boards Angelo had used to repair the back steps. She saw the pale new shingles on the roof of the chicken house, and the spiderweb paleness of the new wire mesh around the chicken-runs, and saw the whiteness of dew on the grass. Everything in the world was dark-silvery or silvery-dark. She lifted up her face and saw the first pale silvering of the sky eastward. But nothing did much good, for that clawing was inside her, so she went back where from the start she had known she would go.

She stood in the now slightly mitigated darkness of Sunder's room, and stared down at the whitish blur that was his face. After a little, she saw the gleam she knew was the opening of his eyes. Then she turned the light on, and saw how everything in the room leaped suddenly to the place where it belonged. It was as though everything had been slyly slipping from its proper place on some illicit, secret project of its own until, caught in that blast of light, like a policeman's whistle, it jerked back into place.

She shaved Sunder. That gave her something to do. That would give her time to get ready to stand the clawing she would have to stand till the thing got tired.

Then, afterwards, she could get back to the other room.

It was funny. How if a thing went on long enough it got different. It got to be a way of living, and you did not remember any other way, and this way had its own happiness, too. You could be happy just going into the room and sitting by the bed, holding his hand while he slept. Or you could slip into the room at night and, with your clothes on, lie on top of the bed on the far side and hear his breathing, and then you might go to sleep, too. You would sleep until that thing woke up inside you and began to stir around, and then you had to leave the room and go outdoors in the dark. But, after that, you could always go in Sunder's room, and look down at him till the clawing wore itself out.

It was that way for three days. Then—this was Wednesday afternoon, and Angelo had come back on Sunday—she was holding his hand and being happy in the new kind of happiness, but all at once, she knew he was not asleep. He was watching her all the time. His eyelids seemed closed tight, but they weren't. They were just the slightest bit open, a thin line of gleaming showing under each lid, and he was watching her.

Carefully, she laid the hand down, as though she were trying not to wake him, and tiptoed out of the room. Outside in the hall, she leaned against the wall for a minute, not knowing why she felt so faint and weak. Then she went on to Sunder's room. She lay on her old cot, looking at the ceiling. The leaves outside, moving in whatever stir of air there was, made a kind of rippling reflection on the ceiling. She stared at the ceiling and tried to figure out how this reflection could be up there, but that didn't do any good, and whatever was happening in her kept on happening.

Suddenly she found herself standing in the middle of the floor. Sunder made a noise, but she did not even look at him. She knew she had to go to the other room and say something to Angelo quick, and make him say something to her. Even if she did not know what that would be.

She went down the hall, and thrust open the door.

He wasn't there.

She ran down the hall, hearing her brogans banging the

hollow boards. In the backyard the sudden blaze of light made her reel. For a moment she paused, then ran to the barn. He wasn't there. She had gone round the barn and was staring across the fields toward the west woods when she heard the shot.

She stood there, frozen.

Then she realized that the shot, far off, had not come from the west woods. It had been from the other woods, off to the left, up the ridge.

She ran back to the house, breathing hard now, down the sounding hall, to the room, and got to the closet and jerked back the burlap. The shotgun was gone. That was all. He had just gone hunting. He was well. He was well enough to go out hunting. That was the shot she had heard.

She threw herself across the bed, and pressed her face into that pillow. It had the smell of Angelo.

After a time, far off, muffled by distance, by the walls, by the pillow, there came another shot.

Everything was ready, the plates laid, the plastic flowers in a vase, the bottle of wine—the last one he had brought—open, the bottle of whiskey by his plate. The radio was there, too. She touched the bottle of whiskey, then withdrew the hand. No, she would not take another drink.

But the one she had taken had done her good. She had gone to his room to get the bottle—for the table, just to have it ready when he came in from hunting—and the instant her fingers closed on it, she knew she would put it to her mouth. This was the last thing she had thought of doing, but, suddenly, she was doing it. She took three big, gulping, burning swallows. It was then that she got the idea of putting on the red dress.

After she had it on, and the black underwear, too, she took another drink, then went to stand before the mirror in the bathroom, to fix her hair. The hair being fixed, the ribbon tied, she stood there smiling at her reflection. Then she began practicing pretty smiles. She found a bright, brittle smile. She held that on her face and stared at the new image in the glass until she didn't even know who she was, but whoever it was, was very pretty. She carried the smile carefully back to the kitchen.

In the kitchen she stirred the sauce, and put the pot of water on for the spaghetti. They would have spaghetti. She would show him how well she could make it.

She turned on the electric light. It was now dark enough for that. She took one more drink, quick, from the bottle.

He came in with the shotgun under his right arm, a dead rabbit hanging from his left hand. She waited for him to speak. But he didn't, so she spoke to him. Yes, he had been hunting. Yes, he got two shots, missed one. He flung the rabbit on the drainboard of the sink, washed his hands, prepared ice for his whiskey, and sat at the table.

She felt the smile on her face, pretty and bright, but it kept cracking and slipping. Twice she discovered that he was staring at her, that he seemed about to say something, and each time she quickly got the smile back in place. But each time, he dropped his gaze.

After the meal, he dressed the rabbit. He sat in a chair, a big pan on his lap, and did the work. When the knife split down the white velvety belly, with that tight, thin, ripping sound, she thought she would faint. She didn't know why, for she had dressed a lot of rabbits, but now she felt the ripping right up her own belly. She had turned her chair from the table to watch him, but now the insides of the rabbit, gray and bluish and red, spilled out, and watching, she nearly fainted. There was blood on his hands.

Seeing the blood on his hands, she felt the pain begin, just under her bosom.

He put the dressed rabbit into the refrigerator, then dumped the hide and offal into the garbage pail. He washed the blood from his hands. Then, across the distance from the sink, he was looking at her.

He came slowly across the distance and stood looking down at her. At first, she thought he was about to draw her up to dance with him, even if the radio wasn't on yet, but he did not. He kept looking down at her, into her eyes, and she kept putting the smile back into place, but it was dry and brittle and cracking and slipping worse than before. Two or three times she saw his tongue come out and wet his lips as though he were about to say something, but he did not.

He turned suddenly away, picked up the bottle of whiskey and the radio and left the kitchen.

She went in and lay down on her cot in Sunder's room, with the red dress still on. She kept falling asleep, but every time, she began to dream about the rabbit, and what had come out of the rabbit, the insides, and blood on his hands.

Finally, after the last time and the worst, she got up, and went to the icebox and took out the rabbit, and went into the backyard. She went as far as the fence, then she flung the thing far off into the darkness. She stood there a moment, catching her breath, then she heard the sound. She must have flung the thing further than she thought. It must have gone into the hog pen. She heard the noise the hogs made.

She stood there and heard the grunting, huffing, grinding sound the hogs made as they shoved each other and fought over it and crushed it in their jaws, yonder in the dark.

When she got back to the kitchen, she saw that blood was streaking her hands. So she washed them in the sink.

Then she went to Angelo's room, crept silently in, barefoot, went around to the far side of the bed, and stretched out on the bed, on top of the covers, beyond him.

It was 2:00 in the afternoon. It was the next day. It was Thursday. She was lying now on her own cot, in Sunder's room, when she heard the noise, and knew it was a knock at the front door. She knew who it would be.

"The time has run out," Murray Guilfort said. He stood in the middle of the room, in front of Sunder's bed, and the reflection of light from stirring leaves outside rippled on the ceiling like upside-down water, or like the surface of water, if you were deep down and looking up at the surface.

He was saying: "No doubt he told you some cock-and-bull story, and no doubt you believed it, but last Saturday afternoon, he got beat up in Parkerton. I have taken great pains to ascertain all the facts. On that afternoon, in the company of a Negro girl, he attempted to purchase tickets at the Negro entrance of the Lyric Theater, and when refused, insisted, maintaining he was a Negro. That fact should indicate to you something of the character of this man, for it is difficult to see how even an Italian can be so lacking in self-respect as to claim to be a Negro. Further, it is difficult to conceive the degree of idiocy which permitted him to make the claim. He has been going back and forth in the streets of Parkerton for months, and he must realize that everybody would know who he is. And whatever the people in Washington, D.C., may do, Parkerton is not ready for race-mixing. There is one thing those people in Washington neglect, the very nature of law, I may say—how the folkways and mores of a society are related to—"

He stopped himself. He seemed to discover her presence.

"Listen," he said, "I don't pretend to know your motives,

Cassie, but I know that you would have none that my dear friend, who lies here before us, would not applaud. But I also know that you are laying yourself open to grave misinterpretations. Listen—that man must leave."

She looked at him, saying nothing. The light rippled on the ceiling.

"If he doesn't leave," he said, "I can promise you that the parole will be revoked."

"No—" she cried, but couldn't go on.

"Yes," he said, "and I am this very instant going into his room and tell him so."

He strode from the room, an erect figure in a well-pressed, well-cut gray suit that almost concealed the sagging belly of his age, his hair gray, his face gray, a gray figure moving through the light and shadow of the room, under the rippling reflection on the ceiling. He went out the door, into the hall, and she followed. He pushed open the door to that room, and entered, and she followed. The bed was empty.

With joyous relief, she recognized the fact, even as she caught the glitter of the spectacles as they swung toward her.

"He's gone hunting!" she said joyously. "That's where he's gone."

"Hunting," he finally said. "Yes," he said, "and one can surmise what he is hunting for."

He rapidly opened the bureau drawers. With a snap of authority he shoved them shut. He pulled aside the burlap over the doorway of the closet. He thrust his hand into the pockets of the plaid town jacket there. He drew something out and held it up for her to see. "Ah," he said, with satisfaction. "A man on parole may not carry this. It is a lethal weapon."

She stared at it. "It's just a hunting knife. Sunder, he used—"

"Sunder was never convicted of a crime of violence," he said. "Look—" and he pressed a button and the blade flicked out. "A switchblade—and more than four inches long. Illegal, parole or not. And look—a hilt—that shows what it's for. Not to sharpen pencils!"

He snapped the blade back, and examined the haft. "Brand new," he said. He looked accusingly at her. "The laws aren't enforced," he said, peevishly. "Little stores on back streets. Jews in pawnshops. Anything for a dime." He held it up again. "Look!" he uttered in outrage. "It's even got the price label pasted on the back."

Still holding it in his hand, he moved toward the door, ignoring her.

Back in Sunder's room, he said, "I'm going to wait. I'll wait as long as necessary to tell him he must go."

"You needn't wait," she said, evenly. "I'll tell him."

He inspected her face. "All right," he finally said. "But let it be clear. That man can have his parole revoked for that brawl last week. In fact, I used my influence or it would be revoked already. Tell him—" He paused. "Now here's my idea," he said. "If that fellow just went away—quietly away—I don't think anything would happen. Out of the state. Mind you, I'm not promising, but it would be just one dago less in Tennessee, and save the state some money. Otherwise—tell him—it is the pen. The P-E-N. Get that?"

Humbly, she inclined her head before him. "I'll do everything I can," she said.

"That's a sensible girl," he proclaimed. "Now I—" he stopped. "Why, I almost forgot," he said. He laid the knife down on the table by which he stood, and reached for his wallet.

He gave her the money. She signed the receipt. He picked up his hat from the split-bottom chair.

"You be sure to do it," he cautioned, giving her a last inquisitorial glance.

"Yes," she said. She could not wait for him to leave.

He came close, staring into her face. His voice, no longer in the tone of public address, began, and he was closer, leaning, his spectacles glittering. "Do you know who that girl was?" He demanded, very low, in almost a whisper.

She did not answer, fascinated by the glitter of the spectacles.

In that new tone, that was like the sly, whispering slickness of a blade making an incision in flesh, he was saying: "That girl—that nigger gal—she's from right here, on this place— that shack down the road, right under your nose." He was closer, the whisper even more whispery: "Now can you take that, her kicking up dirt in your face?"

But he had suddenly straightened up. It was as though he had never leaned, had never whispered. The public voice was back now: "But I feel it is my duty to insist that—"

But her own voice cut in, with a clear ring of triumph in it which, for the moment, was glorious, but which she could not understand. Her voice was saying: "Do you know, Murray, who that girl—that nigger gal—is?"

Then, while the eyes behind the glitter of the spectacles blinked at her, she said: "She is Sunderland's daughter."

And she began to giggle. For a moment she felt light-headed and giddy, like a girl giggling at a party.

"I don't believe it," Murray was saying, and that made everything seem funnier than ever.

Then, all at once, nothing seemed funny. The giggling stopped. She felt the giggles go dry in her throat, as though somebody had forced a big handful of dry bran into her mouth. She sat down on the split-bottom chair.

"Please go," she said.

He stood there, gaping like a fish.

"I'm tired," she said. "Tired."

He went out.

. . .

As soon as she heard the car start, she ran down the hall, into Angelo's room, and jerked back the burlap. The shotgun was there. Even in the dark corner of the closet, even if the metal wasn't bright like new, you could see it.

He had forgotten to take it. That was the awful part. He had not even bothered to remember to take it.

She could see him against the clear sunshine of the open place. She crouched by the hazel clump, which was coming into pale leaf now, and looked down the slope at him, while he, at the last edge of trees, was looking beyond, out into the open place. He stood there stiller than a post or a rock, but even at that distance, and with the back of his head toward her, she knew how sharp the breath would go in and out of him, and how hard and bright his eyes would be, like a bird's eyes, watching.

The shape that had been so still, like a post or a rock, was moving further away now, and it kept moving, on out into the open where the sunlight was. Then it stopped. There was another shape, and the two shapes were close together.

The other shape was a girl, with a bucket hanging loose from the end of each arm, and when the shape that was a man put its arms around that other shape, the arms were wide so that the arms of the girl-shape were crushed to her sides and the head of the man-shape bent down, forward, to make one shape.

Cassie Spottwood saw the back of the man-head, far off there, as it was bent forward. She held her breath. The head stayed bent, and she did not think she would ever breathe again. Then she saw the buckets come loose and fall, one on each side. The buckets made no sound falling, they were so far away.

The two shapes, which, even though moving now, were

almost one shape, went into the little stone house there, with the ruined roof. The buckets stayed outside, on the grass.

Cassie had given no name to those shapes: not to the man-shape, not to the girl-shape. She had pretended they had no names.

But now she moved down the path, swinging wide to the left, and slipped toward the wall of the stone house, at the end away from the open place. She pressed herself against the wall, her arms spread out against the rough stone, her fingers spread and her fingernails trying to grip the roughness. Her right cheek was pressed against the stone.

After a little, her legs got weak and shaky, and she slid down the wall, till she was on her knees. She slid lower, on the grass, crumpled against the wall, the left arm still upward, the fingers gripping at the stone.

The sound she heard—she did not know whether it came from beyond the wall, coming out through the holes in the roof, or whether it was only in her head.

She had lain there a long time, with her eyes shut, when the voice said: "You kin git up now."

She lifted her face from the stone and opened her eyes. There was the woman. Those old tennis shoes had made no sound. The woman stood some six feet away, so close that, with Cassie looking up from the ground, the head was swinging against the sky.

"They done tore it off now," the woman said, out of her twisted mouth. "Tore off that-air piece, and done gone." The woman waited. "Yeah," she said, "and I'se gonna go home and I find two buckets of fresh water on the table. And thar Charlene looken at me. Jes a-looken, and not keer. But I tole her—" She was shivering, as though with cold. "I tole her," she said, bitterly. "I say she do it again and I shoot the son-a-bitch, shoot him daid. I swore I'd—"

She discovered the shotgun she held, lifted it, shook it in the air, proving something. Then, all at once, with sad incredulity, she was staring at it. "Naw—" she said, shaking her head, "but naw. I did'n do nuthen. Nuthen 'cept lay in them cedars and watch you clawen to git in."

She took a step, in outrage demanded: "And you know why I did'n do nuthen!"

Cassie stared up at her.

"If'n I kills him," the woman said, "then they kills me, 'lectrocute me. Then who take keer of my Charlene?"

She drew back, and seemed to sink into herself. The shotgun, like a great weight, dragged down from her stretched-down right arm, flat against her skirt.

"But what I ought-a done," she said, slow, "and done long back. Kill that-air Sunder." She waited. "And then, long back, they kills me, and ain't no more me, ain't never no Charlene."

She waited, her face high above Cassie, darkening against the bright sky, the eyes gleaming from that shadow, saying: "That time I tole him—tole him 'bout me knocked up—yeah, then I ought-a done it." She paused, resumed: "Done jes crawled in the baid, and I says to him how I was knocked up. And he say—you know what he say, Sunder Spottwood say?"

Cassie stared up at her. She could not answer.

"I tell you what he say," the woman began again. "He laugh and say, hell I'll make it twins, and he roll over and make a grab, and I fights, but he gits me, lak a chimley fall on me, and he take it. Next thing, he layen thar snoren, and I git up and I stand on the floor. Doan know how long I stand thar, nekkid. Then I git me that butcher knife."

She waited, sunk into herself. The sky behind her was paling now.

Cassie, on the ground by the wall, staring up at her, almost whispering, asked: "You really got it—the knife—"

The woman's eyes remained fixed across the space, into the darkening trees: "Had that knife in my hand, and him layen thar, snoren. But he open his eyes." She turned to Cassie. "And you know what he done?"

The eyes of Cassie Spottwood, who was now propped higher against the wall, were on the woman's face.

"He jes look at that knife," the woman said, "and laugh. He say, durn, Arlita, if'n you wasn't gonna cut my thote. But look a-here, Arlita, he say, you lay that ole piddlen butcher knife down and crawl right in this baid. He laugh, and say, git in here, gal, and I'll bust you lak a ripe water-milyun been layen in the hot sun. Say, gitten late, gal, and got time jes to rip off one more, a-fore I got to go home to supper or maybe git my thote cut. He laugh, and me standen thar. Nekkid in the afternoon." She paused, sank into herself.

Then: "Maybe me not standen thar nekkid a-ready, in the middle of the afternoon, I would done it. Maybe I'd a-cut his thote." She sank again inward, into some torpor of memory. In a moment, struggling upward from the depth, she said: "But me nekkid, and him looken at me, I jes laid that-air knife on a cheer. And I crawls in that baid."

Cassie kept looking up at her, but the woman's eyes were again away. Until Cassie, the words wrenching bitterly out of her, said: "You got forty acres."

The woman looked down at her again. "Forty acres," she said. "Figgered with forty acres I get some man, help for Charlene, or who the baby be." Looking down at Cassie, she said: "But durn—ain't no man fool enough to come out here. So me—I work it. Work lak a dawg. Break myse'f down. Look at me!" She threw her arms wide, the shotgun held out there in the right hand. "Done got ole," she said, "ole and a-fore my time!"

She paused, studying the woman at her feet.

"But you—" she said then—"you ole, too!" She laughed, then stopped. "Yeah," she said, "you had'n been ole, would'n be layen thar. With the young 'un layen inside that-air wall, gitten it, and you layen out here clawen, yore slobber on the rock."

Cassie shut her eyes, and tried not to hear anything.

"Open them eyes," the voice said.

Cassie opened her eyes.

"Gonna say one thing," the woman said, her voice gone flat and weak. "I'm leaven here. This ain't no place for Charlene, her so young. Ought a-gone long back. But that Eye-tal-yun, you keep him off till I git gone. And if'n you caint larn how to keep holt on a man—" Her face was swinging above Cassie, the eyes gleaming in that shadowiness, the quick, dry laugh coming again out of that mouth, the voice strong again, demanding: "You know what Sunder say?"

"Sunder—" Cassie echoed.

"Yeah—Sunder," the woman said, "he say you warn't better'n a bolster."

Cassie was scrambling to her feet. "No!" she cried out. "No— he wouldn't—not to you—not even Sunder—"

The woman was looking at her, slowly and studiously. "You mean," she said, "he would'n say that 'bout no white woman. Not to a nigger. That what you mean?" She waited a moment as though for an answer, then added: "But old Sunder, he lay up in my baid and say it, and laugh."

Cassie stood there. She felt cold all over.

"But fer that Eye-tal-yun one," the woman was saying, "if'n you cain't do it one way, you better larn another. Lay a shot-gun on him and say you pull the trigger. Take a butcher knife, him in bed, and tell him you cut his thote." She paused. "Lak I ought a-done. With that Sunder."

She turned away.

"Listen," Cassie cried at her, at her back, "I don't believe it—about Sunder—about what he said—he wouldn't—"

The woman was four paces off. She stopped, but did not turn her body. She merely swiveled her head around on the shoulders. "Doan nobody keer what you believe," she said. "Not me, ner God."

Then, with weary indifference, the head swiveled the other way, and the woman was moving into distance.

Cassie had not entered the house till long after dark. It was still full light when she got there, but she had waited, crouching by the barn, out of sight. After dark, she saw the light come on in the kitchen, but from the angle where she crouched she could not see inside. She waited a time, then the light went off.

Now, lying on her cot, in Sunder's room, where, at last, she had groped her way, she was afraid. She was afraid that dawn would come. She did not know what would happen if dawn came, and she lay there shaking cold in all her clothes, even the brogans still on. It was about 2:30—still pitch dark—when she got up.

She turned the light on, the old floor lamp. Sunder was awake, she saw the eyes move, but she paid no mind. She was watching her hands as they did what she knew they would do, and she was humming a little song to herself. She knew that everything would be all right now, it was so easy.

The hands took off her clothes. She looked down at the whiteness of her body and saw the hands draw on the black lace panties and then adjust the black lace brassiere. The hands put on the red dress. Then they took the comb and brush and the red ribbon and fixed her hair. Looking at the mirror, she hummed the little song, which was pale and sweet, and which she did not know the name of.

Then, with the black patent-leather slippers on, she tiptoed down the hall.

Very gently, she opened the door and found her way to the far side of the bed, beyond his body. She lay down there, on top of the cover, looking up at the darkness, hearing his breath. After a while, she said, softly, "You're awake."

There was no answer.

"I know you're awake," she said, even more softly. "But don't say anything. You don't have to say anything."

Then, after a while: "I know—Angelo—I know you've been trying to say something—ever since—"

But she could not go on. The words she could not say were up in the dark above her, but they would not come down so she could say them. So she waited a long time, and heard his breath.

Then she said: "Murray Guilfort—he came. This afternoon."

She was sure that she heard the catch of breath.

Then: "He says you have to go."

Then: "If you don't go, he says they will put you back in. In that—that place."

She knew that that breath in the dark had stopped. It stopped for a long time. Then she heard it again.

And said: "But I won't let them, Angelo. We'll fool them, Angelo. We'll fool them." She began to giggle. She giggled deliciously in the dark. "We'll just put you upstairs," she began when the giggles were over. "I'll tell him you're gone. We'll fix this room like you're gone, and he'll see it. Then that part of the month when he comes—it's always around the first—you'll just stay away from the house. In the afternoon. It's always afternoon when he comes."

She reached out in the dark and found his hand on the cover. It was as though she had been able to see in the dark, the way she found it. The hand she found was nerveless and limp as though he were asleep. It was not heavy, but it lay like a dead weight in her hand.

She said: "But there's something else, Angelo. You've been wanting to talk to me, I know. But you didn't have to. For I know—yes, Angelo, my darling, I know how it is. And remember, I told you—remember that night when I told you— how I didn't ever want you to feel locked up again. How I wanted you to feel free to go out the door. I still want you to— Angelo. If you have to."

Then, softer than ever, she said: "And when you come back —when you come in the door—I'll be there—for you love me a little—yes, Angelo, you did love me a little, didn't you?"

She was sure she felt the hand tighten on hers, even if it wasn't awfully tight.

She lay there a long time holding that hand in the dark. Then she heard the sound from down the hall. She knew immediately what was wrong. She had left the light on, and if you left the light on at night, Sunder would not be able to sleep, and he would make his noise.

She crept out and went to that room. But after she had turned off the light, he kept making his noise, so she knew she had to take care of him. It was almost half an hour before she came back.

But the door was shut. It was shut and locked.

She crouched against the door, not believing that it was true that she was crouching against that locked door. After a time, she lay on the floor against the door, with her eyes shut. In that way, she tried not to exist at all, and if she could make herself not exist then nothing would exist.

But as she lay on the floor, they all were standing there, all of them—Sunder and the woman, Murray, the girl, Cy Grinder, and Angelo. They were all laughing.

Even Angelo.

(224)

CHAPTER NINE

🌲🌲🌲🌲🌲🌲🌲🌲🌲🌲🌲 In the first flush of waking it was like being young again. Or had he waked from a dream of being young, to find the dream flooding into the moment when his eyes opened to the June sunlight and birdsong?

Then, remembering what day it was, he felt the sense of power come to focus. It felt good to be Murray Guilfort. He got up.

In the bathroom, on impulse, he did a few tentative bends to touch his fingers to his toes. He looked at his belly, then shook his head with disgust. He would go to a masseur, he would get a set of exercises, he had the old stables here on the place, and he would keep horses. He had, all at once, a vision of himself standing on the front steps, in early sunlight, before breakfast, trim in the waist, wearing jodhpurs, while a grizzled Negro man led up a fine, nervous, glistening bay mare. He would swing to the saddle in the dappled light.

At the office he would say, "Well, there's nothing really like a brisk canter before breakfast, I mean—to brace a man, and—"

By this time he was taking a cold shower. He had not taken one for years.

As he opened the white gate between the white wooden gateposts, he looked up the brick walk to the house. The house, it was not quite as pure—that was the word he liked—as his own house, which had been Bessie's house, but which, since her death, had become his own, not merely in the legal sense but in a deeper way, with a mystic history replacing the dreary factuality, hanging like a nimbus about the image of the house as it floated in his mind. But if the Parker place, the gate of which he was entering, wasn't as pure as Durwood, it was still the best thing on Parker Street, and had stood here long before there had been any town at all.

He looked up the crumbling brick walk, shaded by maples, up to the white bulk of the house. He turned and looked back at his new convertible—again a white one—now only three weeks old. It waited there beyond the white gate, in the sunlight beyond the shade of the maples, beautiful like an advertisement. Feeling strong and young, he strode toward the house.

Yes, he had arranged things well. Today when Cassie Spottwood came out of that front door side by side with Edwina Parker, she would come clothed in the triple brass of respectability. *Aes triplex,* Murray murmured.

As for Edwina, she could use the money. He had made it discreetly clear that everything would be worth her while, financially speaking, not to mention giving the old fool a ringside seat at a murder trial and a respectable reason for being there at all, and not to mention the inside track of chaperone to the widow-and-star-witness.

Miss Edwina, the mush-mouthed old gossip herself, opened the front door, even before Murray's fingers had released the knocker. Obviously, she had been lurking at the door, waiting. There she stood, just inside the shadowy hall—the white hair, so white it looked blue in the shadows, piled in a complicated way on her head, her blue eyes shining bright as a baby's, her baby-pink wattles shaking ever so little with the motion of her head, which, he surmised, was trembling with expectancy and pleasure, her diamond pendant decorously gleaming against the bosom of the black silk dress. She laid a hand on his arm, came close to him, exuding an odor of orris root and peppermint, and said: "Shush, shush," before he could utter his greeting.

On tottery tiptoe, she led him into the front parlor. In that place of glimmer and shadow, she stood beside a table whereon a great bell of glass housed waxen warblers perched on a massive garland of waxen orange blossom, and again touched his arm, and, with the odor of orris root and peppermint now overwhelmed by that of furniture oil, said: "I think she's all right."

"Yes," he replied, studying Miss Edwina's now preternaturally bright eyes.

"Except," she said, "she is still in a state of shock. Even after all these weeks. If others cannot see this, I can."

"Yes," he said, wondering if he had taken Cassie out of that nursing home in Nashville too soon, had exposed her too soon to Miss Edwina's merciless sweetness. But he had told Cassie, over and over, to keep her mouth shut. She was a witness—she was the key witness in a trial for murder—did she understand? So she should say nothing until she was on the stand. Now looking into the avid gleam of Miss Edwina's china blue eyes, he knew that everything was all right, she hadn't got a shred of real information out of Cassie.

"She wants to confide in me," Miss Edwina was saying. "For the last two nights I have sat by her bed, and she held my hand like a child till she fell asleep." Then she added: "I know she wants to confide."

"I'm sure she does," Murray murmured.

"She tries," Miss Edwina said, and shook her head in such vigorous commiseration that the baby-pink wattles swung from side to side in the shadows. "But it's the shock," she explained.

"Yes—the shock," he murmured.

"I hope you will approve of the way I have dressed her," Miss Edwina said. "Poor thing—out in that remote spot. She had forgotten what the world is like."

"Yes," he said.

"I took her to Nashville," Miss Edwina said. "In a city like that she wouldn't be a matter of comment. Nobody would know who she was."

"Very wise," he said, dutifully.

"I hope I didn't spend too much. But you said you wanted things very nice. Dignified and nice and refined."

"Yes," he said, and in that instant saw, with a sound like the brass gong sounding for dinner in an expensive resort hotel— he saw what lay in the brown paper bag, in the safe, in his study at Durwood. It was what, that morning while Sheriff Smathers and the deputies and Dr. Blanton were in the old dining room with the body, he had drawn from the firebox of the range in the Spottwood kitchen, and concealed in a brown paper bag, under his raincoat, and taken out and locked in the trunk of the white Roadmaster. The fire in the range had been too low, and had done its work very imperfectly, and now, standing in the gloom of Miss Edwina's parlor, he saw it all: the red silky cloth, with the black charred holes in it; the one surviving slipper, blistered and warped by heat, but with patches of patent leather still bright on it, with the heel intact, tall and spiky; the black lace, in tatters but identifiable as underwear—yes, he knew what it would be like over the white flesh.

Nausea gripped him, his knees shook. He managed to extract his watch from the watch pocket of his trousers, and stood there holding it with the Phi Beta Kappa key dangling. He got control of himself. "We must go," he said.

"She's waiting in the back parlor, the dear thing," Miss Edwina said.

"We must hurry," Murray said, standing there in the shadows that smelled of furniture oil, the watch in his hand. "We have a duty," he said. "That monster—he must not go unpunished. Sunderland Spottwood was my friend."

He snapped the watch shut. The click was tiny and precise in the shadows, a glinting sound, like the point of a needle catching light.

Suddenly, Murray again felt young and victorious. He would avenge the friend.

"Please get her," he said.

"Listen, Jack," he had said to Jack Farhill, who was to conduct the prosecution in his stead, he being a witness, "there's just one thing to remember about this list." He put a well-manicured, waxen finger on the nearer of the two sheets of the jury list on top of the great mahogany desk in his study at Durwood, under the discreet glow of the lamp.

Jack Farhill looked at him in deferential question. "Yes, sir?" he said.

"Women," Murray said. "There are seven on the list and only two are safe."

"Yes, sir?"

The white forefinger found one name, then another. "Mrs.

Buckner, Miss Poindexter—they're safe. And you know why?"

"No, sir."

"In their eyes anything Miss Edwina Parker has ever touched is sacred. Even the garbage coming out of the Parker place. And she has touched Cassie Spottwood. Get it?"

"Yes, sir."

"As for the other five, be sure to reserve challenges to take care of them if need be. Some of them might be, shall we say, suffering from female envy of Miss Edwina. And that young Gracey woman, she went to one of those girls' colleges up East somewhere and no telling what ideas she got."

"I hear tell she's sort of a secret nigger-lover," Jack Farhill had said.

"She might be a secret dago-lover by the same token. But women and juries, it's bad medicine. This dago, now, he has the sort of look some fool woman getting middle-aged might go for. Looks like those old dago movie stars, and that fact and the menopause don't make for a dispassionate weighing of the evidence, you might say."

"Yes, sir," Jack Farhill had said.

And here was the duly impaneled jury, already beginning to sweat, even if it was only morning and the accustomed fans had been distributed and were in motion—fans made of tough, glazed cardboard stapled to a wooden handle with, on one side, the picture of an Indian maiden in a birch-bark canoe, and on the other, an advertisement for Billingsboy's Furniture and Undertaking, which firm always provided complimentary fans for a summer jury.

Murray hadn't bothered to attend the preliminaries of the trial, which had occupied the last three days of the week just past. Jack Farhill would do well enough, he had thought.

Now scrutinizing the faces of the jurymen, face by face, he decided that Jack had done well enough, too. Run-of-the-mill, he decided. And a run-of-the-mill verdict, that was what you wanted.

He looked across at the table where Leroy Lancaster sat beside the dago, tall, thin, head bald with a fringe of sandy hair, horn glasses, blue suit unpressed. Leroy wouldn't cause much trouble. Poor Leroy, a good legal education, University of Virginia, but there he was, forty-five years old and didn't make $5,000 a year. Always trying to get elected to something on some fool platform. Well, this case was his level. Assigned by the court to defend a pauper, an ex-con, a dago, and, he added grimly, guilty as hell to boot. Natural rope-bait. Only in Tennessee, they got fried.

No, Leroy wouldn't make any trouble. Leroy was a gentleman.

He stole a glance to his left. Miss Edwina, straight as a ramrod and unsweating in her black silk, a black hat with a small tangle of black veil set high on the complicated structure of white hair, stared straight over the well-populated courtroom as into infinite vacancy.

Cassie Spottwood, between him and Miss Edwina, was looking steadfastly down at her own gloved hands, clasped on her lap.

He could see that the hands inside the black gloves were straining in the clasp. He leaned at her. "Try to relax a little," he whispered. "Everything is under control."

Yes, everything. He looked sidewise at the dress she was wearing. Mourning black, but it wasn't a bag. Miss Edwina had spent some money on this. But more important, Miss Edwina had taste. The hat, just another black hat, but more than that, too. Funny, not one person in this hick courtroom would see anything except just another black dress and black hat, but they'd feel something. The way that dress was at the waist, and at the same time dignified and refined. You couldn't be too careful about details.

The cardboard fans in the jury box stirred the bright air. Now and then a fan would stop and a juror would stare at the print on the back of the fan. Now the sergeant-at-arms stood by to supervise an old Negro man who was handing a glass to each of the jurors. This done, he brought a white enamel bucket full of water in which a ten-pound chunk of ice gently bobbed, and with a white enamel dipper filled each glass.

Murray was thinking how Bessie, after she put on weight, used to sweat inside her clothes.

It had been summer when Bessie died, and even if there was an air-conditioning unit in their bedroom at Durwood, they had to change the sheets three times a day, she sweated so much. Now, he sat there in the courtroom, with a grinding, indefinable misery, and thought of Bessie's sheets wet with sweat. In an access of the old, irremediable awfulness, he let his face sink into his hands, and demanded why did everything in the world have to be the way it was. What was happening to him now—this very moment—was what had happened in the church where the funeral was; he had suddenly sunk his face into his hands, thinking of those sheets.

But now this was not a church and it was not a funeral, and everything—yes, everything—was under perfect control.

So he jerked his head up and swept the room with a glare to freeze everything into its proper place.

The story unfolded. It unfolded with magisterial certainty and hypnotic ease, moving toward the predictable conclusion, but even in that predictability, suspense was sustained by delays, by waverings, by acceleration, by the pacing, by the dramatic silence when Jack Farhill would unexpectedly dismiss a witness to leave the last word of the witness hanging in the air.

Yes, Murray decided, that Farhill boy was learning his trade. Well, hadn't he taught Farhill?

Pace, he would say to Jack Farhill, yes, pace is the secret.

On the morning of Friday, April 11, at 9:25, testified Micah Spann, white, aged 67, of Spottwood Corners, storekeeper, Cassie Spottwood had entered his store. She had sort of hung on the door a second, the rain dripping off her hair, for it was raining, then she stumbled to a coil of rope and sat down—fell down, you might say. She said they had done killed Sunder. For him to call Murray Guilfort, in Parkerton. She got that much out of her mouth, then keeled over.

He yelled for his old woman—wife, he meant—to come from the house, and she came, the house being set just back and to one side of the store. They got Cassie Spottwood to the house and laid her down, and he called Mr. Guilfort, not even bothering to reverse the charges, and told somebody who worked for Mr. Guilfort, Mr. Guilfort not yet being at his office. But they must of got him quick, for he came to the Corners pretty fast, with the Sheriff and Dr. Blanton and two deputies.

First they went in his house, where Cassie Spottwood was a-laying on the bed. She had come running and falling down, there in the mud on the road. You could tell from the shape her dress was in. She was too done in now even to talk. They got holt of Dr. Tucker, who lived at the Corners, to come take care of her.

Then Mr. Guilfort and them, they all went off.

That was the way the word had got out. The wires of the telephone at the Spottwood house had been cut, so Miles Cardigan, the deputy who had made the discovery, testified.

Not close to the phone, where you could see it easy, but at the baseboard near the front door. The Corners was the nearest phone. It was three miles.

At 10:36, as Sheriff Smathers testified, the Sheriff and deputies, followed by Murray Guilfort and the doctor in the former's car, arrived at the Corners. It was 10:52 by the time Dr. Blanton examined the body of the deceased. Dr. Blanton set the time of the death at approximately 7:30 a.m. The death was caused by the blade of a knife, entering the lateral ribcage in the posterior portion of the left axillary area between the third and fourth ribs, to puncture the lower lobe of the left lung and pass through to puncture both the ascending portion of the aorta and the left auricle. The wound, Dr. Blanton said, had apparently been made by setting the tip of the blade under the lifted body and applying pressure from above. There had been a minimum of external hemorrhage, because the knife had been left in the wound and because the victim was in no condition to resist and widen the wound. It was testified by Dr. John Tucker, resident at Spottwood Corners, whose patient the victim was, that the victim had been paralyzed for twelve years, from the neck downward.

At this information, a woman in the courtroom began to sob loudly. Between sobs, she would cry out, "And oh—he couldn't even move!"

After the woman had been quieted, Jack Farhill received from the clerk an object which he offered to Dr. Blanton, now recalled to the stand. Dr. Blanton identified the knife, a switch-blade, as the lethal weapon. He had, he testified, drawn it from the wound in the back of the deceased, in the presence of Sheriff Smathers.

Jack Farhill recovered the switchblade. With the blade now recessed in the handle, he held it high. He touched the button, and the blade flicked out, glittering.

"This weapon," he proclaimed, "is what is commonly known as a frog-sticker. It is a switchblade. Regard it well."

Leroy's objection was overruled.

Farhill stood toying with the object in his hand, apparently forgetting all the eyes fixed on it. Then he lifted his head, and spoke in a ruminative tone. "It is not designed for innocent utility. Nor—" and his voice rose sharply "—for innocent sport. It is designed for one purpose, and one purpose only!"

Farhill's voice was loud, overriding the cry of "Objection, objection," and continuing: "And that, I assert, is the purpose to which it was put!"

Judge Potts sustained Leroy's request that the passage be struck from the record. "I instruct the jury to disregard it," he said.

Farhill bowed to the Judge, ever so slightly, and stepped to the jury box and handed the knife to the first juryman.

The juryman played with it, making the blade flick out, sheathing it, making it flick out again. He was happily engrossed, like a boy. Reluctantly, he passed it on. It went from hand to hand, while Farhill patiently waited.

When all had examined it, Farhill, with a bow of thanks, received it, and restored it to the clerk, requesting that it be marked as Exhibit A.

And all the while Cassie Spottwood was staring down at her clasped hands.

When Murray, Miss Edwina, and Cassie got back to the house for the noon recess, Dr. Lightfoot, Miss Edwina's physician, was already there, just in case. But Cassie said she was all right, if she could just lie down a little before lunch. Lunch, as a matter of fact, was served her in bed—broth, a chicken wing, ambrosia, coffee. Then she lay on her back, eyes closed. Dr. Lightfoot, now and then saying something in his soothing voice, sat beside the bed in the darkened room, until time to get ready.

In the hall, Miss Edwina lurked, waiting for him to come out. "She'll make it," he whispered, "I think."

"Thank you," Miss Edwina said, and with eyes going as bright in the dark hall as the diamond of the pendant at her breast, laid hand to the doorknob, and entered.

Back in the courtroom, Cassie sat as before, black-gloved hands clasped on lap, head bowed. Now and then, as the testimony proceeded, Murray surreptitiously studied her. Suddenly, he knew. He knew that, in spite of the position of the head, the eyes were not fixed on the gloved hands. The eyes were fixed on that man, the dago, who, wearing a fresh white shirt, no tie but the collar buttoned, no coat, with hair slicked down as though nothing mattered but that shoe-polish slickness of hair, sat there at the table, not giving a damn it looked like, sitting there with eyes now bright and watchful but somehow relaxed and unconcerned.

Murray looked at him across the space, and longed to leap up and shout: "I'll show you!—you won't sit like that when they throw the switch."

Instead, hearing the beating of his own heart, he leaned at Cassie. "Don't you worry," he whispered, "we'll fix him. Never again will he—"

He stopped. *Never what?*

For a fraction of a second, while no word would come as answer, he saw the woman's body on a bed, glimmering white in darkness, and a door was opening. It was opening. Then, that picture for which there was no word, and whose existence he had refused to recognize even as he saw it, was gone.

He wet his dry lips. Then the lips said, whispering: "He'll never escape."

Cassie's head was still bowed, but now he saw that she was really staring at the hands.

He leaned at her again: "He won't look toward you. It is a mark of his guilt."

She gave no sign of having heard.

He leaned again: "You'll be next," he said. "Now just relax. Just tell what happened. What you told me and the Sheriff. As simply as you can."

She did not make a sign.

He leaned closer. "Look at me," he whispered, but with command. "Look me in the eye."

She raised her eyes to him.

"Good," he whispered. "Now when you talk you look directly at Jack Farhill. Jack is your friend, remember."

Her name was being called.

All right, Murray reflected, watching her black-clad figure move toward the witness chair. She had lifted her head when Jack Farhill spoke to her. She had focused her eyes on him. It was all right.

He didn't have to worry. She was looking straight at Jack Farhill. Her eyes had never wavered. It didn't matter that you could scarcely hear her voice. In that quietness there was the whispery voice.

This was fine, this strange whisperiness. The fact that everybody was straining, and the jury too, made it all the more important to attend to every syllable. It made every word seem more true.

That whispery voice was saying that she got up at 5:00 a.m. to take care of her husband. Then to bathe him and change the sheets. She tried to change the sheets every other day, but she sometimes couldn't make it, especially in winter when it was harder to wash and dry sheets.

"Poor thing," a woman's voice was saying from back in the courtroom, not a whisper, out loud, "all them sheets!"

The gavel of the judge came down.

Good, Murray was thinking. That kind of remark, that sympathy, was not wasted on the jury.

She had shaved her husband, the whispery voice was continuing. It was 6:40 when she shaved him. This was what the clock in the kitchen said when she carried the pan of soapy water back there to pour out. Then he—the man—came in.

"Now, Mrs. Spottwood," Jack Farhill interrupted, "please excuse me, but who came in?"

"An-gel-o Pas-set-to," the voice said, in a slow, careful way, giving each syllable its separate value, like saying a lesson painfully learned.

"You mean the accused?" Jack Farhill demanded, leaning toward her, looking her in the eye, one arm pointing toward Angelo Passetto.

She did not follow the gesture. Her gaze wavered from Jack Farhill's face, but then dropped to fix on her own hands, clasped there on her lap.

For a moment, unease took Murray. But then he knew it was all right, for she was again looking at Jack Farhill and her voice was saying that the man had brought in an armful of stove wood. He was a little late doing it that morning. He usually did it before she got back to the kitchen. Had she noticed anything else unusual? Yes, he had on his town pants and shoes. The patent-leather shoes. She didn't think much of that at the time. He sometimes went to town. He went in the car. Sometimes he went to get stuff for the work he did around the place. He was always a good worker, she would say that for him, good at fixing things.

No, she didn't know for a long time he had to go to town to see a man about his parole from the penitentiary. She didn't know till Mr. Guilfort—Mr. Murray Guilfort—told her. Mr. Guilfort told her to tell him—that man—that he had to leave the place.

But what was funny, that morning, even seeing the patent-leather shoes, she forgot it was the day he said he would leave for good. That morning she'd been so worried about Sunder, she'd just forgot. She'd told him the day before he had to leave right away, but now she forgot.

Yes, after he left the kitchen she made up the fire. Later she thought she heard a car start, but decided not, not ever thinking he'd take her car, thinking he'd walk to the Corner and catch a ride.

When had she thought she heard the car?

She didn't know for sure, but the coffee was coming to a boil by then.

A little later, she wondered why he didn't come for his breakfast. She always served him first, so she wouldn't be rushed with Sunder. Sunder, he couldn't feed himself. It took time to feed him.

She was sorry, she didn't mean to get off on that. But when he—that man—didn't come, she went into the hall and called. She didn't want his eggs to get cold. Even if he was going to leave today, she didn't want anybody to eat eggs cold and getting tough like whit-leather, and eggs cost money. Her own chickens weren't big enough yet to be laying and—

Her eyes weren't on Jack Farhill's face anymore. She stopped, and her gaze fixed again on the clasped hands.

Jack Farhill begged her pardon, but would she please tell what she did next.

She got her eyes back on his face, and said she was sorry. What she did next, she said, was to put the eggs in the warmer, even if they would get tough as whit-leather, to wait for him to come. And she fixed Sunder's breakfast, and took herself a quick cup of coffee, like she always did before feeding him, for it took a lot of time to feed him and a cup of coffee always helped. No, she couldn't say exactly what time it was then. She just picked up the tray for Sunder. Then she—

She stopped.

"Yes?" Jack Farhill said, in gentle question.

She was staring at him, as at a stranger.

"Yes?" he said. "And you went to the pantry door?"

"The pantry door—" she echoed. "I went to the pantry door." She stopped again.

"Yes, Mrs. Spottwood?"

"I went to the pantry," she said, the whisper lower than ever.

She stopped. She tried again. When the sound came, it was as thin as silence: "I pushed open the door and—"

The mouth moved but made no sound.

Farhill had stepped to her side. "Did you go in the room?" he asked, almost in a whisper.

Nodding, she managed a sound which must have been yes.

"Did you go to the bed, Mrs. Spottwood?" he asked.

Finally she nodded.

"What did you see, Mrs. Spottwood?"

She stared at him in a wild beseeching.

He leaned at her, and smiled pityingly, and his voice was a whisper. "What did you see, Mrs. Spottwood?"

The eyes were wider. The mouth made its motion without sound.

He stood, waiting in patience, smiling the pitying smile, never taking his eyes from her face.

The mouth was moving, with no sound.

Quietly, Farhill turned toward Leroy Lancaster. "Your witness, sir," he said, in an almost inaudible tone, the tone one uses in turning from a sickbed. He bowed toward Mrs. Spottwood, and stepped aside.

The defense declined cross-examination.

Yes, Murray thought, he had known that Leroy wouldn't cross-examine. Leroy would have been a fool to hack at a lady suffering like that, and a widow to boot. To cross-examine under those circumstances—it would have been suicide.

Not that it could matter much anyway. Whatever Leroy could do, it was all play-acting. Play-acting just for the sake of appearances. He looked at Leroy, there by the dago in the white shirt, with no tie and the collar buttoned.

He realized all at once that the court was being adjourned.

At Miss Edwina's house, as they all sat with Dr. Lightfoot and had some of her good coffee, Murray said: "Now, Cassie, you have done splendidly. You will not be called tomorrow, as Leroy Lancaster assures me, and it is my private opinion that you will not be called at all. So you and Miss Edwina might go to a movie tomorrow. Get your mind off things."

Miss Edwina's face had, all at once, shown a trace of cloud.

"No," Cassie said.

"But—" Murray began.

"No," she said, "I'll go. To court, I mean."

"But—"

"I've got to go," she said, in a voice as flat, distant, and final as a voice dealing with what had already happened, not with what might happen or not happen.

"Oh, yes," Miss Edwina was saying brightly, perking up no end, "we'll go!" Then turning to Cassie: "That is, my dear, if you really feel you must."

By noon the next day things were shaping up nicely.

The knife, the switchblade, was identified by Mr. Spann, recalled to the stand, as one he had sold that "Charley gal." Well, her name was something like that. He had sold it to her on April 9. It was Wednesday, he was sure. Mr. Spann was, in fact, excessively anxious to be exact, to please in all respects.

And well he might be cooperative, Murray mused. Jack Farhill had pointed out to him that to offer for sale such a weapon was illegal, but this time the offense might just happen to be overlooked.

There was only one question under cross-examination by Leroy. Did he, Mr. Spann, know the father of Charlene?

Mr. Spann did not. He didn't have time to go around sorting out fathers of niggers.

The remark received a gratifying public response, even as the gavel fell.

Why the hell, Murray asked himself, hadn't Jack headed it off with an objection?

But how could it matter? For the girl Charlene admitted buying the knife. He—the dago—had asked her to. He had been beat up in Parkerton. Yes, trying to go with her in the door for colored at the Lyric Theater. He said he was colored, and folks beat him up, for they knew he wasn't, and he was race-mixing in the Lyric. He didn't fight back, just took it, and later on he told her he knew she thought he was a coward, and she said no, she looked at him that way because she was so sorry and him beat up, but he said he would never take another beating, not even to keep her out of trouble, for her to buy him a knife, he had seen a knife at the Corners, so he gave her the money and she got it like he said. He was too beat up to go get it hisself.

She was weeping on the stand.

"And when did you give the knife to Angelo Passetto?" Jack Farhill was asking, softly, soothingly.

There was no answer, only the sobbing.

"When?" Jack Farhill demanded, in a voice that was, suddenly, cold and bright, like the blade flicking out.

The sobs stopped. She looked up. "Wednesday," she said. "Wednesday afternoon. Down to the ole dairy house."

"And Sunderland Spottwood—Mr. Spottwood—was killed Friday morning—the next Friday, April 11. Is that right?" Jack Farhill said, in a voice again soft and soothing.

The girl finally managed to say yes.

There was only one question under cross-examination. "What is your date of birth, Charlene?"

This time there was an objection. Farhill had, Murray observed to himself, waked up.

The objection was sustained.

The pattern came clearer and clearer, and by the end of the third day it was complete. The fight at the Lyric Theater was amply documented. The outline of the flight up into Kentucky, heading north, was established: the car had stopped twice, once for gas, once for food, observed by reliable witnesses. The officer in charge of the roadblock on the south end of the bridge over the Ohio to Evansville, Indiana, had described the arrest. Arlita Benton had testified as to the time of her daughter's disappearance.

Except for the handling of Arlita, the defense had been sluggish in cross-examination. The evidence which she had offered was simple. When Charlene hadn't come back from the spring with the morning water, she had gone to hunt her. She had found the buckets by the old dairy house and figured that that Eye-tal-yun had her off in the woods. Yeah, he'd been chasing her a long time but she—Charlene, she meant—held him off till lately.

She hunted all over them woods, then she found the place of fresh car tracks in the grass, clear marked, for that morning it was raining off and on, and mud was fresh. Then she come to the big house. Come to the kitchen door, and the door was open, but she knocked and yelled a-fore she went in. She

knocked and yelled at the door to that-air pantry, then she
went in. She never got to whar Sunder was. She was sorry, she
meant Mr. Spottwood.

Soon as she got in the pantry she heard voices coming in the
kitchen door, the Sheriff and them men. She told 'em how she
was hunting Charlene and that Eye-tal-yun, and they said, by
God, they was hunting 'em too. They brought her to town and
helt her. She was a may-tearl witness, they told her.

Yeah, she knowed the time Charlene left out for the spring.
She seen the clock and it was late. Twenty-nine minutes to
eight o'clock. It was five minutes to walk to that-air spring.

Arlita was the only soft spot, Murray had long back decided.
Leroy would naturally go after her, even if the time was wrong
for her to have stabbed Sunder. It was the only thing in the
way of a shadow of a doubt.

Leroy, of course, took the witness back over the period of
hunting in the woods, every spot, tree, stone, and leaf. Having
completed the tour, he demanded: "Are you sure?"

When she said, yes, she was sure, he said: "You have a
splendid memory, Arlita. Now tell me, the relation of the bed
in which Mr. Spottwood lay, to the big table."

"I—I—" Arlita began. Then: "But I never went in thar."

"Never, Arlita—never in your life?"

"What I mean, was—"

"When, Arlita?"

After a long pause, while her yellow face grew streaked and
strained, she said: "That week—Sunday 'twas—a-fore he got
kilt—"

"Before who got killed?"

"Sunder—" she began, then stopped.

"Who do you mean to say, Arlita?"

"Mr. Spottwood."

"Were you accustomed to call Mr. Spottwood by the name of Sunder, Arlita?"

The objection was sustained.

"Why, Arlita, did you say you were never in that room?"

"I thought you was meanen—"

"Was meaning the morning of the murder? Is that it?"

"Yassuh." This sullenly.

"Well, why didn't you simply say yes. You knew about the bed. Why didn't you tell the simple truth, Arlita?"

She stared at him in her smoldering rage, the yellow of her face again streaked. "You did'n give me no chanst," she managed.

Then Leroy Lancaster made her repeat the wanderings in the woods. "Now," he said, "we're back to the room, Arlita."

"But I ne'er went in that-air room, and you ain't gonna—"

"Oh, but you did go there, Arlita. You said so yourself. Sunday before the murder." He tightened, quickened. "And why did you go? Who was there? What happened? What did you do?"

"That's not one question, that's four," objected Farhill.

"Objection sustained," Judge Potts said.

Leroy bowed to Judge Potts, then turned to Arlita: "Take them one at a time. Why did you go there?"

She stared at him.

"Why did you go, Arlita?"

"To tell her—" and she pointed suddenly to Cassie—"tell her to keep that-air Eye-tal-yun off Charlene."

"Who else was there?"

"Sund—" she caught herself.

"What were you going to say, Arlita?"

"Mr. Spottwood. He was thar."

"In the bed?"

"Layen in the baid."

"Did you mention his name while you were in the room?"

After a long wait, she said: "I doan rick-o-lict."

"In the woods, after the spring house, where did you go next, Arlita?"

"Up the hill, south, tow'ds that ole dead-fall pine tree."

"You see, Arlita, you have a splendid memory. For small things. Now for a big one. In that room, on Sunday, the sixth day of April, in the middle of the afternoon, did you utter the name of Sunderland Spottwood?"

"I doan rick-o-lict."

"All right, you don't recollect that. But did you touch him?"

She stared again, her face again drawn and streaked, the yellow gone ashen about the mouth.

"Listen, Arlita. Did you, in any way whatsoever, make bodily contact with Mr. Sunderland Spottwood?"

She stared, waiting.

Finally: "Yassuh."

"How?"

She waited.

Then: "I tetched him with my finger."

"I object!" Jack Farhill was shouting.

She held the right forefinger in the air. She was looking incredulously at it, as though alone.

Christ, Murray thought, *you can't cover everything.* You certainly couldn't cover everything if your only source of information was Cassie Spottwood, who was a very imperfect source. Well, speaking of sources, how the hell did Leroy know what had happened in that room?

Then, looking at the dago, sitting there in his white shirt, not even sweating to speak of, Murray knew. A triple play. Arlita to Charlene to dago. And dago to Leroy.

But muddy the waters—that was all Leroy could hope for.

For, like the old joke, the man stole the hog. The dago had killed Sunder.

"Where did you touch Mr. Spottwood?" Leroy resumed.

"On the fahr'd," she said, saying it even before the objection from Jack Farhill.

The objection was sustained.

Leroy hesitated a moment. "At what date," he began, "did your common-law husband—one Jackson Benton, they called him Jabbo—leave Spottwood Valley, not to return?"

As before, even before the objection could be uttered, the woman had flared out of her sullenness: "Yeah, him, run off soon's war got goen, got hisself kilt and me no 'surance, ne'er named me to git it, his sister, she—"

The gavel had drowned her out.

Leroy waited patiently until her breath got back to normal: "What, Arlita, was the date of the birth of your child, Charlene?"

The objection was sustained.

What did it matter, Murray thought, if everybody in Cardwell County did know that Sunderland Spottwood had knocked up a yaller gal? It mattered exactly nothing. The man stole the hog. The dago had knifed Sunder.

So why did Leroy have to rub a lady's nose in the fact that her husband had a hankering for poontang—had, in fact, betrayed her with a high-yaller wench?

Leroy was a gentleman, yes. But he was also a lawyer.

No, you couldn't blame Leroy. He had to make the motions.

He looked sidewise at Cassie. She was staring at the clasped hands. He was sure she was looking there, not across at the dago.

Or was she?

. . .

Leroy had Arlita again going through the woods. Coming to the kitchen door. Entering. Entering the pantry.

He was demanding: "And you never stepped beyond that pantry? You are sure, Arlita?"

He stepped silently to her. He said: "You hated him, didn't you, Arlita?"

"Objection, objection!" Farhill cried out.

But that woman, the face streaked pale and the eyes wide, was shouting: "I knows what you tryen to do. Make lak I kilt Sunder—yeah, he knocked me up, if that's what you mean and I ought-a kilt him—kilt him long back, but—"

The gavel was pounding out the sound of her voice.

The court was recessed. After the recess Murray himself took the stand. He rehearsed his warnings to Mrs. Spottwood. Yes, he had urged her to send the accused away. Even if her need was desperate for help on the place, and no other help was available. He had tried to persuade her to move into town. But she had refused. Out of sentiment, he had supposed. But after the events at the Lyric Theater, Mrs. Spottwood had consented to send the accused away.

He identified the black purse, which had been found on the floor of the back of the Spottwood car, when the arrest was made, up in Kentucky—the black purse which he had seen every time he had brought the money to the Spottwood house. As for the money, the receipts, dated and duly signed by Cassie Spottwood, were offered in evidence, and checks, signed by Murray Guilfort and marked *For S. Spottwood*, but made to *Cash* and paid at the People's Bank.

He described the hiding place of the purse, the loose brick, the cavity in the chimney. The bills recovered from the accused he could not identify, but there had been 15 tens and 10 fives, all new and crisp, and the amount spent by the accused on the road as established by the prosecution, brought the sum up to only a few dollars above the amount given Mrs. Spottwood on Thursday, April 10.

With corroborative testimony from Miss Batts, who for twenty-three years had been secretary to Murray Guilfort, who always cashed the checks marked *Spottwood* and kept the Spottwood file, the prosecution finished its presentation.

"I have done what I can do," Dr. Lightfoot said. "I have urged her to rest tomorrow. All she keeps saying is, she's got to go. I could put her under sedation, but, under the circumstances—"

Standing in the parlor of Miss Edwina's house, Murray studied the fine, firm ash of the cigar. Looking at it, he said: "It must be she feels it a loyalty to Sunder to stay there—to see justice done."

"Whatever it is," Dr. Lightfoot said, "it amounts to an obsession. Now, if in the light of her—her medical, her psychological history—you wish me to bring in a psychiatrist—"

"God, no," Murray said, surprised at his own violence of feeling. "It's just shock. You said so yourself."

"She couldn't sleep last night," Miss Edwina said. "She was walking about. I heard her, and I went in and sat by her bed and she held my hand. Then she slept."

"I am leaving the pills," Dr. Lightfoot said. He hesitated, then added: "It's not exactly my province, but what happens after the trial? I should suggest a nice rest home. Perfect quiet for a time. Now, there's a nice place in—"

"There's a place right here!" Miss Edwina interrupted. "In this house, and I hope it's nice. She's a dear, lost thing and she can stay right here until she wants to leave."

Looking at Miss Edwina, Murray wondered what she would

say if she knew that Cassie Spottwood was a pauper. *Well,* he thought, with irony, *I'm not.* He hugged the thought with a grim satisfaction.

He put the cigar to his lips. The expensive smoke was as acrid as an old shoe smoldering on the town dump.

It took courage. Putting the dago on the stand in his own defense. Desperation, the mother of courage. The mother of idiocy, rather. For who but an idiot could expect anybody but an idiot to believe that cock-and-bull story? That Cassie Spottwood had called him—him, the dago she was throwing out for good and sufficient reason—had called him into that very room where her husband lay in bed and told him he had done good work and she was sorry he had to go and then gave him two hundred dollars in a leather purse to speed him on his way, and in her car?

That was the core of the defense, and who could believe it?

Muddy the waters, that was all. And Murray grinned grimly to himself, thinking how the only thing that Leroy could have used to really stir up mud was the very thing he wouldn't dare to use.

That was what he had told Jack Farhill, long back.

"What if Leroy springs that dress on us?" Farhill had asked.

"He won't," he said to Farhill.

"Everybody in town knows about it," Farhill had said. "A red dress and black lace underwear and black stockings and slippers and perfume. That fellow bought that stuff. There are no secrets in Parkerton."

"Listen, Jack, you know that is hearsay. And we know that Leroy could not possibly have got anything from the Spottwood house. If he has that dress, he got it from Arlita's shack. If so, what good will that do him?

"None," Jack had agreed. "But—"

"If you mean to imply," he had cut in before Farhill got out another word, "that something—something irregular—transpired between the accused and—"

"Oh, no, no sir," Farhill had hurried to say. "It's just that—"

"Listen, Jack, all Leroy can possibly have is hearsay. But even if he did have that dress and all the accessories in his hand, and could prove it came out of the Spottwood house, he wouldn't offer it. Not to this jury. You are back home now, son, you are not in the Yale Law School. You are in Cardwell County, and if Leroy Lancaster should even hint that there was any hanky-panky between that nigger-loving dago and a white woman—listen, son, in the eyes of this jury, that Angelo fellow is not much more than a spit and a holler from being a nigger himself, and if Leroy tried to work up an angle like that—well, Leroy would sure have one fried dago on his hands."

At that moment, remembering that scene, now sitting in the courtroom in broad daylight while Farhill was cross-examining Angelo Passetto, Murray suddenly, clear and distinct as though physically before him, saw the red dress: saw it, and the black lace, the black slipper, the black stockings, what was left, all in the brown paper sack he had put them in that morning back in April standing there in the Spottwood kitchen, before he went out to the car to put the sack in the trunk and lock it.

He again saw those objects, but as they were now, in the safe in his study at Durwood, as though his eyes had, suddenly, the power to see all that distance, to see through steel and see those objects glowing in that enclosed darkness. And at that moment, the crazy fear struck him that another eye than his might even now pierce all the miles of distance, and pierce the steel, to see those objects glowing like live coals in the enclosed darkness of the safe.

The palms of his hands were sweating. He felt like running out of the courtroom and driving with the accelerator flat to the floorboard, to dash into his study and lock the door and draw the shades tight and build a fire, even if it was summer now, and burn the red dress and all those things so nobody could ever find them. So he would never have to see them again, or even remember them.

He promised himself he would do that—soon, soon. And so felt better.

At least, he felt better until he began to wonder why he hadn't already destroyed those things. Until he began to ask himself why, on two occasions, at night he had gone to lock himself up in his study, and pull all the curtains tight, and take out those things and stare at them.

Sunk in that question, he did not really catch the name of the burly man in the old blue serge suit who was on the stand. Then he caught it: *Grinder*. And remembered the name, the old man up the creek, with his still, and the daughter who had risen in the world to be a whore in Nashville instead of giving it away for free to sawmill hands in the bushes. Yes, there had been a boy. So this was young Grinder—this strongly built man with the thickening belly and the sweat-streaked, weather-creased face incongruous above the blue serge, who was saying how he saw the buck he had been stalking jump up from the brush by the creekside in front of the old Spottwood place, and he snagged it right in the air with an arrow—he was sure he hit it in the air—and a man was coming down the road in the rain with a little piddling newspaper package in his hand. Yes, that was the one sitting right there now, that Angelo fellow.

Grinder said how he called to the man to help him drag the buck across the road to a tree by the creekside to hoist and nut and gut it, but just then Cassie Killigrew—yes, sir, Spottwood now—came out her front door and said not to touch that buck,

it was kilt on her ground, and he kept dragging because he
knew it was his buck, and that man standing there and not
helping, he sided with Cassie—Mrs. Spottwood, he meant—
about where the deer was kilt, and then she shot the ground
out from under his feet—his own feet, yes—so close the red
clay mud blowed up on his pants and—

At the objection from Farhill, Judge Potts directed the jury
to erase the statement from their minds.

Whereupon Leroy changed his line of interrogation. How
long had the witness known Mrs. Spottwood? For thirty—no,
more'n thirty years, since she was a little-bitty girl in school,
she then being Cassie Killigrew. Was it true that at one period,
in high school, he had taken the said Cassie Killigrew out? That
they had been courting? Had been what you might call sweet-
hearts?

The objection of the prosecution was sustained.

But the man on the stand, the graying, weather-faced man
with the thickening belly that pressed against the tight-but-
toned blue serge of the coat, was not, apparently, hearing
what was going on around him. He was staring at Cassie Spottwood's face, across the distance of black oiled and imperfectly
swept board floor. The face was lifted to him, with dark eyes
wide and wearing an expression of puzzled effort and painful
appeal.

Then the white face dropped. The eyes were staring down
at the hands clasped on the lap. But the witness continued to
stare at the woman, across the distance.

The witness had to be addressed twice before he responded.

What had this amounted to? That Cassie Spottwood was
capable of picking up a shotgun and firing a round into the
mud to scare off a man who had, she maintained, killed a deer
on her ground. That Cassie Spottwood had fired a blast under

the feet of the man who had once—how long back—been her sweetheart? That Cassie Spottwood—

But everything had been struck off the record. Then Murray caught himself looking sidewise and secretly at the figure on his left, clad in that decorous and expensive black, with hands in black gloves decorously and innocently clasped, and in that instant he had a vision of her as she had undoubtedly been—black hair disheveled and face white above the leveled shotgun, and the barrels pointing at you, they looked like a little figure eight lying on its side, and then the flame came, and the blast.

No, nothing is ever off the record, he thought, and suddenly everything he himself had ever done, said, thought, or even had not dared to think, was standing at his back, presences silently crowding. There, at his back, they were silently crowding, numberless presences, waiting.

Waiting for what?

Nothing was ever off the record.

And, suddenly, he knew that his own name had been named. It hung in the air.

He was being recalled to the stand.

"—and you have turned over to Mrs. Spottwood a certain sum every month for—yes—twelve years and four months?

"Yes, sir," Murray said.

"And you hold signed receipts for same?"

"Yes, sir."

"For the amount—including the last check, of $200—coming to $15,000 exactly?"

"I haven't added it exactly, but it must be in that neighborhood."

"Do you want to add it, Mr. Guilfort?"

"No, it's in that neighborhood."

"That is a sizable sum, is it not, Mr. Guilfort?"

"I regard it as such."

"I am sure—" and with the word *sure,* Leroy Lancaster swept his conniving and poverty-stricken gaze over, first, the jury, and then the entire courtroom, to elicit an appreciative and financially self-deprecatory titter. "I am sure," he repeated, "that we are all agreed that $15,000 is a sizable sum. And, Mr. Guilfort, was this the income on investments which, in behalf of Sunderland Spottwood, you, as his attorney, managed?"

The afternoon light fell bright across the room. The light flickered from the somnolent movement of the fans in the hands of jurors. The fans made no sound in the slow curdling of bright air. The silence was like the pressure in the depth of a bright sea. Murray felt, behind him, the massing of nameless forces.

But the answer was so pure and simple: the answer was: *no.* He said it. And felt, suddenly, how life was beautiful when it could be encysted in a single, simple word. If only it, life, could always be like that—single, simple, no shade, no shadow: truth.

Leroy Lancaster was speaking: "—and are we to understand that this sum—$15,000—is money which you, Murray Guilfort, gave, free and outright, to Cassie Spottwood?"

Murray hesitated, wet his lips, felt again that shadowy gathering of forces at his back. He said: "To Cassie Spottwood *and* Sunderland Spottwood."

Leroy Lancaster was studying a sheet of paper he held in his hand. He lifted his head. "Mr. Guilfort," he said, "have you ever heard the name Mildred Suffolk?"

A grip, like the grip of an icy hand, took the back of his neck. The cold ran down his spine.

"Take your time," Leroy was saying. "I want you to be very sure of your answer."

If that grip on the back of his neck were released, he would be able to speak.

"To refresh your memory," Leroy's voice was saying, "the lady who is professionally known as Mildred Suffolk, but whose real name is Mildred Dawson, lives in Chicago." The voice stopped, waiting.

"Or perhaps," the voice resumed in the friendliest fashion, "you remember her better as Midge? Her intimates called her that." The voice waited, then asked: "Mr. Guilfort, have you ever heard that name?"

"Yes," Murray said.

"Are you, or have you ever been, personally acquainted with the said Mildred?"

"Yes," Murray said. Or rather, incredulous, he heard his own voice saying the word.

"Did you, Mr. Guilfort, ever, at any time, have what might be termed business or professional relations with the said Mildred?"

The bright light fell across the room. In that light the fans from Billingsboy's Furniture and Undertaking puddled the hot air with no sound. The face of Leroy Lancaster hung there in the bright air, staring at him.

"Yes," he heard his voice saying.

And suddenly, he knew what had happened to bring him to stand here and sweat with all those eyes on him. If he had not been a fool! If once in Chicago, when, another time, the Bar Association had met there, he had not encountered Joe Bates, from Nashville. If he had not sat with Joe Bates in the very bar where he had once sat with Alfred Milbank, who by this time was dead but who had once leaned across the table and breathed out the hot whiskey breath. If he had not taken too much to drink, sitting with Joe Bates, whom he had never liked but whom, that night, he somehow needed. If looking at the slick, vain face of that fool Joe Bates, at that face younger and firmer than his own, he had not had the sudden, appalling, and unconquerable impulse to lean at Joe Bates, feeling strong and victorious and fulfilled even as he was appalled to hear his own voice saying, like an echo: "Look, Joe, illusion is the only truth, and as for me, I solemnly affirm that, within the hour, I am going to lay out $100 for a juicy chunk of illusion. With—" and leaning closer to Joe Bates, he had laughed "—hair on it. And Joe, I'll fix you up, too."

And so Mildred had brought that girl named—named what? —and they, the four of them, had drunk the champagne, there in his, Murray's, sitting room, for he always had a sitting room those days when he went to Chicago, and then Joe Bates had taken that other girl off to his room, and that was all.

All—except that Joe Bates must have remembered the name of Mildred, Joe Bates who had come to no good, who was disbarred long back, who, no doubt, had seen this trial coming up in the paper, who had hit a mark with his wild guess, who, no doubt, had sold the information to Leroy Lancaster.

But the voice was speaking.

"To be sure that we all have understood you correctly," the voice of Leroy was saying, "I repeat the question. Have you ever had any business or professional relations—her profession, not yours, Mr. Guilfort—with the said Mildred?"

"Yes."

"Was not the profession, or business, of this Mildred what is known as a call girl? A high-priced prostitute?"

And in that instant Murray saw the naked logic of it all. He, Murray, had paid money to a call girl named Mildred. He had paid money to Cassie Spottwood. But Sunderland Spottwood had refused to die, and so—

And even as, in that same instant, Jack Farhill's objection was sustained, Murray Guilfort heard his own voice, loud and clear: "Whatever you mean to imply, Mr. Lancaster, I state that I am proud of having been able to do my humble best for the friend of my boyhood when he was stricken and penniless, and I am only sorry I could not do more, and if a man's attempt to be faithful to a friend is a cause for shame and a provocation for the obscene leer, then—"

The gavel of Judge Potts drowned his voice, but he stood there with his head erect and defiant, feeling lifted up in his heart.

Somebody in the back of the courtroom clapped his hands, once.

In the restored silence, Murray Guilfort humbly apologized to the bench. It was clear that he still labored under a powerful emotion, even if it was now under control.

After the adjournment, as Murray moved across the court-house yard, following Miss Edwina and Cassie, three men, one after another, stopped him and shook his hand. "You got 'em told," the first said. "That's telling 'em," the second said. "You laid it on the line," the third said.

That evening when he went to the drugstore to get a box of cigars, the kind they ordered special for him, Doc Milton, the proprietor, short, fat, bald, with dentures, handing him the wrapped box, said: "Well, Murray, how 'bout taking me with you the next trip to Chicago?"

And the loungers at the soda fountain all grinned. The grins were the kind that made Murray stop on the pavement outside the drugstore and look commandingly up and down the street, feeling great. The lights from the store fronts glittered.

Everything was great.

The arguments, brief and predictable, were finished by noon the next day. The prosecution asked for the death penalty. Judge Potts' instructions to the jury were succinct and, Murray decided, eminently satisfactory. The jury was escorted to the MacAllister Arms Hotel, where they were being housed, and were installed in the room on the mezzanine ordinarily used for displays by drummers and for meetings of Kiwanis. A little later lunch was served there to the jury.

It was just after 3:30 when Jack Farhill knocked on the door of Murray's private office to say that the jury was ready.

"Fast work," Murray said. "I guess we know what that means." He rose and slipped on his dark tropical worsted coat. "Hold off till I get 'em," he said, picked up his Panama hat, went down and got his car and drove to Miss Edwina's. By 3:40 he was escorting the ladies to their seats.

At the table, beside Leroy, sat the dago, in his white shirt. The shirt didn't look to be much sweated into. The face above the white shirt was closed, secret.

Cassie Spottwood stared down at her hands.

Judge Potts spoke: "Mr. Foreman."

The foreman of the jury rose. The slow, puddling motion of the fans stopped.

"Mr. Foreman," Judge Potts demanded, "have you reached a verdict?"

"Yes, your Honor," the foreman said.

"Will you state the verdict," Judge Potts said.

The verdict was: guilty of murder, in the first degree.

The words were scarcely out of the foreman's mouth when Cassie Spottwood, who, until that very instant, had been staring into her lap, leaped up, and her voice rang wild and silvery in the hot air. "No! No!" the voice cried out. "I did it, I did it— I killed him!"

She stood there, panting in the bright silence.

BOOK
III

CHAPTER TEN

✟✟✟✟✟✟✟✟✟✟✟ **P**ast 10:00 at night, Leroy stood on Main Street, in Parkerton, with most of the lights already gone out, and thought how everything looked strange to him: as though he were caught at night with a bad bus connection in a town he didn't even know the name of.

He thought: *I have lived here all my life.*

He had lived here all his life except for the years away at college, at Washington and Lee, and at law school, at Charlottesville, and except for his time overseas, in the war. But those periods, once over, had never seemed real to him. And now, it struck him with sudden terror, if Parkerton stopped being real, what, what in the world, would be real for him?

He thought: *What's wrong with me?*

So he stood there and wondered why, after coming out of Judge Potts' chambers, he had acted on the sudden impulse to call home and tell Corinne that he wouldn't be able to get to dinner, that he had to work on the hearing for tomorrow. But only fleetingly he wondered that, for his mind jerked back from the question he had asked himself, as the eye flinches from a sudden blaze of light.

Past 10:00 now, and he hadn't yet gone to his office, much less got to work. Instead, he had sat at the Greek's, in the most remote and shadowy booth, near the service door where nobody wanted to sit, and, with no hunger, had picked at the blue-plate special, and then had continued to sit there with coffee turning cold in the cup, until closing time. After that, without direction, he wandered the streets of Parkerton.

Out to the abandoned sawmill, where the great saw used to fill the summer afternoon with its snarl and shriek of lyric agony, but where no saw was now, only rotting piles of sawdust from which great clumps of burdock sprouted. In the dimness of starlight, he could not see what they were like, the great burdock plants, but he knew in his mind's eye, the leaves big as elephant ears and soft with a dusty-green piling, and fat stalks shading from pink to cream-color at the base; and the plants were, somehow, horrible.

To the school building, where he had once been a serious, stubby child with bifocals.

Down the streets of houses, where lights were going out, trying to remember what child had lived where, what that child or this had looked like, what was the name of the child who had been drowned in the millpond.

To the ruined railroad station, where no traffic ever moved now, but where he, the college boy, used to arrive home on the evening train—for Christmas, for summer—and see below him, as he stood in the vestibule of the Pullman, his mother, dumpy, red-faced, smiling, in her best dress and shining spectacles, and his father, gaunt and slow, in blue serge, with the high, stiff white collar, and above the collar the face as incongruous as the carved, weathered stone face of the statue of some hero who had died in some cause now forgotten, and whose name nobody could remember. So he, the son, who had now lived near half a century, stood by the ruined station and felt again the old surge of guilt and unworthiness that he used to feel as he looked down from the vestibule of the Pullman upon those uplifted faces, and the manifest joy.

Was that, he demanded of himself, looking at the ruin of the station, why he had come back to Parkerton? Because, years ago, standing in the vestibule of a Pullman, looking down at those faces, he had confronted that love and joy? Because, at such a moment, he had known the overwhelming emotion of guilt and unworthiness?

Had he come back to pay a debt for something? To expiate something?

Why hadn't he stayed in Richmond, Virginia, or even gone off to Nashville or Louisville or Chicago to get rich? What had obliged him to come back and set up shop as the Conscience of Parkerton?

The phrase was in his head, and he felt, physically, even in the literal curve of his lip, the sneer, the delicious self-contempt, that was in the phrase.

He thought: *What is wrong with me?*

And he stood there shivering in his sense of dislocation.

At that moment, two blocks away, across the foot of Main Street, where it debouched into the Courthouse Square, he saw, under the arc light, the white Buick convertible of Murray Guilfort slip majestically across, and disappear.

It had to be his. There was no other big white car in town.

Past the stores, all darkened but the drugstore, Leroy moved toward the Square, crossed it, stopped. Yes, there was the Buick, parked in front of the office where Guilfort and Farhill would now be. Yonder, in the second-story window, the light was showing. Guilfort would have just come from Edwina Parker's house, and Leroy imagined the shadowy bed where

Cassie Spottwood lay, the dark eyes staring up from the whiteness of flesh, from the whiteness of linen, and Murray Guilfort
leaning, saying something.

Saying what?

What could he say?

She had confessed in open court, hadn't she?

Sure, he—Leroy Lancaster—knew the nature and limitations
of that fact, for he was a lawyer, wasn't he? Even if he wasn't
the greatest. But the great Guilfort, no matter how great he
was, he couldn't change the simple, objective fact of that confession, no matter how much or how little it was worth. She had
surged to her feet, with a sudden energy like flame, her eyes
had flashed their blackness across the space, and she had cried
out: "No! No!—I did it, I did it—I killed him!"

The words had seemed carved on the air, on the silence.

When it was over he had gone directly to Judge Potts'
chambers.

"Judge," he had said, "I reckon you know why I'm here."

For a moment Judge Potts said nothing, making a tired gesture toward a chair, for him to be seated, then divesting himself of his robe. His shirt was stained dark with sweat, at the
armpits. He took a glass of water, drank it, then faced Leroy.

"I reckon I know why you've come," he said, studying Leroy's
face. And added: "And I reckon you, being a lawyer, know why
a judge sometimes lays awake at night."

"Judge," Leroy said, "it is a full confession in open court, and
it has cast substantial doubt on the verdict as rendered. It has
made available new evidence which, if known in time, would
have—"

The Judge waved his hand in the same tired gesture.

"All right," he said, "all right. So you want a hearing."

"Judge," Leroy said, "I am going to move that the statement

made in open court by Cassie Killigrew Spottwood be included in the record."

Judge Potts ran a finger under his collar. "Ten o'clock tomorrow morning," he said. Then added, fretfully: "It's this damned heat. It's killing me. I'm not so young anymore, I'm fleshing up, and it's killing me. Ought to be a law, a death penalty for all folks that get tried in the summertime. Automatic—innocent or guilty."

One of the fans donated by Billingsboy Furniture and Undertaking lay on his desk. He picked it up, and began to fan himself with a finicky, peevish motion, a motion like an irrelevant ripple at the margin of his bulk.

"Ten o'clock tomorrow," Judge Potts said.

Leroy rose. "Thank you, Judge," he said.

When Leroy got to the door, Judge Potts said: "I'll be laying awake all night."

The fan had stopped. It was, clearly, doing no good.

"With this heat," Judge Potts said. "All night with this heat. And that durn fool woman."

Leroy had reached the door before the Judge said: "Why didn't she keep her fool mouth shut?"

"Conscience, maybe," Leroy said.

"Yeah," the Judge said. "Yeah, and maybe because he screwed her blue. Black, blue, blind, and witless. And she just can't bear to think of that tool getting fried."

The Judge was again moving the fan in the air, hopelessly.

Leroy went out.

It was then, standing outside the deserted courthouse, under the old maples where the starlings bickered and let their droppings spatter down, splotchy-white on the time-crumbled bricks of the walk, that Leroy had the overmastering impulse to call his wife and say he would not come home.

So he sat at the Greek's as long as possible, and then, in the early dark, he walked the streets of Parkerton. He even walked as far as his own house, the house his father had lived in all the years when, in his time, he had been the lawyer in Parkerton who somehow never had many cases you could win, or get paid for even if you did win. And now, in the dark of night Leroy stood and stared at the house where his father had lived and died: a medium-sized frame house in a big yard gone to the kind of weeds that grow in shade, for forest oaks grew there, left over from the first clearing of land.

The house was on the edge of town, the last house with a sidewalk to it, disintegrating concrete with smartweed crawling in the cracks, and beyond this point, open country. Leroy stood on the concrete at his own gate, and saw the one light beyond the darkness of the oaks, knowing that it was the light of the kitchen wing, knowing that Corinne would have waited as long as possible before eating and was now there, seated at the kitchen table because she was alone, eating delicately, meditatively, in that realm of silence she always seemed to inhabit, even in a room full of people, and into which, for so many years, he had tried to penetrate. She would smile at him sweetly as though through a momentary break in coiling mist; or her voice, even if enunciating the words of courtesy or endearment, would sound as though coming from a distance, cut across, now and then, by a lift of breeze.

He stood in the dark and looked across the yard at that dim light, the single bulb by which she was eating, and he thought that she had lived in that house for nearly fourteen years now.

She had come here because she loved him.

She was the daughter of an Episcopal bishop, and he had met her at a party at Charlottesville, when she was only eighteen and he was a first-year student in the law school there.

She was not pretty, with a face a little too sharply molded, the nose too thin and aquiline. But it was the sort of high-bred face that, though not pretty for a young girl, gives promise of a fine-grained handsomeness in later life. The gray eyes were clear, and the ash-pale hair curled mistily about the brow. Her legs were thin, and the hips and buttocks rather small.

Or perhaps they were not small. Perhaps they merely seemed so, because the breasts were decidedly larger than might be expected on that torso, or beneath a face of that cut. In their first moments together, the girl had seemed embarrassed about her breasts. She seemed to be trying to conceal them, to cover them with the left arm, to be secretly trying to compress them, to be trying to distract him from them with some excessive gesture into distance with her right arm while she covered them with her left. All the while, what she succeeded in doing was to rivet his attention there, and when he did tear his eyes away and looked into her face, he flushed with his own embarrassment as though caught in a shameful act. Some part of his mind kept thanking God for his bifocals, for maybe, through them, she couldn't tell how his eyes kept wandering down.

Her embarrassment was part of the cause of what was happening to him, but not all. The cause lay, rather, in a disproportion, a disharmony, between those breasts and the rest of the body that was Corinne Melford. The thin legs, the small hips and buttocks, that in themselves seemed almost sexless, were, in contrast to the slow, lush depth and weight of the breasts, infected with a powerful, derivative sexuality, powerful because derivative. He had the abrupt image of that body lying naked, on the back, and the legs would be active, agile, curving, reaching, groping, gripping, prehensile, and the very toes sly, subtle, gifted for secret, sudden tickling, the buttocks athletic or tricky, with slow undecipherable hitches and retardations. The breasts would be the deep soft center, the relentless fulcrum, and the legs, the feet, the arms, the sharp fingers, would be outriders, scouts, beaters, prickers-on, drivers, whippers-in, and in all the discords and contrasts there would be a miraculous and merciless unity.

He had stood looking into the girl's face, trying desperately not to look lower, and all the while his imagination swirled with images of confused activity, scarcely discernible white flashes in a coiling obscurity, like the momentary gleam of fish bellies in black water. Then, striving to disregard the body that was Corinne Melford, striving to see, literally, only her face, he became aware of another discrepancy, even more inflaming. The chiseled clarity of her face, the innocence of the brow mistily framed by the pale hair, and the spirituality of the clear gray glance, were irrelevant to the deep promise of the breasts from which he could not keep his eyes, but even as he strained to fix his attention on her face, the face, too, by reason of its very purity, became infected with, connived corruptly with, that overwhelming sexuality. He saw how the eyelids would flicker, how the clear gray glance would go opaque with a terrifying inwardness, how the lips would tighten back to expose the sudden white teeth, how the nostrils would quiver with the abrupt passage of breath.

But it had never come to pass. At least, not that way. When, after the two years of engagement, they were married, she gave herself to him sweetly, gravely, graciously; and then she held his head on her shoulder and gently patted the damp tangle of his hair and told him that she loved him. He told himself that he loved her, and he did. He told himself that he was glad that he was a virgin when he came to her. He resolutely put away, in some dark corner of his mind, the fantasy which had obsessed him during the period of the engagement—a period during which, in fact, he had rarely seen her.

They had been married in June, 1938, just after his graduation from law school, and Leroy had gone to Richmond to a

firm dominated by one of Corinne's uncles. Leroy, studious
and conscientious, had done well enough there, but by 1941,
when Pearl Harbor came, he had become aware of a blankness
in life that he had no name for. Then came the war, and his
period overseas. Just as he got back to Richmond and again
became aware of that unnamable blankness, his father, far
off in Parkerton, died. His mother was already dead. Leroy
knew, suddenly, that he would spend the rest of his days in his
father's old office on the Courthouse Square, in Parkerton, and
the rest of his nights, with Corinne lying by his side in the
dark, in the shabby white house under the last cluster of
forest oaks.

The years began to slip by. She accepted the restricted life
there, and the disrepair of the house under the oaks. In the
early period he would go to the Episcopal church with her.
Then, when that sect had withered away before the en-
croachment of the Baptists and the booming onslaught of the
Church of Christ, she went with him to the Presbyterian church,
where his father had been a deacon and of which he was nomi-
nally a member. Then the Presbyterians were, in their turn,
devoured, and the church building was remodeled as a dwell-
ing, and Leroy and Corinne began to attend the Baptist church.

She was quietly busy with good works. When a family was
in trouble she would be there. She tended babies, she nursed
the sick, she bathed those who were wounded, filthy, and infected, she prayed with the dying, and at last it was assumed
in all Parkerton and the outlying country that Corinne Lancaster
would be found in any house, white or black, that had been
struck by disaster. Long since, Leroy had got used to the midnight telephone call, or at the back door the voice of some
Negro child saying, "My mammy, she sick, she lak to die, kin
you come?"

Then Leroy would get out of bed, if that was the way it had
to be, and drive her to whatever place it was where she was

(271)

needed. Sometimes she told him to go on home. Sometimes he waited in the car, staring at the light in the window of a cabin or shack.

On the wedding night, just as he drowsed off, she had slipped from the bed. He had seen her kneel by the bed, her hair, visible in moonlight, damp and curlier than usual, her breasts pressed against the bed's edge as though to mortify them. She had groped out for his hand, had found it, and clutching it, had prayed, silently. Every night thereafter and always, after her silent prayer, she had slipped back into bed and held his head on her shoulder.

They had never had a child.

So, now, he stood on the disintegrating cement, and stared at the light beyond the darkness of oaks, and knew how she would be sitting there in the kitchen. The years had scarcely touched her. The ash-pale hair had begun to slip imperceptibly into gray but had kept its glimmering mistiness. The gray eyes still had their clarity. The pale skin was soft and scarcely lined. If now, in the kitchen yonder, she should rise from the chair, her figure would be the same that had inflamed his imagination at the moment of their meeting almost twenty years before.

He stood there, staring at that distant light as though he could spy on her loneliness. He had the impulse to enter the yard and creep toward the window. He would have to be careful. The old acorns that strewed the ground would crackle underfoot in the dark. He imagined himself secretly peering into the window where she stood, alone in that pale light.

What would he see there?

His breath came short.

Then, all at once, he felt old and dry. He wondered where life had gone.

He thought: *When will I be done with illusion?*

. . .

Back on the Square, he regarded the white Buick parked by the curb under the lighted window of the room where Murray Guilfort and Farhill conferred. He turned and looked toward the courthouse. He saw a light in the window of the Judge's chambers. He wondered what Judge Potts was thinking.

He went to his own office, turned on the light, and sat at his desk. He had said that he had work to do. But there was no work. He sat there and thought of the afternoon:

The cry of the woman, silvery and absolute, burst forth, and Leroy stared at her across the bright air. This had to be a dream because it was what he had so often dreamed —the dream in which, miraculously, the guilty declared themselves, the innocent were saved and did not have to suffer, the crooked way was made straight, and justice was redeemed.

The dream, too, in which—at last—Leroy Lancaster was victorious.

That was the final thing that certified this as only a dream: for Leroy Lancaster's only victories had been in dream.

There was the woman standing there, arms slightly lifted as though at the beginning of the motion of an embrace, and face lifted, not looking at anybody. She was actually there, but, even so, he could not believe that this was true. In the total silence of the courtroom that seemed to last forever, he stared at her in the joy of all the old dreams and the pain of the present incredulity.

Then he became aware that Angelo Passetto, his client, was on his feet, leaning forward, and had, in fact, cried out.

Leroy suddenly realized what Angelo had cried out.

(273)

He had cried out: *"Piccola mia—piccola mia!"*

Across the distance, irrelevant to the disorder and the banging of the gavel, the woman's gaze was now directly on Angelo Passetto, who had just cried out to her, and her face was shining.

Leroy stared across at the woman's face.

Then his professional instinct stirred. He snatched his gaze from the woman and inspected the jury. In the midst of the tumult and the banging of the gavel Leroy studied the face of the nearest man. He was a backcountry man, a hill man, in middle age, his lank, bony frame wrapped in a faded blue shirt and khaki pants, his hair a sandy red, uncut, his face long, bony, lantern-jawed, the jaw moving slow on the quid of tobacco, and the pale, flat, faded blue eyes, the color of his shirt, were fixed on Angelo Passetto.

Then, even as Leroy watched, the juryman's pale, hard gaze left Angelo and turned to the woman, whose eyes were on Angelo and whose face was shining. The jury-man's jaw, in mid-grind, stopped its motion on the quid, and the pale gaze swung from the woman to fix again on Angelo Passetto. The quid of tobacco the juryman had been chewing was now thrust to one side of the mouth to make a neat round bulge in the cheek, and as he stared at Angelo his jaws tightened, the jaw muscles bulged hard, and the man's eyes, steady on Angelo's face, squinted slow as though he were staring out from the cover of under-growth in the instant before the rifle is raised.

Leroy turned his head slightly toward Angelo. "Sit down," he ordered in a hard, tight voice, very low, out of the side of his mouth, not looking at Angelo.

Then, as Angelo, seeming not to hear, remained stand-ing in that vulnerability, Leroy swung toward him, and in a voice still low, but with a vibrant intensity, said, "God damn it, you fool, sit down!"

Slowly, not turning to Leroy's voice, still looking across the space at the woman, Angelo sank into his chair.

Looking at him, Leroy thought: *The fool.*

The fool: to call out to her, to stand there in the sight of all, bemused in the full shining of the woman's face. To proclaim whatever might have been in the ruined house, the dark grapplings, the tangling of sheets, the torn-out cries. To invite the hard, targeting eyes of all those people who, like the hill man in the jury box, stared unforgiving at him from the thorny shadow of their own deprivations, yearnings, and envies, as from a thicket.

They—all of them—the judge, the jury, Farhill, Murray Guilfort, and all those people—would kill Angelo Passetto because he had stood there in the full shining of that woman's face.

Leroy Lancaster felt sick at heart.

He thought: *My God, that's the way it is.*

That was the way it had been, and that was the way it was again in his head now tonight, as he sat before his desk, not at work. The office was dark. He had not even bothered to turn on the light.

He sat there, and suddenly knew why he had called his wife and said that he would not come home.

He had not dared to go home, because, as he now knew, he wanted to cling a little longer, just a little longer, to the dream of victory—even if an unearned victory. But it was only a dream.

If he had carried that dream home, she, the instant she saw him, would have recognized the unadmitted knowledge of the new failure to come showing on his face, hanging about his shoulders like a threadbare coat, emanating from him like a smell. She would have met him with her grave smile and the

level gray-eyed gaze that saw everything and forgave everything. She would have given him the cool tenderness of her kiss.
As they sat at the table to eat the food she had prepared, she
would have reached across to lay a hand on his.

That was what he could not bear.

As he sat in his office, where the rays from the nearest arc
lamp in the Square angled upward through the window to
strike the ceiling but left him in darkness below, he knew that,
sooner or later, he would have to go home, and that, no matter
how late, his wife, when he came to bed, would be awake and
would turn to him and give him the cool tenderness of her kiss.
She would murmur that she loved him. She would, after a little,
offer herself to him, gravely and sweetly, and after the execution of what would have come to him as a merciless and contemptuous command, she would hold his head on her shoulder,
with little consoling pats, as though he were a child.

As though he were the failure that he was.

Yes, that was it, he thought, and rage filled him. It was always when he had failed, or when she, in her pitiless clair-
voyance, knew he was about to fail, that she offered herself
thus, with that special gravity and sweetness.

So she thought that that would redeem failure? Like a bone
flung to a dog, or a bright object offered to a child to distract
it from crying? Did she think that getting between her legs was
such a prize?

His head was about to burst with sudden pain.

Or was this, he demanded, but another of her good works?
When, after their coupling, she patted his head, was that the
motion she used to soothe all those children, not her own, that
she held in her arms in those cabins, shacks, and falling-down
farmhouses? When she touched his body was that, in some
secret way, the way she touched the body of the sick? When,
kneeling in prayer and pressing her breasts against the bed's
edge, she held his hand, was that the way she held the hand

of the dying while she prayed? Had she, in the first place, married him because she could, even then, smell the failure on him —married him so that this object of good works would be always available for her charity?

Or had she, by her charity—by her love, for she said that she loved him—made him the failure that he was?

He felt demeaned, outraged, emasculated.

And, in that instant, he saw, blazing in the darkness of his head, the whiteness of Corinne Lancaster's body moving and twisting in the old frenzies and weaving arabesques of the long-forgotten fantasy. And the weight that implacably bore down upon her bosom to inflame the flickering white of her motions was the naked body of Angelo Passetto.

After a moment, sitting there, he knew that that afternoon, in the courtroom, his own eyes had fixed upon Angelo Passetto as unforgivingly as those of the juryman from the hills. He had wanted Angelo Passetto to die.

He sat in the dark office and shivered in a rage that was like truth.

Me too, he thought, sitting there, shivering. *Me.*

Suddenly, without formulated intention, thrust down as by a great hand laid on him, he found himself kneeling by the chair. There in the dark office—totally dark now, for the arc lights on the Square had long since been extinguished—he was praying. He had not prayed since he was a boy, but now, out of guilt and despair, he was crying out in his heart, even as, aloud, he uttered the words, "God—God."

As he prayed he kept telling himself, in some corner of the mind, that he had done all possible for Angelo Passetto, he had worked hard, he had done all anybody could. He believed what he told himself, but it didn't seem to have any bearing on things, it didn't do any good.

For something else was happening in him. A great stifling substance seemed to be swelling in his chest. No, it was as though pain itself were a fluid, as though he were bleeding internally and it would not stop, and he knew that whatever he had done for Angelo Passetto would not help this. This was deeper and more awful. He could not breathe.

So he struggled to his feet, and there, in the dark office, stood gasping for air. He caught air, and then, to his total surprise, marveling even in the midst of pain because the words being uttered had never even been in his mind, he heard the voice that was his own voice but sounded so strange and far away: "God forgive me—I have blasphemed against my own life."

All at once, mysteriously, for no reason he could name, the tears were coming.

When the tears stopped he sat down. He wiped his face with his handkerchief, and blew his nose. The sound of blowing his nose struck him as marvelously funny, and the funniness had a sort of sweetness. He felt weak and shaken, but the pain was gone. He felt high and clear-headed too, as he had once felt standing on top of a mountain, one bright fall day long ago in Virginia, but there was no thought in his head, only a kind of bright, windless openness, like the sky.

Slowly he became aware that he wanted to go home. That was what he wanted to do.

Somehow, he felt that he could go home now.

At 10:00 the next morning, in open court Leroy repeated what, in Judge Potts' chambers, he had already said: the whole case against Angelo Passetto, his client, had been circumstantial, and the full confession, offered in court, had cast substantial doubt on the verdict rendered, and had made available new evidence which, if available earlier, would have precluded the verdict against his client. He moved that the statement of Cassie Killigrew Spottwood be included in the record.

Farhill countered by maintaining that there is nothing inherently wrong with circumstantial evidence. As for the alleged confession, that confession was, he said, naked and unsupported, and could not be made part of the record, for the jury had already reported its verdict before Mrs. Spottwood uttered a word. It was simply the hysterical outburst of an overwrought woman. This woman, who had given years of notable devotion to a paralyzed husband, had, as must have been common in the course of her daily domestic duties, left him unattended, but on this occasion, when she found him murdered, she felt that she herself was guilty in that she had not been present to defend him. Then, under the strain of the trial, which she had insisted on attending to see justice done, the reliving of the tragic event had momentarily inflated the superstitious sense of guilt into the hysterical outburst. Furthermore, Farhill added, it was generally known that Mrs. Spottwood had at one time been under treatment for hysterical—

At this point Judge Potts had cut him off, saying that neither the psychological theorizing nor an account of the medical history of Mrs. Spottwood was relevant to this hearing. That second question, indeed, might emerge as relevant in another context, but for the moment, in this hearing, the issue was more narrowly technical.

Judge Potts proceeded to rule that no judical basis appeared for including the statement of Mrs. Spottwood in the record. The trial had been completed in full compliance with the rules of law before her utterance. However—and he paused here and looked down from the bench at Farhill—the State, in the light of that utterance, had the privilege, even the obligation, as some might construe it, of further investigation, which perhaps might culminate in an indictment of Cassie Killigrew Spottwood. But it should be clearly understood—and here his gaze rested on Leroy—that the judicial branch was not an investigatory agency. He wished to add, he said, still addressing Leroy, that though there was no ground in law for including Mrs. Spottwood's utterance in the trial record, an affidavit to the same effect, duly executed by her according to the forms of law, could be presented in the motion for a new trial.

At this moment, Leroy looked across at the face of Farhill. He was sure that he saw the lips of that full and handsome mouth lift slightly in an incipient smile. At that moment, Farhill abruptly excused himself, and was gone.

Leroy went directly to his office and began work on his motion for a new trial.

Thirty minutes later, he shoved his chair back. "To hell with this," he said out loud, and got up. He stood there, thinking of the incipient smile he had seen on the lips of Farhill.

He went into the outer office, told his secretary that he didn't know when he would be back, and not bothering to pick up his hat, marched out into the hall, and down the dim stairs. At the outer door of the building he hesitated a moment, straightened his shoulders, took a deep breath like a diver getting ready to plunge, and stepped out into the June glare. He moved diagonally across the corner of the Square, abandoning the pavement—a tall, angular figure in an unpressed blue suit, moving in an abstracted, awkward loping gait, apparently not noticing a car right on him, but managing to dodge it at the last minute, his balding, hatless head outthrust on the long neck like a heron in its cranky flight. His spectacles glittered in the sun.

He entered the doorway of another building, and climbed the stairs there, which were dim like his own. At the top, before a door, he stopped and took a deep breath. All at once he felt just great. He went in.

Yes, Mr. Farhill was in, the secretary said. Mr. Farhill would be delighted to see him.

He was delighted to see him, Jack Farhill said. He had, he

said, smiling ruefully, been thinking things over as deeply as he could, and he was glad to have a chance to talk. He wasn't, he said, exactly a heavy-praying man, but he had been wrestling back and forth all night with their question. It was, he said, a tough one.

"It's the question of a man's life," Leroy said.

Farhill was looking at Leroy out of his large, moist brown eyes, with a gaze that, for a moment, made Leroy feel drawn, in weakness and stupidity, into some dire complicity. Farhill was saying: "It so often is that, isn't it? The question of a man's life?"

Farhill's gaze, which invited complicities, was removed. It was now directed out the window, into distance, and his clear profile was exhibited, with his chin lifted. He said: "But we have to play by the rules."

He swung the soft, enveloping gaze back over Leroy, like a net of a thousand delicate filaments. "Don't we?" he demanded, ever so gently.

"Sure," Leroy said, "sure. But right now I'm interested in a little justice, too."

"Do sit down," Farhill gently invited.

Leroy sat down.

"Yes, we all want justice," Farhill said. "But"—and he smiled winningly—"can we get it except by the rules? In the end, in the long haul, I mean. Yes—this trial now." He shook his head thoughtfully. "You sure gave Arlita—that colored woman—a hard time. You know, and I know, that she didn't kill Spottwood." He lifted a hand calmingly, just as Leroy stirred in the chair. "Oh, no offense, I know you had to do it. But if she had just accidentally been a little earlier coming to the Spottwood house that morning, you might have done her a grave injustice. Like getting her electrocuted. You even made a pass at the great man, old Guilfort himself. Well"—he smiled—"that backfired a little. But you see—"

Leroy thrust himself forward, about to say what the question right now was.

But Farhill forestalled him, smiling, continuing: "—it's only by the rules that things get sorted out. Arlita, old Guilfort. And you even made a pass at poor Mrs. Spottwood—"

"And she"—Leroy stood up—"has confessed in open court, and the question is, what are you, as an investigatory agency, as you were defined this morning by Judge Potts, going to do?"

Farhill paused thoughtfully, then lifted his head, in decision. "I am going to try to do the right thing," he said.

Leroy looked at Farhill and felt that he was being lured into a trap, and when he had taken the next step, as he must, that smile would suddenly leap forth, just as the trap was sprung. But even in that instant of realization, he felt very gay. *To hell with Farhill and his games,* he thought. So he said: "More specifically, what?"

Leroy stood and waited for the smile to arrange itself on the handsome mouth, for the lips to curl to form the answer.

The answer came.

"Nothing," Farhill said, and the smile, rueful and contemptuous, was there on the handsome, smooth-skinned young face that so resembled the face of a matinée idol in the old silent films.

Then, even as, totally unexpected, Leroy felt a peculiar, thin stab of pity for the man, Farhill again spoke: "Oh, do sit down."

Leroy ignored the invitation. "Listen," he said, "you will, of course, cooperate on the matter of the affidavit?"

"Of course," Farhill said. "I mean that I would, of course, like to. But—" He interrupted himself, making a gesture of courtesy and saying, "Oh, do sit down and be comfortable."

Leroy sat, and Farhill leaned at him. "But," he said sympathetically, conspiratorially, "we do have to be practical.

You're a practical man, Leroy. And besides you were an honor man in a fine law school, and—"

As Leroy stirred in the chair, Farhill lifted his hand as though to soothe him. Then his voice continued, still soothingly: "Now about Mrs. Spottwood. We might conceivably have got an indictment—and that's what you'd really like me to do, isn't it, Leroy?—as of yesterday. But—"

Farhill spread his hands in a little gesture of helplessness. "You know, Leroy," he began again, "it's a damned funny profession we're in."

"No doubt," Leroy said.

"About poor Mrs. Spottwood, for instance," Farhill continued. "Just a little while back you were trying to sneak into the record—no offense, I don't blame you—the fact that she had been off her rocker and therefore might, like taking the pot shot at that old hillbilly sweetie of hers, have just happened to knife her beloved husband. No, you didn't accuse anybody— just casting a shadow of a doubt by hinting that she had been crazy. But me, I didn't want her crazy. Not then. But it's all the other way around now. You want her *compos mentis,* all set to make affidavit, and me *au contraire.* Now isn't that funny?"

"Very," Leroy said.

"Only," Farhill said, "it does look like I'm the lucky one today. You see—" He paused, put the tips of his strong, slick, white fingers together, and sorrowfully shook his head, then resumed. "You see, she went real nutty last night. Nutty as a whooping crane stuck in flypaper."

"Well, it's no wonder," Leroy said, "with what went on yesterday, and—"

"Oh, I'm not referring to a little female crying fit," Farhill said. "I mean the real McCoy. Real wild." He looked down at the left sleeve of his well-pressed and unstained palm beach coat, flicked away an invisible bit of lint, then lifted his gaze. "You see, Dr. Lightfoot had to put her under sedation. And at first dawn—"

He paused, and shook his head.

"Let's get on to the facts," Leroy suggested.

"It's very sad. But this morning they had to take her away."

Leroy got up. "Listen," he said, "you can't just fling somebody into the booby hatch. There are certain safeguards, certain—"

"Of course," Farhill was saying. Then suddenly, in the abstract singsong of a classroom recitation: "Two doctors must offer certificates to support the complaint, the county court clerk must issue an application, the county judge must view the patient—" He paused, smiling in camaraderie. "Hell, you know all that. And that," he added briskly, "is exactly what they did. In the middle of the night. When she was howling like a banshee and no mistake."

Leroy stood surrounded by the elegance of the office. *So that's the way it is,* he thought.

"You see," Farhill was saying, "Dr. Lightfoot thought she ought to be under care at the earliest possible moment. She was really wild. Suicidal. He didn't want the responsibility. But"—he brightened—"everybody was very sympathetic. Very cooperative. Old Judge Meeker got right out of bed, in the middle of the night."

"Where did you take her?" Leroy asked.

"*I* didn't take her anywhere," Farhill corrected.

"Well, where did *they* take her?"

"Where she was before. When she had that other hysterical breakdown." Farhill put a slight emphasis on the word *hysterical.* "Long back, you know. That time when they say she burst out laughing at her mother's funeral."

Leroy looked down at the man sitting before him, studying him. "It's very tidy," he said, calmly.

Farhill was looking up at him. The expression on Farhill's face was one of slowly thickening puzzlement, like a drop of vinegar spreading in milk.

"Very tidy," Leroy repeated, in a tone of admiration. "But you know," he added, "maybe not quite tidy enough."

Farhill stirred in his rich maroon leather upholstery. The chair, for all its solid and expensive structure, creaked ever so little with the not inconsiderable weight. "Leroy," Farhill said, slowly, "you're damned funny this morning." He hesitated, "I do believe something has come over you."

Leroy kept looking down at the large, slick, handsome face curdling in its puzzlement. He found the sight very funny. "You know," he finally said, smiling down in the friendliest fashion possible, "I do believe so myself."

At the door he turned. "Goodbye," he said, "and thanks."

Back in his office, he sat again at the desk with the appeal papers before him. He did not touch them. Instead, he rang for his secretary. She came in, and sat with pad on knee, waiting.

"It's to Thomas Bowie Atwood," he said. "New York City, but I'll have to hunt up the exact address later." He began: "Dear Tom." He hesitated, cleared his throat, began again:

This is a voice from dear dead days beyond recall, but I hope you remember the late-night, beer-and-bull sessions at Charlottesville during which you and I settled the destiny of nations and the problems of philosophy. I have always been meaning to write you, but my news is always so unthrilling. Since the war (in which I neither got shot nor shot anybody), Corinne (who is still beautifully untouched by time) and I have been living happily together in the little town where I was born and which always seemed the right place for me, and where she devotes herself to the welfare

of others and is much beloved. My only complaint is that
we have no children.

I have followed in the press your predictably splendid
career, and have gloried in it from afar. Now I turn to you
for help, for you as an old Alabama boy will intuit something
of my problem, and because I hope that you—and your Civil
Liberties Union—will agree with me that here is a tragic
miscarriage of justice. I am enclosing, of course, a transcript
of the trial, but I should add some background material. At
the very moment when the jury returned the verdict, the
widow of the murder victim, who, as you will see from the
transcript, had been a witness against the accused, leaped
from her seat and—

For a moment after Angelo's cry, Cassie stood there in her
exaltation. Even as hands were laid on her to draw her down, a
wonderfully sweet weakness took her, and she sank back in
the chair. They hurried her out of the courtroom, through the
gabbing crowds, to the car, and back to Miss Edwina's house,
and to bed. She tried to talk, to tell how something was over and
she was glad, but nobody would listen, they kept saying, hush,
hush, and then she was in the cool sheets and Dr. Lightfoot gave
her a glass of water, or whatever it was, to drink.

It was late at night when Murray Guilfort came into the room
where she lay in the strange state of lassitude that amounted
to fulfillment. He came in with no sound, and stood in the
shadow above the rays of the night lamp by the bed, looking
down at her. Then he sat in a chair by the bed, as a doctor
might, with only the faint light from the night lamp falling
across his face and glittering on his spectacles. He asked her
how she felt, and before she could answer, he said that he, that
everybody, knew what a terrible strain she had been under,
that everybody understood how it—how the unspecified *it* that
his voice underscored—had happened.

(286)

She tried to tell him how she felt light and free now, but he said, hush, hush, he knew. He said she hadn't needed to feel guilty in the first place. When she rose up on her elbow to insist that, yes, yes, she was guilty, he smiled and reached to pat her hand, and said it was natural for her to feel guilty—very natural —that everybody understood how, after those long years of selfless devotion, it had been a shock to find that, in the brief moment when she had left her husband unguarded by her love, that terrible thing had happened. It was natural for her to feel —it was the very index of her love, for her to feel—that she was the cause, that she was guilty. And natural for her to feel guilty because she had insisted, even after he had told her the man was a convict, that he stay in the house.

She pushed herself up again, but he lifted his hand, and said, no, he would not dwell on that, he had not come to accuse her, to offer recrimination, all he was here for was to say that in spite of the fact that, under the circumstances, it was natural for her to feel guilty, her feeling was a delusion.

No, no, she cried out, she had done it.

But he seized her hand, pressing it hard, saying that it was all delusion, that believing in that delusion was what made her sick, that believing that was her sickness, but they would make her well, she would be surrounded with love and attention, and soon it would all be nothing but a bad dream.

No, no, she cried out, it was true.

But he pressed her hand harder, and the spectacles glittered closer, and he was saying that he would save her from the consequences of her delusion, asking her if she didn't know what the consequences might be if she had her way, asking her if she realized exactly what she was asking for, saying that she might be shut up forever in a prison—no, no, she might even be strapped in a chair and—he gripped her harder, with both hands, with the spectacles glittering out of the dimness so she couldn't see his human eyes—saying that the electricity would rip into her body, it would jerk and twist her horribly, and she would be dead.

She struggled to pull her hand free from his grip, managed to get it free, and was sitting upright in the tangle of bed-clothes, asserting that she did not care, that having the electricity rip into her so she would die, that was what she wanted—oh, that!

He seized both her hands in one double grip now, and as she writhed and struggled to get free, and cried out that she wanted to die, he leaned closer, telling her to listen, he would protect her, she was the wife of his dear friend and he would protect her.

But she cried out again, and while he gripped harder, his voice sank almost to a whisper, though a whisper that was vibrant, controlled, taut, and penetrating, telling her that he was a lawyer, that what she had said in court meant nothing in the law, that there was no supporting evidence for her naked confession, that every day thousands of people confessed, they were crazy enough to confess but nobody believed them, that nobody, least of all the judge, would believe her, that every-body would just laugh at her, because she had once been crazy too, she had been locked up for crazy.

But she screamed that she was not crazy, that she had done it.

To which he replied, his face closer, his voice lower and more vibrant, that everybody would be sure she was crazy, if she was crazy enough to want to be strapped in the chair and have that electricity rip into her till she died.

But that was what she wanted. She wanted to die. She was screaming it, over and over.

He released the hands, and suddenly stood up. Looking down at her contorted face, with the round black hole there from which the scream came, his heart was filled with pity, virtue, and victory.

(288)

"But listen," he said, "listen, Cassie. Nobody will ever believe you. Nobody in the whole world!"

Miss Edwina had burst into the room.

"Call Dr. Lightfoot," he commanded. "Please, please, hurry. She is completely hysterical."

The woman in the bed was screaming that she wanted to die.

At dawn the next morning the white Roadmaster convertible rustled the gravel up the drive of Miss Parker's house, followed minutes later by the wine-red Chevrolet sedan belonging to Dr. Lightfoot. Some fifteen minutes later, the red Chevrolet slid down the drive, passed through streets where closed shutters or curtains drawn blankly beyond glass declared that a blessed gloom yet prevailed for those men and women who, within, were clinging to the last moment of sleep.

Then the red Chevrolet had shaken free, and was on the west road, moving fast between fields where a drop of dew glittered at the tip of the bending corn blade and therein was globed all the fractured colors of the world, and where a field lark, with song, flared up from the grass, flicking wetness from its wings.

At the wheel, alone in the driver's seat, was Murray Guilfort, eyes fixed on the road. In the back seat was Cassie Spottwood, looking pale and torpid as though still sunk in a dull shimmer of sleep, like the water of a pond. She was flanked on one side by Dr. Lightfoot, and on the other by a vigorous, red-faced woman of middle age, who wore a white uniform. Dr. Lightfoot's black bag, slightly open, was on the floor at his feet.

They had gone some twenty miles before any difficulty with the patient occurred. Then, Murray Guilfort, at a word from Dr. Lightfoot, drew the car over to the side of the road and stopped, and Dr. Lightfoot, while the red-faced woman competently grappled the patient, made recourse to the black bag and the prepared hypodermic.

By 8:00, as prearranged, Murray Guilfort and Dr. Lightfoot were closeted with Dr. Spurlin, the owner of the sanatorium, a man who, with his fine leonine head of iron-gray hair brushed straight back, his Vandyke beard, and his heavy horn-rimmed spectacles, looked like an advertisement for a book on how to create the happy marriage or how to achieve social and business success by ten easy psychological rules. But Murray tabulated such items as the frayed cuff of the tropical worsted sleeve, a bitten nail on a nicotine-stained finger, a crack in the plaster on one wall, a small hole in the nigh extinct Persian rug, and an electric cord from the desk lamp inexpertly repaired with once-white adhesive tape; and then, recollecting to the penny the sum of the mortgage which he, as a member of the board of directors, knew the Parkerton Bank held on this property, proceeded to give a detailed account of the events leading up to his telephone call of the previous evening. He concluded his remarks by saying that Dr. Lightfoot, who had been in continuous attendance on the patient during the ordeal of the trial, would, of course, supplement this layman's account. Fortunately, Dr. Lightfoot had been present the previous evening when the patient was at the peak of one of her hysterical seizures with the fantasies of guilt and suicidal yearnings in full bloom.

Dr. Lightfoot, after insisting that he was just a G.P., not a psychiatrist, gave his professional account.

Dr. Spurlin thanked them both for their most perceptive and cogent presentation, and laid aside his clipboard of notes.

Murray said that he wanted the patient to have every possible attention and comfort, that she had been through a most tragic experience, that Dr. Spurlin would, he knew, spare nothing that would make life endurable for the patient, that he himself—and now he gave the seedy spruceness of Dr.

Spurlin a slow assessing glance, not entirely lost on the object of his attention—would immediately forward a letter declaring his financial responsibility for the whole affair.

Dr. Spurlin nodded in approbation.

Murray now affirmed that the patient was the widow of his dearest friend, and that he could do no less than give what protection and comfort were possible in memory of his old affection for the murdered man.

Dr. Spurlin murmured that such friendship was all too rare in the modern world, and then, in a firm voice, promised that the patient would not only have the constant attendance of his brilliant staff, in whom he had the greatest confidence, but of himself.

Murray said that Dr. Spurlin was to telephone him at any hour, day or night, and that in any case, he would come out in a few days to get, personally, a report of progress. He shook hands with Dr. Spurlin. Dr. Lightfoot shook hands with Dr. Spurlin.

At the door, Murray turned for a moment to repeat that that very day he would dictate the letter assuming all financial responsibility.

Once outside, standing beside the white Buick, Murray cast a critical eye over the building. Clearly, the roof was in bad repair.

He stood staring at the point of the roof near the chimney, where the slates had cracked and slipped most alarmingly. Then, suddenly, he was in the clutch of a dry, unaimed rage. He felt seized by the throat and shaken like a rat in the dog's jaws.

The paroxysm passed. There was only a dusty misery inside him. He had an interior vision as of dust motes settling slow in some attic after old junk had been disturbed.

He became aware of Dr. Lightfoot's gaze upon him.

Dr. Lightfoot got into the driver's seat, for it was his car.

. . .

For two weeks, whenever people came together—at the drugstore, at 10:30 in the morning by the sticky-wet marble counter of the soda fountain, under the ceiling fans that slowly puddled the air, sipping a Coca-Cola or a cherry smash, at the Greek's for an afternoon beer, on the benches in front of the courthouse, at the church on Sunday morning after the service —they talked of the trial.

Then, all at once, nobody mentioned it. Everybody knew that it was not over, but, all at once, you did not have to remember it. You would not have to remember it until the Supreme Court of the State of Tennessee said you had to. Everybody knew that Leroy had taken that dago's case up there when he couldn't get a new trial here after that crazy Cassie busted out in court, and you never knew what those high muck-a-mucks would do. But you had to live in the world, and you could forget Angelo Passetto.

Meanwhile, Dr. Spurlin and his chief assistant, Dr. Bradsheer, reported that Mrs. Spottwood was in need of further treatment, and the county judge extended the commitment by sixty days, the maximum extension permitted by law without a lunacy hearing. This event passed unnoticed.

The lunacy hearing itself occurred, by the recommendation of Dr. Spurlin and his assistant, twelve days before the expiration of the sixty-day extension. Trial by jury not being mandatory and being waived by the guardian *ad litem* of the patient, the proceedings took place in the chambers of Judge Meeker. The guardian *ad litem*, a poor hill boy just beginning his practice, had been appointed by Judge Meeker at the request of Farhill, who had said: "It would be nice, Judge, if you threw that fifty dollars in the direction of Sam Piercy. He hasn't had a square meal all summer." Later, to Sam Piercy, Farhill said: "Son, if I were you, I'd just keep my mouth shut. Now and later. I'm sure you agree that, as gentlemen, we should try to spare Mrs. Spottwood any gossip, poor lady."

Sam said he sure agreed. And Sam kept his mouth shut. Everybody involved kept his mouth shut. Not that public gabble would have mattered. People knew that Cassie Spottwood was nuts. And when word finally did drift around about the lunacy hearing, everybody thought it was an act of fidelity to an old friend for Murray Guilfort to take on the grief, not to mention the expense, of having Cassie, since she had no kin, committed to his care instead of being sent to the Asylum over at Nashville. Now she could stay in that little sanatorium Dr. Spurlin ran, where it was more homey, and Murray could sort of keep an eye on things.

By this time the lawyer from the ACLU had visited Parkerton. He had declined the hospitality of the Lancasters, staying at the hotel, but he did spend a full day in Leroy's office reviewing the case and the background situation. The following day he had interviewed Farhill, Judge Potts, Dr. Lightfoot, Judge Meeker, and Murray Guilfort. The next day, after a trip to interview Dr. Spurlin, he had been driven to Nashville, to catch his plane back to New York.

A week later Leroy received the official reply. Dismissing ultimate ethical questions, the reply ran, there seemed to be no ground on which the organization might fruitfully act.

The heat of summer had peaked and passed. In the creek bottoms the corn was laid by, and clods hardened, gritty as sandstone, in the corn-balk. Water shrank in the ponds, and over dried mud the green scum hardened with a sheen in the sunshine like corroded copper. Back in the hills, the hill people had their revival meetings. Many were convicted of sin, and were felled by Divine Grace to the earth, where they lay weeping. Some received the gift of tongues.

That fall the corn yield was good, and the price held. The football team of Parkerton High lost the West Tennessee Championship by only three points. The oldest inhabitant of the section, a Negro man who had been born a slave, died, and there was a story on the front page of the Parkerton *Clarion*. The story had the headline: THE PASSING OF AN ERA. There was a light snow for Christmas.

On January 6, the decision of the Supreme Court of Tennessee was handed down. The conviction of Angelo Passetto was sustained.

Late that afternoon, back from the visit to Angelo to report to him, to pretend that he was working on a new idea, to promise that there was yet hope, Leroy sat down at his desk and began to write. By midnight he had finished and had retyped his work. Then he wrote a brief letter. He put the manuscript and the letter into a large envelope, addressed and stamped it, and on the way home dropped it by the post office. It was addressed to the magazine called *The New Nation*, in New York City.

Looking at the dark slot into which the envelope had disappeared, Leroy wondered what good it would do. Even if they published it. How many people would read it? Ten thousand? Five thousand? Five hundred? How many in Tennessee? And if anybody read it, who would care?

He wondered if the Governor of Tennessee would read it if he sent it to him with a letter asking for an appointment.

He was suddenly aware of the silence here in the post office, of the blankness here under the one dingy overhead fixture.

Well, he thought, *I guess I had to do it.*

He went out into the dark street.

Anyway, it was something to do.

He could not sleep that night. Every time he almost slipped off, he jerked wide awake in a panic of suffocation. He told himself that this was the way the world was, and a man had to deal with that fact. He told himself it was not because people were wicked. He told himself that he must not believe himself surrounded by wicked people. He was surrounded, he told himself, merely by people, and he was like them. He told himself that things simply came out this way, in this world. That you had to recognize this fact and keep on trying to do what you had to do. The world moved slow, and you had to do the best you could. But none of the thoughts seemed to help him very much.

He reached out in the dark and found Corinne's hand, and held it.

By daylight he was dressed and on the road to Spottwood Valley. He had not even had a cup of coffee.

He found Cy Grinder. Would Mr. Grinder retain him, Leroy Lancaster, to draw up a petition for a writ of *habeas corpus* for the release of Cassie Spottwood, who might then be willing to submit to psychiatric examination by impartial experts? Leroy explained to Cy that to retain him was merely a legal technicality.

Cy said that he would do it. Even if it hadn't been a technicality and would cost something. He said he thought anybody, if he was trying to tell the truth, had a right to be listened to.

A week later, the hearing was held before Judge Potts, in his chambers. Leroy and Cy Grinder were there, with a psychiatrist in tow, a professor from the Medical School in Nashville. Farhill and Dr. Spurlin, with an assistant from the sanatorium, presented Cassie. A nurse, in uniform, stood in the background. Judge Potts stated that he had carefully read the record of the commitment proceedings, and asked Leroy if he could point to any irregularities in that document. Leroy replied in the negative. Whereupon Farhill offered to Judge Potts a packet of letters which, he said, the patient had written but which Dr. Spurlin had thought it inadvisable to mail—for reasons which no doubt would emerge. However, Farhill said, Dr. Spurlin would not wish to withhold such material from the court. In fact, Dr. Spurlin was sure that the letters might be valuable to the court in reaching a decision.

The Judge put on his spectacles, furrowed his brow, and began to read. "Dear Governor—" he began.

Very respectfully, the professor from Nashville interjected that, though he was not completely conversant with court procedure, he wondered if it were medically advisable for the letters of the patient to be read aloud before a group of people.

Judge Potts took off his spectacles, paused for a moment, and then, thanking the professor, explained that he was here to establish the admissibility and competence of all the evidence placed before him, and that he did not want to do so without making that evidence available to all properly present.

He reset his spectacles. But the light was bad. The day was rainy, and the ceiling fixture, a big washbowl-shaped receptacle of frosted glass, was flyspecked and dusty, and was covered, in the bottom, with generations of dead moths. The Judge switched on his desk lamp, and inclined his head.

The large shadowy room was silent except for the occasional hiss of steam in the radiators, the plash of rain on the windowpanes, and the irregular breath of Cassie. The room was too hot. Sweat was on the bald head of Judge Potts.

"Dear Governor," Judge Potts again began the reading. "You

are the only person in the world who can help me now. I killed Sunder. I had to do it. I did it with a knife but his eyes were closed. No, they were open but he did not care. Every time I went to wake him to shave him in the morning he might jerk and cut himself and blood came. He couldn't shave himself after his stroke and when I tried to wake him I stroked his arm and then I pulled his hair but the blood came out and he never would have made it to the door. It was springtime, that is what it was. Oh, Governor, Governor, help me. I want to die, for he was coming down the road, he was coming—"

The Judge stopped reading. The sweat was on his forehead now in bright little drops. He lifted his head and met the woman's eyes. "Mrs. Spottwood," he said, moving toward her with the letter in his hand. "Mrs. Spottwood," he repeated, standing before her, with his free hand now laid on her shoulder, "did you write this letter?"

Seated, like a little girl with her hands primly folded on her lap, she stared up at him. Slowly, she nodded at him. "Yes, your Honor," she murmured.

All at once, she had slid to her knees, reaching up to catch the hand that held the letter, seizing the hand, crying out. "You've got to believe me, you've got to," she cried. "He was coming down the road, it was like a torch coming through the rain, like a lightwood torch and the flame so pale you couldn't hardly see it in daylight, but I saw it, and the rain couldn't put it out, and it was coming—"

"Stop, Mrs. Spottwood, stop!" the Judge was commanding, trying to pull his hand free.

He had pulled his hand free, tearing the letter in the process, but she was now clutching him about the knees, pressing her body against his legs, looking up at him, saying that it was like a torch coming through the rain.

As she knelt there, clutching the Judge's knees, the psychiatrist from Nashville stepped forward, but stopped himself in mid-motion, and stood with one hand frozen, outthrust in the air.

The nurse had come to release Cassie's grip, standing behind the kneeling woman, leaning over her, strongly grasping the wrists together so that the hands appeared, for a moment, to be in a gesture of supplication.

The nurse made Cassie return to her chair. The sound of her weeping filled the chamber. The Judge took off his spectacles and wiped his face with a handkerchief. He looked over at Cassie, then at the company.

"Gentlemen," Judge Potts began. Getting his breath better, he began again. "Gentlemen, it is clear that this woman is suffering from a severe mental disturbance. She has been under the care of two physicians who are graduates of schools of medicine legally empowered to grant degrees, and these men are duly licensed by the State of Tennessee to practice medicine."

He paused, wiped his face.

Leroy seized the moment, and respectfully suggested that, considering the gravity of the situation and the question of justice at stake, might not the court order a psychiatric examination by a board of—

He was summarily interrupted by Judge Potts.

If the physicians in charge of Mrs. Spottwood wished to call a consultation, that, Judge Potts affirmed, was a matter beyond the jurisdiction of this court. Further, he added, the petition for the writ of *habeas corpus* presented in this case could not be sustained. The law on the point was clear and distinct, as affirmed by the Supreme Court in the case of *Giles et al. versus State ex. rel. Giles* (191 Tenn. 538), December 9, 1950. By the said decision of the Supreme Court of Tennessee, the petition in a *habeas corpus* proceeding would be dismissed, unless some substantial irregularity in the proceedings was apparent from the record or the decree of commitment was not valid. Here no such irregularity or invalidity appeared, and as the mental condition of the defendant could not be inquired into in a *habeas corpus* proceeding, the petition must therefore be dismissed.

Out on the Square, after the psychiatrist from Nashville had driven off, Leroy stood in the cold drizzle and waning light of late afternoon. He had known all the time what the law was. But there was always the off chance. You had to try.

You damned well had to try.

He put a hand to the pocket where the letter from *The New Nation* was. It had come that very day, but he had forgotten it. The letter said that *The New Nation* would be very glad to publish his piece. Standing there, he thought how he had never written an article before, not for any magazine, had never even tried, and here he was, getting on toward fifty and had written one and it was being published in an important magazine like this. He saw, in his mind's eye, the magazine, the title of his article on the cover—"Chivalry Is Not Dead in Dixie"—and his name. Suddenly, as though jerking back a slow, incredulous finger from touching the literal cover of the magazine, he jerked back from the image.

He thought of Angelo sitting in his cell, waiting.

He would get a copy to the Governor. The magazine had promised to rush it out. Out in three weeks, they said, three weeks from now. He wondered if he might get a contempt of court out of this. Writing an article. But no, he decided, the case was over. The Supreme Court had been adverse. The *habeas corpus* proceedings had been repulsed. The case was over. They couldn't get him on contempt. All they could do was kill Angelo.

Unless the Governor did something. He would wait about the Governor. Wait till the piece came out. The piece would say it better than he could, face to face.

He had forgotten to put up his umbrella. Here he was, standing in the rain, with people looking at him, the few who went by this time of day, toward dark and the weather like this.

He put it up now and, in his long-legged, awkward loping motion, crossed the Square. By the time he turned into his own street, the lights were coming on in the houses. The light would be on in his own house, back beyond the leafless old oaks. He increased his pace. Under the umbrella his long neck was outthrust.

Tomorrow he would try to think of something else he might try. If there was anything. But now he was just hurrying to get home. He wanted to see Corinne. She would smile at him.

Maybe he could think of something in the morning.

CHAPTER ELEVEN

✝✝✝✝✝✝✝✝✝✝✝✝ Now, honey," Miss Edwina was saying, "you've had a very tiring day, and the doctor, he wants you to take one of these." She held out a stemmed wineglass; in the glass was a red capsule.

Cassie, propped on the pillow, looked at the capsule and thought it was just like Miss Edwina to give you a capsule in a wineglass, an old-fashioned cut-glass one, too. At the sanatorium the nurse gave you the capsule on a saucer. The saucer was not always very clean.

She picked up the glass and poured the capsule into the palm of her left hand. Letting it lie there in her palm, she smiled up at Miss Edwina. "I reckon I *am* a little tired," she said. Then added, "Oh, Miss Edwina, you're so good to me!"

She was watching Miss Edwina's face. All that white hair above it, that was so white it looked blue, seemed to be giving off sparks in the light from the wall bracket beyond her, and the diamond pendant against the black silk of her breast, catching light from the little lamp on the bedside table, was giving off sparks, too.

Suddenly, at her words, Miss Edwina's face had seemed to go all to pieces with pleasure, curling and creasing and crinkling and cracking in all directions, and the old blue eyes sparkled. Watching the smile on Miss Edwina's face, Cassie thought: *It doesn't take much to make a person happy.*

The thought made her, in an instant, feel happy herself, and the feeling surprised her. She had forgotten what it felt like. She slid down the pillow and was happy and closed her eyes and let herself be taken care of, while the smile was in the air above her.

But she remembered.

So, with the awkward, greedy gesture of a little child, she put the left hand to her mouth as though cramming the capsule in it was so good, but catching it with the damp tip of her tongue, drawing it in, working it under her tongue, while her right hand reached toward the tumbler of water—that, too, cut-glass—on the silver tray on the little table.

Miss Edwina handed her the glass, and she took a sip, ever so carefully, coughed, pretended to take more water, then reached the glass back. As Miss Edwina took it, she slid flat into the bed and hunched the covers up, her cheek flat into the pillow.

"You poor, dear child," Miss Edwina was saying, "you're so tired," and reached down to pat her on the shoulder. To avoid opening her mouth, Cassie slipped her own hand up to give Miss Edwina's hand a little squeeze of gratitude, then thought, *My God, she's going to sit down and hold my hand,* and that would spoil everything.

But Miss Edwina must have conquered the impulse, for as

Cassie could see from between eyelids narrowed to a slit, she was tiptoeing out of the room.

The instant the door was closed, Cassie heaved herself up and fumbled in the dark for the box of Kleenex on the table, got one, crammed it against her mouth, and spat. The skin of the capsule she had held under her tongue was almost dissolved. She could taste the bitter oozing out.

She slipped out of bed, and on bare feet went to the bathroom. She rinsed the bitter out of her mouth. Then, just in time, she remembered that the toilet made a lot of racket. So she wadded the Kleenex up in some toilet paper and put it in the wastebasket under the basin.

All at once she did feel tired. But she pulled herself together. She would have a long time to wait. She knew they were still downstairs, talking.

She stood there, cold in the dark, and knew they were talking about her.

While the last stroke of midnight was echoing from the clock on the courthouse, she rose from the straight chair where she had been sitting to keep from going to sleep. She stood in the middle of the dark room and thought how the sound of the last clock stroke was dying away over all the roofs of the town, and there was nothing but the stars shining down on the roofs, and under the roofs all the people lay in their beds asleep. But she couldn't lie down.

Still barefoot, but wearing a dressing gown, she slipped into the hall. She drew the door shut behind her and stood listening to the absoluteness of the silence. A little light burned dimly in a wall bracket at the first landing of the wide stairs, and threw the vertical bars of shadow of the railing at the top of the stairwell upward and against the wall where she stood.

For an instant, she felt that the bars of shadows holding her fixed there were of iron, not shadow. But she knew that was crazy. So, setting her feet down softly, very white on the red carpet of the stairs, she descended.

She thought: *I don't even know what day it is.*

Below, there was enough light for her to make her way to the parlor, then back to the library, but there was nothing there. She retraced her steps, and passed through the dining room. In the butler's pantry, she dared to turn on a light. She looked in the cabinets under the shelves.

In the kitchen she was afraid to have any light except what filtered around the swinging door to the pantry, for Miss Edwina's bedroom was in the back and a light here might throw a glow into the yard. So the search was slow. Not in the storage closet. Not on the latticed back porch, where she felt her way. Then, back in the kitchen, she spied the door. She opened it, shut the door behind her, pressed the switch, and a bulb hanging from a cord leaped to life. She stood on a landing at the head of the stairs leading down to the cellar.

The landing was wide, with recessed shelving on both sides.

There they were.

Her hands were trembling. The first one was the *Nashville Banner,* but she saw beneath it a copy of the Parkerton *Clarion.* She seized it.

Nothing.

Seven or eight papers down the stack, she found another *Clarion.* Again nothing. Again, and again nothing. Her breath was coming shorter. She did not think she could stand it much longer. She tried not to think of what she was hunting.

Then she found herself looking right at it, at the headline, and not knowing what the words meant. She did not even know how long she had been staring at those black marks, not knowing what they meant, and now no breath coming at all. There were the black marks:

GOVERNOR REJECTS PLEA

She sat down on the top step of the stairs, under the electric bulb hanging on its cord, and shut her eyes and let her head go forward so that the forehead pressed against the paper spread on her knees. Her mind was telling her that it was something else the old fool governor was rejecting. She giggled. Of course, it had to be.

But it said:

> Citing the fact that the conviction had been upheld by the Supreme Court, Governor Detwylie last night refused the plea of clemency made by Leroy Lancaster, of Parkerton, on behalf of his client Angelo Passetto, currently in the death cell of the penitentiary at Fiddlersburg. Passetto was convicted in June of last year of the murder in the first degree of Sunderland Spottwood of this county, the last surviving member of a prominent family, who was found stabbed to death in his bed. The case attracted statewide, and even national, attention when the widow of the deceased rose—

She could not go on.

She felt again how that cry had come bursting out of the darkness inside her into the bright air. It had come as though it tore loose and left everything bloody inside, but that pain was like joy. She saw again what night after night she saw when she closed her eyes: how, hearing the glittering cry that tore out of her, Angelo Passetto had leaped up, there in the middle of all those people, crying, *"Piccola mia—piccola mia!"* and his face was shining.

She shut her eyes, but this time did not let her head sink forward. She was sitting rigidly erect, and she was feeling how he—how Angelo Passetto, whose face had been shining— would be strapped in that chair, so tight it hurt, and how the electricity would come roaring into his head like lightning and down his spine with all his nerves screaming. She felt her own nerves screaming as it flashed down her spine.

She opened her eyes. She was shaking, and the sweat was worse. But she wasn't dead. It was Angelo Passetto who was going to be dead.

Then she thought: *Maybe he is dead already.*

She leaped up. She stood under the bulb, clutching the paper. It said: ". . . date of execution fixed at 12:05 a.m., March 21."

But what was today?

There was no calendar in the kitchen. None in the pantry. None, of course, in the dining room. She thought of the library, of Miss Edwina's desk. She again found her way there, telling herself to move slowly, not to make a noise.

A little moonlight came into the library, but not enough. She would have to risk turning on the little reading light on the desk.

In a drawer she found the engagement book. She opened it and began to look at the dates, a date to each page. She began to cry. What a fool she was! She had thought that somehow a calendar would tell you what day it was. All she knew was that it was March now. She sat down on the chair by the little desk, weeping out of vexation and weariness.

All at once she realized she was not weeping because Angelo Passetto might be dead, just because she was such a fool. The tears stopped. She found herself looking at the telephone on the desk.

With the tears drying on her cheeks, she picked up the phone.

No matter how hard he worked he didn't sleep so well anymore. Once, he had been able to sleep any time, any place —even curled up with his dog and one blanket in a cedar thicket, back in the hills in a foot of snow. Or on the wet ground and the temperature 90 at midnight and humidity absolute, in the jungle, when he was in the Pacific. Or on a bare hard floor, and rats running over him. Or on a pool table and no pillow. But now he reckoned he was getting old. Or he reckoned, that maybe, if you lie in the same bed every night and know that the day you have just lived through is just like the day you are going to live through tomorrow, and that this night is going to be like all the other nights after those days to come, then you don't sleep so good anymore.

He was awake, or near awake, when the telephone rang.

His feet found the floor. As he moved toward the door, he took a backward look at Gladys, knowing even as he looked at her piled up there in the moonlight, that she wouldn't wake up, not till day, and then she'd come floating up, sodden and slow, from her heavy inner darkness, her face pale and glutted and her lips slightly puffed, like a drowned person rising at last, trailing weeds that were slickly dark and tangled in the hair.

He got to the phone, there in the hall, before it woke up the kid.

The operator asked if this was Cy Grinder, Mr. Cy Grinder, and he said yes, suddenly coming full awake, wondering who would be calling him, now, in the middle of the night.

Then the voice said: "Cy—Cy—"

As he stood there in the dark hall, his feet bare on the cold boards, the voice came in a dry, tight whisper out of the thing he held to his ear. He took the thing from his ear, and for an instant stood looking stupidly at it. Then again, a sound came from it, nothing now but a tiny, brittle crepitation that came from he did not know where, and would be his name.

He put it back to his ear. The whisper, tight, dry, urgent, said: "Cy?"

He wet his lips, and said: "Who's that?"

The whisper said: "What day is this?"

He couldn't think what day it was. He felt a cold prickle run over his scalp. Something was happening in darkness, and he did not even know what day it was.

"What day of the month?" the whisper was demanding, drier, hoarser. "What day is tomorrow morning, Cy Grinder?"

"The twentieth," he said, suddenly remembering. "Who's that, who's that?"

There was no answer, only a dry choking sound that came over the wire, through the dark, from somewhere.

"Damn it," he said, in rage now, into the mouthpiece, "who's that—or I'll hang up!"

After a moment of dead silence, he heard the voice, little more than a whisper: "It's Cassie."

He stood there, and knew that, night after night, year after year, he had lain in his bed and had known that some night, in the middle of the night, the telephone would ring, and he would stand in the dark, his feet bare on cold boards, and the whisper would come.

The whisper was saying: "Yes, it's Cassie Spottwood, and you—you listen, you got to do something for me. Because it was you, Cy Grinder, that caused everything, and now—"

"Look here now—" he interrupted.

"You listen," the whisper said, "you went out that door and never even turned your head—oh, yes, you did, and—"

"Listen here, Cassie—"

"—yes, and you know it," the whisper was saying, "and then, in that courtroom you stood there and were afraid to look at me, you were ashamed, and now you're going to do what I say. You know that Parker house in Parkerton. There's an alley running behind it. Tomorrow afternoon, at 2:30, you be at the south end of that alley. In your car. You wait till—"

"But—" he broke in.

But he heard the click, far off.

He held the phone in his hand and looked at it, feeling, all at once, that everything was off-center, that things were swaying and losing outline as they do in the woods when the thaw has come with no warning, and the night settles down and the air is soaked, and suddenly above the coldness of the not yet melted snow, there is nothing but the white coiling of mist where the black trees had been.

He put the instrument back to his ear. There was the hollow sound as of the wires being thumbed by wind, and the wind blowing in, all that way, from the darkness between stars.

It was a sound like trying to remember.

Miss Edwina was slow over lunch. She obviously wanted to talk, but now and then she'd break off in the middle of a sentence as though she had been about to say something she suddenly remembered she shouldn't say.

"They've told her what not to say, Cassie thought, *but those are things she's just dying to talk about.*

But Miss Edwina was taking forever to eat.

At last Cassie got up. "Miss Edwina," she said, "please excuse me, but I've got to get upstairs to my nap," watching Miss Edwina's face go blank in disappointment, like a candle blown out. "And you—" she added, "I know you have to take a nap too. It's Dr. Spurlin who makes me be prompt about my nap, he says if you're always prompt you really go to sleep."

Miss Edwina's face was not merely blank now, it was like a crumbling cookie. It was all to pieces with disappointment. So Cassie had to go around the table to the poor old fool and kiss her, and thank her for being so good to her.

Miss Edwina brightened immeasurably, and her pink wattles shook.

Cassie had to struggle not to run up the stairs.

She kicked off her shoes and lay down with an afghan over her, just in case Miss Edwina should poke her head in. But finally she heard Miss Edwina's door close. She leaped up, and looked at her watch. She had less than twenty minutes. She got the best dress out, the one she had worn to court, got into it, got the shoes to go with it, the hat. She opened the door, and peeked out.

Downstairs she felt safe. In the hall she paused an instant, listening to the muted noise from the kitchen, where the cook was finishing up, then slipped out the front door, into the sunlight, around the house to the right, keeping close to the wall where the hydrangeas were. She got her nerve up for the one dangerous place, the space between the wall and the old carriage house that served as a garage. The garage door, she thanked God, was open, so she made a dash for it, slipped past the old Reo that Miss Edwina never used, and out the back door, into the alley.

There, at the foot of the alley, the car—it must be his car—waited.

There he sat, wearing his good suit, the old blue serge that now was much too tight. She got into the car.

"Hello, Cassie," he said.

She looked at him. "The Nashville road," she said, breath still uneven from the effort she had been making.

He let the clutch out, the car moved down the street. At the corner, he took the right turn. Then he looked at her again. She was looking straight ahead. "Hello, Cassie," he repeated.

She turned toward him with a sudden, wide, wild, naked look that frightened him.

"Hurry!" she said.

They gathered speed.

"Hurry," she said.

"I don't want the constable on my neck here in town," he said.

She was leaning forward, as though the impulse of her body could lend speed.

(3 1 0)

They jounced over the railroad tracks, and past the lumber-yard.

"Now," she said, "now," not looking at him, staring up the road. There were no houses now. The car was up to fifty-five. "Faster," she said.

"Not on this road," he said. "I'll bust a spring here. We get on the slab and I'll put her past seventy. This old De Soto, she's in better shape'n she looks. I keep a car up. Mechanically, I mean."

She wasn't listening, he knew. She was staring up the road. There were woods on both sides up the road. The woods were brightening now with buds just bursting.

Past the woods they stopped at the stop sign, then wheeled onto the highway slab.

"Now," she said.

He put the De Soto up to seventy, then seventy-five. The car began to shiver a little.

"Faster," she said.

"No," he said. "She's in good shape, but she's old."

She was still leaning forward, straining.

"They're going to kill him," she said.

Not looking at her, he said, "I figgered it was something to do with that."

She made no answer, straining forward.

After a time, still not looking at her, he said: "I'll carry you wherever you say, Cassie, and I know it ain't none of my business." He paused. "But what you aim on doing when you get there?"

"I'm going to tell him," she said.

Still not looking at her: "Tell who?"

"The Governor," she said.

Still not looking: "He's been told."

"Not by me," she said.

(311)

Still not looking: "He won't believe you."

"If I tell him, if he sees me standing there telling him—but, oh!" she cried out. "That's the trouble, not one person, nobody, not a single person, ever let me tell. When I shut my eyes, it's like it's happening all over again. I'll shut my eyes and I'll see it all over again, and Sunder, he'll look up at me, and then I can tell that Governor so he'll have to believe it!"

She struck her forehead with a clenched fist, and held the fist pressed there. "It's in here," she said, "it's happening in here, and I'll tell it."

He was looking at her now. The car was slowing down. "Cassie," he said, quietly. He could hear her breath as she sat there, leaning forward with the fist pressed hard to her forehead, her eyes now closed. "Cassie," he said. "Open your eyes. Look at me."

Looking at him, she said: "I can see it with my eyes open."

"Look at me anyway," he said.

"I see it," she declared. "It was that knife Murray found in Angelo's pocket. In the pocket of Angelo's coat. He—"

"I don't want to hear it," he said.

"Murray laid it down," she said, ignoring him, "he laid the knife down, on the big table, there in Sunder's room, and forgot it. Then it was next day and I gave Angelo the money, and I told him to take the car and get the girl and go. I told him I loved him and wanted him to be happy, for he had made me beautiful like I never was, and happy, and he—you know what he did?"

"God damn it, I don't want to know."

"He knelt down and kissed my hands," she said. "That's what he did, and he called me *piccola mia,* and I was happy for I wanted him to be happy. I almost fell down I was so happy. Then—" She stopped. "Then he was gone," she said.

She was silent.

Cy stared up the highway, into the distance. He could hear

her breath. He was sure he could hear her breath.

"I saw them driving off," she resumed. "I was looking out the big front window when they passed, going fast down the road, the car splashing the mud, for it was raining. Angelo and the girl. It was raining like the day he came. Then—"

She stopped again.

When she resumed the voice was different, thin and pale-sounding, like something remembered. "Then," she was saying, "I went back there. Back where Sunder was. The knife—it was just lying there on that old table. Where Murray left it. My hand—it picked it up. I knew my hand was going to pick it up. But it surprised me, too. And then—"

"I told you I don't want to hear," he said, not looking at her.

"I got to say it," she said. "I never said it to anybody. It's what I've got to say to him—the Governor—when I get there." She waited, then in a rush, began again. "Sunder was looking at me, and I laid it on the cover, and took both my hands to lift him up some. I had to hold him up so I could get it set—the knife—and not see it go in, so I held him with one hand, and—"

"God damn it," he burst out, suddenly loud, "I told you I don't want to hear!"

He was not looking at her, but he could hear her breath.

Then she said: "He was looking up at me. It looked like he was getting ready to smile. Then he was smiling, I was sure he was smiling. And then you know what?"

He wouldn't even look at her.

"Then I was smiling down at him. I could feel my face doing that. And he was smiling up at me—oh, I'm sure—"

What was about to burst out of Cy Grinder rose up in his throat, swelling and hard, like he might break a blood vessel. But a car from behind surged past with a hot, searing sound, and flashed into the distance, spattering the sunlight.

"You're slow," she said, "you've got slow again!"

He looked down at the speedometer. It was just under

forty-five. "I'm sorry," he said, and jammed down the accelerator and watched the needle climb.

After a long time her voice said: "He'll believe it."

He said nothing, not turning.

"When you tell him to," the voice said. "When you tell him to believe it."

"Me?" he demanded, swinging toward her.

"You," she said. "You know me better'n anybody in the world, Cy Grinder. You know I'm telling the truth." She waited. "Don't you know it?"

After a moment, he said: "Yes."

"And you'll tell him," she said. It was not a request, not a prediction. It was a simple statement of fact.

"So," he said, staring up the highway, "that is what you called me up in the middle of the night for. For me to get on to Nashville more'n a hundred miles to tell that durn Governor it was you who killed Sunder Spottwood. Me to tell 'em so they can let that durn nigger-loving dago go, and grab holt of you to do whatever they'll do. So you pick me to do it. Three and a half million folks in the durn state of Tennessee, and I'm the one gets called in the middle of the night to do that."

"Yes," she said. "You."

And after a time, she added, quite factually: "Yes, and you'll tell him, too, how I shot at you and nigh killed you. That'll help him believe. You'll tell him that."

He seemed not to have heard, staring up the highway into the brightness.

Finally, he said: "You wasn't really gonna shoot me, Cassie."

She did not seem to be paying him any mind. He had almost forgotten what he had ever said, when the voice came.

"No," it said, "I don't reckon I was. Not you."

He kept staring up the highway. The motor was turning over good. Any machinery, even a pore man's, had the right to be kept in good shape. The highway sliced straight here between the hills, far ahead.

They kept boring into that bright emptiness.

Toward sunset, threading in from the low hills to the west, they came to the openness of meadows greening, backed to the south by other hills, where woods showed the first thin, white tatters of dogwood bloom. In one meadow, four horses, three bays and a sorrel, stood just inside the white boards of the fence. They glistened beautifully like enamel in the leveling light. On each side of the road, now and then, would be limestone gateposts, and beyond, the white gravel drive leading far back to the grove where a big white house stood, or sometimes red brick, long since gone mellow.

"Them high muck-a-mucks," Cy said, "that's where they live."

"It's getting late," she said.

"Hadn't been for that durn puncture," he said. "It cost us time."

The houses were thicker now, but still set far back, among the big trees. Then the highway was turning into a street. Traffic thickened. They came to the first traffic light. Then groceries, drugstores, a filling station. Then again houses, big still, but not as big as before, not set in groves, only in yards, and some of the yards looked shaggy. Occasionally a house had a sign: *Tourists*. Traffic got heavier. They kept missing lights.

"You know how to get there?" she asked.

"You can see it, it stands up high," he said. "That tower thing on top. What some folks call the silo."

They were downtown when she said: "That must be it, up yonder. That tall thing."

"Yeah, but it's a one-way street," he said.

Finally, he hit it right, and there across the open space, on its little hill, the building stood, with stone steps spilling, it seemed in that perspective, down too steep, too narrow for its height, with columns too many and too thin, the stone smut-streaked to gray, and set on top of it, the tower reared up like a silo or a big spool, of the kind thread comes on but enormous, capped with a shape like a saucer upside down but with the rim fluted back up to make a sort of crown. The crown was silver, and the silver glinted in the smoky light. Except for that smoky-glinting silver, the whole thing looked like an engraving tinted in shades of gray against the impure pink that was the sky, an engraving by an artist who had never really learned how to draw.

It was the Capitol.

From the parking space the man and woman moved up the incline to the foot of the steps, and began to mount—a thin woman of indeterminate age, in a black dress, with a black hat somewhat askew, a dark gray coat over an arm, and a man in a blue serge suit, too tight around the middle and shiny at the seams, a white shirt, not adequately starched, with neck button off and the knot of the black tie slipping down, with an antique dark brown fedora on his head, the hairiness of the fedora gone patchily thin like the hide of an old mule, the fedora itself pulled down to the man's ears, pressing on them. The hat brim, wide in the style of a past time, was sagging down, dispiritedly and unevenly.

The breath of the climbers came heavy. Their faces were fixed on the big doors at the top of the steps. The woman's lifted eyes were dark and preternaturally bright. The man's eyes were pale, flat-seeming, and in their flatness, irreconcilably purposeful. Neither he nor she noticed the people who, coming down, stared at them.

Inside the great doors, to one side, stood an aging white-haired and very black Negro man in a white jacket. In the stillness, height, and emptiness of the space, where electric lights were already on but seemed to be bleached out by the lingering daylight, that figure seemed lost and irrelevant, and patient in its lostness. It did not even seem real. Only the whiteness of the jacket seemed real. It was as though a starched white jacket had been hung on a single post in a darkening field.

Cy stepped to the man.

"This lady," he said, "she's got to see the Governor." And added, gravely: "It's a matter of life and death, please."

The aging Negro said for them to go on upstairs, please. "But like as not, he's done gone," the Negro said. "Got his private way for goen and comen."

"Thank you kindly," Cy Grinder said.

Upstairs a Negro janitor was in the reception room, nobody else. But Cy heard some noise in a side office, where the door was ajar, so he knocked. A young woman was there, putting a hood on a typewriter.

The Governor was gone, she said.

Did she know where he lived, Cy wanted to know.

She said he couldn't go out there.

"I—I've got to—" Cassie broke in, but Cy suddenly crushed her hand so hard she gasped. Then he was talking fast.

"Lady," he was saying, "I'm a taxpayer and a registered voter. In Cardwell County. I voted for Timothy Detwylie, and I ain't ashamed to say so. We come a long way, and all we want is to see where he works and see the house he lives in."

"Oh," the young woman said. Then: "It's sort of in the country. Out the Franklin Pike. Do you know where Curtiswood Lane is?"

"No, mam," Cy said, "but you tell me, and I'll sure find it."

So she told him.

·   ·   ·

It was full dark and lights were on in the great house at the end of the long drive. A very large Negro wearing a white jacket answered the door. He said that the Governor and Mrs. Detwylie had gone out to dinner. He did not know what time they would be back, but the Governor had said it would be late, not to wait up.

Cassie began to cry. The man said he did not know where the Governor had gone to dinner. No, there was nobody who knew. At least, nobody he knew of.

The Negro stood there patiently holding the door, and Cassie was crying. Finally, Cy got her down the steps to the car. Even that far away he heard the solid, rich-sounding *chink* of the big door of that house when it shut.

In the car she kept crying, her head bent over her knees. At last, he started the car.

Once they were out on the road and in full motion, she lifted her head. The lights of cars passing flicked whitely over her face. When they had finally got back on the highway going west, she said: "You know what I'm going to do?"

He said, "No."

"All my life, as long as I live," she said, "I'm going to keep telling people. Before I die I'm going to make somebody believe me."

"I believe you," he said.

"You don't know the awfullest," she said. "It's how part of you yourself doesn't believe you did it. You have to look in the mirror—look at your own face and say, it was you did it—and keep saying it, until something happens to that face in the mirror, till it goes all white and sick-looking, then suddenly, you know that that face believes it."

He tried not to listen.

But she was saying: "Then—then after you know that that face believes it, you can sleep. You can go to sleep."

He was trying not to listen.

"You aren't listening," she said.

"I heard you," he said.

They had made it past the western rim of hills before she uttered another sound. Then she broke out laughing, a sudden burst of gaiety. She stopped. "Oh, I was so smart. I planned everything. How they would catch Angelo and kill him. Because he locked the door and I had to lie on the floor, with the door locked, in the dark, and—"

"I don't aim to hear it," he said.

"I was so smart. I planned everything, even cutting the telephone wire."

The moon had come up now, and from southward the light fell, rinsing the highway bone-white. He tried to hear nothing but the way the engine turned over.

But there was the voice: "And everything came true, everything I planned. That's the awful part, it's just like the fairy story about getting your wishes, only worse, for there's no last wish to wish them untrue with. What I wished was that folks would believe Angelo did it, and that's a lie, but my wish came true, the lie came true, and it got to be the truth, it's like it was the truth, and I—"

"Lean back," he ordered her. "Shut your eyes."

"It happens behind my eyes," she said, "what they will do to him."

But she obeyed. She lay there a long time, her body lower, her head now falling back against the seat, as they moved through the flood of light as cold and white as phosphorus.

The hills on either side were as black as ink. Here and there, the ink-black of the woods spilled down to the bone-white of the highway, and they ripped through pools of blackness, like water. Her arms hung lax at her sides, palms upward and open. On the sweep of a curve her head would roll sideways in a slow motion of abandonment.

When, at last, she opened her eyes, he said: "You went to sleep."

She was sitting erect again, looking forward into the moonlight. "Look at the moonlight," she said.

"Yes," he said.

Then, after a little: "Do you think he can see it?"

"What?"

"The moon," she said, "do you think he can see it? Angelo— in the room where he is?"

"How would I know?" he demanded, in anger.

After a little: "I read somewhere they shave your head."

He said nothing.

"He won't want them to shave his head," he said. "Angelo was proud of his hair. He would comb it and comb it. Till it was shiny black as silk. It felt soft like silk. To feel."

Later: "Do you know what they do?"

"Yes," he said.

"They strap you down tight," she said.

"I know," he said, "you don't have to tell me."

She was sitting rigid in the seat, staring ahead, her arms tight to her sides, but the forearms stiffly horizontal and forward, as though strapped to the arms of a chair.

"They strap your legs," she said, and pressed her legs together and back against the seat. "They put that thing on your head. And then—"

"Why don't you hush up?" he demanded.

But she didn't hear him.

She was saying: "—then it comes, the electricity, it jumps into you and it hits you on the head, it runs up your back, it's like fire, it's cold as ice, and it jerks you and throws you, and—"

"Shut up!" he said.

"—and they'll do it to him, but—I wish it was me—and oh—"

The car was drifting, his hands lax on the wheel. He was looking at her as she jabbed her feet against the floor and thrust her body back and threw her head back, her eyes wide, again saying, in a gaspy exhalation, "—and oh, I wish it was me!"

It was then, letting the wheel go, that he leaned over and with his left hand slapped her hard on the right cheek.

"Now will you shut up?" he demanded.

A minute later, he said he was sorry. "But you know," he added, "it sounds worse than it is. You don't feel anything. It's just bang, like that. It is the chop."

"I wish it was me," she said, in a far, thin voice.

"Shut up," he said, wearily. "It's always thinking makes things bad. If you just don't remember nothing. Just don't wait for nothing. Just keep *now* in your head. A man can stand anything if it is only just that second. If a man just keeps *now* in his head, there ain't nothing else."

He was breathing hard.

Catching his breath, he said: "And that little wop bastard, if he just thinks *now*—don't remember nothing, and don't wait for nothing—he'll make it all right. To the chop."

A quarter of a mile on, he said: "We got a way to go yet. You better try to get some sleep." And added: "Prop over against me. If it'll help."

"Thank you," she said, and did.

She had slept some twenty minutes when she woke. He realized, even if she did not sit up, that she was awake.

Her voice said: "Cy."

"Yes," he said.

"Cy," she said, "do you think I'm crazy?"

He thought for a moment. "No." Then, after another moment:
"No, you just had to do what you had to do."

She closed her eyes, and again seemed to sleep. They had
almost reached the cutoff to Parkerton, when she stirred. This
time, still not lifting her head, she said: "That time you walked
out of the hospital door, and left me. Went out the door and
not turn your head? Not even to look back at me? Did you
have to do that?"

He did not turn toward her. The words were coming from a
long way, and a long time off. It was as though he had heard
them long back, and forgotten them, and now they were
nothing, just a remembering.

Quietly, he said: "How do I know? I just keep doing the
things I do."

At they approached the cutoff to Parkerton he noticed the
lights of the roadhouse. "You ought to eat something," he said.
"Something to stay your stomach." Then he added, with a
flicker of heartiness, obviously false: "I reckon I ought to stay
my stomach, too."

When they got there, she obediently went in.

They sat in the varnished pine booth, under the dim light
of an electric fixture designed to imitate a candle with wax
dripping down the side, the fixture set on a bracket that jutted
from the wall. They looked down at the bare board of the
tabletop, while across the barnlike space a jukebox was playing
"Red River Valley."

Occasionally he took a sip of the highball. Hers was untouched. He said: "You ought to take your drink. It'll help
you."

She took a sip.

"Drink it all," he commanded, and she did.

The waitress set the hamburgers in front of them, the bottle of catsup, the boat of relish. When the waitress left, he slid the relish toward Cassie. "You still take relish?" he asked.

"Yes," she said, and smiled in a wispy way.

"Me, I still take catsup," he said.

But he took nothing now, holding the empty highball glass in his hand, looking down at it. At last he set the glass down, and picked up the bun and took a bite.

"You forgot the catsup," she said.

He looked at the bun as though discovering something. "That's right," he said. "Thank you."

He opened the bun and smeared on the catsup.

They ate in silence. They took small careful bites, chewing slowly.

"This is a place we came once," she said.

"I don't remember," he said.

"The jukebox was playing then, too. It was playing something else. People were dancing to it."

"I don't remember," he said.

He signaled the waitress, ordered pie and coffee for both. He had not consulted the woman who sat there. The order came and they began to eat, as before. After a few bites, she laid her fork down. "It's good," she said. "I always did like apple. But I just can't eat. Not any more now."

"You ought to," he said.

But she couldn't.

"All right," he said. "Drink your coffee."

She began sipping the coffee, fastidious and slow. Then she set the cup down, and looked across at him. "They had colored lights here then," she said. "In the ceiling. They swung around and around, the lights did."

"I told you I don't remember," he said.

She returned to her coffee, her eyes down. Then again she looked across at him. "It's funny," she said.

"What?" he demanded.

"You and me sitting here. Just like you hadn't."

"Hadn't what?"

"If you hadn't walked out that door," she said, "and never even turned your head. We might be sitting here just the same, like now. Maybe we live in Parkerton, and you an engineer working for the power company. Maybe we're driving back from Nashville, been to see our boy in college over there. Maybe we just got hungry on the road coming home. Maybe—"

"Excuse me," he said, suddenly, and heaved up from the booth, his belt buckle catching on the edge of the table with a scraping sound.

In the men's room, he stood in front of the mirror and saw the heavy, roundish, weathered face there above the thick neck and the popped button of the shirt collar, and stared into the pale, flat eyes that regarded him with outrage. He was saying to himself that he had just come in here to piss, that was why he had come. If he just did what he had come to do, that would be the reason he had come.

So he did it.

But as he washed his hands, he saw the pale eyes in the mirror looking at him, swollen, red-rimmed, and outraged, and when he heard somebody outside the door, he knew, in a flash, that if somebody came in here and said something to him—no matter what—he might just haul off and knock him down, so he got quick inside the can door and latched it, and stood there, waiting till the man out there did his business and washed his hands, and maybe his face too, and combed his hair, he took so long.

Cy Grinder stood and thought how his whole damned life had been working to bring him here to stand shivering, locked in a can like he was afraid, saying, *now, now,* for if you could just live *now,* no backwards and no forwards, you could live through anything.

But a man can't. He was finding out that a man can't. For

something was like a big hand reaching through his ribs, a hand big enough to grab his heart like a wet washrag and squeeze it into a wad, and then that hand was tearing his heart out by the roots while he stood there trapped in that atrocity of anguish and could not breathe.

When he came out, Cassie had left the table. He saw her coat there on the rack. He sat down to wait. After a little, he thought he might as well call the waitress and pay her, so he did. After nearly fifteen minutes more, he called her again and asked her to go into the ladies' room, and see if everything was all right, the lady with him wasn't feeling too well and she might have got sick in there or something.

The waitress came back. There wasn't anybody in the ladies' room, she said.

He stood up, and put his hands in his pockets for the keys. He remembered then that he had put the keys on the table by his hat, next to the wall. It was a bad habit, laying keys down. He reached to pick up the fedora.

There were no keys there.

Long afterwards, even after his fondest ambitions and most cherished projects had been achieved, Murray didn't like to remember the final night at Miss Edwina's. He was a tidy man, his desk was always in perfect order, the hedges at Durwood were always perfectly clipped, the shoes in his shoe closet, firm on the shoetrees, were always arranged side by side with military precision. Looking back, he always told himself that it was the untidiness of the events at Edwina Parker's that had appalled him.

It had been as though a picture on the wall, even as you looked at it, were turning slowly and maliciously askew. As though a bureau drawer, even as you looked at it, were sliding silently forward to gape open, and some pink silky thing slid over the edge like a snake, to hang there in hideous irrelevance, the way things used to hang from a drawer in Bessie's bureau, for Bessie never was very tidy.

It had all happened, too, just when everything was about to be over and tidily forgotten. That was the outrage of it. By God, Edwina Parker—you'd think she'd have enough native wit, without having to have things spelled out to her, to know that she was supposed to keep an eye on somebody as unstable as Cassie Spottwood. That was what she was being paid for, to put it brutally—even if with Miss Edwina there had to be that song and dance about money, money being so low a topic that you shouldn't mention it directly.

But oh, no, Miss Edwina had not been keeping an eye on anything, she had been upstairs snoring away like a dray-horse all afternoon till six o'clock—she ate like a horse, too, as you noticed if you weren't deceived by those ladylike little nibbling bites and began to count them. Lying on her back with, he bet, her dentures in a cut-glass tumbler for elegance and her black kid shoes unlaced for comfort, and then telling him she hadn't looked in that room because it was Cassie Spottwood, the poor dear, who needed her rest.

The hell it was. It was Edwina Parker, the poor dear.

Six o'clock before Edwina Parker even knew she was gone, and by that time clear to Nashville. And 8:00 before Edwina Parker had got hold of him. Not in his office, she said. Well, in the ineffable name of the Most High, how many places in Parkerton did she think a man could locate a thing enough resembling a dinner to be able to choke it down? Why hadn't she called the hotel and had him paged in the dining room and save two hours?

Then, her whole attitude had had something about it. If you caught her face when she thought you weren't looking, you could tell she was gloating. Positively gloating. Why wouldn't a man spin out of control for a second?

But no, he came later to admit to himself with perfect candor, a man should never spin out of control. He had built his career on control, hadn't he?

That night had been enough, though, to crack a saint. When he called that goateed fakir out at the sanatorium to ask what to do when they caught his patient, the fakir couldn't have cared less. Just put her under sedation, he said, cool as a cucumber. You didn't know what she might have been up to, and he says put her under sedation. Oh, yes, have a doctor on hand. It was no wonder even he, Murray Guilfort, cracked enough to demand why had he, a doctor, ever let her out in this condition in the first place. Then to have that goateed fakir, cool as a cucumber, start blaming him—saying that he, Murray Guilfort, had wanted her out, and that he, the fakir, had taken a calculated risk. What did that goateed fakir think he was being paid for? To take calculated risks at somebody else's expense?

Murray supposed, in fact, that it was the conversation with Dr. Spurlin that had really set him off with Edwina. When he came into the parlor from the library after the telephone conversation, he realized that Miss Edwina had been eavesdropping. Her face had that bloated gloating look, and her eyes were as bright as a hophead's and with a tone of most loathsomely artificial pity and sincerely gloating condescension, she asked him if he didn't think some hot coffee might do him good.

No, he said, not *no thank you,* and watched her jerk so sudden her dentures slipped. No, he said, no hot coffee, but begging her pardon, and if she would be so kind, he'd greatly like some cold bourbon.

She may have jerked the dentures loose, but she did get the bourbon, and one for herself too, which, until the ice melted, was, he noticed, the rich color of a cowhand's well-used saddle and nearly as opaque, and the ice did not have time to melt anyway, for the old girl belted it down with the prompt aplomb of a horse-marine, whatever a horse-marine was. Meanwhile, anent his conversation with Dr. Spurlin, he remarked as soon as he had taken a drink, that it was absurd for a man who fancied himself a psychiatrist to have let a patient out in the world in the obviously hysterical condition of Cassie Spottwood.

"But I thought you wanted her out," Edwina Parker said, in a tone of innocent surprise, as though it had just popped out.

But how innocent was that innocence? That was what got him. And if it was innocent, she was idiotic. So somewhat acidly, he had to admit, he said: "Of course, I wanted her out. I want her out—but well and happy. You see"—and he took on the professional air of patient explanation—"if a client comes to me and says he wants something, I, as a lawyer, do not blandly agree to get it for him. I explain the legal position. So, whatever my desires, it was the role of Dr. Spurlin to put them in the proper psychiatric context and—"

"But," Miss Edwina interrupted, with more of that innocence, "I just thought you wanted her out before—"

She stopped.

"Before what, pray?" he asked.

"Before—" she stopped, then plunged on "—before they got that man killed."

"And why that?" he demanded, hearing his own voice distantly, as though it belonged to somebody else, and in that instant, even as the words came out, feeling as though he had missed a stair in the dark.

"So," she began again, paused, flushed, went pale, continued: "So people wouldn't be able to say that you kept her locked up until that man was dead. So you let her out a little before so nobody could say—"

She sat down, as though she had, all at once, come to the end of her energy.

He stepped to the edge of the parlor table and touched his hand to that surface whereon stood the great bell of glass housing the bright colored waxen warblers that perched at random on the garland of waxen orange blossoms. He fixed the glitter of his spectacles full on her. "Do you think," he demanded, "that I am concerned with village gossip? I have done what I think right. I have striven to protect the unfortunate woman who is the widow of my poor slaughtered friend from the consequences of her own mental unbalance. And I should like to point out to you that what I have done has had full legal sanction. As the courts have indicated."

He caught his breath, then went on, feeling his voice icy, elated in a sense of perfect control now, saying: "And it is no wonder, therefore, that I am disturbed. Because that poor woman has now been allowed to run in the night to what pain and mischief—"

"Do you, Murray Guilfort, mean to imply," Miss Edwina was saying, "that I—"

"I am implying nothing," he said, high and icy. "I simply comment on the fact that Cassie Spottwood is being allowed to run somewhere in the dark, this very moment, in her terrible delusion—"

Miss Edwina had risen from her chair as she spoke. She seemed, all at once, refreshed. She had taken a step toward him. The table was now between them, light glittering on the great glass bell, the warblers seeming suddenly alert among blossoms symbolizing the devotion of sexual bliss.

"Delusion?" she asked, in almost a whisper. Then as he stared, her face took on the look of cold, slowly dawning inward certainty. There, in a whisper, in a voice that seemed to be in awe of its own secret, she said: "I—I believe her."

The words echoed in his head. His fingers jerked up from the polished mahogany of the tabletop, as from a hot stove lid. "So," he burst out, in a ringing tone of angry triumph, "so that is your way of confessing that you connived, that you—"

Mis Edwina again sank back down. She looked drained now, her face gray-streaked, the wattles at her throat hanging loose and without color. She was slowly shaking her head. "No," she said, "no, it is not that."

"Well—" he began.

She looked up at him, interrupting. "But perhaps I should have. Connived, I mean. Long back."

He was looking at her now in a calm bemusement that he himself could not comprehend. He could not comprehend why he just stood there and stared at her in this strange torpor. As though his whole body were under Novocaine, existing but not knowing its existence.

Very low, very tired, her voice was saying: "I knew you wanted something out of me, Murray. Wanted to use me some way. But I wasn't smart enough to understand right off. But I ought to have known. For—yes—Murray, you always use people."

The old woman who sat in the chair under his gaze, who wore that not-new black silk dress, whose voice had trailed weakly off into silence—she was just another old woman. But Murray stared at her as though she were truly remarkable, were undergoing a mythical metamorphosis, were splitting the chrysalis of that not-new black silk to emerge in some new form of appalling brightness. He could not take his eyes off her.

She came out of her inward groping, and lifted her gaze to meet his. "You know, Murray," she said, "I never understood you. Not all these years. All I know is, you did something to people around you. You sucked something out of them. Like poor Cousin Bessie."

"She's dead," he heard his voice distantly saying, and heard the marvel in the voice, as though he had never believed it true till now.

"Yes," the woman's gray, drained face was saying, "she is dead. You didn't kill her. You just made it so it didn't matter whether she was dead or not." She paused, looked down at her hands in her lap. "Oh, I don't mean those women in Chicago. I mean something worse. Long before that, I don't know what to call it."

She looked down at a forefinger that had begun to smooth the black silk over her knees. She began to speak again, her eyes on the small task being performed by the finger, her voice abstract. "Bessie wasn't a pretty girl, not exactly. She was bean-pole-thin. Like I was too fat. 'Eddie,' she'd say to me, 'they ought to boil us down together and then take half and half and make you and me over, then we'd come out better.'"

The old woman waited again. Resumed: "No, not pretty, and she didn't have anything in front. But her eyes sparkled, and she was awfully good-natured. People liked to be with her, she was fun to be with. And—" She paused again, the finger ceased its work on the not-new black silk, and she looked at him with an air of sudden dismay: "And she was crazy about you. In the beginning."

She was, he realized, now staring at him with a hard appraisal.

"I never understood why," she answered. "I told her so."

"No," he said slowly, "no, you never liked me," and again, as when he had heard his voice so irrelevantly declare that Bessie was dead, he caught the marveling in the tone. In the silence the ormolu clock on the mantel was ticking.

"No," she agreed. She fell into thought. "Not even when you were poor," she said. And added: "Less, now that you are rich."

She stood up, looking straight at him. "And as for me—I'm tired, sick and tired, of pretending to be rich. I'm sick of being in this house like a jail, just because old General Parker built it. I'm sick of lying awake at night and thinking of money. I'm sick of—"

"But, Edwina—" he burst out in a tone that had in it a glitter of confidence. He took a step around the end of the table, toward her.

"Edwina," he was saying, feeling relief, exculpation, hope, "if I had only known you were upset about money, if you had only given a hint, if you'd only brought your financial problems to me, then I—"

Her face—some unapproachableness, some completeness he had never seen on it before—stopped him in his tracks.

"I don't want anything you've got," she said. She stared at him in a glittering rancor, adding: "Listen here, Murray Guilfort, I wish I *had* connived with that girl. I wish I had taken her out—out of this house—to everybody, and made people, made everybody, believe her. I wish—"

The telephone was ringing.

When he came back from the library, where he had dashed to answer the phone, he found Miss Edwina's gaze again on him.

"Have they found her?" she asked.

"No," he said, feeling dull and drained. "It was Farhill. The Warden had called him from the pen. That Italian was pronounced dead at 12:17."

She studied him.

"That's all you wanted, isn't it, Murray Guilfort?" she said then, very low, as though asking a secret.

Standing there in the middle of the floor, feeling heavy and numb, he said nothing.

"I don't know why you wanted that," she said, "but you've got it now. I hope you are satisfied."

But he was not satisfied.

He stood there, realizing for the first time how, on that morning when he had stood above the bed where Sunderland Spottwood's body lay with a knife in the back, he had experienced a towering, massive, glittering sense of vindication, like a snow peak in sunlight. In that glittering instant he had felt fulfilled in the justice of the world.

And now the dago was dead, and he stood there, and in his interior darkness a tide, black, thick as slime, and nameless, was sluggishly flooding upward. His breath came hard. His nostrils were full of the odor characteristic of this room, the odor of furniture polish mingled with the odor of dusty disuse.

He heard the sound of the clock and could not bear the thought that soon he would be lying in the bed in a hotel room where he would spend the interminable night. He knew that he would lie there, and all night the viscous, lightless tide would be slowly rising in him. It would be like an internal drowning.

And that was the way it was.

Until the telephone rang.

The call came at 3:40 in the morning. They had found Cassie Spottwood. About 11:30 she had tried to gain admittance at the gate of the penitentiary in Fiddlersburg, and had been turned away. Because of the various formalities of an execution, the report from the gate was not called to the attention of the Deputy Warden until almost 1:00, at which time the State Police were notified.

State patrolmen found her, in a semiconscious condition, in a clump of brush, huddled against the stonework of the wall, twenty-five yards south of the main gate, at the base of one of the towers.

EPILOGUE

CHAPTER TWELVE

✟✟✟✟✟✟✟✟✟✟✟ **I**n November 1918, when World War I ended and when Cassie Killigrew was three years old, the State of Tennessee had a population of 2,140,624. It now has a population of 4,049,500. In 1918 the gross income was $655,000,000. It is now $11,151,252,000. Nashville, the capital, with a population in 1918 of 155,815, was a modestly prosperous little market city, with some manufacturing, with banks of a total capitalization of $4,150,000; with four institutions of higher education—a small university, of 982 students in all schools, a teachers college, and a college and a medical school for Negroes—all four institutions founded by Northern philanthropy, which institutions gave the city the claim to be called the "Athens of the South"; and with a replica of the Parthenon, for whose pediment, some years later, the figure of Ganymede would be modeled from a child who was later to become an important American poet. Nashville now has a population of 469,400 with banks of a total capitalization of $37,800,000. In 1918 the gross income of the city was $29,950,000; it is now $1,589,083,000. And the poet who, as a child, was the model for Ganymede is dead.

As for Spottwood Valley in that earlier period, there was a population of 192. On the six farms of the Valley owned by whites, the families of the owners accounted for 37 persons. On each of these farms there were two to four families of Negro tenants, accounting for 82 persons. The difference of 73 persons was made up by the families of Dr. Tucker, the owner of the sawmill, the storekeeper at the Corners, and the hillbillies, like the Grinders, who scratched a few corn patches up the creek and watched the soil wash away, ran a few hogs, hunted and fished, worked for the sawmill, and did some distilling, illegal of course.

The total income of the 192 inhabitants was, in 1918, something around $70,000. Of this, approximately $45,000 was earned by the six large farmers, including the Spottwoods, Killigrews, and Guilforts, and something under $10,000, by the Negro tenants; $3,285 by Dr. Tucker; $2,544 by the owner of the sawmill; $1,823 by the storekeeper; and again something under $10,000 by the hillbillies. The figures for the Negroes and the hillbillies are, at best, rough estimates, interpreted rather liberally.

Today the Valley is largely under water, a dam having been constructed near the Corners. The total population is now 17. Cy Grinder, his wife, and only child, a girl named Gladys for her mother, live on the old Grinder place, which has been greatly improved since the days of Old Budge, the jug-fighter, moonshiner, brawler, jailbird, and generally hard case. Fourteen people live at what is called the Landing, on the edge of the woods bordering what once was the ruined cornfield above the Spottwood house. There are three dwellings at the Landing, tight little prefabs bright with new paint, a snack bar and cold-drink stand, and a stand where tackle and bait are for sale, and where boats can be rented or moorings reserved.

The place is called the Landing because the new road to Spottwood Lake ends there. The woods, which border the lake, have been thinned and cleared of brush, and there are neat picnic tables of oiled redwood, and stone fireplaces. The whole area is now a State Park and game preserve. Cy Grinder is the game warden, head of the rangers, and when occasion demands, the fire boss. One ranger and his family live at the Landing. The other two and a couple of maintenance men do not live in the Valley at all—that is, on what remains un-flooded and still available for human habitation—but on the slope of the ridge to the west of the old Valley, which is also part of the park.

The total income of the Valley is now some $37,000. The people at the Landing do well, in a good year making around $21,000, this including the salary of the ranger who gets $7,200, and does some moonlighting for tourists and fishermen. Cy Grinder's salary is $9,500, but in addition, he clears, with his thrift and ferocious energy, some $7,000 a year feeding cattle for market. The old Grinder place had some bench land level enough and well watered, and Cy has long since cleared that and sowed it to pasture, and has one good corn bottom. As for the family living, all vegetables, fowl, and meat, including pork and venison, are taken fresh off the land, or from the deep-freeze locker which he built into the cellar of the old house when he renovated and enlarged it.

Cy has prospered. He has managed to increase his land holdings, and land prices are rising. He has, in government bonds and savings accounts, over $65,000, and an equity in an insurance policy for $25,000. He is devoted to his daughter, a senior at the Cardwell County High School, who is pretty and graceful, for several years has been a drum majorette of the school band, and makes wonderful grades. He has laid aside money in a special fund to send her to a good college. His only nightmare is that something will happen to her. When he wakes at night, he always slips out of bed and goes to her room and looks at her as she sleeps.

In the period after the trial of Angelo Passetto, Cy Grinder learned to be, on the whole, content. He could be in the woods as much as he liked, alone. He could be happy for hours watching a red-tail hawk in the sky, a deer feeding, or a beaver working on his dam, for now, after a century of absence, beaver have come back. He could be happy, too, thinking of the time when his daughter would grow up and he would have a little grandson to take with him to the woods, to teach quietness to, and all the sleights and knowledge he had grown into over the years. He would like to teach the little boy, for somebody ought to carry on those hard-to-come-by things, even if folks out in the world never seemed to care anymore. Meanwhile, he had a good friend in the biologist from the State University who worked on the Wild Life Survey, and who gave him books and pamphlets, and with whom he worked on several projects.

His health remained vigorous, and except for the nightmares about his daughter, he usually slept well. He had learned the trick of thinking, every night before trying to sleep, of what he could do the next day, what task he would turn his hand to, where he would go on the Reservation. So he almost never thought of the past.

This was his great achievement, for during the first ten or twelve years after he had come back to the Valley, almost any bend in the road, a dell by the creek at the season when leaves were turning, the view across a field in spring, the glimpse of the old fallen-in schoolhouse, might strike his heart a bruising blow that made him gasp like an apoplectic. In those days he even sought out such moments of pain, like an addict, for, somehow, only in such moments did he feel real.

After such an episode he might come back to his house and drink a half-pint of whisky, and sit sullen all evening. Or, in the period after his marriage, he might come back to wreak himself and his pain, in a cold rage more painful than the pain it assuaged, on the shapeless mass that was the body of Gladys Peegrum Grinder.

But finally he learned to move untouched through the corridors of haunting and fierce symbols that the Valley was. So a tree became only a tree, a stone only a stone. And when the Reservation had acquired the new land and announced the project of flooding the Valley, Cy began to feel that the past itself would be flooded and he would be free to live in the contentment that was possible in the life of each day. He came to feel, in fact, that part of his own being was already under water, and he thought of the shadowy depths with a kind of cold contentment.

It was like the feeling he had whenever he went to the sanatorium, as for several years he regularly did, to see Cassie Spottwood.

She always recognized him. She would speak affectionately to him, as to child or brother. She might even refer to the past—except for that part of it which, in her delusion, she had now blotted out or revised nearer to her heart's need. After a time she seemed to have triumphed over the past, living in a calm joy. It was only from this calm joy, Cy Grinder came to believe, that his own secret life had been possible. He had learned to draw off, decant, and dilute that joy, converting it, thinned out, into the careful contentment by which he lived.

As for Murray Guilfort, a good part of the time now he was not in Cardwell County, having an office in Nashville, where most of his business was centered, with Jack Farhill there as partner and manager. But Murray kept the office in Parkerton, too, with Sam Piercy in charge. Sam, in spite of his humble hill beginnings, had shaped up well since the days when he was lucky to get $50 for serving as guardian *ad litem* for Cassie's commitment. Sam, however, had not been Murray's first choice. Leroy Lancaster had been that.

Murray had been very pleased with himself when he first struck on that idea. To begin with, something had certainly happened to make Leroy shape up, no doubt about it. He had left off his bumbling and had hit his stride at last. He had got hold of, and won, two pretty big cases. People said that what had come over Leroy was finally getting Corinne knocked up and having that boy—which was almost as much of a trick, they said, as Abraham knocking up old Sarah and getting Isaac. Sure, Leroy was bucked over the boy, Murray thought, with faintly contemptuous tolerance, but whatever it was that had come over Leroy had come earlier, he calculated, back in the Passetto business. People simply forgot the fight he had put up for the dago, because back then they had mostly been against what he was up to. It was later that they caught on to the new Leroy, and to everybody's surprise, including their own, voted him in as prosecutor, over Farhill.

Murray had been surprised at this, too, and had been, in a way he didn't understand, quite upset. But he quickly realized that it was because Farhill was really an urban type, and had, for all his ability, merely a stand-offishness rather than the kind of dignity that country people respect. So Murray decided to send Farhill to Nashville and take Leroy on at Parkerton. Leroy was certainly good, and besides, Murray reflected with satisfaction, it would show that he held no grudge for the trouble Leroy had caused, and that Leroy didn't hold any grudge, either. It was all in the game. So he made Leroy a very handsome offer, partnership and all.

The only trouble was, it didn't work. At first Leroy hemmed and hawed, and said that he didn't think he was the man for the job. Murray insisted that he was too modest, he certainly was the man for the job. No, he wasn't, Leroy repeated, and then, in the calmest way in the world, so calm Murray simply couldn't believe his ears when it came out, Leroy said: "Besides, Murray, I just don't want your fucking job."

Murray wasn't going to forget that in a hurry. He reckoned he swung enough weight, politically speaking, to make Sam Piercy prosecutor next round. By God he'd make him county judge. Sam had that hill twang in his voice and he'd find votes Leroy didn't even know existed. When those hill boys were smart, they were really smart, and Sam had tasted blood now. Yes, Murray thought, he would take care of Leroy.

Murray was, indeed, a power to be considered. His years of cultivating political influence had paid off. In spite of his stiff manner, he had a knack for hospitality, and if the guests who came to Durwood for the weekends of quail-shooting, black-label sour mash, and vintage wines, had originally thought him odd and fussy, they began, after the trial and the revelations about his hidden life in Chicago, to regard him in a new light. The very contrast between his stiffness, fussiness, and Phi Beta Kappa key on the one hand, and the vision of elegant debauchery with expensive call girls in Chicago on the other, titillated their sense of the dramatic, of the ironies and quirks of life. And the heartier specimens got the habit of clapping him on the shoulder by way of greeting, exclaiming, "Murray, you old cocksman, you!"

It is true that the aroma of high living and sexual license that now emanated from Murray Guilfort offended the nostrils of the more churchy elements in a place like Parkerton. But the same trial that had divulged the secret of his capacity for debauch had also divulged the secret of his capacity for self-sacrificing friendship. Not many men would fork over hard cash, year after year, to take care of a ruined friend like that Sunderland Spottwood. And what he said in court, when Leroy

Lancaster tried to make it appear damaging—how did it go? Oh, yes:—"and if a man's attempt to be faithful to a friend is a cause for shame and a provocation for the obscene leer, then—"

Murray could sure swing the English language. But it wasn't just a speech either, something cooked up for a purpose. It had just burst out, there in court. It was sincere. You could trust a man like that. All the newspapers had printed what just burst out of Murray Guilfort.

Three years after the death of his friend, Murray Guilfort was Attorney General. Three years later he was a member of the Supreme Court of the state. It was a popular appointment, and when he attended meetings of the Bar Association, he found the respect he had craved.

Or assumed that he found it.

By this time people had, however, long since stopped talking about the trial. After the excitement of the execution, it became uncomfortable to talk about. For one thing, if that crazy woman's confession was true, an innocent man had been executed right in their midst. Maybe he was not innocent of being a nigger-lover, and at the same time not much better than a nigger himself, and had been fooling, maybe, with a white woman. But was that enough to execute a man for? Maybe shoot him for, maybe lynch him for, if folks got worked up, but execution was different someway. It got mixed up with what law was. The thing was uncomfortable to talk about. You found yourself saying things you weren't too sure you believed, whichever side you took, whatever you said.

Guilty or innocent, the thing was uncomfortable to talk about in another way. It was lonesome. It was lonely. It was lonely to think of yourself paralyzed, trapped in yourself that way like you were your own coffin, and somebody picking you up carefully and setting a knife to go into your back. It was lonelier than getting stabbed, face forward, of a sudden. It was lonely to think of that young fellow—the dago—and that old woman lying up there together, at night, in that fallen-in house, and that paralyzed man in the next room. It was lonely to think of that woman, even if she was crazy—but was she crazy then?— driving to Nashville and trying to see the Governor and not seeing him. It was lonely to think of having something in you that made you try to get into the pen just when they were getting ready to strap the dago on the hot squat, and not getting in. It was lonely to lie beside that stone wall of the pen, in the brush, at night, and grab the stone till your hands bled, trying to get in, you loved somebody so much, if that was what you call loving.

It was even lonelier for the dago, if you chose to regard it that way.

It was, then, the loneliness that made people uncomfortable when they talked about the trial. But it was the loneliness, strangely enough, that made people keep on remembering even if they did not talk. You thought of it at night just before going to sleep. Or woke up just before day and started thinking about it. You might be walking home from the store or office and suddenly think that your wife was getting old and shapeless and when you came in the door she would look at you as though she didn't know you. Or you might realize that you yourself were old, and you might suddenly wonder what was in her head. Or if you were a woman, you might be sitting in a room shuttered shadowy against the heat on a summer afternoon, and wonder what that crazy Spottwood woman had got out of life that you never got, and the loneliness would suddenly overcome you like lostness and too-lateness, and a grief you had no name for.

So out of all this loneliness, nameless grief, unspecified guilt, and a need to atone for everything and to forget something, you voted for Leroy Lancaster.

As for Murray Guilfort, he wanted to forget, too. It made him uncomfortable to go and see Cassie Spottwood. It made everything, even his success, taste like ashes on his tongue. So he quit going. He paid the monthly bill and tried to forget the whole business.

But he could not. He thought about it at strange times. He came into a room, and the thing would be standing there, patiently waiting. The sunlight might fall through it and it cast no shadow, but there it stood.

On a bright afternoon in May, at the time when the dam was under construction, Murray drove slowly beside the creek, up Spottwood Valley. Coming into the Valley for the first time in years now, he stopped, just above the Corners, to look at the work on the dam that would create Spottwood Lake. Now he was on his way to the Spottwood farm. He had told himself that, as executor for the estate, he should take one last look at the property to see if anything was worth salvaging—for the terms of the sale had given this right. He was sure that there was nothing there. But you couldn't be too careful when you had an obligation. A man ought to be conscientious. He had even leaned over backward about Edwina Parker, after all the mess she had made for him. He had sent her a check for a sum that would amply repay her for her time and trouble, and when the check came back, neatly torn in half, accompanied by not a word, he wrote her a letter that he considered to be logical, conciliatory, and dignified, with, of course, another check. That letter came back unopened. But when, a few months later, her house came up for sale, he had his opportunity.

Seven years earlier he had founded the West Tennessee History Association, and bit by bit, under his unobtrusive guidance, it had developed into what he regarded as a significant organization. What now the Association needed most, he soon decided, was an appropriate center, a building to house its records and growing library and to provide a gracious background for its activities. Old General Parker's house, especially if its splendid library could also be procured, would be appropriate in all ways. An anonymous gift to the Association took care of everything. The price of the house was, relatively speaking, low; it was easy to outbid the Morning Glory Funeral Parlor, which was anxious to acquire the property for its headquarters. Furthermore, Murray stood in need, at this moment, of tax relief.

So, willy-nilly, Miss Edwina got taken care of. It did not matter to Murray—in fact, it gave him a certain ironic pleasure —that when he met Miss Edwina on the street she would cut him dead. That is, if there were no spectators. If there happened to be spectators, she would manage a stiff bow. She was, Murray was bound to confess, a lady, and did not make a private difficulty into occasion for public comment.

Murray had some obligation to Miss Edwina. She was, after all, a kinswoman of Bessie. But he had even leaned over backward to take care of that colored woman Arlita—though what obligation he had to her would, God knew, be a hard thing to define. The State Park people had needed to buy her forty acres, and since taxes were in arrears, they might have simply waited for a tax sale. But he, Murray Guilfort, had taken it upon himself to put an investigation agency on the trail of the woman. They had found her, in Chattanooga. She had a job as a wrapper in a department store. He took some comfort in that information. Yes, she was clean and energetic and not without intelligence, and it showed what one of them could do, if they put their mind to it.

He had to go to Chattanooga anyway, and, on impulse, he decided he might take care of the business. If some half-baked young squirt from a law office in Chattanooga was sent down he would probably get her all confused, and things would end in a tangle. But Murray would know how to explain things so she would understand, she would know he wasn't trying to rob her, and after all, she was from Spottwood Valley and that fact, in a peculiar way he did not scrutinize, gave him some sense of responsibility in the matter.

He found the address, a shotgun bungalow in bad repair but with the patch of yard clear of the trash that had accumulated around similar houses to each side. The interior was clean, and smelled clean. There was a picture on the wall, of a waterfall, the blue and white of water, the green of forest, and blue of hills beyond. It was the sort of picture you buy in what used to be called a dime store, but it was a picture. On the dingy sofa, there were two new sofa pillows in some sort of tapestry design. A framed photograph was on the mantel, the rather fuzzy enlargement of a snapshot of a child of three or four, with a big bow on her hair. That, he assumed, was the girl. What was her name? Charlene.

The woman gave no trouble. He carefully explained how the price per acre was the same as that paid for the Spottwood land (he had documentary evidence to offer on that point, he knew how suspicious they sometimes are), how if she refused, eminent domain would probably be invoked, and so on. She said, "I'll sign," and waited while he went out to call in the cab driver as a witness.

She looked up from the signing, and said: "It ought-a been drownt out long back."

Then she burst out laughing.

The cab driver, finishing his careful signature, looked at the face contorted in that sudden mirth, shook his head, and went out.

Murray was looking at that face, too, thinking that she had a right to laugh, she had just got an unexpected and unpre-

dictable $6,ooo for having got on her back a few times for
Sunderland Spottwood, and that was high pay by any standard,
especially for her brand of commodity. Then looking into the
contorted and aging face he wondered what had ever made
Sunder want to get into bed with her in the first place.

As the face convolved and writhed, he looked down at the
yellow slickness of skin, at the palpitating swollenness of veins
faintly blue-green in the neck, at the sliding of flesh and
musculature under the yellow skin of the face as it worked in
laughter, at the wideness, the slight bulginess, the yellow
depthlessness of the eyes glittering like tears in that mirth. As
he stood staring at her, the thought slowly formed in his head:
She was young then.

And in that instant he was engulfed by such a wave of lust,
envy, sick fear, revulsion, and nameless yearning, that his
head spun, his throat clamped shut, and his knees shook as he
stood there, and he had to reach out and put his hand to the
back of a chair to stay himself.

"Anyway, Arlita," he then heard his voice, in a dry, gritty,
distant vengefulness, saying, "six thousand dollars is a lot of
money."

"Yes," she said, "it's a lot of money."

"Well," he said, and wished his voice would stop, for he
wanted to leave, to go away, never see her again, "you got
that. And you got that Passetto fellow executed. You wanted
that, didn't you?"

Abruptly, she stood up. Her face had lost that yellow slickness. It was streaked with gray, like wood ashes. Her eyes did
not glitter. "A lot of good six thousand dollars'll do," she said.
"Or that Eye-tal-yun being dead, neither."

She moved toward a door that led to a room beyond, and
pushed it open. "Come here," she said. No *please,* no *please,
sir:* just *come here.*

(3 4 9)

He obeyed.

"Look yonder." She gestured into the dimness of that further room.

On the floor, in the bar of light that came from below a pulled-down window shade, a shoe lay on its side. Across a straight chair, trailing the floor, a green dress had been flung. The gesture of weariness and contempt that had flung it seemed yet fixed in the air. On the bed was a body swathed in a patchwork quilt. Even in the heavy wrapping the body looked skeleton thin.

"That's her," the woman said.

Looking across the dimness, wanting to leave, to get out of here but feeling trapped, he managed to think of something to say: "Is she sick?"

"Naw, she mainline-en."

He looked at the woman in question.

"Doan even know what mainline-en is," she announced as to an unseen and jeering audience.

"All right," he retorted in anger, "what is it?"

"Dope," she said, "you pump it in."

She studied the figure on the bed. "Long time after they done let her out, she did'n do nuthen but set. Eat and set, and sleep. Did'n take no in'rest. Got fat and poochy. Little fat rings round her wrists, she got so fat and poochy. Then she got so she go out some. I come home from work and she say she done taken a walk. I figgered she done started to take a in'rest, go out the house. Fat begun to sweat off. But naw—"

She stopped, resumed: "Dope. She'd go git it. Go on the street. Mainline-en a'ready." She studied the figure on the bed yonder as though she had just discovered it. Then burst out: "God-durn, warn't my fault! Could'n be here all day and make no liven, me worken."

Murray turned from the door of the room where the girl lay.

"Six thousand dollars," the woman said, "it'll buy a lot of dope."

"I've got to go," he said, and caught the apology in his tone.

He crossed the sitting room, got to the front door, laid his hand to the knob. He was surprised to find the woman there at his elbow, silent in her old tennis shoes.

"That Eye-tal-yun," she said, "they burn him."

His hand was turning the knob.

"But—" she began, thrusting her face closer, then saying: "They done burn the wrong 'un!"

"Now look here, Arlita," he cut in angrily, "the court—"

She was looking at him in a wild and yellow-eyed derision that filled the dim air with a brilliance worse than laughter.

"Yore ole coh'ts!" she said.

As now the white convertible slouched luxuriously over the ruts, up Spottwood Valley with the creek on the right and the Spottwood land now on the left, Murray Guilfort was not remembering what had happened in Chattanooga. He was trying to remember nothing. He was thinking that soon, when the land lay under the dark suffocation of water, there would be nothing to remember.

Then he was at the house, and went in.

The light of afternoon, a shadowy gold streaked with blue, a light cool and sourceless, hung without motion among the newly fleshed leafage of May beyond the windows, and filled the house like the stillness of water. His body drifted from room to room, slowly, weightlessly, as though floating through that medium. He moved without recognition, room after room, for in his knowledge there was no need for recognition. Each object was monolithic and wrapped in its mystic repose, as though he, the boy who, a half-century before, had moved through these rooms, had never existed any more than the man he was existed now, as though whatever existence he might, in some cosmic whimsy, have been conceived to have, had long since been totally absorbed by these forms whose eyes, unseen but seeing, broodingly stared at him from the frieze of the world.

No—whatever eyes might be there, were not fixed on him, they were fixed, he felt, on the empty space in which he was supposed to be but was not. He felt air move in that space. Light, he knew, flowed through that space.

Standing in the middle of the floor of the room which had once been the dining room, but was the room in which Sunderland Spottwood had passed the last years of his life and had died, he closed his eyes and tried not to breathe. If, far off, a towhee called, that isolated, musical lament was only part of the silence. The sound of the beating of his own heart was no more than the pulse of the silence. It was as though nothing had ever happened.

It was then that he heard his name.

In the precious nothingness which was the darkness behind the closed eyelids, even as a clutch came at his heart and his scalp prickled, that name came as clearly as though somebody had spoken it: *Murray Guilfort!*

And somebody had.

For when he opened his eyes, there the form was, framed in the doorway to the hall, assuming shape, color, identity, a strongly built not-tall man, black felt hat slouched on head, red flannel shirt, corduroy pants stuck into boots, a hand ax hanging from belt.

"Murray Guilfort—durn if it ain't," the man was saying. "But I never meant to give you heart failure, Mr. Guilfort, like I thought I had done for a second there, you was so white in the face. But"—and the man came a step into the room—"it's Judge Guilfort now, ain't it?

Murray was staring at the man. "You—" he said, "you're Cy Grinder."

"That's me," Cy Grinder said.

Cy took another step toward him, inspecting him, saying: "You sure you're all right, Judge? You look white and shook up."

"I'm all right," Murray said.

"Sorry I skeered you," Cy said. "But these-here boots, they're soft-sole. And I guess I got the habit, being out in the woods, of just not making no noise. Anyway, it's my business to sort of keep an eye on things. I was up to the west ridge and seen a car."

"Yes," Murray said.

"Back a time," Cy said, "lots of folks come, you'd be surprised. Two, three years after the trial. Come to look at the place. It warn't none of my business back then, me not being warden then. But I seen 'em. Folks come by daylight, just looking. After sundown they come to screw. All this way just to screw in a place where something happened. To git a diff'rent kind of a jolt, I reckon. Now ain't that peculiar, Judge?"

"Yes," he said.

Cy approached the bed on which Sunderland Spottwood had spent all those years, and looked down at it. "Ain't nothing changed here," he said. "All them years now and that sheet, what ain't rotted off, still laying there. That"—and he pointed —"that's the spot where the blood come out of Sunder Spottwood and soaked in. But you was here that morning, warn't you?"

"Yes," Murray said.

"Then you seen it fresh," Cy said. He studied the dusty brown stain, then said: "But the funny thing is, word being round the country about goings-on here, some fellow used to come to screw right on this-here bed. Bring some woman all this way to screw her on this-here bed. Now ain't that something?"

(353)

"Yes," Murray said.

"I seen them cundrums throwed on the floor," Cy said. He continued to study the stain, his gaze sharpening with the effort, his face clouding. Finally, not lifting his head, he said: "It was a long time back." He continued to study the stain. "Now all gonna be drownt out," he said. He looked up suddenly at Murray. "Sunder Spottwood dead. The dago cooked. You a judge, and yore name in the papers. Me—I'm game warden. And—" He took a step toward the other man, peering into his face. "Was it you," he demanded, "made that-air durn doctor stop letting me see her? See Cassie?"

Murray wet his lips. "Dr. Spurlin—" he began, then stopped. Then said: "I am sure Dr. Spurlin follows his best medical judgment."

"Shit," Cy Grinder said. "But you don't have to be worrying no more about it. Ain't nobody cares now. You don't ever have to worry no more about her." He studied Murray's face. "When the last time you seen her?"

"Well"—Murray began—"not that it's any concern of yours, but—"

"Three years," Cy interrupted triumphantly. "I sort of tricked a nurse into saying it. But if you'd been going out there lately, you'd know yore worries are over."

"I can't imagine what you are talking about, Mr. Grinder," Murray said icily.

"She's done changed her tune," he said. "That's what I'm talking about. She's done forgot how things were, how it was her put that knife—"

"Listen, Mr. Grinder," Murray cut in, "if the doctors have been successful in curing the poor woman of her delusions—"

"Delusions, shit," Cy said. "I don't care if she stabbed Sunder Spottwood every Sunday in the month. Nothing to me, except I want her to feel good as she can. If it was telling the truth it took to make her feel good, OK by me. But now—"

He stopped, gave a quick laugh, bright as an ax blade.

"Well," he resumed, "the truth has done gone and changed on her. She's got a whole new kind of truth."

He was grinning at Murray. "You ought to go see," he said. "If'n you can spare the time. From the judge-business."

Then he was gone, and Murray was alone in the room.

He had sworn not to do it. Not to come. But here he was, in the waiting room surrounded by the flaking calsomined walls of institutional green, amid the furniture of bird's-eye maple and the stacks of old magazines with boldly colored covers that proclaimed the importance of the world, and the door was opening. Cassie Spottwood was there.

She was wearing a dark skirt, a gray pullover with a white collar showing, black-and-white saddle shoes. She had put on a little weight, but was still slender enough. The black hair, piled loose, showed no gray. Her face was pale, and the dark eyes glittered. She was looking at him across the room, a smile on her face, bright and unexpected as a new tin pie plate you hang on a cherry tree to turn in the breeze and keep the birds off.

"I know who you are," she said, brightly.

"Cassie," he said, "I'm sorry I haven't—"

"You're Murray Guilfort!" she announced triumphantly, and smiled the smile of a little girl waiting to be congratulated for her recitation.

He came and put out his hand. Politely, she offered hers, and he took it. The flesh of the hand was dry, cool, boneless. To his pressure the hand was as unresponsive as a small rubber glove filled with sawdust. When he released the hand he was surprised that it did not fall to the floor, like a detached object.

"Let's sit down," he said. He was tired.

With the smile like a tin plate turning lightly in the breeze, she obeyed. She sat primly on a straight chair of bird's-eye maple, crossed her ankles, laid her hands in her lap, palms up in a kind of little-girl parody of ladylikeness, and looked brightly, expectantly, at him.

"Cassie," he began, quite formally. "I'm sorry I haven't been by lately. But work—you see, I've got new and heavier responsibilities—I am now—"

He heard his voice trail off. He did not want to hear his voice saying what it had been about to say, and he was glad the voice had changed its mind. He felt very tired.

She was looking at him in a posture of attention so perfectly polite that it was inattention. A robin out there would not stop its mellow, drowsy, petulant note: *gluck,* silence, then *gluck,* like water dropping.

"Cassie," he began again, "I just wanted to come by and see how you are."

"Oh, I'm fine, Mr. Guilfort," she said brightly.

"You used to call me Murray," he said.

"Oh, did I?" she said, with not the least flicker of memory across her face, or in her voice.

"You always did," he said. "From the first time I saw you. You remember, I was Sunder's oldest friend."

He paused. "His best friend."

"Oh," she said, as though remembering, "Poor Sunder."

"Yes, poor Sunder," he said.

He looked at the hands lying so passive on the lap over there: not large, lying palm up, inert, empty, weak.

Then, suddenly, he saw those hands gripping the shoulder of Sunderland Spottwood, straining, lifting the body, the veins standing out blue on the whiteness of the hands. His head twitched sideways as in a spasm of chill, or denial. The shudder passed.

(356)

"The doctor," he said, "he writes me that you are feeling much better."

He wished he had not lied. Whatever the doctor had written he had not read, but then, the doctor must have written that.

"Oh, yes," she was agreeing, in social brightness, "for a long time now. You see," she continued in the tone of cheerful chattiness, "it is always hard at first. When you've had to make yourself do something. Even if it's something you know is right. You know how it is, don't you?" Then, tentatively, as though trying out the sound: "Don't you—Murray?"

She looked at him brightly, as though expecting an answer. But he had no answer.

Then she was going on. "Even if it is right," she was saying, "it may hurt you," and as she spoke, the hands on the lap stirred, lifted, the palms still upward and open, the fingers making delicate little weaving motions as though engaged in some invisible game of cat's-cradle, or in an effort at some too subtle explanation.

"Even if it has to be," she was saying, "it's a shock to you. It takes time to get over it, even if you are glad. It is like—" She stopped, then pressed the hands, hard, over her heart. "Like you tore your heart out," she resumed, "and threw it away." She stopped again. "No," she said then, the shadow of thought passing over her face now. "Not that. Not throw it away. No—" she said, and the brightness came suddenly back, not the brightness of a smile hanging like a tin pie plate, but, all at once, as she rose to stand before him, a luminousness from within.

"Murray"—and she cast her gaze full on him, in a deep, enveloping, not-to-be-denied demandingness—"did you ever *love* anybody, Murray Guilfort?"

The gaze was on him, even as he shifted in his chair trying to escape.

(357)

"Yes," he said, with dry lips, but the question kept on echoing over and over, down the dark corridors and recesses of his being.

She was saying: "If you have loved somebody, you know how it is, how you tear your heart out, just to give it away, and that is a great joy. Even if it hurts and even if they don't want it, even if they just look at it and laugh and drop it, like it was nothing, and walk on away—but Murray, listen, and I'll tell you something!"

She came closer.

"It doesn't matter," she said, "because it—your heart, I mean —it belongs to them anyway. Even if they just drop it and walk away, you're happy. It may be terrible, but you are happy. Listen, Murray—"

Her voice had gone calm and factual.

"Let me tell you how he came," she said. "It was drizzling rain and I saw him, far off, coming down the road, in the mud, and it was like he was a torch of some kind with a white flame. It was like it was a flame so white you could hardly see it in daylight, him moving toward me in the rain, but the rain was not putting the flame out."

She stopped, then took a step closer, demanding: "Do you know what he did?"

"No," he said.

"He made me feel beautiful," she said. "He made me feel a way I'd never been—he called me *piccola mia*—" She repeated the words with great care, sounding each syllable. "But the time came," she said.

In the moment of silence, Murray could hear, far off and faintly, the rattle of cutlery. They were getting ready to feed the patients.

"Didn't you ever love anybody?" Cassie asked, and not waiting for an answer plunged on. "Yes, I loved him—but all of a sudden, I was old, and I said, 'Take the money, take the car and the girl, and go—go where you want to go—but be good to her.' And you know what he did?"

Murray shook his head.

"He knelt down. He took my right hand in both of his, and he kissed my hand. Then he went away, but—" She had stepped back from him, not looking at him now, her head lifted, looking far away. "He has gone away," she was saying. "Somewhere far away, and he is happy. And I'm happy too, because I made him happy, for oh, I loved him—"

Her hands were lifted as though to frame a face, caressing it. Her eyes were staring into the empty space between her hands. Then the eyes closed. Her body swayed as she stood there as though surrendering to an embrace. He saw her hands held there in the air, saw them caressing the face that was not there, in the empty air that was not empty.

"Stop it!" he commanded, rising from his chair, kicking the chair back.

Her eyes opened. She turned toward him. Her face was fresh as a child's on waking.

"Do you know where he is," he demanded, "that dago?"

Before she could respond, while her face yet hung there in that dewy brightness, he stepped at her, thrusting his face at hers, saying: "He's dead—that's where!"

As she became aware of the words, she was looking at him with a pitying, indulgent smile.

"Dead in the electric chair," he said. "Convicted, executed—and do you know why?"

She was smiling the pitying smile.

"For murdering Sunderland Spottwood," he plunged on, lifted out of himself, high and free in that instant when wind from great spaces seemed to be whistling past him. "For stabbing him to death. But look here—" He stopped. He gathered himself to say it, thrusting his face at her, saying: "But he was innocent!"

(359)

He was breathless, dizzy. He knew what was going to happen.

"It was you," he said.

It had happened.

But, with the pitying smile, she shook her head, saying: "Why, Murray—Murray Guilfort—you just made up every word of that, not a word's true."

His breath came back. "God damn it," he burst out, "it's true and you know it. For you—"

"That's the silliest thing I ever heard," she said. "Poor Sunder, he was sick, he—"

"Listen here, Cassie—" he uttered, feeling the blood beat in his head. Then: "God damn it, don't you remember!"

But she was pitying him with that smile, across a great distance, saying, "Of course, how Angelo—how he went away—and he's happy."

As he drew the door closed behind him, he looked back, and through the narrowing slit, he saw her yet standing there, her face calm and pure, not looking at him, but into distance, like a lamp in the darkening room.

In the hall a nurse stopped him to say that Dr. Spurlin would like to speak to him. He couldn't wait, he said, and fled to his car.

He started the car and slid down the drive, where the first intimations of dusk were gathering under the old maples, a subaqueous, cool, unswaying green. High beyond the maples, he caught sight of the sky, lemon-pale and bright.

He came out into the full light of the road, saw the openness of fields, the distance of hills, the height of sky, and, fleeing furiously into that emptiness, felt a sudden relief. He was fleeing from the luminous joy on the face of that woman.

What right did she have to it? He hated her because she had

it. So he fled into the empty distance of the world.

But the world was not empty.

He saw it ahead, coming at him, every detail mystically precise in the opening brilliance of the world: the little house set in a yard that was simply the squared-off corner of a field with a wire fence, one tree, an enormous cedar, in the yard, the house once painted white but dingy now, the tin roof rusting, the tumbled-down barn, the mule in the lot by the patch of mud pond gleaming in the evening light, the backhouse of weathered boards, the wisp of smoke crawling blue and sleepy up the air, every detail whirling at him in that merciless microscopic clarity, the flecking of rust on the no-longer-bright tin of the roof, the line of wash hung out in the yard, the chicken tracks on the damp bare earth by the kitchen door where dishwater had been flung out.

He could see it all. His head was full of vision. All, everything, every detail, however minute, came flying into the enormous, wounded, bleeding eye that was his brain. He was spared nothing.

Everything was flying at him. The woman in a straight chair under the cedar, he saw her now, and saw that she was giving suck to a baby, saw the whiteness of the orb of the breast, saw the black hairs that ringed the brown nipple slick with wetness for a moment when the nipple was withdrawn from the baby's mouth, saw the tiny hand like a pink bird-claw of fierce feebleness clutching against the orb of the breast.

He saw everything.

He could have forgiven everything if the children—two others, young, hanging on the wire fence—had not cried out to him, and waved. No, he could have forgiven even that.

If the woman had not waved, too.

What right had she to smile when the unsayable thing was swelling in his chest? He hated her.

He hated the man who would come in from the field. His

brogans would clump on boards. His blue shirt would be dark across the shoulders, for the sweat was not yet dry. She would smile at him.

He fled on down the road, faster. The light filled the high sky. The fields swayed and swung and pivoted like cards splayed from a deck. In a field, far off, a man was riding a yellow tractor across the high black swell of field. A flight of grackles flared upward across the height of sky, in the sweep of their ever-shifting and re-forming pattern, like the pattern of a wave, glittering darkly like purple seed flung inexhaustibly upward into that lemon light.

He fled on.

But there was no flight *from*, that was the terror, only *toward*. *Toward:*

Two little boys were fishing in a stream. They looked up as the car whirled over the bridge. He saw their faces lifted, pale and pure. They would be late for supper.

An old Negro man was walking slowly along the edge of the highway. He was carrying a basket in one hand, with the other leading a little Negro child, a girl, in a stiff-starched red dress and little red ribbons tied on the teats of her hair. The car was racing toward them. The old man grinned. Why did he grin? He was old and poor and black, and he grinned.

Two lovers were entering a woods. The girl wore a yellow dress. The man wore khaki pants and a blue shirt. His arm was around her waist. He was much taller than she. His hand was big at her waist, on the yellow dress.

An old man was hoeing in his vegetable patch, in the evening light. When the blade of the hoe rose, it caught the light, it was polished so bright. All at once, the old man stopped work, leaning on the hoe while he wiped his bald, sunburned head with a red bandanna. The light glittered on his spectacles. An old woman, fat, with white hair, was coming from the house, a tray in her hand. On the tray was a tall glass of what looked

like iced tea, with a sprig of mint in it. She was bringing it to
the old man.

There was no emptiness in the world.

In the world there was no place to flee, from the joy on the
face of Cassie Killigrew Spottwood.

The world was full of people.

He had originally intended to spend the night in his apart-
ment in Nashville, but here he was at Durwood, which had
once been Bessie's house, but which was now his own, for hadn't
he bought it ten times over, with its swelling meadows, clipped
hedges, rose garden, fences white around the pastures, stables
glistening white? Bought it with all the money and judgment
and everything else—what? but he did not name what else—
that he had poured into it.

In the hall, feet set on the burgundy-colored Aubusson, under
the glitter of the big chandelier suspended unlighted from the
upper dimness, he caught a glimpse of himself in the great
pier glass framed in gold, himself a graying man talking to a
graying old Negro in a white jacket obviously just jerked on,
for the collar was twisted inward. Murray Guilfort was saying,
no, he'd just have something light, just a light supper, he wasn't
hungry, he was sorry he hadn't let Aunt Delfie know he was
coming, no, he wouldn't ride in the morning, he had to get on
to Nashville, but had the vet been to see about Starlight's
strained tendon?

He took a bath. He put on a gray checked shirt with a soft
rolled collar, a dark brown tweed jacket with elbow patches,
gray flannel slacks, and slippers, and came downstairs. In the
study, Leonidas had set out the whiskey and ice. He took a
drink. Not once had he looked at the wall, where, behind an
oak panel, the safe was. He had taken two drinks before
Leonidas announced that his dinner was ready.

After dinner, again in the study, he had a brandy. He did not once look at the wall. After he had heard the nine o'clock news, during which it crossed his mind, with a twinge of bitterness, that if he were ten years younger he might hope to be senator, he went upstairs, carrying a highball for a nightcap.

Carefully, ceremonially, he made all the preparations for bed, put on pajamas and lay down: propped on pillows, a magazine in his lap, the yet untouched highball on the bedside table beside the lamp. In the shadowy room, no other light was on. He lay in the little cone of light, safe, and all the world beyond was shrouded in shadow.

When the nightcap was finished, he yet lay there, in a massive lassitude of mind and body, like a great stone perched on the edge of an abyss. He made no motion to cut off the light, staring across the room at the shadows.

It was well after 10:00 before he got up, put on a dressing gown and slippers, and went back downstairs, again to the study. He threw the bolt of the door, and inspected the curtains on the windows. Then he went to the wall, slid back the panel, touched the coldness of the steel knob.

Under a single light, he sat in the reading chair with the objects on his knees, on the brown paper grocery sack from which they had been drawn. Lightly he ran his fingertip over the slick shiningness of the unburned part of the red dress.

He made me feel beautiful: that was what she had said.

Beautiful in that sleazy red rag. He touched the patent-leather slipper, the surface cracked and pimpled by heat. Beautiful in that sleazy red rag, standing in shiny black slippers with those awful heels, in the middle of the kitchen floor, with that dago coming at her, his hair slicked down slicker-black than patent leather.

But, by God, the dago was dead, that was that, innocent or guilty, and that was that. He felt his whole being closed hard like a fist, ready to strike.

(364)

But there was the letter, too, waiting. It was lying there patiently, waiting for him to read it again, as he had read it many times before, at night, sitting in this chair, the door bolted, the curtains drawn tight.

It was waiting to say:

> I want you know I thank you. You try to save me, I thank you very much. Nobody think you say truth, I not know why. You did good to me and you bella and I want to love you. It no work rite. I try. You got good hart, give Angelo money, give car. I see smile on your face when I kiss your hand. I keep promise like you say, be good to girl. Now they kill me quick. But they no scare Angelo. I love you but it no work rite. You try save me and now I kiss your hand, I thank you.
>
> Respecly
yours
Angelo Passetto

Murray Guilfort sat there, on his knees the letter the dago had written in the death cell, in indelible pencil, on a school tablet of dingy gray paper ruled in blue. You could tell where he had stopped to think and had put the pencil to his mouth, for just after such a point there would be the spreading stain of brighter purple.

The letter had been mailed to the office of Leroy Lancaster, who, in turn, had mailed it to the sanatorium, where Dr. Spurlin had given it to Murray. Cassie Spottwood had never seen it. The doctor had been afraid of its effect on her.

Well, what difference would her seeing it have made?

For sitting here, Murray suddenly saw again, as through the narrowing slit of the closing door, her face uplifted, luminous with its inner light, in that room where the first dusk was encroaching.

Love, he thought, and the word rang hollowly in his head as in a great cave.

He rose sharply from the chair, went to the safe, crammed

the stuff in, slammed the door shut, spun the lock.

He left the study. The air in the dark house was thick to his lungs as though charged with a dry and furry dust. The walls of the house seemed to be slowly constricting. He stood in the great hall, under the high chandelier that was hanging above him like ice in a dark cave, and felt how the walls drew in, how the mass of cruel and glittering ice hung perilously above his head.

The house was a prison.

He thought of Angelo Passetto in his cell, at night, breathing.

His own breath was difficult. The shadows were heavier. The walls were closing in.

He was in himself and he could not get out.

He had always been there inside himself, and he had always been trying to get out. To be Sunderland Spottwood galloping up the lane on a gray stallion, great hoofs flinging red clay like blood. To be Alfred Milbank, with his bulging eyes, leaning over the bar table in Chicago, hotly breathing out the fumes of whiskey, saying: "And as for me, I solemnly affirm that, within the hour, I shall lay out one hundred dollars for a big juicy chunk of illusion." To be a judge on the Supreme Court, so people would respect him. To be—even—Angelo Passetto, in a dark house.

But if the self was the prison, then what was trying to get out?

His mind slowly fumbled that thought like a stupid child turning a strange object over and over in awkward hands. He stood under the icy weight of the chandelier—it might fall any instant—and was afraid to turn his head, for there was the great pier glass and if he did turn, he might look into the glimmering darkness of its depth and see nothing.

He was fleeing from the hall, up the wide stairs, when, as clearly and chillingly as that afternoon, Cassie Spottwood's face again looked luminously at him, but now from the air floating in the dimness at the head of the stair. And again she demanded: "Did you ever love anybody, Murray Guilfort?"

For a moment, frozen on the stair, in the darkness, he started to cry out: "You!"

But he knew it was a lie.

He stood there, on the stairs, and thought, marveling, that he had never even known her. How could you love somebody if you never even knew them? Long ago, the door of the old Spottwood house had opened and there was the white face of a girl floating toward him in the shadows of the house that belonged to Sunderland Spottwood, and that was all he had ever known: a dream. It was the dream he had been forced to dream.

He went on up the stairs, to his room.

The light was still on by the bed. In its rays, which dwindled across the length of the room, he saw on the mantel the large photograph of Bessie, propped in its easel, in the heavy silver frame. Slowly, he went to it.

It was the picture of Bessie taken just before their marriage, the face of a young girl, the face thin and sharp, but with eyes smiling in innocent roguishness. Murray studied the face, tried to remember what it had, in reality, been like. The eyes were blue, yes, the hair medium brown, really pretty with a sweet smell. Her skin had been very pink and white—an old-fashioned complexion, people used to say, he remembered. He also remembered that she had bruised easily, in great black spots, with tiny tendrils of purple reaching out into the surrounding whiteness.

Miss Edwina had said: "People liked to be with her, she was fun to be with."

He tried to remember if that had been true. Had he had fun being with her? He tried hard, humbly, but he could not remember. Studying the picture, he did remember, however, that the expression on the face there, that smile, was what happened just before she would get the giggles—she sometimes got the giggles like a child. And he heard, in abrupt, outrageous obscenity, a burst of that ghostly merriment.

He studied the picture, but the face kept on smiling in its idiotic, uninformed, blasphemous courage.

Oh, didn't she know what was going to happen! Didn't she know how everything would be! He longed to take her by the shoulders and shake her till those little white teeth—they always looked too small, like a child's teeth—rattled and that silly grin got wiped off her face. He would stop that giggling.

If he told her how everything was going to be.

How it wouldn't be long before she'd stop making her silly jokes. How the grin would bleach off her face, and leave nothing but the not quite symmetrical bones showing sharper and the mouth pulling down at the corners. How then she would take to eating too much, and get up at night and go find chocolates, and get fat, and—

And suddenly he remembered that for one brief period when she was first putting on weight he had again liked to go to bed with her to handle the new soft rondure of breasts and belly and buttocks. But then he remembered how soon the soft rondure became a bulging unwieldiness, and with that memory, he looked again at the face in the photograph and thought, vengefully, that one thing would certainly wipe that smile off.

If he told her how she, a mass of bulging and sweaty unwieldiness, would die.

For Bessie had died in this room, in this bed, in the sweat-soaked sheets. One evening, shortly before the death, when the doctor was here, bending over Bessie on one side of the bed, while the nurse, with the help of Aunt Delfie, was changing the sheets on the other side, he had stood at the foot of the bed watching, in what had long since become a schooled numbness. Suddenly, on impulse, he had turned and gone to the picture on the mantelpiece and looked at it, really looking at it, peering at the thin, asymmetrical, courageous face with its ignorant smile. He could not endure it.

He had fled from the room. He had never looked at the picture again.

Until now; and now looking at it, he thought what Miss Edwina had said: "She loved you." And now, with a cold blaze, like truth, he thought what he suddenly knew he had always believed but never dared to think.

That if Bessie had loved him, it was only because she wasn't popular, boys might gather round while she talked and giggled, but she was too skinny (nothing in front, Miss Edwina had said), and she danced badly, like bones hung together on a wire (yes, he hated to dance with her, for he danced very well, he liked to dance with some girl whose breasts brushed you ever so softly, who curved into your movements), but yes, she was sly, she was cunning, she had known his weakness, she had known that he would marry her in the end. For her house, for her money, for her friends, for her name.

But she had loved him.

Well, if she had loved him—and he tested the edge of the thought like sliding your thumb down the honed edge of a knife—her love was the mark of her inferiority, her failure.

And of mine, he thought, even as he desperately tried to stop the thought: *of mine!*

And at that he knew he hated her.

"She loved you," Miss Edwina had said.

Love, he thought, *so that is love.* To dream a fool dream like that fool Bessie Guilfort, to dream a fool lie like that fool Cassie Spottwood, to dream a lie and call it truth. And he thought of all the people moving over the land, moving in streets, standing in doorways, lying in the darkness of houses, all in their monstrous delusion, and so he swept the picture from the mantel.

He heard only the tinkle as glass broke on the hearth, for he had turned away. He stood in the middle of that room of luxurious shadows, laughing.

Laughing, but only for a moment.

For the thought, like the sound of a slow bell, came into his head: *The dream is a lie, but the dreaming is truth.*

He stood there, absorbed numbly in that thought, trying to feel what it meant, not knowing what it meant, but thinking that, if so many people moved across the world as though they knew what it meant, it must mean something.

So he cried out in his heart: *But nobody told me—nobody told me!*

People passed on, across the world, and sometimes smiled and waved at you. That woman had waved at him from under the cedar tree, and she was smiling. The little boys fishing, they had looked up at him, their faces pure in the evening light. Now he stood there shuddering in the intolerableness of the never-having-known.

Slowly, he took off the dressing gown.

He hated them all.

He got into bed, and stared up at the shadowy ceiling. He thought how many times he had stared up at that ceiling. He pushed himself up on an elbow and fumbled in the table drawer for the box. He took one of the capsules, did not even look at it, slipped it, with a gesture like secrecy, into his mouth.

Now he would sleep.

But he did not sink down. Propped on his elbow, holding the box in the hand of the arm on which he was propped, he took another capsule. He swallowed it. When a little saliva had again gathered, he swallowed a third. Then a fourth.

He thought, with a calm marveling, as from a distance: *What is happening to me?*

Propped on the elbow, waiting for saliva to gather, he had no answer for that question. All he could do was wait, each time, for a little saliva to gather. When the box was empty, he let himself down and stared at the ceiling.

After a moment, he reached out, not looking, and fumbled at the lamp until he found the switch.

At one point he thought he was looking out of the window of a jet as it plunged into cloud and, lulled in the unremitting, unheard thunder of its passage, saw that swirling, swelling, dove-gray envelopment flush the color of rose with the exhaust of the engines.

Then he was not in a plane at all. He was falling free—no, deliciously floating free, alone in the rose-flushed vapors.

But something changed. For an instant, like plunging into icy water, he realized what was happening to him, what he had done, and in that instant, like waking to a blaze of light, he knew that he must undo it, he must go back and walk in the world, for that would be enough, that would be bliss, merely to be in a world where people, each walking in his dream, looked at you from within the individual glow, and smiled at you, perhaps waved. With this, he struggled upward, over, reaching out, struggling to get up, to call out.

Leonidas would come.

He did not hear the lamp crash from the table, or the table fall.

Before the end, Murray Guilfort experienced one more flicker of consciousness. He seemed to see a hand reaching into the darkness of the safe, where, like fox-fire, the red dress, the slipper, the letter, lay gleaming coldly in darkness, and he felt, distantly and numbly, the terror of discovery: *They would know, they would find out.*

But the terror was fading as he sank deeper, sinking into truth, into the truth that was himself, whatever his self was, as into joy, sinking there at last.

That evening, Cy Grinder did not go to bed early. He knew that he wouldn't sleep. Now, as in that period long back when he had suffered from chronic sleeplessness, he let Gladys go on to bed, and sat in the living room to watch TV. It was a big, pleasant, tumbled room, with a big stone fireplace and chimney, the only visible relic of the old structure which had been incorporated here, and with walls paneled in chestnut from the dying trees taken off the Reservation.

On one wall was the gun rack and the guns, the dull oiled sheen of metal and of polished walnut. Near it two bows lay on pegs in the wall, and a quiver hung alongside, with arrows. Beyond, the fly rods lay on pegs. On the floor, near the hearth, was a bearskin rug, and to one side a low table and on it a five-foot bow, hickory, in the last stages of manufacture, clean and polished, the pieces of window glass for scraping and some sandpaper yet lying there, and the coil of rawhide and the gluepot ready for winding the grip.

On the mantel shelf were a box of shotgun shells, a green glass vase full of spills made from newspaper for lighting a pipe, a battered creel, a bottle of liniment, two hunting knives, a revolver, several bananas, a pair of binoculars, a tin of tobacco, and a near-empty pint bottle of good-quality bourbon. Above the mantel, jutting from the chimney stone was the head of a ten-point buck, blank and imperious in spite of the band majorette's shako hanging coquettishly askew from one antler prong, and the silver baton propped against another.

There was no fire on the hearth. On the wall, near the door to the hall, a bracket lamp gave the only light except what filtered from the TV screen. The volume of the TV was so low that now and then you could hear the soft, sad batting of moths on the screening at the open windows, or the click of some horny insect zooming in from the dark air to be blocked there.

Cy Grinder sat in his easy chair, staring at the TV, but attending to nothing. His pipe was long since dead, but he had no matches in his pocket. He held the pipe clamped cold in his jaws. He would sit there till the late news from Nashville. Then he would risk going to bed.

The news came. Cy saw the image of the newscaster, the handsome, heavy, slightly ravaged face, the well-tailored shoulders, the careful tousle of dark hair. He saw the mouth moving, but with the volume so low the words were scarcely more than a whisper, coming from that world that was not his. He leaned heavily back in his chair. This was the world he had made.

Then out of the whispering, which was only a little louder than the breeze turning the first pale new leaves out there in the dark, he caught a word, and in that moment, realized that the word was more than, and different from, the other whispering sounds, and then, jerking up, he leaned forward:

> . . . to the hospital in Parkerton. It is reported that attempts at resuscitation are continuing, but a spokesman indicates that little hope is held out. Mr. Guilfort, long known as a brilliant lawyer and now a member of the Supreme Court of the State, has of late years been prominent in . . .

Cy Grinder had risen, and cut it off.

He went down the hall to the kitchen. For a moment he stood in the middle of the floor. Then, very deliberately, he went to the sink and drew a glass of water from the tap. Moonlight fell through the window above the sink. He stepped back from the whiteness, and slowly drank the water, and then stood with the empty glass in his hand.

"Well," he said at last, out loud, "durn if he didn't go and do it." His voice, to his own ears, sounded dry and unused.

He looked with slow wonder around the room. It was his kitchen, but everything seemed strange to him. He was, all at once, overcome by a terrible loneliness.

What did you do when you stood in an empty kitchen, in the middle of the night with moonlight pouring in the window, and held an empty glass in your hand, and your throat was still as dry as though you hadn't drunk a drop, and even if you'd always been the kind of a man who could be alone all day and all night, off in the woods or some place, and not even know or care, you now felt lonesomeness creeping over you like a last chill? What could you do?

It was like everything that had ever happened had fallen away and had never even happened, and he stood there shivering cold in the lonesomeness.

Numbly, he set the empty glass down on the table, and went out into the hall. He leaned over and took off his shoes. Holding them in one hand, he cautiously pushed open the door to the daughter's room, and tiptoed to her bed. The curtain was drawn tight and he could see nothing of her face, only a soft blur of whiteness. But the blurriness did not matter. He knew what that face was like. For a long time he stood there staring.

He went back into the hall, and made his way to his bedroom. He lowered his shoes to the floor beside a chair. He looked across to the bed, at the sleeping woman. The curtain at the window had not been fully drawn, and light was leaking into the room. It fell across the pillow where the sleeping head lay.

He tiptoed across the room to stand by the bed, looking down at the woman's face with a slow, sad, studious attention. Before he turned away to undress, he realized that the face on the pillow was very much like the face of the little girl who lay in the next room. He had never before observed that fact.

Naked, he stood in the middle of the moon-shadowy room,

and did not know what to make of that fact, or of anything.

His nightshirt was on a chair, where his wife had left it for him. He pulled it over his head—an old-fashioned flannel nightshirt that wasn't too easy to get into. He went to the bed and carefully slipped between the sheets. He knew he wouldn't be able to sleep. But he lay there as still as possible.

Then he was wondering if there would ever come a time when the little girl in the other room would be heavy and slow-footed and short of breath and would lie sleeping in a room where moonlight seeped, in a bed beside a stranger who, wakeful, was listening to her breath and did not know or care who she was.

The thought was too terrible to bear.

He rose on an elbow and again stared at the face across which moonlight washed, and everything, everything in the world, was too terrible.

He got up.

He took his old bathrobe off the peg near the door and, barefoot, went down the hall, then out to the back porch. He stepped off the porch and stood under the great white oak there, looking out over the world of pale, watery moonlight. The tree was only leafing now, but he felt the need for the protection of what shadow it gave, and stood there scarcely breathing, waiting.

He looked out over the valley where, far below, the treetops swam in the watery light. The breeze had died down, but the air smelled sweet of rain coming. He heard the musical rustle and stitch of the stream that spilled down from the upper pasture along the rail fence of the yard and, further down, yonder in darkness, to the creek, where, before long now, the lake would be. Over the valley, the sky was milky with mist.

He knew the kind of moon he would find in the sky when the time came for him to step forth from the shadow of the tree. The moon, not yet westering, full, in a vapory vagueness of concentric circles, would be swimming high, and from it would spill the pearly glow to fill the vastness of the world.

But he stayed there, under the new-leafing boughs, his bare feet set on the cold new grass, aware of the slow, heavy, pulsing numbness in his chest, like a bruise that has not yet begun to hurt. He let his head sink forward until his chin pressed on his chest. He closed his eyes and tried to think of nothing, nothing at all.

But after a little, there in the inner darkness, was the face of the woman who, back in the house, now slept in his bed and had slept there every night for now so many years.

Yes, that face was like the face of the little girl. All those years, and how had he failed to see it?

With the image of the woman's face so clear in the darkness of his head, he began to wonder what she thought, what she felt; and his wondering was mysterious to him. He wondered what she had ever thought, what she had ever felt. He realized, slowly, that never, in all the years, had he wondered that before.

The realization was, all at once, an anguish to him. But that was, he somehow knew, what he had to stand there and suffer.

When the time came, he stepped out of the shadow of the tree. He looked up. There was the moon, with the sky, and the whole world, in its light.